KT-559-706

The People's Act of Love

James Meek

The People's Act of Love

CANONGATE
Edinburgh · New York · Melbourne

First published in Great Britain in 2005 by
Canongate Books Ltd, 14 High Street,
Edinburgh EH1 1TE

10 9 8 7 6 5 4 3

British Library Cataloguing-in-Publication Data
A catalogue record for this book is available on
request from the British Library

ISBN 1 84195 654 6 (hardback)
ISBN 1 84195 662 7 (paperback)

Typeset in Sabon by Palimpsest Book Production Ltd,
Polmont, Stirlingshire
Printed and bound by Creative Print and Design,
Ebbw Vale, Wales

www.canongate.net

– Busy remaking the world, man forgot to remake himself.

Andrei Platonov, *Nursery Of The New Man*

Samarin

When Kyrill Ivanovich Samarin was twelve, years before he would catch, among the scent of textbooks and cologne in a girl's satchel, the distinct odour of dynamite, he demanded that his uncle let him change his second name. He didn't want to be 'Ivanovich' any more. The Ivan from whom the patronymic came, his father, had died when he was two, soon after his mother, and he had lived with his uncle ever since. His uncle's name was Pavel; why couldn't he be called Kyrill Pavlovich? When his uncle told him he couldn't change it, that this was the way things were done, that dead fathers had rights and required respect, the boy went into angry silence, pressed his lips together and looked away, breathing loudly in and out through his nose. His uncle knew these signs. He would see them every few months, when one of the boy's friends let him down, or when he was told to put his reading lamp out and sleep, or when he tried to stop his uncle punishing a servant.

What the boy did next was not familiar. He looked at his guardian and grinned, and began to laugh. The effect of the boy's deep brown eyes looking up into his uncle's, together with that laugh, not a man's yet – the boy's voice hadn't broken – but not a child's either was unsettling. 'Uncle Pavel,' said the boy. 'Could you call me just "Samarin" from now on, until the time when I can choose my own names?'

So the twelve-year-old came to be called, at home at least, by his family name alone, as if he were living in a barracks. The uncle was fond of his nephew. He spoiled him when he could, although Samarin was hard to spoil.

Samarin's uncle had no children of his own, and was so shy in the presence of women that it was difficult to tell whether he liked them or not. He had little rank to speak of, and a large fortune. He was an architect and builder, one of those charmed individuals whose practical usefulness transcends any amount of snobbery, corruption and stupidity in the powers on whose patronage they depend. As Samarin grew up, people in Raduga, the town on the Volga where he and his uncle lived, stopped thinking of him as an unfortunate orphan and began to refer to him as schastlivchik, the lucky one.

It didn't harm the good name of Samarin's uncle among the conservative gentry that he took no interest in politics. No circle of chattering liberals met at his town house, he didn't subscribe to St Petersburg periodicals, and he refused to join reform societies. Reformers would keep asking him to sign up, all the same. He hadn't always been aloof from causes. In the mad summer of 1874, long before Samarin was born, his uncle had been one of the students who went like missionaries among the peasants in the villages, urging them to rebellion. The peasants had no idea what the students were talking about, suspected they were being mocked, and asked them, with embarrassed whispers and some jostling, to leave. Samarin's uncle was fortunate to escape exile in Siberia. He never recovered his lost pride. Once a month he would compose a long letter to a woman he had met in those days, who now lived in Finland, and, just before posting it, he would burn it.

Samarin seemed to take after his uncle in politics, though not in his dealings with women. He went through school and on to the local university, where he enrolled as an engineer, without joining any of the debating societies or discussion clubs or semi-underground Marxist circles populated by the radical students. Nor did he enjoy drill, or mix with the militant anti-semites who would loiter on the university steps, gawking at hooknosed, bloodsucking Jewish caricatures in pedlars' chap-books. He read widely – his uncle would buy him any book he wanted, in any language – went to dances and, in his late teens, took long summer trips to St Petersburg. When a friend asked him about luggage labels in German, French and English on his travelling trunk, he smiled and said that buying the labels was much cheaper than actually travelling abroad. He had a great many friends, or rather a great many students counted him as a friend, even though, had they stopped to think about it, most of them would have been able to count the hours they'd spent with him on the fingers of one hand. Women liked him because he danced well, didn't try to get drunk as quickly as possible when the means were to hand, and listened with sincere interest when they talked. He had a way of devoting attention absolutely to one woman, which not only pleased her during their conversation, but left her with the feeling afterwards that the time they'd spent – no matter how brief, and usually it was brief – was time offered to her from a precious store, time which could and should have been used by Samarin to continue a great task. The fact that nobody knew what this great task was only intensified the feeling. Besides, he dressed well, he stood to inherit a large estate, he was clever, and everything about him, his wit, his strength, even his looks – he was tall, a little gaunt, with thick collar-length brown hair and eyes that shifted between serene remoteness and a sudden sharp focus – suggested a man holding himself back from revealing his full self out of consideration for the less gifted around him.

The voices which spoke of alternative Samarins never gained a patient hearing, not because they were thought to be motivated by envy, but because their slanders were deemed too obscure. They were received like the small paragraphs in newspapers reporting bizarre happenings in other small provincial towns similar to Raduga (though never in Raduga): they were read with interest, but not believed, let alone acted on. There was the story of how somebody had seen Samarin and his uncle walking together when the nephew was fifteen, and how it had been the nephew talking, gesturing as if explaining something, and the grey-haired uncle who was listening, silent, nodding, hands behind his back, almost respectful. In those days there was unrest in the countryside. Manor houses were being burned down by peasants angry at the compensation they still owed landowners for the privilege of being freed from serfdom forty years earlier. Samarin's uncle would be called on to supervise the reconstruction of the manor. He would take Samarin with him to visit the families of the burned-out gentry. What one witness said, and it was only his word against everyone else's, was that he had overheard uncle and nephew together after one such visit, to a family of the most minor nobility, who had lost everything, and that the two of them had been laughing about it. 'I heard the boy laugh first, and then the uncle joined in!' So the witness said.

In 1910, when he was 21, Samarin began spending time with Yekaterina Mikhailovna Orlova – Katya – a student in his class and the daughter of the rector of the university. They went for walks together; they talked in the corner at parties; they danced. One day in early spring, Katya's father ordered that the relationship end. Samarin had humiliated him, he said, during his annual address to final year students. When Orlov had talked about how fortunate the students were to be young in an era when Russia was becoming a wealthy, enlightened democracy, Samarin had started to laugh. 'Not a snigger, or a chuckle,' said Orlov. 'A great roaring, bellowing laugh, like a savage beast in our academic groves.'

There was a holiday, and Orlov took his daughter to the country house of one of the university's patrons. Samarin found out that another student had arranged to meet Katya in the grounds of the house, to read her his poetry. Samarin persuaded the student that they should go together to the gates of the estate. Samarin warned him that Katya preferred men to be dressed in light-coloured clothes. Not long after the two men set out along the country road to the house, Samarin on a bicycle and the other on a horse, there was an unusual accident. The horse, normally docile, threw the poet, just as they were passing an area of deep, wet mud. The poet's white suit and beige English raincoat were covered in dirt, and he hurt his ankle. Samarin helped him onto his mount again and the poet turned back. Samarin offered to deliver the poems to the house before riding back to chaperone the poet safely home, and the poet agreed. They parted.

A mile short of the house, Samarin dismounted and walked on, wheeling the bicycle with one hand and holding the student's poems in the other. The verses were heavily influenced by the early work of Alexander Blok. The words 'moon', 'darkness', 'love' and 'blood' occurred with great frequency. After reading each one, Samarin stopped, tore the paper into eight neat squares, and dropped it in the ditch running along the side of the road. There was no wind and the paper spread out onto the surface of the meltwater run off the fields.

A watchman stood at the gate of the estate. One student looked much like another to him and, when Samarin introduced himself as the poet, it didn't occur to him that the young man might be lying. Samarin asked if he could meet Katya at the summer house by the pond and the watchman went to fetch her. Samarin wheeled his bicycle over to the summer house, a sagging, rotten structure being claimed by bright green moss, leaned his bicycle against a tree, and sat on a dry patch on the steps. He smoked a couple of cigarettes, watched a snail working round the toe of his boot and ran his hand through a clump of nettles till he was stung. The sun came out. Katya came through the wet, uncut grass, wearing a long brown coat and a broad-brimmed hat. She smiled when she saw it was Samarin. She bent down and pulled something out of the ground. When she sat down next to him she was holding a bunch of snowdrops. Samarin told her what had happened to the poet.

'I'm not supposed to see you,' said Katya.

'He gave me his poems,' said Samarin. 'I lost them. They weren't good. I brought something else to read to you. Would you like a cigarette?'

Katya shook her head. 'Are you writing poetry now?' she said.

'I didn't write this,' said Samarin, taking a folded pamphlet out of his inside jacket pocket. 'And it isn't poetry. I thought you'd be interested. I heard you intend to become a terrorist.'

Katya leaned forward and laughed. 'Kyrill Ivanovich! What stupid things you say.' She had perfectly regular little teeth. 'Joking all the time.'

'Terrorist. How does it sound? Because you need to get used to the word. "Terrorist."'

'Be serious! Be serious. When have I ever said a word about politics to you? You know better than anyone what a light-minded creature I am. Terror, I don't even like to say it. Unless you're talking about when we set off fireworks behind the ice fishermen at New Year. I've grown out of that. I'm ladylike now. Fashion. Ask me about that! Do you like this coat? Papa bought it for me in Petersburg. It's pretty, isn't it? Enough. So.' Katya put the flowers down on the step between them. The stems were crushed where she had squeezed them in her fist. She folded her hands on her lap. 'No wonder Papa doesn't want you to see me if you're going to make fun of me. Well, read, go on.'

Samarin opened the pamphlet and began to read. He read for a long time. At first, Katya watched him with the kind of wonder that shows on people's faces when somebody says something out loud which corresponds to their most deeply buried thoughts; equally, it could have been what shows when one person makes a lewd proposition to another much earlier than expected in their courtship. After a while, however, Katya's blue eyes narrowed and the last patch of red faded from her smooth white face. She turned away from Samarin, took off her hat, brushed the gleaming blonde wisps from her forehead, took one of his cigarettes and began to smoke, hunched over her forearm.

'"The nature of the true revolutionary has no place for any romanticism, any sentimentality, rapture or enthusiasm,"' read Samarin. '"It has no place either for personal hatred or vengeance. The revolutionary passion, which in them becomes a habitual state of mind, must at every moment be combined with cold calculation. Always and everywhere they must be not what the promptings of their personal inclinations would have them be, but what the general interest of the revolution prescribes."'

'Listen to this part, Katya: "When a comrade gets into trouble, the revolutionary, in deciding whether they should be rescued or not, must think not in terms of their personal feelings but only of the good of the revoutionary cause. Therefore they must balance, on the one hand, the usefulness of the comrade, and on the other, the amount of revolutionary energy that would necessarily be expended on their deliverance, and must settle for whichever is the weightier consideration."'

'What does this strange document have to do with me?' said Katya.

'There's a story of a plan to entrust you with a device, and a target.'

'You should mind your own business,' said Katya.

'Don't take it. I believe the intention is to spend you, and mark you down as a cheap loss.'

Katya gave a short, thin laugh. 'Read more,' she said.

Samarin read: '"The revolutionary enters into the world of the state . . ."'

Blowing out smoke and looking into the distance, Katya interrupted him. '"The revolutionary enters into the world of the state, of class and of so-called culture, and lives in it only because he has faith in its speedy and total destruction,"' she recited. '"He is not a revolutionary if he feels pity for anything in this world. If he is able to, he must face the annihilation of a situation, of a relationship or of any person who is part of the world – everything and everyone must be equally odious to him. All the worse for him if he has family, friends and loved ones in this world; he is no revolutionary if he can stay his hand."' There. Now if you're working for the police you can blow your whistle.'

'I'm not working for the police,' said Samarin. He folded the pamphlet and tapped it on his knee. 'I could have lost this, with the poetry, couldn't I? You memorised the Catechism of a Revolutionary. That was clever.' He lowered his head a little and turned his mouth in a smile that failed to take. It came out as a grimace. Katya tossed her cigarette stub in the weeds and leaned forward to catch the expression of doubt in his face, an expression she'd barely seen before. Samarin turned his head away slightly, Katya leaned further forward, Samarin twisted away, Katya twisted after him, Katya's breath was on Samarin's cheek for a moment, then he straightened up and looked around. Katya made a little sound at the back of her mouth, scorn and amusement and discovery all at once. She put a hand on his shoulder and he returned to her, looking into her eyes from almost no distance. It was so close that they could tell whether they were looking into the filaments of the other's iris, or into the black ports of the other's pupils, and wonder what significance either had.

'It's a curious thing,' said Katya, 'but I feel I'm looking at the true you for once.' Her voice was the voice of closeness, not a whisper but a lazy, effortless murmur, a cracked purr. With one finger Samarin traced the almost invisible down on her upper lip.

'Why is it so unbearable?' said Samarin.

'What?' said Katya.

'To look into the looking part of the one who's looking at you.'

'If you find it unbearable,' said Katya, 'don't bear it.'

'I won't,' said Samarin. He put his lips on hers. Their eyes closed and they put their arms around each other. Like a feint, their hands moved decorously across each other's backs the more eagerly they kissed. It was on the edge of violence, on the edge of teeth and blood, when they heard shouting in the distance and Katya pushed him away and they sat watching each other, breathing deeply and sullen, like opium eaters over laudanum they'd spilled squabbling.

'You have to leave,' said Katya. She nodded at the pamphlet. 'There. In there. Do you know Chapter 2, Item 21?'

Samarin began leafing through it, but before he could find it, Katya began to recite it, pausing to gulp breaths: '"The sixth, and an important category is that of women. They should be divided into three main types: first, those frivolous, thoughtless and vapid women who we may use as we use the third and fourth categories of men; second, women who are ardent, gifted, and devoted, but do not belong to us because they have not yet achieved a real, passionless, and practical revolutionary understanding: these must be used like the men of the fifth category; and, finally there are the women who are with us completely, that is, who have been fully initiated and have accepted our programme in its entirety. We should regard these women as the most valuable of our treasures, whose assistance we cannot do without."'

It was months before Samarin saw Katya again. One morning he waited for her at the station. The university had a poor library and at intervals the authorities would send railway wagons, fitted out with bookshelves and desks, from Penza to give the students access to specialist titles. Samarin had all the books he needed at home but in the hottest days of May, when the railway library came, he was outside. Katya arrived, wearing a white dress and no hat and carrying a large, almost empty satchel. Her pale skin had burned and she was thinner and more anxious. She looked as if she had been sleeping badly. There was a hot wind and the poplars were hissing in their row beyond the station. Samarin called to Katya but she didn't turn round. She went into the library wagon.

Samarin sat on a bench on the station platform, watching the wagon. Something was burning in town, there was black smoke spreading over the roofs. The wind was so strong and hot there was bound to be a storm but the sky was clear, just the smoke spreading. Samarin sat on the bench and watched the students come and go. The bench was in the shade of the station roof and sheltered from the wind but planks in the roof began to rattle. The students were moving through clouds of dust, their eyes closed, the women bunching their skirts with one hand and holding their hats with the other. Samarin could smell the smoke from the burning. The trees would rustle and then roar like a waterfall. When there were no students still waiting outside in the wind Samarin began counting the ones coming out. He could smell the burning. The clouds were coming. They were thick and they heaved while he watched them. No one else was left on the platform. The air stank of dust and smoke and ozone. It became very dark. The sky was a low roof. The last of the students came running out of the wagon. Samarin got up and called to him. The student ran round the wagon and across the rails and off towards the fields with his collar turned up. He turned round once without stopping and looked at Samarin. It was a message from the future. He'd seen something he didn't want to see again and all he wanted was to look Samarin in the face once more, to be able to say: 'I saw Samarin that day.'

Katya was the only one who hadn't come out. Samarin went over to the wagon. The reading room was empty and the desks were clear except for the copy of *Essentials of Steam* Katya had been using and some of her notes. She'd written a poem. 'She loved like suicides love the ground they fall towards,' she'd written,

> It stops them, embraces them and ends their pain,
> But she was falling over and over, jumping,
> Hitting the ground, dying and falling through again.

Samarin closed the book, went to the door of the librarian's office and pressed his ear against the wood. The wagon was creaking in the wind so loudly that he couldn't hear. He couldn't tell if he could hear whispers on the other side of the door or if it was the wind and the roaring of the trees. A gust caught sand and straw and sent them pattering along the wagon chassis like a flood of rats flowing through the wheels. Samarin moved away from the door and heard a woman cry out. It came from outside. He ran out of the wagon into the dust and looked up and down the platform. There was no one. He could hear bells from a fire brigade in the town. He heard the woman cry out again, as if not from fear or pleasure or anger, just for the sake of making a sound, like a wolf or a raven. It was a long way away. A stone hit Samarin in the shoulder, and another on his head, and one on his cheek, drawing blood. He covered his head with his arms and ran under the platform roof. The sound of the wind was drowned out by a sound like cannonballs being poured onto the town from an inexhaustible bunker and the air turned white. The hailstorm lasted two minutes and when it ended the remnants of leaves hung from the trees like rags. The ground was ankle-deep in ice. Samarin saw the door of the wagon open and Katya climb down with a satchel on her back. Something heavy inside it weighed the satchel down. She looked up and saw him. Samarin called her name and she began to run away down the line. He moved after her. She slipped in the hail and fell and he came up to her. She was lying in the ice, half on her back, half on her side. Samarin knelt down and she looked up at him as if he'd come to her in the morning to wake her up after nights and days of sleep. She touched the cut on his cheek and slowly drew back her fingertip with the smudge of blood on. She was beginning to shiver with the cold. She asked Samarin: 'Where to?' Where to. Samarin took her hands and pulled her up out of the softening hail. She was dripping wet and shivering. She took a few steps away from him, took off the satchel, looked inside it, held it against her chest and laughed. Samarin told her to give it to him. She went on laughing and ran away down the track. Samarin ran after her and caught her round the waist and she fell face forward. She was strong and she tried to cover the satchel with her body. Samarin wrestled with her, trying to turn her over, his shins wet in the ice, his knees against her thighs, his hands delving in under her to where she held the satchel against her belly. He smelled her hair and the wet cotton of her dress, and her soft strong middle twisted in his hands like a fish. He drove his right hand in between her legs and his left hand up to her breast and without crying out she let go of the satchel, squirmed round and tore at his hands with hers, their soft chill palms on his knuckles. He seized the satchel, rolled away from her and stood up.

'Give it back,' she said, lying still, looking at him.

Samarin opened the satchel. There was an explosive device in it. He took it out and threw the satchel to her. Katya began to shiver.

'Better me than you,' said Samarin.

'Romantic,' said Katya in a flat voice. 'You've failed before you've begun.'

'My throwing arm is stronger.'

'You'll throw it in the river. You'll never use it.'

'Why not?' said Samarin, smiling, looking at the heavy package weighing down his hand. 'It's better than plans.'

Katya stood up, the melted ice leaving dark streaks down the crumpled front of her dress. Fragments of hail hung from the ends of her hair. She looked down, began to brush herself, then stopped and looked at Samarin. A change came across her face. It became warm, hungry and interested. She came up to Samarin, pressed her body against him, wrapped her arms round him and kissed him on the lips.

'Do you really like me so much?' she said.

'Yes,' he said, and leaned his mouth to hers. Katya grabbed the bomb from his distracted hand, hooked his ankle with her toe, snatched him off his footing, and ran away before he could catch her.

Two weeks later, she was arrested and charged with conspiring to commit an act of terrorism.

The Barber and the Berry Gatherer

In the middle of October nine years later, in that part of Siberia lying between Omsk and Krasnoyarsk, a tall, slender man wearing two coats and two pairs of trousers came walking from the north towards the railway. He followed the river, walking through the wild garlic and rowans and birches on the rocks above the rapids in the couple of miles before the bridge. His ears stuck out from coiling tails of dark hair reaching to his collar and his tongue slipped from the tangled beard to moisten his lips. He looked straight ahead and walked steadily, not stumbling, not like one who knew the way so much as one who had walked for months towards the white sun and was intending to walk onwards until killed or blocked. He ducked down and with his right hand touched a piece of string keeping his boots together. He kept his left forearm pressed tight against his chest.

He was a few hundred yards from the line when he heard the whistle of a locomotive. There was no wind and the trees shuddered from the sound to the horizon. His certainty and direction were sent awry and he looked around him with his mouth open, licking his lips. He squinted up at the bright grey sky and began to breathe deeply. The whistle went again and the man smiled and made a noise which could have been a part of a word or him having forgotten how to laugh and trying all the same.

When the whistle sounded for the third time, closer, the man ran forward, round a bend in the river, and saw the bridge. His face closed and he ran to the water's edge. He squatted down and with his right hand scooped up water and splashed it over his face and drank some. He looked quickly at the bridge and behind him through the trees and let his left hand relax and pulled a package out from inside his coat. It was wrapped in a linen rag. He took a heavy stone and stuffed it into the cloth and tied two ends of the cloth tight in a knot. Stretching his arm back he hurled the package out and it disappeared into the water of the river. He put his hands into the water and washed them, took them out and shook them, rolled up the sleeves of his coats above the wrists and washed his hands again.

The locomotive came over the bridge, a dark green beast streaked with pale corrosion, like malachite, creeping across the thin span with a string of cattle wagons in tow. The whistle sounded down the gorge and the weight of the train bore down on rotting sleepers with the groan of wood and the scream of unlubricated iron and steel. It crawled on as if there were many ways to choose instead of one and flakes of soot and pieces of straw drifted through the air towards the river. One of the wagons was rocking from side to side and above the noise of the engine and the train there was a hacking sound as if someone was taking an axe to a plank.

The door of the wagon shot open and a man in army breeches and a white shirt was in the doorway, with his back to the outside, holding on with one hand and trying to catch the bridle of a horse with the other. The horse was rearing up and flailing at the man with its forelegs. There were more horses behind, their heads lunging madly towards the light. The man fell from the wagon as it rocked towards the river and toppled over the rail. He fell fifty metres into rocky shallows. His limbs worked as he fell, as if he was trying at the same time to fly, to land feet first, and to brace himself for the moment of impact. His eyes were open and so was his mouth but he did not scream. His cheeks were stretched back and he hit the water belly down. The water lifted white skirts high around him and when they came down again the man was not moving, beached on gravel, lapped by quiet eddies at the river's edge.

The horses, five of them, tumbled out of the wagon after the man. They were caught between the moving train and the low rusted guardrail of the bridge. One fell off the edge of the bridge immediately, landing on the edge of the river close to the fallen man with a crack on the water like a mine going off. The others fought for space on the bridge parapet. One stocky chestnut got dragged forward by a wagon, her harness caught by a projecting hook, and was hauled trotting and skipping and struggling against the mouth of the tunnel at the far end of the bridge, where her neck was broken.

The three surviving horses tried to shuffle to safety between the train and the rail. There was only space for them to move in single file, and barely that, but one of the three, a big skinny coal black horse, was trying to go in the opposite direction to the others. It reared up and its feet came down on the horse blocking its way, a bay. The black one got its balance back and reared again. The bay pushed forward and the black one ended up on top, its legs hung over the neck of the other.

While the bay and the black were locked together, like punch drunk boxers, the train must have given the third horse, a white stallion, a shove, or it had gone mad, because it charged the guard rail and dived head first over the edge into the river. It was roped together with the bay and the bay was snatched out from underneath the black horse and went down after. Bay and white flew down, so unlike Pegasus, graceless in the air, their limbs frozen, and smacked thunderously into the skin of water over river pebbles.

The survivor, the black horse, took a few paces back, stopped and cantered forward, against the motion of the train, back the way it had come. The space between the guard rail and the wagons widened as the horse moved on and it picked up speed as the last wagon swung across the bridge. The wagon disappeared into the tunnel and the horse was gone west at a gallop through the bracken and deep grass by the railside.

The man by the river stood still and listened until he could hear no sound from the train. He unbound his boots, took off both pairs of trousers and went out into the river to the place where he had thrown the package. The water came up to his thin white thighs. He searched for an hour, slowly, scanning the clear waters pace by pace, back and forwards. Twice he reached down and closed his hand round a pale stone.

He came out, sat down and put his boots and trousers back on. 'A fool then,' he said aloud.

He walked along the water's edge till he came to the base of the bridge. The bay was still alive, its head flailing in a shimmering cloud of mosquitoes, the rest of it paralysed with the water rushing round it, a great soft warm rock of flesh. The soldier who fell from the train and another of the horses were washed up on the shore. The soldier was dead. His breeches were of fine material and his boots were imported. There was nothing in his pockets. The man took off the boots and tried them on. He couldn't get his feet into them. He put the boots back on the corpse, turned the body over face down and took a knife out of his pocket. It was a single long, thin, rectangular piece of steel, sharpened to an edge along one side and with a strip of felt tied round the end for a handle. He went over to one of the dead horses, the white one, cut away a strip of hide from the leg, cut off a strip of flesh and put it in his mouth. He went over to the edge of the trees, picked a handful of sorrel leaves and squatted down, chewing the raw meat and leaves, looking round and watching the soldier. When he had finished he drank water from the river. He pressed his ear against the stanchion of the bridge and listened.

He went over to the soldier and picked up his right hand. He looked back upriver the way he had come, placed the soldier's wrist on a stone washed by a thin stream of water and cut off his hand, sawing through the ligaments and parting the joints by pressure rather than the sharpness of the blade. Blood darkened the stone, clouded out into the waters and swirled away into the current.

The man let the soldier's arm fall into the river, took the severed hand and ran into the woods. He walked for a mile away from the river and dug a hole with his hands through the mud and leafmould and earth. He buried the hand and covered it up. He returned to the river, cleaned his hands and began to climb the rocks up to the railway tunnel.

His toes with jagged broken toenails clawed out through the ends of the boots and when the way became steep he took the boots off and rammed them into the pockets of the outer coat. Thirty metres up there was a stanchion founded on the rock but the last ten metres up to it were steep, sheer almost, with no bushes to hold. The man stood on a ledge, breathing hard, the dying sun in the west hot on his back through the thick coat-cloth, and tracked the cracks in the rock with his eyes. He took the first handhold, stretching his left arm out straight up, and hauled his right foot up to a lip of rock. He crawled up limb by limb until the rock became smooth and the crack he had seen curving up to within reach of the stanchion turned out to be the shadow of a downfacing leaf of sandstone. He was pressed against the rock with his arms and legs splayed out like a newborn creature trying to suckle and embrace a stone mother vast beyond the scope of his senses. He had climbed too high to let go and fall. There was a vein of quartz slanting up towards the stanchion. The man felt the rock about to leave him. He made a sound, half grunt, half sob, and grabbed for the quartz with the fingernails of his right, then his left hand, getting half the purchase he needed from the translucent bulge to stop him falling, and the rest from his toenails. The long hard right big toenail scraped down the rock a couple of centimetres and slotted into a hidden crack. All the man's weight slid back onto the brittle plectrum for an instant before he used it to shove himself back up and, in the moment before the nail tore off, snatch the rusted iron spar of the bridge stanchion with one hand. He hung for several seconds, then got hold with the other hand and pulled himself up so that his feet were resting on the metal.

He climbed up the stanchion. It was easy, like a ladder. The pain beat with his pulse while he climbed. There was a hatchway at the top onto the walkway by the line. He went through and sat on the painted metal plates. The sun was about to sink behind the trees. He lay down along a smooth stretch of metal between rivets and closed his eyes.

He heard feet moving on the stone chips bedding the sleepers and turned his head towards the sound, not getting up. The clouds had cleared and the sky in the west was orange with the skyline torn by the black pines and the twin humps of blasted rock on either side of the cutting. The being coming was on foot and alone, about thirty metres down the line, a small, broad, dark form moving slowly in the twilight. The man stood up and spread his arms out. 'Brother!' he shouted. The approaching form stopped. 'Don't be afraid! I'm alone, without weapons!'

The other figure took a few steps closer.

'Come on, let's not frighten each other.' The two men came near enough to see each other's faces. The man from the west had a hat and an overcoat and downy fuzz on his chin. He was carrying a carpet bag.

The man who had climbed up said: 'I've been gathering berries. Samarin, Kyrill Ivanovich.' He held out his hand.

'Balashov, Gleb Alexeyevich.' His hand was long, cool and soft-skinned. Samarin's was rougher, hot and chapped. Both men were about the same age; thirty.

Samarin sat on the rail and lashed his boots on. Balashov watched him, holding the bag in front of him with both hands.

'Why are you walking?' said Samarin. 'Are the trains too fast?'

'There are no trains any more. Only military ones. It's forbidden to travel on them.'

'I saw a train.'

'That was a military train. A Czech train. The Czechs shoot at you if you try to climb onto them.'

'Czechs? Is this still Siberia?'

'Siberia.'

Samarin looked carefully at Balashov, as if trying to work out whether he was a liar, or an idiot. Balashov cleared his throat and looked away. He squeezed the handle of the bag till the leather creaked. He looked round, behind him, over the edge of the bridge, craning his neck. He cried out, dropped the bag and grasped the guard rail. When the bag hit the ground it fell on its side and objects spilled out of it. Balashov paid no attention.

'There are horses down there!' he said. 'Injured!'

'They're dead,' said Samarin. 'They fell from one of the wagons in the train. I saw them fall.'

'Poor beasts. Are you sure? I should go down. Perhaps one of them is still alive. When will men start leaving the horses out of their wars?' He looked at Samarin as if he hoped for an answer.

Samarin laughed. 'You won't get down there. I almost killed myself climbing up. Well, you have me. All this time I've been gathering berries and the first man I meet when I come out of the forest is someone who cares more about the horses who went to war than the men who went with them. It's like the Englishwoman who went to hell and saw millions of the damned being tormented by demons while they loaded burning hot coals onto donkey carts with their bare hands, and she said: "Oh, those poor donkeys!"'

'Horses don't go to war,' said Balashov. 'Men take them.'

'There's another dead horse up there,' said Samarin, nodding towards the mouth of the tunnel.

Balashov turned, drew in breath, and ran towards where the dead chestnut lay, about fifty metres away. Samarin watched him go and when he saw him bend over the animal and place his hand on its neck he squatted down by Balashov's bag. A small, heavy, bound roll of canvas had spilled out of it. There was a loaf, a jar of pickled peppers with a Chinese label, and a pamphlet called *Nine Secret Ways To End Sorrow*. Looking over his shoulder to check on Balashov, Samarin opened the canvas roll. A set of surgical instruments was there, a whole crooked jaw of points and blades and scissors in cosy gums of cloth. Samarin rummaged comfortably inside the bag and found a litre bottle of raw spirit, which he sniffed at and took a swig from. He took out a large cloth, once white, now stiff with dried blood. He pushed it back in the bag together with the pamphlet and took out the last item, a dog-eared cardboard wallet the size of an envelope, fixed shut with a piece of elastic. He opened the wallet and pulled a photograph from a grease-proof paper pocket inside. It was the portrait of a young woman, not a stiff Sunday-best provincial studio shot but something intimate, real and close; she was resting her head on her hand and perhaps looking too intently into the camera lens – it was too dark to be sure, or make out details. The back of the picture was blank. He put wallet and photo inside his outer coat, set the bag upright, put the bottle, the roll and the cloth back in, and began cramming the bread and peppers into his mouth. He ate quickly, with his head bowed and his eyes lowered.

'I'm sorry,' said Samarin, chewing, when Balashov returned. 'The food fell out of your bag. I was hungry. Here.' He handed Balashov the remains of the loaf with one hand while draining the brine out of the pickle jar into his mouth with the other.

'Don't worry,' said Balashov. He waved the crust away. 'Your health. It's only an hour's walk to Yazyk.'

'Can I get an express to Petersburg from there?'

'You've been gathering berries a long time.'

'Yes. Yes, I have.'

'I told you. There are no trains,' said Balashov. He was looking inside the bag. His hands fluttered against the inner sides like a trapped bird, getting madder. 'Did you see a cardboard wallet? It had a photograph inside.'

'A wallet?' said Samarin. 'No, I don't believe so. Who was the picture of?'

'Anna Petrov- but you wouldn't know her, of course.'

'Anna Petrovna! Your wife?'

'No, I have no wife.' Balashov was on his hands and knees, searching the track bedding. It was almost completely dark by now. 'An acquaintance, that's all. She asked me to take it to Verkhny Luk in relation to some documents but . . . nobody is giving out documents now.'

'What a pity you've lost it! And what a pity I can't see it. Anna Petrovna. That's the kind of name that allows you to imagine any kind of woman, doesn't it, Gleb Alexeyevich? Blonde pigtails, short red hair, a young student, an old babushka, maybe with a limp, maybe without. On a name like that you can draw your own picture. It's not like, I don't know, Yevdokiya Filemonovna, who could only be a brunette, with warts and a big bosom. Anna Petrovna. A highly moral person, probably. Or is she a bit of a slut, I wonder?'

'No!' said Balashov. 'She's the widow of a cavalry officer, she has a young son, and she is of the highest possible moral character.'

'Excellent. And how admirable that you make it your business to be her errand boy.'

'I'm a storekeeper in Yazyk. And a barber, sometimes. I was going to Verkhny Luk on business. It's two days' walk back that way. I have a stall. I cut all their hair, I shave those who want it' – Balashov was speaking faster and faster, opening and closing the bag.

'Gleb Alexeyevich!' said Samarin, putting his hand on Balashov's shoulder. 'Don't worry. You don't have anything to explain. You're a peaceful, law-abiding citizen, going about your business. Look at me, now. Am I not the wild one? Should I not be the one explaining myself?'

Balashov laughed nervously. 'It's dark,' he said.

'Not as dark as it'll be in the tunnel,' said Samarin.

'Oh,' said Balashov. 'Are you going to Yazyk too?'

'It's the nearest town?'

'By far.'

'Then I have to warn them about the man who's following me.'

The two men walked along between the tracks, just visible in the starless night. As they passed the dead horse at the tunnel mouth, Balashov crossed himself and murmured a prayer.

'Usually when there are two of us walking through the tunnel at night, we hold hands,' said Balashov.

'Well, we are in Asia,' said Samarin. Balashov took Samarin's hand and led him forward into the tunnel. Their feet began to sound mighty in the gravel and the blackness fizzed infinite around them. Samarin coughed and the cough took off, alive, along the invisible brickwork. After a few hundred metres Samarin stopped. Balashov tried to walk on but Samarin tightened his grip on his hand and, rather than struggling, Balashov waited.

'Are you afraid?' asked Samarin's voice.

'No.' Balashov's voice wavered.

'Why not? I am.'

'God is here.'

'No,' said Samarin. 'There isn't one of them. This darkness is what there is to be afraid of. To go to sleep here, to wake up in darkness and silence.' He let go of Balashov's hand. 'Alone. And with no way of determining who you are. You can listen to the sound of your voice. But is it really you?' He seemed to be speaking from far away, as if the being behind the words was attending to many things at once.

'I am not alone!' shouted Balashov. His voice rolled back and forward down the tunnel, sizing it to the heightened perception of their ears. It was no longer infinite. Samarin grabbed Balashov and embraced him. Hesitantly, Balashov put his arms around Samarin and gave a weak hug in return.

'I'm sorry, my friend,' said Samarin. 'Of course you're not alone. I'm here. Here's my hand. I've been away for too long.'

They walked on. 'Once I was lost in the forest for a week,' said Balashov. 'It was this time of year. At night I was terrified of the wild beasts but I didn't dare light a fire in case outlaws saw it. I lay in a blanket in the dark after walking all day, trying not to fall asleep till I thought my eyes were about to bleed from the pain of it. Sometimes I heard wolves. The silence was worse. You would long to hear frogs, or an owl, even though they sound like souls begging to be allowed to move on, and instead an hour would pass in silence and then there was a rustling nearby and you would think of the teeth of the beast snatching at your leg and jerking you out of the stillness and you screaming and pleading but knowing the animal couldn't understand you and had no good or evil in it to reason with. Even in the midst of the fear and the pain of staying awake I began to see that the horror in the beast when it came would be all within me. I would feel cruelty and the pain of a death alone in the wilderness but it wouldn't be of the wolf's making, the wolf is only part of God's workings, and God is good; all the horror of it I was carrying with me, as fear, and the wolf would take that from me and there would be nothing between me and God any longer.'

'What if it wasn't a wild beast? What if it was another man?' said Samarin quietly.

'That couldn't have been so terrible. Up to the very moment of death you'd hope they would save you from the horror in themselves, that they'd change their minds. You'd believe they were mistaken. But the beasts didn't come that time, nobody came in the night. In the end I fell asleep, and instead of nightmares, the dreams I had were beautiful, of paradise and the memory of an eternity of joy. When I woke up, when I realised I'd woken up, I was miserable, as if the one I loved the most had died. I walked through the day and the memory of the dream would fade until by night I was terrified again. One evening I saw the lights of a village and I knew I was safe. But a new terror came up in me, stronger than the old one. I was afraid that all the nightmares I hadn't dreamed in my time in the wilderness would come to me at once in the first night of sanctuary.'

Samarin stopped and came close to Balashov. His breath touched Balashov's face. 'Did they?' he whispered. 'Did that happen?'

'No!' said Balashov, trying to pull his face back from Samarin's hot breath. 'They never came.'

'Of course not,' said Samarin. 'Of course not. Good. On.'

The two men walked out of the tunnel into the smell of the larches on either side of a cutting. A clouded night had come and there was nothing to be seen but a sheen where the rails were and the faint black serration of the trees against the sky. A flock of geese flew overhead, crying like a shutterhinge in the wind. Samarin's broken boots made a slithering, flapping sound on the track bedding.

'What year is it?' said Samarin.

'1919.'

'There's still a war, I suppose.'

'It's a different kind of war. One where you can't understand who is on which side. In the old war, the one against the Germans and the Austrians, it was ours against theirs. Now it's more ours against ours. There are Whites and there are Reds. The Whites are for the Tsar – he's dead now, the Reds killed him – and the Reds are for everybody being equal.'

'What are you for, Gleb Alexeyevich?'

Balashov was silent for a long time. Eventually he said, in a stretched voice: 'Everybody is equal before God.'

'But how do you live that?'

'What kind of a convict are you?'

Samarin, who was in front, stopped and turned round. The moon had risen behind the clouds and a bare ration of light daubed the men's faces in infant shadows. Samarin's face had lost its animation and settled into an empty stillness.

'I thought in Siberia people referred to us as "unfortunates,"' he said.

Balashov took a pace back. 'So we do, but . . . you don't talk like a convict.'

'That's good after five years among them.' Samarin's features began to unfreeze, and once his face animated, it was as if the dead emptiness that had come across it could not have truly happened. He snapped off a piece of fern and began picking off the fronds. He sang a few lines of a song too faintly for Balashov to make out the words, except for the phrase *among the worlds*.

'I did break the law, and I have escaped from a labour camp,' Samarin said. 'But I'm not a criminal.'

'A political.'

'Yes.'

'You're an intellectual. A socialist.'

Samarin laughed and looked into Balashov's eyes, knowing and familiar. 'Something of that breed,' he said. 'I ran from the White Garden. Have you heard of it? It's a thousand miles to the north of here.'

'Was there gold there?' said Balashov vaguely. 'I didn't know there was a labour camp at the White Garden.'

'There was labour, but there was no gold,' said Samarin. 'I suppose you'd like to know why I was a prisoner there.'

'I don't need to know,' said Balashov. 'It seems to me that curiosity about strangers is a kind of sin, in a way.'

'Heh! That's a very congenial way of thinking. Are you sure you've never done time yourself?'

'No. I was never a prisoner. Except in the way all our souls are prisoners of our bodies. Kyrill Ivanovich.'

'Oh yes, the soul body thing. Yes. Well. If you believe in that, I suppose.'

'In Yazyk we do. We believe in salvation. Most of us have been saved.'

'Salvation,' laughed Samarin. He began walking on and Balashov followed a few paces behind. Neither man spoke for a time. Occasionally Samarin stumbled or coughed. Balashov moved quietly, stepping from sleeper to sleeper as if he knew each one even in the dark. He broke the silence.

'Of course, Kyrill Ivanovich, if you want to tell me why you were a prisoner, it would be a sin to prevent you,' he said.

'No, you were right,' said Samarin curtly.

'Only I remember you spoke earlier about a warning. About a man who was following you.'

'Yes. Perhaps it would be better if I turned back. Did you hear the story about the monk who arrived in a small town in Poland one time, rang the bell in the marketplace, gathered all the citizens and told them that he had come to warn them of a terrible plague which would soon afflict them? Somebody asked him who was carrying the plague. The monk said: "I am."'

'I see,' said Balashov.

'I was an engineering student in a town near Penza. There was a girl, another student. Katya. Well, the name doesn't matter. We were friends. She got mixed up with the wrong sort of people. So did I. Katya went further than me. This was back when the Tsar was still in charge. She ended up carrying a bomb. I liked her, and didn't want her to be arrested, so I stole the bomb from her. Then I was arrested. They sentenced me to ten years' hard in the White Garden.'

'So far north,' said Balashov. 'It must have been difficult there.'

After a while, Samarin said: 'You can't imagine how far, how cold, how forgotten. One night I went out with the intention of not going back. The darkness seemed twice as dark as this. The wind was so strong you felt like a piece of straw in it. I thought about what they'd say about me and understood it'd be nothing. I was part of no human movement and if all five hundred of us, the convicts, walked out of the barracks and lay down in the snow the snow would cover us and we wouldn't have touched history. Do you understand? We would have left no mark. We were the history of the moon. We were the history of air and water. There were holes waiting for us in the ice, we'd be the colour of ice and fit the holes. I thought if I ran to the wire and hit it hard enough I wouldn't feel anything, I'd sleep just the same, the wind'd shake me like an anchor in a storm and the cloth of the coat'd get caught in the barbs, and when they found the body and took it down they wouldn't be able to pick all the threads off the wire, and the wire'd fall and rust but the threads'd be there, my outline, a sign that some man ran against the wire, some time, and it'd be some tiny atom of the future better world, the memory of a man running through the darkness to his death, not lying down to let the snow cover him.'

'God was surely watching over you to bring you here,' said Balashov.

'God didn't bring me here,' said Samarin. 'A man brought me here. The man who is following me now. The Mohican. Have you heard his name?'

'No. I mean, I know the novel, of course.'

'This Mohican is no older than you or me, and he has the respect of all the great thieves, from Odessa to Sakhalin. They're afraid of him. The Mohican climbs over bodies to get where he wants to go just as lightly as you're stepping on those sleepers there. Even in prison, he was the freest man I ever met. The ties that form at once between two people, whether they're brothers or complete strangers like us, don't exist for him. He doesn't deal in honour, or duty, or obligation, or care.'

'And yet he took you with him when he escaped.'

'Yes. He took me for food. We ran in January, when there is nothing to eat in the taiga, let alone the tundra, and the deer herders are too far south. He took me with him intending to slaughter, butcher and eat me, like a pig.'

'God have mercy on us.'

'What could be better than food that walks alongside you, carries your goods, and keeps you company until the day you eat it?'

'Christ in Heaven, Kyrill Ivanovich, did he try?'

'He tried. I ran. I'm a day ahead of him, I reckon.'

'But if he made it this far, why would he need to . . . there's not much food in Yazyk, but . . .'

Samarin laughed and punched Balashov on the shoulder. 'Gleb Alexeyevich, you should be in the music hall! You're funny! Is that a train?'

The tracks were singing. A grey stroke of light flickered across the sky to the east, from the direction the men were heading. Balashov and Samarin stepped off the tracks, which ran along an embankment. The tracks sang louder and hissed and trembled. The train had a searchlight mounted on a pintle on a flat car. It came round the curve in the track, heading west, with two white lamps shining from the locomotive, trailing red sparks, and the searchlight sweeping the trees, blinding the owls and driving the panic-stricken martens miles away from the line on either side. As it came past Samarin began to run. Balashov shouted at him to stop. There was a flash of light and a report. Samarin jumped, grabbed at a chain hanging from one of the wagons, lifted his feet off the ground, swung for a fraction of a second, then fell and slid down the embankment, rolling into a coil of limbs in bracken at the foot. Balashov came over and pulled him to his feet.

'Your hand is cut,' said Balashov.

'Let me put some of that spirit on,' said Samarin. Balashov hesitated. 'I had a swig earlier.'

'I know,' said Balashov. 'I smelled it on your breath.' He took a handkerchief out of his pocket, soaked it in spirit and cleaned the cut. He asked Samarin if he had heard the gunshot. 'I think the bullet broke a branch over there,' he said, nodding at the trees. 'You were lucky. As I said, you can't understand who's on which side now. The old war didn't end cleanly. There were remnants everywhere in Russia, leftovers, like the Czechs. Russia took them prisoner in the old war, when they didn't have a country of their own. Now they do, and they're trying to get back to it, but they've got caught up in this new war. They're White, officially. But half of them are Red. There are thousands of them all over Siberia. They've taken over the whole of the Trans-Siberian railway, can you imagine? None of it makes any sense.'

'Everything makes sense,' said Samarin. 'Except you.'

Balashov laughed. 'We should go,' he said.

They walked on in silence until Samarin said: 'No, I mean it. Really, you are the one who makes no sense.'

'I don't understand,' said Balashov, his voice wavering as his throat dried up.

'You're not a barber. Unless you're a very *bad* barber. Barbers don't use scalpels and spirit and make their customers bleed like hogs.'

'Sometimes my hand slips when I'm shaving.'

'Shaving what? Shaving a throat with a scalpel?'

'Please, Kyrill Ivanovich, you must understand how far we are from the nearest hospital. Sometimes I carry out small surgical procedures.'

'I can believe you belong to one of these crackpot Siberian sects. I can believe everyone in your, what was it, Yazyk, does.

But you're too well born to be a barber, or a storekeeper, and you're too stupid to be a political exile.'

'Mr Samarin, I'm begging you. You've already said how content you are to avoid deep inquiry into other people's lives, when they do not want their lives inquired into.'

Samarin stopped, turned, and put out his hand to stroke Balashov's chin. Balashov turned sharply away. 'I know what you are,' said Samarin. He sank to his knees, held back his head and laughed at the sky, a full, long, savoured laugh. He levelled his head and looked at Balashov, shaking his head. 'I know what you are. I know what you've done, and I know what you've lost. Extraordinary. Do the Czechs know about this? No, obviously not. They probably think you're just regular crackpots. Well, this is very funny, although I'll bet the man – man? Boy? – in Verkhny Luk isn't laughing.'

'Not lost,' whispered Balashov.

'I'm sorry?'

'You said: "What we lost." We lost nothing except a burden, and gained a new life.'

Samarin yawned and nodded. 'I'm cold,' he said. 'As soon as I start thinking about being inside a warm building, I get cold.' He began to move and Balashov followed, keeping a good ten paces behind, now.

'What are you going to do?' said Balashov after a while.

'I'm headed for Petersburg.'

'But there are no trains. And there's fighting in that direction down the line.'

'I'll just have to persuade your Czechs to put me on one of their trains. Matula, is that his name? Their commander here?'

'Yes,' said Balashov. 'But he is not altogether normal. His soul is sick.'

'It's curious that you say other people are not normal.'

'Kyrill Ivanovich, please, whatever you do, don't speak of our nature aloud in Yazyk. The Czechs, as you say, don't know. We told them the children of the town were sent away to Turkestan to keep them safe.'

'Turkestan! You old entertainer. And what about your friend Anna Petrovna? And her son Misha?'

'Alyosha, not Misha.'

'So he's called Alyosha.'

'Please don't hurt Anna Petrovna.'

'Why should I?' asked Samarin. Up until this point he had been speaking without looking back at Balashov but now he turned. He sounded curious. 'Is she worth hurting?'

Points of light appeared between the trees ahead.

'There's Yazyk,' said Balashov.

Samarin stopped and looked at the lights.

'Poor little town,' he said. 'Listen. There's something you've got to tell me. Has a Tungus shaman been bothering the people lately? Some native charlatan who wandered out of the woods not long ago on a mangy reindeer, talking prophecies and trying to cadge drinks?'

'There's one who sleeps in the yard outside Captain Matula's shtab.'

'The devil there is. How many eyes does he have?'

'One.'

Samarin stepped up to Balashov. 'One good eye, you mean,' he said.

'One good eye, and two bandages, one over his bad eye and one over his forehead. He claims to have a third eye there, but no-one has ever seen it.'

'Mm,' said Samarin. 'Poor fellow. I fear he's the first on the Mohican's list.'

'You should wait here until the morning,' said Balashov.

'There are Czech soldiers on the edge of town at night. There's a curfew. You don't have a pass.'

'Give me the bottle,' said Samarin.

'It's not good for drinking, Kyrill Ivanovich.'

'I told you to give it to me.' Samarin's voice had altered. It sounded more as it had in the darkness of the tunnel, an older voice quite shorn of anything of a passionate man's highs and lows.

'I – I don't feel inclined to give you the bottle, Kyrill Ivanovich.'

'You're not a fighter.'

'No, but you should not take the bottle if I don't want to give it to you. You said you were not a criminal.'

Samarin's hand darted inside his coat and pulled out his knife. He pressed it against Balashov's cheek. 'Give me the bottle before I finish what you started.'

Balashov put the bag on the ground, bending away from the knifeblade carefully, brought out the bottle and gave it to Samarin.

'Now I've got no good reason to kill you,' said Samarin. 'You'll say nothing about meeting me tonight, as if it didn't happen. I'll say nothing about what you were up to in Verkhny Luk. We never met. I hope that's understood. What's on the other side of those trees?'

'A meadow.'

Samarin kicked away, ran through the trees and disappeared into the dark meadow, with Balashov calling after him to wait, and not to hurt Anna Petrovna. He heard Samarin's voice calling once, his younger voice: 'Comedian!'

Mutz

Lieutenant Josef Mutz, of the Czechoslovak Legion in Russia, sat at a table in his room, engraving with a skew chisel on a piece of cherry wood by the light of a kerosene lamp. Every minute or so he brought his nose close to the wood before consulting a smudged newspaper clipping with a photograph of Thomas Masaryk. He blew on the engraving and pressed it against an ink stamp. He took a small, rectangular piece of blue paper from a pile in front of him. On the paper, in Russian, Czech and Latin, were printed the words 'First Slav–Socialist–Siberian Bank of Yazyk: One Billion Crowns', and the number in figures. Mutz breathed on the woodcut and pressed it onto a blank area of the paper. An image of the first president of Czechoslovakia dried into the note. Masaryk's glasses came out smudged but the fine detail on the wrinkles round his eyes was there, and under the beard, Mutz had caught the faraway smile with which, for decades, the president had listened while fools talked. Mutz took a fine-pointed gouge and worked over the spectacles again. It was important that Masaryk didn't look as if he was wearing dark glasses. In Mutz's mint the eyes of good men would always be seen.

The lieutenant's mint was made of a large printer's tray set on its side to form pigeonholes, with a backgammon board nailed horizontally to the bottom, stained with the indelible brains of the Left Socialist Revolutionary Chupkin, whose head had been punctured by a sniper just when Mutz had been about to beat him, as he always did, although Chupkin refused to recognise any previous defeat, a stubbornness which had permeated his nerve cells and made scrubbing at the mess with sand and water as futile as trying to change his mind about the role of the bourgeoisie in the class struggle when he was still alive. The board held Mutz's chisels and gouges. The pigeonholes contained the short history of inflation in Yazyk under Czechoslovakian martial law, notes from one to 100 million crowns and the wooden plates to go with them. There were not many one-crown notes left. They had lasted a whole two months, while Mutz had been able to hold Matula to a standard, tying the value of money printed to the amount of food in the district. They were worn to limp softness and had lost all worth. Mutz took out the one-crown plate and ran his fingertips over the grooves. It was so long since it had been used that the ink had dried and left no mark. Mutz set down a fresh blank, inked the plate and printed a new copy. The image he had devised for the one-crown note was a woman representing Liberty. The word 'Liberty' was written underneath the woman, who might otherwise have been mistaken for someone famous, or at least someone in particular rather than a symbol, because he hadn't shown her full length, storming the barricades, but only her head and shoulders. Her head was bare, with a mass of long kinked hair bound at the back. She had a pointed nose, and her upper lip was fuller than the lower, finely outlined and a fraction upturned. She was gazing out of the note at the bearer with round dark eyes which she had used for so long to devour the world, and laugh in delight at the comedy of it, that even when there was nothing left to laugh at she hadn't been able to make them look away.

Mutz looked at Liberty for a time, his face burning. He

worked his neck, cold fingertips on the warm muscles, put the one-crown note in his shirt pocket and the one billion-crown note between his lips, got up and began clearing the clutter from his bed. He laid mammoth teeth, white lumps the size of bricks, on the floor, stacked specimen boxes containing mounted Siberian moths on a shelf, put a sheaf of Bolshevik propaganda cartoons in chronological order and slotted the draft of an account of the geology of the upper Yenisey into the library of notes in a trunk by the door. He lay on the bed and held the billion-crown note up to the light. No watermark. In Prague now they'd be using new Czechoslovakian money, with watermarks. With fewer zeroes. One day, let it be soon, a hundred men in ragged uniforms would disembark from a train in Prague and march towards the pub, and for the men in new suits and women in new dresses stopping in the street to stare the war would have ended a long time ago, and they would be embarrassed by these armed soldiers marching among their fashions, insisting like madmen that they'd been fighting for Czechoslovakia in Siberia. And the men of Captain Matula's company of the Czech Legion would walk into the pub, quiet, licking their lips, and try to pay for a drink with the Imperial money they'd carried in their pockets for five years, across Eurasia and America and the Atlantic, and the landlord would shake his head, and show them the new money, the Czechoslovakian money, didn't they have any of that? And one of them would dig in his pocket again and bring out a wrinkled billion-crown note from the first Slav–Socialist–Siberian Bank of Yazyk, and whack it on the bartop, and demand one hundred beers. And the landlord would serve them, perhaps out of pity, perhaps out of fear, perhaps because for a moment he might see his customers lined up in scruffy parade in a town on the steppe on the other side of the world, waiting to go home.

Mutz heard voices from the yard below his window, where

Captain Matula kept the shaman chained to a kennel. It was almost midnight. Mutz got up and opened the window. He was on the upper storey of the Czech shtab, which had been Yazyk's administrative building. The only other light, apart from his own, was the sentry's lantern, which hung on a hook in the archway leading to the yard. He saw the silhouette of Sergeant Nekovar in the archway. Nekovar turned round and moved out of sight.

Mutz called down to the shaman. He couldn't see him but heard a body slithering in the mud and a chain clink.

The shaman coughed through deep curtains of phlegm and said: 'Everyone will have a horse.'

'Have you been drinking?' said Mutz.

There was silence, and the cough, and in it the answer: 'No.'

'Sleep then,' said Mutz, and closed the window. Captain Matula was jealous of the shaman's dreams. The captain – who had attended seances in Prague before the war and seduced a black-eyed medium with hair the colour of Carpathian rock oil, believing her to be of Brahmin blood, only to find when they lay warm and damp in her unhooked perfumed silk and linen that her blood line had gone no further than Pressburg since the Stone Age – believed that when the shaman slept, his spirit roamed the taiga. The captain wanted to know what the shaman had seen, and how he made his spirit mobile, and in which worlds he walked; was it possible that the astral plane visited by European spiritualists was a busy, gossipy, modish place, like a Viennese coffee shop, all fern fronds and delicacies and ostrich feathers, where friends became lovers and lovers glanced at neighbouring tables, and news from the living was a waiter's murmured call to the telephone; while the shaman's upper and lower worlds were wide plains where heroes, demons and reindeer raced and fought, places of blood and iron? When the shaman had first come to Yazyk, looking for a drink, the captain gave him a room and a bunk and a little vodka and ordered him to pass on his shaman secrets, to help the captain establish order over the lands north of the railway, up to the northern ocean, to help a hundred Czechs partake of the mysteries of the larch forests. The shaman had asked for more drink, and then fallen asleep. When he woke up he started coughing blood and called Matula 'avakhi', which means 'demon' in the Tungus language. He called all the Czechs and Russians avakhi. He said an avakhi had blinded his third eye in the forest and his spirit could no longer see anything. Matula said he'd open his third eye, and ordered him to be chained up to stop him escaping or finding drink until he began to see again, and revealed his secrets.

Mutz lay down on the bed. There was a shuffling of boots outside the door and he heard Broucek calling his name. Mutz ordered him in.

In the doorway Broucek stood holding his rifle so that the muzzle bobbed a few centimetres off the floor, fidgeting with his collar with the other hand.

'Humbly report, brother,' he said. 'Mr Balashov. Wants to talk to you.'

'You don't have to say "Humbly report" any more,' said Mutz. He swung his legs off the bed, sat on the edge and wondered aloud what Balashov was doing out after curfew.

'Mr Balashov is very nervous,' said Broucek.

'He is nervous.'

'More nervous than usual.'

'Sit down.'

Broucek sat on the bed next to Mutz, holding onto his rifle muzzle with both hands. He was dark as a gypsy, although he said he wasn't one, and insisted, without ever getting angry about it, that no gypsy had ever come close enough to his mother to have contributed to the conception, or to have popped a changeling in the crib. He was tall and moved his height around with shambling grace. His mouth was slung in a permanent half-smile and his big inky eyes looked down on everyone with innocence and interest. He was not witty, he had no stories to tell, and he was not a good liar or flatterer, but in the course of the journey from Bohemia to Siberia he had found how attractive to women he was and, without intending to, had picked up, from them, the language that he could use to charm them. His friend Nekovar, who had devoted his life to identifying what he described as the mechanical basis of female arousal, was constantly badgering him for data. In the meantime, they were a farm hand and a draughtsman made soldiers. On the worst day of their reluctant service, in Staraya Krepost, Broucek had hung back, not wanting to take part, and never noticed how the women's screams choked into a horror more silent and terrible when they saw the fresh, clean, unlined face of Broucek, beautiful and unworldly, among their tormenters, when the women realised that angels and devils were far closer to each other than they would ever be to them.

'Here's the new money,' said Mutz, showing Broucek the billion-crown note. Broucek took it and studied it for a long time.

'There are nine zeroes,' he said.

'Yes. It's a billion. We're all going to be billionaires.'

'A billion is a lot.'

'It's a hell of a lot. It's a thousand millions.'

'A thousand millions!'

'Yes!'

'When I was working on the farm in Bohemia we got ten crowns. Ten!' Broucek grinned and his hands sprang fingers.

'You could buy all sorts of things with ten crowns. Kilo of coffee, or playing cards, or a handkerchief, or a bottle of cognac, or a pair of boots, or a day ticket to Hradec Kralove, or a newspaper, or an English hat, or an axe, or a mousetrap, or a mouth organ, or a bunch of carnations, or a bag of oranges. And the last time we were paid we each got, how much?'

'Five hundred million crowns.'

'Yes. And there wasn't anything to buy, except sunflower seeds, and they cost a hundred million for a packet. Maybe it's because Siberia is so big. Maybe that's it. Like the same thing happens with the miles as happens with the money. In Bohemia if you travel ten miles everything changes. Here you go thousands of miles and everything looks the same. Flat, with birches and crows. Is that Masaryk in the picture?'

'Yes.'

'You've drawn him well. When's he going to bring us home, then?'

'I don't know.'

Broucek sniffed and leaned forward to scratch his nose on the tip of the rifle muzzle. 'Must be fine for him in Prague,' he said. 'He'll be in the castle now. He shouldn't have left us here in Siberia, should he. Maybe he's forgotten us.'

'No, said Mutz. 'But you know. When the French and the British and the Americans got together and decided how to carve up the Empire, everyone who wanted a bit of it had to bring something to the table. Something valuable, like gold, or coal, or blood. And Masaryk didn't have any gold or coal to offer.'

'Didn't he?' said Broucek. 'I thought he was rich.'

'Not in those things.'

'So it's blood, then.'

'Yes.'

'Our blood.'

'Yes.'

'We fought the Germans. Wasn't that enough blood for them?'

'That was good, but now that the Germans are beaten, the French and the British and the Americans are worried about the Reds.'

'Because they killed the Tsar.'

'More because they want to divide all the property up and share it out.'

'Yes, I heard that,' said Broucek, nodding. 'It sounds like a good idea. Isn't that what Czechoslovakia is going to be like when we get back?'

'I'm not sure,' said Mutz. 'Is that what you want it to be like?'

'Yes. I don't have any property at the moment. I always wanted a grandfather clock. And a piano. And a suit like the ones the English wear to the horse races.'

'You forgot the gramophone.'

Broucek shrugged. 'Someone else can have the gramophone. I'd like to get back to see about the clock, though. It's time. We fought the Reds already. They seem like Russians. So do the Whites. They all seem like Russians. They don't need us here. They're killing each other well enough without us. Maybe Masaryk wants to make a Czechoslovakian Empire, like the British and the French have. Maybe he thinks if the English on their little island can have the whole of India, the Czechs and the Slovaks can run Siberia.'

'Not Masaryk,' said Mutz.

'The captain, is it, then,' said Broucek.

'Yes,' said Mutz.

'Some of the others think we should kill him.'

'That would be mutiny.'

'Yes.'

'He pays Smutny, Hanak, Kliment, Dezort and Buchar in dollars to protect him, and they have the Maxim gun.'

'You could lead us out of here. You could get us to Vladivostok without the captain.'

There was a timid knock on the door.

'Mr Balashov's outside,' said Broucek, standing up.

'I'll see him. You go down and ask Nekovar if the shaman's all right.'

'Nekovar's not here, brother. He's keeping an eye on the locals gathering in the back room of Mr Balashov's shop.'

'So no-one's on duty outside the yard?'

'There's only the shaman in there, and he's chained, so he can't get out.'

'What if someone wanted to get in?' said Mutz.

They ran out into the dark corridor, past Balashov, who called something after them. Mutz's boots and Broucek's beat the floor in the silence of the corridors and on the threshold the soldier's gunbolt rattled in and out. Outside it had turned colder and begun to rain.

The two men ran through the archway and approached the shaman's kennel, a smudge against the wall by the light from Mutz's window. Mutz's boot kicked against glass. He squatted down and picked up an empty litre bottle. Remnant raw spirit danced out and stabbed his sinuses. He dropped the bottle into the new mud, coughed and wiped his eyes. It was getting easier to see. The shaman was sitting in the mud with his back against the side of the kennel, his drum over his stomach, and his hands folded over the drum. Mutz shook him by the shoulder. The corroded iron animals and coins and folded tin can lids adorning the shaman's coat beat their cat's alley tune. Mutz took a lighter out of his tunic and held the flame to the shaman's face. The rain was washing bile and blood out of his scraggly beard where they had trickled from his mouth. The shaman coughed and there was a smell of stomach acid and alcohol. His good eye fluttered. It did not open.

Mutz put his hand on the shaman's shoulder and shook. 'Hey,' he said. 'Who gave you the drink?'

'Too far south,' said the shaman. The words were faint. He spoke good Russian through a strong Tungus accent and a throat roughened by age, illness and alcohol. In his whisper was the bare trace of a voice, like the last redness in the ashes of a fire. The words were not slurred: he sounded more exhausted than drunk.

'Did someone hit you?' said Mutz. There was a cut in the shaman's lip.

'I told him I couldn't see his brother in the other worlds,' said the shaman. 'I could only hear him, down there, where it stinks. I heard the brother crying that he wanted his body back.'

'Whose brother?' Mutz turned to Broucek. 'Have you any idea what he's talking about?'

Broucek shrugged. 'My father used to get drunk and scream nonsense for hours and nobody asked him what he was talking about.'

The shaman's head lolled over to one side and he began coughing and vomiting. Mutz shook his shoulder again.

'We have to get you inside,' he said.

Broucek said: 'You have the key.'

Mutz felt shame. He began looking in his pockets for the key to the padlock which fastened the shaman to the kennel. The shaman retched into the mud. The reflex seemed to jolt a mild current of life into him and he inhaled and opened his eye.

'Damn,' said Mutz. 'Broucek, run back to my room. The key's on the hook beside my bed. Shaman. Tell me who hit you. Who gave you the spirit?'

'When I had three good eyes, I was a brave warrior,' said the shaman. 'In the singers' stories I was a warrior. They called me Our Man.'

'Please,' said Mutz. 'Try to understand what I'm asking you. You must tell me who did this to you.'

'No,' said the shaman. 'He'll pursue Our Man to the Upper World. He is a cruel demon. He is an avakhi.' The shaman's hand darted into his pouch, pulled out a dry dark fragment, slipped it between his lips and began to chew. 'Our Man'll die soon. He's leaving.'

'Wait,' said Mutz. 'We'll take care of you inside. Wait a little while, just until we fetch the key.'

'Our Man can't see where he's going now, but he can smell larches, and hear a branch creaking where a rope's pulling on it, and smell a birch bark coffin swinging in the wind on the end of the rope.'

'Wait,' said Mutz. 'Live! Heal yourself. You've lived through worse nights than this. What did he say to you, the demon?'

The shaman's voice changed; it had the same barely voiced whisper, but without the accent, and a harsh sneer added, as if he had recorded the demon's voice on an acetate disk. 'You whoring son of a bitch,' said the shaman in the demon's voice. 'What did you come here for? D'you think I'm going to believe your whoring shaman visions and hang myself?' The demon's voice crackled through the shaman's in a distorted European laugh. 'Folk love blind fortune tellers. They think the less they see, the more they know.'

'I can find and punish this man if you help me,' said Mutz. 'Did you know him? Did you meet him before?'

The shaman breathed deeply in and out and shivered violently several times. In his own voice, he said: 'Leaving.'

Mutz heard the sound of Broucek running back. 'There's Broucek with the key,' he said. 'Soon we'll have you inside, out of the rain.'

The shaman put one of his hands palm down in the mud and made a sweeping stroke through it. 'No deer to carry Our Man to the Upper World, and no horse,' he said. 'This mud is soft. Push Our Man through it to the river, push him out into the water, and let the current take him north.'

Broucek splashed up and Mutz grabbed the key from him and unlocked the padlock.

'The keel slides through the mud and floats free,' whispered the shaman. There was a sound in his throat like an injured bird in fallen leaves. 'In the future,' he said, 'everyone will have a horse.' His head fell forward. Mutz lifted his head back, tugged at his jaw to open his mouth a little and held the back of his hand against it. He waved the lighter back and forth in front of the shaman's good eye, and sought a pulse with his other hand.

'Is he dead?' said Broucek.

'Yes. He drank himself free,' said Mutz. 'How does a chained man get hold of a litre of alcohol in the middle of the night in a town like this?'

Mutz looked at the shaman's face, tattooed lengthwise on each cheek and aged with lines crossways as deep and sharp as anything he could cut with a fine engraving gouger. The shaman's other eye was an empty socket, lost to a bear, which the shaman had considered an honourable loss. On his forehead was the deerskin band covering his third eye, which he said was also blind, but which none of the Czechs had seen. He fought and shouted if anyone touched it. Mutz pushed the band up over the dead man's scalp. The third eye was a swelling on his forehead, bone hard under flesh, with a picture of an eye tattooed on it. The tattoo was old, and deformed, as if it had been bestowed on the shaman when he was still young and the bone lump had yet to grow. Over it someone had made a recent, cruder tattoo, cut with a knife point. It was a word: LIAR.

They carried the shaman to the building in his own coat. As they passed through the rain the alcohol stink faded and they smelled wet rusting iron. They laid him down on the tiles at the foot of the stairs. Balashov was waiting there. He cried out to God when he saw the corpse.

'Was he stabbed?' he said.

'Why do you think he was stabbed?' said Mutz.

'Sometimes outlaws come in from the forest. Convicts without a home. Men who have become like beasts.'

'Have you any reason to think there's a convict in Yazyk now?'

Balashov shook his head.

'You don't sell spirit in your store, do you?' said Mutz.

'Respected lieutenant, as you know, this is a dry town. Our beliefs.'

'Yes, your obscure beliefs. Not even for medicinal purposes?'

'Are they so obscure?'

'Obscure. Yes. All I know is you don't use the church, you believe in God, you don't drink or eat meat, you always find a way to turn a straight question, and we never see your children.'

'Turkestan,' murmured Balashov. 'We sent them to Turkestan in a special train, you know . . . while the troubles . . .' He rubbed his mouth and ran his hand through his hair as he looked down at the dead man. 'Who would give him spirits? Perhaps they didn't mean to hurt him. Only to be kind to another unfortunate.'

'What are you doing out after curfew? I don't mind, you understand, but you might have been shot.'

'I was visiting friends on the edge of town. I wanted to see you. I'm afraid Anna Petrovna is in danger. I wanted to ask if you would send some men to guard her house tonight.' He nodded at the shaman. 'Poor man. Something new and unpleasant has entered our town.'

'What makes you think Anna Petrovna is in danger?'

'God told me. One of the Tungus will come to fetch the shaman's body. You should put him in a cold cellar meantime. But please, I implore you, send a soldier to watch Anna Petrovna's house.'

'I'll go,' said Mutz. 'Come with me.'

'No!' said Balashov loudly. When he said it, for an instant, another man entered his face and looked out of it, as different from the familiar Balashov as a wound is from a scar. 'No,' he said more quietly, the other man spinning down to nothing. A smile opened and closed and he put his hands on the lieutenant's sleeve. He said: 'Anna Petrovna won't allow me – has asked me not to approach the house on account of a long-standing disagreement between us. She's a good woman, she's respectable and honest, with a young son, she's a widow, widowed in the war. But you know her, don't you?'

'Yes,' said Mutz.

'You know what a good woman she is.'

'Yes. She is.' Mutz watched Balashov's smile coming and going, then a fit of blinking and a frown as a memory came forward.

'You put her face on your money,' said Balashov.

'Yes,' said Mutz. 'It was a mistake. I should have asked her first. She was upset. I saw her at the gate, watching us when we first came into town. I remembered her face. Faces stay with me. Well, I'll go there, anyway. Go home now.'

Balashov thanked him and left. Mutz and Broucek enclosed the shaman in two sacks and carried him down to a dank, chilly basement storeroom, where they laid him on a bed of straw and smashed crates, in a greater nest of junk, broken furniture and rusted metal parts. Mutz was used to seeing the dead look uninhabited, husks of life, but the shaman looked like something else. Preoccupied, perhaps. As if he truly believed in what he said he could do, walk in the spirit world, and had died focusing on the last big jump there. All he had ever done was to turn his dreams into words. What else was there? It was when people tried to turn their dream words to deeds that things became difficult. Something new and unpleasant. Mutz had never seen Balashov lie so perilously before. 'I'm going to join Nekovar for a while,' said Mutz. 'You go to Anna Petrovna's. I'll see you there later.'

Broucek smiled and nodded.

'Do you like her?' asked Mutz, feeling a sudden churning in his guts. Broucek grinned and shrugged. 'She's nice,' he said.

'Don't talk to her,' said Mutz. He wondered if Broucek could see his face changing colour by the light of the lamp. 'I'm ordering you, understand? See she's all right, wait for me outside her door, and leave her alone.'

Broucek looked hurt and embarrassed. He nodded again and trotted up the stairs.

Balashov

Mutz stood on the threshold of the shtab. There was no light in any window and the sound of the rain on the roof had risen to a roar. He put on his cap and an English poncho and went outside. The square was hidden in the rain and the dark; the derelict church, Balashov's store, the abandoned offices of the pelt broker and the dairy co-operative, the houses, the statue of Alexander III, the kiosks where the Russians sold smoked fish, sunflower seeds, tracts and journals and month-old newspapers, and, lately, personal effects, watches and jewellery and ornaments. Mutz stepped forward, off the little patch of cobbles, into the mud, a layer of liquid, a hard layer below, and between them a layer as lubricious as grease. The ground gave off a thick smell of liberated dust and he felt the weight of water striking his shoulders. His boot went deep into the edge of a rut as he crossed the square and he tugged to pull it out. It came with a snap of air audible over the rain. It took several minutes to reach the other side. Mutz stopped at the corner of a barn-sized log building raised on piles, with a sign across the gable. It was too dark to read it, but he knew what it said: G. A. Balashov – Goods – Groceries. The store, with windows on either side of the door, was shuttered up. Mutz climbed the steps to the door and knocked on it gently. He put his ear to the door, listened for a while, and walked back down to the square.

To the right of Balashov's store was a narrow gap between it and the next building. Mutz walked through the gap, through soaking clumps of dandelion, nettles and chickweed. The store was bigger than it seemed from the square. After a couple of small windows the wall stretched back, blank, for some thirty five or forty metres. The rain had stopped and halfway along, from inside the building, Mutz heard a faint beating, a sound between a drum and a pulse, and something else so indistinct and subtle he took it at first for a tinnitus in his own ears. He'd been to the seashore, near Trieste, when he was twenty. The sound was like that.

A steam whistle cried three times from the forest and the searchlight on Captain Matula's train beat at the darkness beyond the roofs of Yazyk. In the back yards neighbouring Balashov's, roped curs raised their heads and barked back. Mutz reached the far end of Balashov's store. At the back of the building was a compound surrounded by a high, solid wooden fence. Sergeant Nekovar stood against the fence, stubby and thwarted as a shrub, the last of the rain dripping off the ends of his moustache.

'Humbly report, brother, they're all in there,' whispered Nekovar. 'Rotating and pronouncing and prophesying. Three hundred and forty nine individuals, two hundred and ninety one males, fifty eight females.'

'Can I go up?'

Nekovar knelt down and brought up a retractable ladder which he extended and set up against the side of the building. Its components moved with greased silence and the metal rungs were solidly joined in place. Mutz shook his head.

'When you get to the top,' whispered Nekovar, 'lean forward and you find a handle. Pull it very gently towards you and a trap opens in the roof. Push the door upwards. It swivels. Climb in and you'll see a small slit of light where I've cut a port for you to look through. The floor of the roof space is strong but move quietly or they might hear you.' He sounded bored with his skill.

'How did you do all this without anyone noticing?' whispered Mutz, angry for some reason he didn't understand.

'I'm a practical man,' whispered Nekovar. Oh he was bored. Give him something difficult to do.

Mutz began climbing the ladder. Nekovar held the foot. As Mutz reached the top the ladder swayed and bent with his weight but did not seem about to topple. Gripping the ladder with one hand, Mutz reached forward blindly, expecting to touch the wet planking of the roof. His fingers found cold, rain-smeared metal. The handle was in his fist. He pulled, pushed, the hatch opened, and warmth and dryness puffed out, and the smell of Balashov's store, salt fish, cheap tea, dill and vinegar, sawdust, kerosene, mothballs and freshly cut wood. Mutz stepped off the ladder and into the roof space.

The beating sound was clearer. It was the stroke of a foot stamping on timber. Mutz heard the shudder and the rasp and the pain and the many lungs now in the sound of the sea. It was a gathering of people, breathing together. He saw the light where Nekovar had cut his spyhole. He moved towards it as softly as he could in his boots, lay down, and looked through it into the warehouse at the back of Balashov's store. A form turned in space. On either side of the warehouse were lamps and men and women swaying and breathing through their mouths, heads held back, eyes closed, hands knotted together in prayer, but there was a space around the form that spun, a ring of awe and dimness between the breathing circle and the white cloth turning. It would be a man, only a man altered to become a silent turbine, just the beat of his right foot on the floor and the hiss of the edge of his smock cutting the air. The arms were stretched out, the left heel pivoted on the floor as if fixed and oiled, the smock billowed up, and he spun, too fast to see his face, though Mutz believed it was Balashov. The smock and breeches were eyeburning white, turning so fast it seemed like a shimmer standing still, a spinning seed caught between the tree and the ground, held there whirling in a meeting of winds.

A woman fell to the floor, crying out words in a language Mutz didn't know, and lay there twitching and shaking her head from side to side. A man Mutz recognised from the street stepped forward and began to turn like Balashov. The breathing began to fall into time with the beat of Balashov's foot as he spun. The assembly breathed louder, filling and emptying lungs to their limit in a second. Two more people fainted and a man screamed about the spirit. The second spinner collapsed on the floor, shook his head, got to his feet, staggered like a drunk, and prepared to spin again. Balashov whirled on, then he fell, and was caught by two worshippers. He lay in their arms. His eyes were open, but very far away.

Gradually the breathing and the talking in tongues lessened and, without speaking, the celebrants walked to and fro across the warehouse, embracing and kissing each other on the cheek. Some drank tea. The movement began again. One after another, like Balashov, they began to spin, and the whisper of the hems in the air and their breathing and the gentle beat of their moving feet were like a crowd of children running through a wheatfield, trying not to be heard. Balashov rose and spun again, drifting to the middle of the room. An eagle-like woman, with a heavy brow, hooked nose and broad shoulders, was beside him and one by one the others fell or fainted or stopped spinning and stumbled back to the edges. After a time only Balashov and the eagle-like one were left, their faces and bodies half transparent, fogged with speed, spinning with the hands of their outstretched arms crossing, like wheels of a marvellous engine, joined but not touching, in unity and harmony. A sharp sound came from the eagle-like one, arcing out into the roofbeams, and she spun away from Balashov and began to slow down until she stopped and stood still, upright, bright with sweat, hair slicked and wild like a egret, dress sticking to her flat, smooth chest. Was she a woman?

'Brothers and sisters, Christ that you are,' said the eagle. 'I have flown to a high place, in an emerald aeroplane, to the eyes of God. Angels dressed me in a coat of leather, white as snow, and diamond pilot's goggles, and a leather helmet, like pilots wear, only white. I flew for many hours through the darkness until I could see, far away, the great, bright eyes of God burning, like two Londons in the night. As I grew closer I could see the million electric lamps of heaven, millions upon millions of shining lights, and the sound of angels singing from a hundred thousand gramophones. God's words pass to earth through telephone wires as thin as spiders' silk, my friends, as numerous as all the hairs on all the heads in Russia, and the angels most favoured of the Lord drive golden cars, with tyres of pearl, and horns of silver. I flew my emerald aeroplane across the face of God, and far below, on a green hill, by a river of electricity, I saw Jesus Christ our Saviour talking to our Christ, our angel, our brother Balashov. I see him returning now, brothers and sisters, I see Gleb Alexeyevich returning from heaven, with his news, with his messages from God. He is coming back! He is here!'

The cryback came from the wall shadows: 'He is here!'

'Brothers and sisters,' said Balashov. Sweat dripped from his chin. He was swaying and blinking and slurring his words. He inhaled slowly, a long, deep breath, and let it out. He steadied and smiled. The smile turned to an inlooking blankness, as if his spirit was too leaky a vessel to hold happiness for long.

'Yes,' said Balashov faintly. 'Yes, I have been there and spoken with our friend, our brother, the son of God, he who cares for the white doves.'

'He cares for us,' came the murmur back from the wall shadows. 'Not for the dead ones, the crows.'

'He told me that heaven's time is different and that the years should be counted as hours. We've been living in Yazyk through the hours of night, but the dawn is about to break.'

'Amen!'

The responses from the wall shadows brought Balashov further in from where he had been. His voice strengthened. 'In the first hour,' he said, 'the Tsar's commissioners came to our village and tried to conscript those among the white doves who had been men. By the grace and love of God, we made them understand we did not fight, and they left.'

'A season on earth is but an hour in heaven,' came the mutterback.

'In the second hour, the ones calling themselves socialist revolutionaries came, praised our virtue, admired our life in common, and took our chickens.'

The wall shadows laughed.

'In the third hour, the Tsar's men came drunk and called us traitors, unbelievers, they beat the brothers and sisters, they made us kiss icons and drink vodka, and took our horses and left. The Land Captain and his household went with them.'

'Wolves! To steal from the angels!'

'In the fourth hour, the influenza came to the village while we were weak from labouring without horses, and twelve of us moved to live with Christ always.'

'He knows his own!'

'In the fifth hour, the ones calling themselves Bolsheviks came, with their red banner, told us to rejoice that the Tsar, our enemy, was dead, and that now we were free to live as we chose under communism. We told them that we had always lived a life in common. They laughed, took all the food and cutlery they could carry, and left.'

'Crows!'

'In the sixth hour, the Czechs and a Jew came. They searched our homes, took our food, and began to kill and eat our cattle. They shot the teacher. The Land Captain returned. The Czechs promised to leave. They stayed.'

Silence in the wall shadows.

'The seventh hour is coming. The seventh hour is winter, and we are hungry, even though we share.'

'The angels share!'

'But the seventh hour is the dawn. He told me. The Czechs and the Jew will leave, and no more will come, and we will have milk and bread again, and send butter to market. The sun will rise on Yazyk, and the train will come weekly without soldiers. This will be next, brothers and sisters, and we must pray and be patient. No more Tsar's men, no more revolutionaries, no more red banners, no more westerners. We shall live our life in common for all eternity, here on earth as in heaven, without sin, restored to that state of Adam and Eve before the fall.'

'We have mounted the white horse!'

'Yes, sister. We must pray and be patient. Last night in Verkhny Luk I helped a young man mount the white horse and find salvation. He wept and held my shoulders while he bled, praying and thanking God for the strength to find salvation. Look, on my shoulder, the marks of his fingers! Afterwards he stood and threw the keys to hell into the fire alone. You see, even without sin, even without children, our numbers are growing. Patience, it will be soon, by the first hard frosts, they will all be gone.'

'The widow too,' said a woman's voice from the wall shadow. It was not a response, or a question. It was the eagle. She spoke as to weave her prophecy in with Balashov's.

'The widow,' said Balashov, looking down at the floor and wiping his palms on his smock. 'Christ said nothing to me about the widow. She lives here. In heaven, their names weren't mentioned, sister. Friends! It's late. A psalm, then let the needy make their petitions, and our closing prayer.'

Balashov opened his mouth and sang:

My wonderful Eden
How bright was my day
My soul and my comfort
In paradise lay
I lived there with God
Immortal, as one;
He loved me as closely
As his own true son.

'Amen!' came the cryback from the wall shadows. And: 'Immortal!'

Mutz heard footsteps behind him and squirmed round, flailing his boots and arms like an overturned beetle in the darkness. His wet poncho became hopeless batwings in his panic, and he bit his lips together to stop himself crying out. His right foot connected with something mobile in space which, horror, took hold of the bootsole and would not let go.

'Brother!' whispered Nekovar. 'You must go back to the shtab. They've caught a doubtful character sneaking about. Outsider, brother. Knife on him the size of a sabre.'

The Convict

One of the rooms in the shtab had been made into a cell. Several times Matula's enforcers had brought Czech soldiers there to hurt them when they complained too often about not going home. Every once in a while, as now, the forest and the railway, a single track spur off the main Trans-Siberian one hundred miles to the south, threw up the scraps and peelings of war's kitchen. A Cossack deserter from Omsk had been in, purging himself of alcohol and tearfully repenting his rapes and burnings. They let him go after a few weeks and he walked back into the forest. Perhaps he was still there. Perhaps he had walked out in a different place, with a different name and a different history. It was a good time for that. There was a Hungarian who claimed to be an ex-prisoner of war trying, like the Czechs, he said in broken German, to go home. Matula judged him a spy and shot him personally. There was socialist revolutionary Putov, who claimed he was visiting relatives. Eager young fellow, pleasant company, with big eyes and sleeves over his knuckles. He had wandered off somewhere. And the fur-buyer from Perm. They had no excuse to lock him up. He was as Russian as black bread and vodka, and he had papers. But there was no way Matula could persuade him to stay otherwise, and Matula wanted to talk to him about the mysteries and wealth of the taiga. So he put him in the cell for a week, then sent him on his way with a sack of salt red fish and an ugly birch bark nativity scene by way of an apology.

Mutz carried a lantern down the unlit corridor leading to the cell. It was dank and chilly in the night cold after the rain. The light from the lantern raced up and down the corridor as the lantern swung. It flashed on eyes and belt buckles ahead. The voices of Racansky and Bublik, the captors, rumbled. At night in these bare corridors, with parquet floors long since worn clean of varnish, with whitewashed walls and high damp ceilings, any two people talking together sounded like a conspiracy.

'Look, Racansky,' said Bublik as Mutz approached. 'Illumination is for the officers. Now, there's a metaphor for the class struggle.'

'You're right,' said Mutz. 'But I'm not going to give you the lantern.'

'Even the prisoner has a candle,' said Racansky.

'We gave him ours,' said Bublik. 'Rightly.' He lowered his voice. 'I believe we're in the presence of greatness, comrade Jew-lieutenant, sir. His name is Samarin. A political prisoner. Escaped from a place up north. I think he may be a Bolshevik. A revolutionary!'

'And you like that.'

'What good honest man doesn't? The alliance of soldiers, peasants and workers –'

'Then why did you lock him up?'

There was silence. Bublik cleared his throat and fidgeted with the safety catch of his rifle.

'Matula,' said Racansky.

'I know,' said Mutz. 'When are you going to make a revolution against *him*?'

'A revolution without lanterns?' shouted Bublik. He gave

Mutz the thumb-between-the-fingers. 'You'd be next against the wall, comrade bourgeois.'

'He's all right, Tomik,' muttered Racansky.

'In the revolution, nobody is all right,' said Bublik to the floor.

Mutz opened his mouth, then closed it. He desired some form of address for these men. To that extent he was still hiding under the ruins of the empire that he had lived in, and which had died. He had a weakness for categories. Most people did. He was the comrade-jew-lieutenant-sir. He knew what a risk it was to hug old categories to you in days of revolution and civil war and new countries, yet could not resist. He opened his mouth again. 'My . . .' Bublik looked up. '. . . co-functionaries.' Bublik's eyes narrowed and his whiskers seemed to twist back, like a cat's ears. He was contemptuous, but he couldn't help liking the phrase. 'Did you search him?'

'He has the dirt of a man on him,' said Bublik.

'He stinks,' said Racansky. 'And he's got lice.'

'We'll get him cleaned up,' said Mutz. 'What did you find?'

The lantern was guided to a foul rag laid on the floor. On it was a length of metal fashioned into a rough knife, a rolled-up scroll of bark, some lengths of string made from the guts of an animal, and a cardboard wallet.

'Not much, is it,' said Racansky.

Mutz opened the wallet and took out the photograph. His guts lurched. 'This was in his possession? Does he know Anna Petrovna?'

Bublik and Racansky crowded into the light to see the photograph. 'We didn't realise it was her,' said Racansky. 'He said he'd found it in the street.'

Mutz picked up the scroll and unrolled it. On it was scrawled, in slovenly capitals, 'I AM DYING HERE. K.' He put the scroll and wallet in his pocket and asked if Samarin had said anything else.

Bublik put his face close to Mutz's and grinned. 'Somebody tried to eat him,' he said.

Mutz took the key to the cell and turned it in the lock. 'I'll leave it open,' he said to the soldiers. 'Watch for trouble.'

'If you lay a hand on him, you'll have us to answer to,' said Racansky.

Mutz entered the cell and closed the door behind him. He looked down at the prisoner, who had fixed the candle to the end of the iron cot and was sitting cross-legged under its light, on the floor, reading an old copy of *Czechoslovakian Daily*. They were all old by the time they reached Yazyk.

'Do you read Czech?' asked Mutz, in Russian.

Samarin looked up. 'Do you have any cigarettes?' he said.

'No.'

Mutz put his hands in his pockets and regarded the prisoner. Samarin's thin, used face brandished disdain and an impatient, turning mind. His eyes reached out; they could touch, stroke, poke or claw at what they saw.

'I'm sorry we have to lock you up,' said Mutz. 'Strange as it may seem to you, we have the jurisdiction here, and since you have no papers, we have to look more closely into your story.'

'It'd be easier to put me on the next train to St Petersburg,' said Samarin.

'It's two thousand miles to Petrograd, and they're shelling the Omsk suburbs,' said Mutz. 'You know that, don't you?' He crossed the room and sat on the cot. By the light of the candle he saw a tiny movement in Samarin's hair and he shifted further up the mattress. The straw stuffing wheezed under his weight.

'When I was arrested, it was still called Petersburg,' said Samarin.

'When was that?'

'In 1914. I was tried and reached the labour camp at the White Garden in 1915. I broke out in January. Nine months ago. I've been walking for nine months.'

'There'll be a hearing of your story tomorrow,' said Mutz. 'I'd like to ask you a few questions now.'

'Well?' said Samarin. He coughed, hawked and spat into the corner, put his forearm on his knee, and rested his head on it. Mutz saw that he was not just tired. He had been crushed in five years among convicts, and in the wilderness. The life of his old bright, quick mind had flickered up, deceiving Mutz when he first saw him, but now the emptiness was slipping back; he had seen the hollowing out of convicts before, when the emptiness is not an absence of vitality, but vitality is a occasional desperate trick to hide the emptiness.

'How did you cut your hand?'

'It's full of sharp edges out there. A jagged branch.'

'Do you know anything about a Tungus shaman with a deformed forehead?' said Mutz.

Samarin shrugged. 'I met one like that in the forest a few months ago. The circumstances were difficult.'

'How so?'

'Another convict was trying to butcher me.'

'Yes. The attempt at cannibalism. And not since then? Did you bring any alcohol into town this evening?'

Samarin lifted up his head and laughed. Mutz half-stood in surprise. It was as if he had been standing in the hallway of a cold, dark house, having a shouted conversation with a half-asleep, muttering voice upstairs, when suddenly the owner had thrown open the door, put on the lights and lit the stove.

It was not that he had misjudged Samarin but that he had not been talking to him until now.

'Lieutenant Mutz,' said Samarin, getting up and looking down at his interrogator with one hand in his pocket and the other stroking his bearded chin. 'Before you ask, they told me your name, the comrades. Don't you think this is all rather topsy-turvy? Here I am, a student in my own country, a convict only by definition of a tyranny which has now been overthrown, along with the laws under which I was arrested. Yet I am being incarcerated by you. Who are you? A Jewish officer, commissioned by the army of an empire which no longer exists, now serving a country which you've never visited, because it's only a year old, and it's three thousand miles away. It seems to me that *I* should be locking *you* up, and asking *you* what *you* are doing here.'

Mutz looked up at Samarin, who stood over him with arms folded and eyebrows raised. He was tall, and looked cleaner, somehow. Clapping came from the corridor outside and Bublik cried 'Bravo!' Mutz felt himself falling into a well of sadness. He studied his boots, pursed his lips, and said: 'Well. I intend to go to Prague when I can, of course. What's the significance of this scroll?'

He took the scrap of bark out of his pocket. Samarin snatched it away from him and held it into the flame of the candle. It burned so fast he dropped it and trod it out.

'That was nothing,' he said quickly. 'In the White Garden the convicts would throw these out of the punishment block. I don't need to be reminded of that. I didn't know I had it in my pocket.'

'For eight months?'

'K . . . who was K? Kabanchik, I believe it was. A good thief, if it comes to getting in and out through a small, high window.'

'What about the photograph?'

'As I explained to the young Czechs out there, I came into the town from the north, along a stream, and after I passed the first farm, when the path becomes a road, I found the wallet lying on the ground.'

'In the dark.'

'I have good eyesight.'

'Do you know the woman in the photograph?'

'Should I?'

'Well, do you know her?'

'Do you?'

'Yes,' said Mutz. 'I do.' He rubbed his forehead with the fingers of his right hand. 'I'm not a policeman. I'm not a detective.'

'It's fine. Don't worry,' said Samarin. 'And the truth is that I didn't have light to see the picture by, before your men took it from me. May I see it now?'

Mutz took the photograph out and gave it to Samarin, who sat down on the cot and held it in the candlelight by the thumb and first finger of each hand, pincering the white border with his black, broken nails to avoid smudging the print. It was the same Anna Petrovna as Mutz's engraving on the Czechs' one-crown bill, the same mass of kinked hair tied at the back and the same hungry eyes, but a few years younger, and happier: Anna before the war. The dark dress with the high collar would have looked old-fashioned now but by the apparently careless unfastening of the top two buttons, and by the way Anna's head leaning on her hand made a thin pale jagged line of throat visible, it moved outside fashion. Where the studio photographers would have made a smooth white complexion under flat light, this picture was divided into extremes of light and shade. The harsh contrast between the darkened and the lit planes of Anna's face was echoed by the contrast between the severity of the chiarascuro itself and the happiness of her smile. The light – it was hard to tell whether it was sunlight or some theatrical contrivance of electricity – picked out the tiny wrinkles and blemishes even on her young skin, and this against the stark simple way her cheekbones and slightly upturned nose were outlined made her seem youthful and wise at the same time.

'Beauty,' said Samarin. If he'd said it any other way, Mutz would have become angry, and regretted showing him the picture. As it was, he said it matter of factly, as if being beautiful were a profession like carpenter or drayman, and every little town would have its beauty, as a matter of course.

'Not everyone thinks so,' said Mutz. 'Do you recognise her?'

'No. I wonder when this picture was taken. Whoever took it, he's good.'

'It's a self-portrait,' said Mutz. He took the photograph back and put it away. 'Do you have any reason to think she might be in danger?'

'I don't even know her name. I can tell you that everyone in this town is in danger. The second convict has been pursuing me. The Mohican by alias. I don't know his birth name. He's very businesslike when it comes to killing. A few dozen Czech soldiers aren't going to trouble him.'

'Do you know a man named Balashov?'

'No. Tell me, what is that woman's name?'

'It's not necessary for you to know.'

'Is it Anna Petrovna? It is! I can tell from your expression. My guards here were telling me about her. Do pass on my compliments on her photography. That picture will last longer than we will.'

There was a moment's quiet. Mutz sensed Samarin was

watching him. He turned and the prisoner was gazing at him with an expression of natural friendliness. Sure enough, when he spoke, it was with the most delicate, intimate concern, as if the two men had been close for years. For an instant Mutz found himself running back through his acquaintances. Did he know this man? Ridiculous. And yet could men exist with the power, by tone of voice, expression and an ability to read others, to make it seem as if they were every man's friend? To make it *seem* that a second of affection was of no less value than years – that time made no difference? Did memory have so little meaning when it came to putting a value on the present?

'You're fond of Anna Petrovna, aren't you, Jacob?' said Samarin.

'Is – it's not Jacob,' said Mutz. A cheap trap.

'Abraham?'

'My name is Josef. I'd rather keep it formal. Did you know the shaman was dead?'

Samarin shook his head. Then he snapped his fingers and pointed at Mutz. 'Alcohol poisoning!' he said. 'You gave your suspicion away already. Why would I – listen.' He lowered his voice, licked his lips and glanced towards the tiny window in the cell. He was serious and frightened. 'What if the Mohican was already here? The shaman knew what he tried to do to me! This is hard to understand, but while a great robber can boast to other thieves about eating a man, he can't allow the shame of the common herd knowing. And I know he was carrying spirits with him. Please, lieutenant. You can see how tired I am, and this tribunal tomorrow – if one of your sentries isn't on duty under the window through the night, I'll not sleep. Every one I tell about what happened in the taiga is in particular danger. You, now. But tomorrow I tell so many people even he can't kill them all.'

'Bublik! Racansky!' called Mutz, getting up and moving to the door. 'Come in here.' The two shuffled in. Mutz looked around. 'Mr Samarin has asked for some close guarding tonight, and I know you all want to get better acquainted. I suggest you spend the night together.'

'Honoured,' croaked Bublik.

'Don't give him a weapon. Otherwise, share what you have.'

'Leave us the lantern, then.'

'I'm not going yet.'

Bublik stepped a pace forward. 'We are honoured to have as our guest a genuine member of the Russian revolutionary class, an intellectual, an active friend of the workers, a lamp post – a beacon for the peasants, a man who has witnessed from within the nature of the greatest revolution the world has ever seen, who can help us understand the death throes of imperialism, capitalism and bourgeois nationalism, who can be our guide through the works of the great Karl Marx. Comrade Samarin!' Bublik clapped. Racansky joined in.

'Give me a cigarette,' said Samarin. Bublik nudged Racansky and Racansky gave him one and lit it. Samarin smoked greedily.

'Has there been a revolution?' he said.

'Yes!' shouted Bublik, raising his fist in the air.

'I suppose there were flags, marches, a change of government, the punishment of property owners, a certain amount of burning and looting, a redistribution of land and floor space, a quantity of swift justice?'

'Yes!' said Bublik, half-lowering his fist, less certain. 'Everything has changed.'

'And have you changed?'

'Yes!' said Bublik, raising his fist again. 'No!' He slapped his forehead, his chest, banged his rifle butt on the ground, punched Racansky. 'I feel . . . ignorant. That is, uneducated.

It's not my fault. We're all victims of the bourgeois-controlled Austro–Hungarian education system. There are so many . . . processes.'

'I'm only a student, you know,' said Samarin, sucking grey heat into his lungs. 'I'm not a revolutionary, as you say. Five years in a labour camp.' He laughed. 'For a misunderstanding! But, for what it's worth, this is how it seems to me: a revolution happens when it happens in here.' He tapped his head.

'Excellent!' said Bublik, standing up and sitting down several times. 'You see? Concise, direct. Comrade Samarin, what is the best way to carry out this inner revolution? Many of the soldiers and officers . . .'

'There are those who are naturally virtuous,' said Samarin.

'Yes!'

'Naturally generous. Selfless people, who work for the common good, who share without looking for profit, who make sacrifices without expecting gratitude. People who don't need to be organised.'

'Yes! I myself –'

'All the rest have to be destroyed.'

'Destroyed . . . I see.'

'It's very easy to see but it's very hard to look at. It's this way: even though there's no God, a true revolution has got to be like a divine punishment. Its agents must seem to the virtuous like agents of an inevitable, irresistible will – their own – taking the wicked to their doom. Give me a cigarette.'

'Give him a cigarette, Racansky.'

'It's the last.'

'Do you want to be destroyed by the will of the virtuous? Give it to him!' Bublik snatched it away and gave it to the prisoner, who leaned easily into the flame of the candle and lit up. 'Go on, please, Comrade Samarin. Tell us how this destruction is to be carried out. How will the virtuous be recognised? Is there a danger of mistakes?'

'That's for sure,' said Samarin, laughing. He rolled over onto his side and propped himself up on his elbow, waving the smoke out of his face. 'Remember, I don't know how it's going to happen. I'm only a student.'

Racansky said: 'But if the destroyers kill the innocent along with the guilty, don't they also deserve to be destroyed?'

'Shut up,' said Bublik.

'Racansky is right,' said Samarin. 'In the end, the destroyers will destroy each other, and it'll be over. That's why they may permit themselves to behave, as it must seem, like monsters. They're outside guilt and innocence. They're terrible, frightening, bloody. But you don't judge them, any more than you judge a flood, no matter how much it has terrorised you, no matter how many of your kin it has slaughtered. The waters will recede, and the flood is gone, though the land has changed.'

Bublik and Racansky looked at each other, Bublik nodding, Racansky staring at Samarin with his mouth slightly open. He lowered himself to the floor and sat cross-legged, rifle over his lap, looking up at the prisoner. Breathing heavily with effort, Bublik did the same.

'Does anyone know any jokes?' said Samarin.

'You see?' murmured Bublik to Racansky. 'Now he lightens the mood, and draws the peasants and workers in, with entertaining and instructive anecdotes.'

'Here's one,' said Samarin. 'A murderer takes a little girl into the woods at night. It's dark, the trees are moaning in the wind, and there's no one else about. The little girl says to the man: "I'm frightened." And the murderer says: "You're frightened? I'm the one who's going to have to go home by myself!"'

There was silence for a few moments. Bublik's face crumpled, he squeezed his eyes shut, opened his mouth and gave out a long, croaking laugh. Samarin, Racansky and Mutz watched him while he whined, shook his head, wiped his eyes and giggled. 'Home by myself!' he said, and doubled up again. 'Oh dear. You see?'

Mutz came forward into the circle of the three men and put the lantern down in the middle. 'Here,' he said.

Bublik looked up at him and turned back to Samarin. Samarin said to Mutz: 'You're a generous man, Josef, to leave your lantern when it's dark. Of course nobody will see you, either. If you're going to Anna Petrovna's, I'm sure you know the way.'

'I don't like familiarity,' said Mutz. 'See the prisoner is deloused and cleaned, with new clothes, by nine tomorrow. Sergeant Bublik. Please.' And he left for Anna Petrovna's house.

Anna Petrovna

Anna Petrovna Lutova was born in 1891 in a town in Voronezh province, on the European steppe, at a time of famine in the land around. Her mother went into labour on a rainy October afternoon and her father rode for the doctor. When the two men came back her father was pale. While the doctor went upstairs to attend to Anna's mother, her father sat in the kitchen without talking, drinking tumblers of cognac, spilling half of it on the floor because he filled the tumbler to the brim and then his hand shook, and he wouldn't let the maid pour for him, but looked dumbly into her eyes when she tried to prise the empty glass from his fingers. To find the doctor he had ridden out beyond the edge of town. On the way he passed a family by the roadside, three starved-looking children with their faces drawn over the teeth and their ears stuck out, asleep on the wet grass, and their parents standing over them, the father with a black jacket over his smock and a flat cap and his hands behind his back, staring into the distance; the mother with her sodden headscarf stuck wrinkled to her forehead moved forward as the horse approached, and shouted to him. She called him 'sir' and asked for help. Anna's father rode on without stopping. Why had the mother and father let their children go to sleep on the soaking ground, with the rain falling on their faces, and the children so weak and malnourished? It worried him and didn't worry him. On the way back he told the doctor and the doctor looked at him without saying anything until, half a mile further on, he'd stood up in the saddle and turned round and said to Anna's father: 'The children died of hunger, probably.' When they passed the spot the family had gone. The doctor said only the richer peasants were left in the villages, the rest had gone to the cities, or into the woods. People were eating bark and lizards. On the edge of town, they saw the family again, in a cart. The mother and father sat with their backs to the carter. The dead children lay under a piece of canvas with puddles in the folds, and the surface of the puddles puckered as the cartwheels rolled over crossruts and the rain slipped into the water. The parents didn't look up as Anna's father and the doctor cantered by.

Anna heard the story for the first time from her father when she was fourteen. Until then she'd believed what she heard from her younger sister, who'd heard it from the maid, that their father was so frightened at the thought of childbirth that he'd got himself drunk in panic. The father she knew only drank on holidays and picnics, or when he was with his friends, and they drank long, serious toasts to each other and to people with strange names like Obri Berdsley and Gustav Klimt, and Anna had been proud that when she was being born her father felt so deeply about it that he reached for the bottle, and crooned a song in the kitchen for his daughter while she was being born, perhaps.

Her father was an artist. He was self-taught and put it about that landscapes were a dead form. He despised photography, calling it corrupt, degenerate, debased, and refused to allow any member of his family to have their picture taken. Whenever they asked, he promised to fetch his sketchbook a little later, although once he'd finished the business that stopped him drawing – smoking, or reading a novel, or writing a letter – he forgot about the sketchbook. He painted portraits of businessmen, intellectuals and the Voronezh aristocrats, and their wives. He approached them to ask whether they would sit for him, rather than the other way round, but the truth was, sometimes they offered to pay. He waved the offers away, thrusting both palms forward forcefully as if he was penning bulls in a stockade, and said: 'A true artist doesn't work for money. A true artist doesn't need money.' It was true that Anna's father didn't need money, because the income from the brewery the family owned in Lipetsk was enough to pay for the upkeep of their house, the family's clothes, their food, four servants, and the desired things which appeared in the house as the century turned – the bicycle, the gramophone, and electric light.

Anna grew up with the scent of oil paint and canvas and freshly planed wood that breathed out when the door to the studio opened, with the sitters who stalked up the creaking stairs, the landowners who came in from their country houses with frayed hems and dandruff, smelling of damp, the middling bureaucrats stiff in mail-order new uniforms, the tall beautiful women, sometimes in twos, sometimes alone, rustling with hurried grace towards the light that filled the upper floor. After weeks, Anna's father would let her into the studio and show her the painting, and she was astonished at how her father changed his subjects, how the red veins disappeared from the cheeks of the landowners and their noses became sharper, how the bulge in their stomach migrated north to their chests, how the beautiful women became younger and their waists thinner than they really were, how shifty-eyed bureaucrats with dead faces came to look out from their portraits filled with wisdom and a yearning to do good for humankind which you never caught if you saw them on the street. When she was a child Anna thought her father's clients must be very grateful to him for smoothing out all their wrinkles, spots, lumps, warts and squints, for taking so much hair away from women's faces and putting so much on men's heads, for making, in fact, all the women and all the men look almost exactly the same as each other, so that none of them would be jealous. She thought they must pay highly for their portraits, in gold maybe.

One afternoon, a few weeks before Anna's fifteenth birthday, her father called her into his studio to show her his portrait of the local marshal of the nobility. Despite his fondness for contemporary art, in his own work Anna's father was conservative. His subjects were dressed formally and always stood against a dark background, so dark that it was hard to tell whether it represented night, or a curtain, or simply a brisk coat of plain black paint. Perspective was provided by objects in the foreground, like a skull, or books, or a globe, lying on a table, on which the subject's fingers rested delicately. Anna recognised the marshal by the quantity of medals and orders her father had detailed on his chest. On the table her father had painted three harvest mice which seemed to have starved to death. Their ribs stuck out, their haunches were wizened and the skin was stretched over their skulls, their mouths open in agony. He had never painted anything so real or so ugly. Anna saw that her father was excited, and nervous. The paint was almost dry but he was still wearing his smock. He hadn't come down to lunch that day, they hadn't seen him at breakfast, he hadn't even been in to kiss his daughters goodnight the previous evening. There were specks of paint in his beard and rings of weariness and anxiety around his eyes.

Anna knew her father wanted her to ask about the mice, so she did. He told her about the dead children he had seen on the day she was born, and how the marshal of the nobility, who was the biggest landowner in the area, had sold all the grain he had in storage and shipped it overseas while his tenants were dying of hunger, and then had tried to stop other aristocrats and townspeople raising money for famine relief, for fear they might think abroad that there was a famine. Anna looked at the painting, and looked at her father, smiling and frowning and blinking and chewing the end of a paintbrush. Her first thought was that it was very inconsiderate of other children to die on her birthday. Her second thought was that the marshal of the nobility, whom she had seen going stiffly up the stairs to the studio a week before, who had smiled and nodded at her, a small man with grey skin and heavily oiled white whiskers, was a monster. She sat down on the table where her father mixed his paints and a tear dribbled down each cheekbone. Her father put his brush down, put his hands on her shoulders, parted the hair from her face, kissed her on the forehead and told her not to worry, he probably wouldn't be arrested. This did not make sense to Anna, who was crying because it seemed to her a grievous way to disappear from her family's memory, dead and nameless under a tarpaulin in the rain, and she felt responsible, and ashamed that she hadn't been there to help.

She asked him again what the mice meant. He sat next to her and said that they were a symbol of the famine. She asked him why, instead of painting a symbol of the famine, he hadn't painted the famine. Her father blushed and stood up and threw his hands in the air and shook his head and said she had no idea of the risk he was running, offending such a powerful man as the marshal, even with a symbol. He could be sent into exile in Siberia.

Anna wiped her eyes, sniffed and frowned. She didn't want her father to be sent to Siberia, she told him. She said that if he was going to offend the marshal, maybe it would be better to paint pictures of real people on his estates who had died of hunger, so he might be offended all he wanted, but he wouldn't be able to argue about it. She said that if he wanted to offend the marshal he shouldn't have painted him as a tall, strong man with piercing eyes and the same rosy cheeks as all the other men and women he painted, he should have painted him as he was, grey-skinned, old-boned and sly. Her father became angry, grabbed her arm, threw her out of the studio and slammed the door.

A few days later Anna's father wrapped the painting up and left for an afternoon meeting of the city assembly, where he was going to present it to the marshal, who hadn't seen it. When Anna saw how frightened he was she became frightened herself. Her father kissed and hugged her and her sister and her mother as if he might never see them again. A fear had penetrated deep into him. Anna realised it was a shard of the outside world which had cut into her father's heart. She'd never really seen it before, the terrible strength and lack of mercy of the accumulation of all the people you didn't know which could reach inside you and make you afraid. She'd never seen it, and now she saw it on her father's face. After that she only saw it on him two other times, when he heard there was a strike at the brewery, and when he heard he was a bad artist. When she saw it she understood that she'd seen it before, that other people had it all the time, men with dusty suits and frayed caps who walked slowly down the streets as if they were afraid to go home, and the absence of it in her father was a sign of how few dealings he had with that world. It made her want to capture it and pursue it. Later when she met her husband she would see in him neither the fear of the carelessness of the great world, nor her father's deliberate ignorance of it, but a belief in another world still.

That evening her father didn't come back, and Anna and her sister and their mother sat up until after midnight drinking tea and playing cards. Anna's mother told the servants to go to bed and the three of them sat together on the divan, watching the German clock on the wall beside the stove. The girls' mother ran her fingers through their hair until they told her to stop because she was rubbing their scalps too hard and they fell asleep on their mother's shoulder after the clock chimed two. At five there was a battering on the door and the house woke up to news. Anna's father had been arrested by the police, on the orders of the marshal of the nobility, and was being held in the town jail. Anna's mother grabbed a shawl and hat and dragged her two sleepy daughters into the street. It was May, just getting light, and they ran and strode and tripped through the dusty blue empty streets, watched by slow drunks. Anna stood outside the jail, holding her sister's hand, listening to her mother argue for hours with the guard at the jail gate, trying to get to see her husband, weeping and waving her handkerchief in the guard's face and pointing to her children. The guard listened carefully and nodded and turned his moustache to the ground and said and did nothing, while a small crowd of other prisoners' wives, poorer than Anna's mother and angry that she was getting all the attention, gathered at the gate. In the end Anna's mother walked away with her head bowed. She looked at Anna and asked her in a voice hoarse from pleading why she wasn't crying, it would've helped. Then Anna did cry.

Her father was in prison for two days. He wasn't sent to Siberia, fined or tried. The marshal of the nobility was hurt by the painting. The accusation was bad, the fact he had not realised he was being accused at first was worse, they were only three mice after all, and everyone else knew he was being accused, because Anna's father had spent months working his courage up to paint the mice, and had made sure everyone knew what he was about to do. But it was 1905 and the marshal of the nobility was cautious. The council was a nest of liberals, the army used artillery on the streets of Moscow, peasants were setting fire to landlords' properties. One day there was smoke in the city from where the Black Hundreds were laying into the Yids and smoke from beyond the edge of the city where the blind husk of Kulin-Kalensky's manor house fumed from its windowholes. The police were playing their own game, and the papers weren't to be trusted, the editors had lost their proper fear. When the marshal's own daughter told him that she wasn't welcome in some of the best houses in town because he had arrested the artist Lutov, he arranged for Anna's father to be let go.

Anna's father came home in triumph, tenderly embraced his family, and left after an hour for a banquet in his honour held by the leading liberals of the town, where he was praised in speeches as the lion of democracy, and in toasts his name was joined so often to the urgency of a constitution and the establishment of an elected parliament that he came to believe the three were part of a whole, and that one without the others would be meaningless. Over the weeks and months which followed this idea faded from the minds of all the banqueteers except Anna's father, who continued to believe that of all the heroism shown in the struggle for freedom in 1905, his had been the most extraordinary. His family saw little of him, and dust gathered on his palette and brushes, while he smoked poods of tobacco and drank Turkish coffee with liberals and revolutionaries in dark restaurants and stuffy conspiratorial flats. He met the revolutionary Tsybasov, recovering from the wounds he got fighting Cossacks in Odessa, on the run from the police, likely to be hanged if caught, a scar across his jaw where a sabre had almost sliced his head in half. When Anna's father greeted him as a right-thinking warrior who had done almost as much for the cause as he had, Tsybasov – who at the age of sixteen had addressed a revolutionary congress in Vienna, without notes, for an hour – was so astonished that he couldn't think of a reply. Anna's father began spending time at a house that acted as a night school for young women who wanted to learn about Marxism. He was able to talk about Marx to them with more eloquence and conviction than they could muster because he wasn't hampered by any knowledge of the great thinker's writings. Some of the Marxist girls were not much older than Anna.

One sultry evening the following summer Anna's sister's head began to hurt. She became feverish and her nose bled. She lay in bed for ten days, coughing blood, raving and twisting in damp coils of linen. The doctor found a rash on her torso and diagnosed typhus. They sent telegram after telegram to Anna's father, who had taken a cottage in Crimea for July, intending to deepen his study of Marx, but it must have been mislaid, because by the time he returned to Voronezh, his younger daughter was hardly moving. Her hoarse, shallow breaths were the loudest sound in the quiet room where she lay. Anna met her father at the door, they embraced, and they walked upstairs hand in hand to the room. Anna's mother was sitting in a hard chair next to her youngest, talking to her about a ball she'd been to in St Petersburg, and the silk dress she wore. Her daughter's eyes were closed and her lips, slightly open, had a thin crust of foam. When her husband came in, Anna's mother looked up and looked away again, without stopping what she was saying, as if a stranger, a stranger with a reason to be there but still a stranger, had come in. Anna's father leaned down, put his hand on his daughter's forehead and spoke her name several times. She didn't move. Anna's father sighed slowly and deeply, furrowed his brow, and said: 'I must paint her.'

He fetched the easel and a blank square of canvas and began to make a charcoal sketch. Anna watched him. He kept glancing from the sketch to his daughter as if it would be to the life. The figure on the canvas was standing up, though, like all her father's subjects. Anna saw a child version appearing of all the women her father painted, slim, with long, thin arms and legs that curved this way and that as if they were made of rope, pale lips, waves of liquid hair, a little upturned nose and enormous black eyes, while Anna's sister was plump, with a flat nose, small brown eyes and red lips, and fine fair hair that seemed to try to fly apart even when it was lashed into pigtails.

'Papa,' Anna said. 'Papa. I know what we should do. We need to take her photograph. I can run for Zakhar Dmitryevich. You don't have time to paint.'

Her father looked up at her, dropped his materials, pinched her round the top of her arm and pulled her out of the room, closing the door. He asked her what she meant by saying that there was no time. Was she saying her sister was going to die? Wasn't she ashamed?

'She is going to die,' said Anna, looking down at the floor. 'And she'll be buried and we won't have a single photograph to remember what she really looked like.'

Her father went white. He slapped her across the cheek, the first time he had hit her, and told her she was an ignorant little fool. Did she think a mess of chemicals on paper, a gimmick of light and mirrors, could reach into her sister's soul and see her true nature? Was she so cold, did she have so little feeling, that she couldn't understand how her sister's father, who had watched her grow from a baby, who shared his daughter's blood, who had a gift with pen and brush so powerful it had shaken the political foundations of southern Russia, would paint a picture of her in which all her breathing, beating, singing life would be captured for ever, more vitally than a cheap gimcrack contraption for peasants and soldiers to celebrate their ugliness and cheap clothes?

Anna's cheek stung. She was surprised that she didn't cry. She kept her hands clasped behind her back and looked up into her father's face. In wonder she realised her words had caused him far more pain than his hand had left on her face. He was blinking and breathing hard. She wanted to hurt him some more. She said: 'All your portraits look the same.'

Her father raised his hand to strike her again and she squeezed her eyes shut and hunched her head into her shoulders. The blow didn't come and when she opened her eyes she saw he had let his hand fall and was trembling. He screamed at her that she was a monster, that she could not be his daughter, and told her to go to her room.

The door opened and Anna's mother came out. 'She's died,' she said.

When the funeral was over Anna's father went back to Crimea. Up to the time he left he wouldn't speak to her and it was years before she saw him again. Anna's birthday came a couple of weeks after the funeral. Anna's mother came into her room as the sky lightened, while she thought her daughter was asleep, carrying a large, heavy parcel wrapped in cream paper. As soon as her mother had gone out Anna went to open it. It was a French camera, in a hinged wooden box lined with velvet with a handle like a suitcase. Besides the camera the box contained a folding bipod, flasks of chemicals, different lenses, a cable with a plunger for pressing the shutter at a distance, and a thick book called *Principles of Photography*, all trim in velvet pockets.

Anna's first picture showed her standing at the dressing table in her room, with sunlight coming from behind the camera, shining through tall windows. It was early afternoon and the sun falling on Anna was high, bright and hot. In her inexperience and eagerness she hadn't thought about the light and shade and in the picture she floated in a dazzling parallelogram that leaned away from the darkness of the unlit room around, where dim lumps and corners slunk formless to the edges of the paper. Her white dress was so overexposed that it was impossible to make out any detail or texture and in the picture it seemed to shine with a light of its own. She was sixteen. Her hair was tied back in a ponytail and her face came out clearly. She was holding the shutter cable behind her back and having pressed it tried very hard to keep still for a long time in case the exposure came out as a blur. Her head was raised. She looked proud and happy, looking down on the world with eyes moist from the effort of keeping them open in the sun without blinking and lips only just held together as she tried not to laugh.

Anna took over part of the cellar for a darkroom, persuaded her mother to pay for a black felt curtain to be hung from ceiling to floor in the corner behind the pickle barrels, and frightened everyone with the smell of her chemicals and her yelling at anyone who tried to push through the screen when she was developing pictures. She took down her father's oil paintings of her that hung throughout the house, new paintings for each year of her life, and put them on the bonfire of leaves the gardener made in November. Her mother watched and frowned from the window and didn't try to stop her, but the gardener refused to burn them, and said he would take them to his brother in the country, which is how they ended up in a market stall, and fetched a poor price, and disappeared.

In their place Anna put up self portraits and photographs of her mother. She wanted to put a picture of the servants in the hallway but her mother objected and insisted it hang in the scullery. Anna went to the cemetery and took a picture of her sister's grave in the first snows, with a sticky lees of crystals cast on the gravel at the base of the stone, and a bunch of dried, frostbitten chrysanthemums wedged in the angle as if seeking shelter. She had it put in a black frame with a black ribbon across one corner and wanted to hang it instead of her father's last painting of her sister but her mother shook her head, so Anna put it on her dressing table.

Anna took her camera to the market and photographed old peasant women in curdstained aprons standing with their big knuckles resting on the counter on either side of ruined white castles of tvorog, their eyes deep and sceptical behind red cheekbones. Some pulled the edge of their headscarves over their faces and shooed her away and set up a cry that she was putting the evil eye on them. Others laughed and asked Anna to send them a copy, and when she asked for their address, they called themselves Aunt and gave their first names and the names of their villages. Anna took pictures of a work gang loading sacks of grain onto barges on the Don, they all stopped what they were doing and arranged themselves shyly into two sweating lines, and none of them knew whether to fold their arms or to hold the lapels of their jackets or to put their hands behind their backs, they kept moving and sniggering and nudging each other and whispering like girls, till they grew bolder and began asking whether she was married, and would she like to dance, and could they take her on the river, and by the end they were all laughing and singing her songs and capering on one leg until the foreman appeared from a shed where he'd been napping and scolded them back to work.

She got up before dawn one morning to photograph fishermen in small boats, bilges awash with tiny silver fish like pools of mercury, before the sun had burned the mist off the river. She set up the camera on the family balcony to photograph the carrying of the cross through the town, the priests blinded by dust whipped up by a summer wind, their black and white vestments snapping with a sound like a city of geese rising at once from a field, and a crazed indigent in a ragged black suit without a shirt or shoes skipping and hopping backwards in front of the procession, his head lifted up to the golden cross, hands alternately held out towards it and rubbed together as if it was a fire and pressed to the sides of his head. He tripped and fell on his back and the procession stepped over him. Some of the priests kicked him as they passed and one placed the sole of his boot squarely on the chest of the sicksouled one. Eventually he was hauled to the side of the road, bleeding from the corner of his mouth, by a party of nuns, who laid him carefully in the gutter and hurried on after the cross. After a few minutes the lunatic roused himself and followed the dust cloud on all fours.

One day in the autumn of 1907 Anna went to take pictures of a group of students who had set up a swimming, mushroom-gathering and skating club. They swam, skated and gathered mushrooms, but only to hide from the police their discussions of communism. Anna had heard of communism, the word was in the air, but was unsure what it was; she had an idea it was an austere, worthy, artistic–philosophical sect, perhaps with vegetarian tendencies, whose members lived in huts in forest clearings – serious people, long-bearded intellectual men in peasant smocks, women in plain black dresses, who spent their time discussing how the world could be made a better place and, although they were from good and prosperous families, growing and cooking their own food and even doing their own laundry, although how they managed to have enough time for discussion without servants to do all that work was a mystery. Perhaps the women did the laundry and the cooking and the potato harvesting, leaving the men free to organise themselves for discussion. Anna didn't read newspapers, only novels, and poetry. Much of the time when she was reading Alexander Blok she didn't understand what he meant to say but she loved the light, the colours and the space, formless yet intricate, which his words seemed to open a prospect to, and left a longing with her. She asked the students if communism had anything to do with Marxism. A lanky student with glasses and straggling collar-length hair, with thin wrists coming out from the cuffs of an old canvas coat several sizes too small for him, looked at her as if she had asked how many days there were in the week, before beginning, with growing pleasure, to explain. Anna interrupted and asked if he knew a man named Lutov.

'I know the name Lutov,' said the student. 'He says he's an artist. I've seen his pictures. He uses debased bourgeois forms. His style is very primitive. He paints archetypes of pretty women and pretty men. He speaks about himself like a revolutionary, as if he'd placed a bomb under the Tsar's pillow, but so far as anyone knows he's never done so much as handed out a leaflet. He's a parasitic rentier, anyway, he lives off the blood of the workers at some factory he owns. He spends most of his time trying to seduce girls who hang around with Marxists. You're just his type. You should be careful.'

Anna followed the communists to a meeting they'd organised at a dyeworks near the docks. The workers had downed tools after one of their number was drowned in a vat of coal tar and his brother was sacked for taking a day off for the funeral without asking. There were six in the party that strode along a cobbled lane to the plant not long after dawn. The lanky one with the hand-me-down clothes, the chairman of the club, went ahead, carrying a bundle of leaflets, a pot of paste and a brush in a leather satchel over his shoulder. Behind him was a stout, well-fed boy in a black leather cap and a new black leather coat, his face pocked by some childhood malady. He had tightened the belt of the coat so fiercely, with an uncompromising knot that could not be untied except by sitting down and working a spike into it, that he resembled a figure of eight. He had a notebook and pencil in one hand. He was intending to write an article for the underground magazine *Young Social Democrat of South Russia*. A small woman in a brown coat with fair hair tied in a bun and no hat, her skin pale and smooth as wax, her eyes big and watery blue, carried a rolled-up banner made of red cloth. She walked with quick, short steps and her head slightly bowed, as if she was late and expected to be punished. This emphasised the power and grace of the woman next to her, a tall, beautiful communist princess in an Astrakhan coat, wearing a grubby peasant's cap on her short black hair like the season's must have from Vienna. She had fawn skin, high cheekbones and finely narrowed eyes. Her grandmother was a Buryat. She carried a purse in her gloved hand, and occasionally turned to smile at Anna, who was toiling in the rear with the bipod and plates over one shoulder and the camera on a strap over the other. Alongside Anna was a man with a sweet, bristly face, a Jew in an old black bearskin hat that had gone spiky in the raw air, carrying an empty crate. He was trying to explain Marxism to her as they hurried along, and she was trying to listen and understand and at the same time work out what it would be like to be seduced by her father, and what seduction meant, and what it was about the process, when it happened in novels, that made men treat the women so badly afterwards.

There were others moving among them and alongside them,

workers, a thickening drift as they approached the clammy gathering-space in front of the locked factory gates. Standing on brown weeds and half-melted, half-frozen mud and puddles stained by brilliant chemicals were two hundred men, gathered into groups around pairs of the eloquent among them, disputing what they should do. There were footsoldiers at the gates, a group of a dozen mounted Cossacks on a rise between the workers and the river, and in the lee of a half-built brick shed closer to the town, a troop of regular cavalry, watching and smoking and conversing. Anna and the communists followed the chairman to a large man in a woollen coat and a bowler hat with a scrap of red cloth tied around his upper arm.

The two men shook hands and the workers' elder nodded at the other students. His gaze lingered on the women for longer and his eyes narrowed and he turned to the chairman and looked back at the women and nodded again and began to talk to the main communist. He was many years older than the tall student but at some earlier time he had passed through a barrier to understanding and he looked and talked to the chairman not as a worker to a student or a self-taught man to a university-lettered one or as a man who had fought with his fists and sired children to a pale near-virgin who until recently had lived with his comfortably-off family, but as a man with a problem talking to a specialist who offered a solution. The rest of the strikers hushed their champion rhetoricians and moved towards the group. The two women unfurled the red banner and stretched it out. Men's lips moved as the literate among them spelled the words painted in white, which read: For All Workers – Respect, Dignity, Justice. The Jew set the crate down in the mud and the chairman stepped onto it, putting him head and shoulders above the crowd. He gave his bundle of leaflets to the elder who started handing them out. Silence fell over the strikers as they looked up at the young communist, and there was a sense of reverent expectation, such as the practitioners and celebrants of old religions imagine occurred in the miracleworking early days of a faith, when the word was about to be preached for the first time, but when rumour of its efficacy had gone before it. The faint murmur of engines came from the factory, a horse whinnied, and men suppressed their coughs.

When the chairman spoke, in an insistent voice that carried far, diving and soaring like a lark over a hayfield, it seemed to the strikers that he knew their suffering, could name them and describe them, as if he'd been watching them for months, hovering invisible at their shoulders while they tended stills and vats and furnaces. He was acquainted with their trade, and considered them admirable men. He called them respected workers, comrades, brothers. He knew how little they were paid; what long hours they worked; how those who were injured were turned out of the gates without a kopeck to bide them over, and on certain occasions, pursued beyond the gate by bailiffs for damage they were supposed to have done to machinery with their mangled limbs and crushed skulls; how the owner addressed them with familiarity, as if they were serfs or small children; how most of what he paid out in wages the owner took back in rents for the rat- and roach-ridden barracks where the workers and their families lived, and most of what was left in takings at the company shop; how the owner's son had raped one of the workers' daughters, and gone unpunished, with the family given a few gold roubles and sent far away, to Kharkov, and warned never to return; of the owner's latest vile crime, after the drowning, when the victim's brother had held the drowning man's hand for a moment with the pulse still beating before he died, and how when he defied the owner over the funeral the owner had seized him in a frenzy and struck him about the head and beaten him with a pole till the blood poured from his ears, and had to be held back, else there would have been two corpses, and again, no prosecutor would touch the case.

The chairman had captured them; he paused; the workers were still now as well as silent. He went on, adding gestures to his words, clenching his fists and shaking his forearms, punching his open left hand, rocking back and spreading his arms wide, pouncing like a cat, crouching down and sweeping his outstretched arm in a flat arc across the crowd's heads, planting his hands on his hips and cocking his head to one side and then leaning forward and stabbing his finger into their faces, you, and you, and you, all of us. Anna, making space among men's shoulders, in the smell of damp and tobacco fixed into the cloth of their coats, lowered her head to the viewfinder of the camera and in a window of light in darkness saw the chairman straighten up, lean back and look around the crowd, nodding as he smoothed the world of air with his hands. She moved the camera down until only the chairman's shoe and trouser leg appeared in one corner of the picture and the viewfinder was filled with the faces of three of the workers. At that instant, one was shouting out, his eyes on fire between his cap and his beard, the word he shouted, True! not to be recorded on the gelatin and silver nitrate of Anna's plate, but his rage to be witnessed forever, another worker was staring up at the chairman with a face full of silent wonder, as if one of the apostles had walked into the city out of the forest, and revealed that from this day, all rumoured, dreamed of and reported marvels would be witnessed by the common man, and more besides; while the third man, not yet ready to believe, nor ready to lead the sceptics' party, but always ready to laugh, was looking to one side, looking for the crack in the spell he could prise open with a joke. Anna pressed the shutter, pulled out the plate and replaced it with a fresh one.

The chairman spoke on, louder, more confident and with new wonders to ease the workers. He had astonishing knowledge of the owner's finances and explained how much it cost to make the dye, and how much the dyes sold for, and how the owner pocketed the difference. He explained how the difference belonged to the workers, since it was they who made the dyes, not the owner – did he have the skills to make them? Were his hands ever stained with vitriol or carmine? No! They were stained with blood only, workers' blood. The owner was a parasite, not a maker of necessary, useful or beautiful things, a man who had gained the power to steal the fruits of the workers' labour not by skill but by exchanging his humanity, his natural good-heartedness, for the chance to sit with that tiny gang of bandits who ran the banks, the capitalists, and take a share.

Somebody called out that the banks were run by Yids. Others cried Aye. The chairman looked into the eyes of the chorus one by one and spoke on with a voice that was on their side and at the same time made their side so much more magnificent than they had imagined. Jews, Russians, Tatars, Germans, Poles; it was not the kind of blood that mattered, but whether you were one of those that drank it, or one of those that had it drunk.

'That's what the Yids do,' said the dissenter. 'They kill Christians and drink their blood. They do it in secret.'

The elder told him to shut up and not be a fool.

'The capitalists and their newspapers tell you these fairy tales to keep your eyes from the true secret, the greatest and most terrible secret,' said the chairman. He lowered his voice slightly, and even the breathing and coughing in the crowd stopped and the workers shuffled closer to the centre. Far away there was a clinking of metal as the Cossacks adjusted their gear.

'The secret is that there are many of you, and few of them. You are strong, they are weak. When the workers in a single factory rise up, as you have done, they tremble, and they don't fall. But what if all the factories stopped, and not just the factories, but the peasants, and the soldiers? And not just in Russia, but in Germany, and France, and England, and America? This is the secret they do not want you to know: you are not alone. They speak of the people. The people is you, the people is in you and you are in the people; the people is a terrible force, stronger than armies because without the people there is no army, stronger than money because without the people money has nothing to buy, stronger than love, because without the love of the people there can be no true love. The people is you. The people is all-powerful. Znachit, you are all-powerful. Look! Look, brothers!'

The chairman pointed towards the gates of the factory. The soldiers had opened them to allow the owner's car to drive out. Despite the cold the black car was open and the crowd could see the owner sitting in the back, in the middle, bulked in squirrel fur and his own fat and muscle, with an English hat on his head, like the one worn by the English detective Sherlock Holmes. His seat was set high and as the car rolled over the folded waste he looked like a king mounted on a beetle. Such was the spell the chairman cast that it seemed he had summoned the owner from the safety of the factory by an arcane invocation of the people whose power he knew, and some of the workers slipped back from the crate, expecting the two men to face each other in a duel whose fantastic nature they could not foresee. Many more ran towards the car, which turned for the road into town but moved too slowly and was set to be headed off.

Anna looked over her shoulder to the high ground where the Cossacks waited. She saw through their eyes how the men in the open spread and ran black against the field, a ragged, rook solidarity, and she wanted to put it on her second plate. The Cossacks glided off their station, a calm, silent phalanx of horsemen, and when they drew their sabres and rested them on their shoulders, the advancing horses were not alarmed. The regulars had mounted up and held their ground. The chairman of the communists climbed off his crate and his group coalesced around him, except the small woman, who was running with the workers towards the owner's car, with one end of her banner trailing in the mud where the communist princess had dropped it.

The Jew called to Anna that it was time to leave.

'Why?' said Anna. 'Where are you going?'

'Those in the vanguard of the revolutionary struggle are too few to be sacrificed in open warfare with the forces of reaction,' said the chairman. 'That is the task of the broad mass of the radicalised working class.'

He turned and began to walk quickly towards the town with the other four members of the vanguard. After a few paces, they started to run.

The owner's car was held fast by a column of workers putting their weight against the radiator. The driver gunned the engine and the tyres churned round. The owner stood up and the crowd mocked his hat and demanded to know the whereabouts of Dr Watson and his Georgian dog, Baskervili. There was laughter and a stone hit the owner on the shoulder. He pulled out a revolver, the crowd jeered, and a man cried: 'Murderer!'

'What kind of a murderer am I, you idle fuckers?' shouted the owner. 'You'd be dead of the hunger if I hadn't built this place. Go back to the village if you like it there. I pay you too much. I've seen the clothes you wear on holidays. My father was a peasant and a serf and he had all of two shirts. What, are you believing the Jews now when they tell you you're miserable?'

The crowd asserted that they knew that already, without any help from any Jews, and began to rock the car from side to side. The owner fired in the air, dropped the revolver from the kick of it, and toppled over. The driver pulled himself out over the windscreen and slid into the ruck. The cry went up of Cossacks and the horsemen were among them. It was speed and horse-muscle and horsebreath and harness, and men in dark coats leaning down, losing their grace in the saddle, they struck with the blunt weight of their weapons. Anna looked through the viewfinder of her camera, the rush of fleeing men around her while she stood as still as she could, aware of her feet planted cold square on the stiff ground, she centred on the car turned on its side, the owner stood with his back to it, afraid but curious for an old man with his mouth open and one flap of his Sherlock hat hanging down, a man lay face down nearby, his arm twitching and his scalp spiky with blood, one of the workers had found the gun and cocked it and pointed and fired as comfortably as if he was hanging his coat on a hook, the kick didn't bother him at all, and the Cossack's horse was hit through the breast and buckled and went down and another horseman leaned over and with the sharp tip of the sabre drew a line from the man's forehead to his waist, the line thickened in a second and he fell down with the two sides of the line not together. Anna watched it through the viewfinder as if it was happening only there and when one of the Cossacks tore down the banner and rode round the blind side of the woman holding it, who looked in the wrong direction, confused, it was tight horsemanship, and the Cossack grabbed the woman's hair and wound it round his fingers like reins and pulled, and the woman put both hands on her hair and tried to pull it away, and the Cossack was laughing, the woman did not scream or say a word, and Anna pressed the shutter. The Cossack took the back of the woman's coat in his other hand and dragged her up onto his horse, slinging her over the pommel, face down.

A Cossack put his boot against the camera. Anna looked into his face high up and dark and beating with fighting rage.

'Eh, báryshnya,' he said. 'What's the apparatus, what's it for, what are you here? Studentka! What's the apparatus, eh, clever you, godless studentka?'

'I'm taking photographs.'

'What photographs?'

'Of the things that happen.'

'Lord, what a clever bitch,' said the Cossack, and swung back his sabre arm. Anna put her arms round the camera and hunched her head into her shoulders. The Cossack put down his sabre and stepped his horse back. Another horseman was beside Anna, a regular cavalryman, a hussar.

'Back,' said the hussar to the Cossack.

'She was with the scum, your honour,' said the Cossack. 'Yid agitators, and these mutineers.'

'Can't you see she's a respectable girl?'

'Your honour, respectable girls don't carry cameras.'

'Do we cut girls' throats now because they have cameras?'

'Da nu, bárin,' laughed the Cossack. Half his mouth was gold and his nose was broken and he was a goodlooking red tanned southern boy. 'Bit of the blunt edge of a little sabreling, nothing terrible,' he said. 'Something for her to remember us by.'

The hussar looked down at Anna, and her face burned and then went cold, because she understood that before that time she had never pleased anyone in the way that she pleased the young horseman, and yet she'd not spoken, and she didn't know what it meant, to delight a man only by the way she appeared, to be looked at as if time was running backwards and he'd come face to face with his dearest memory before she was a memory, knowing her completely in the first instant and unknowing her in a life.

'I can take you home,' he said.

She nodded, and he dismounted and helped her up. She sat side saddle, and the hussar led her off towards his comrades, who were coming to meet them with a spare mount.

Anna looked over her shoulder, she saw the soldiers from the gate and the owner and driver righting the car, and two of the workers who couldn't have been workers turning the dead workers over with the toes of their boots and searching their pockets, when the cut one rolled over his insides spilled, and the Cossacks in a mounted huddle around the shot horse, a yelp from the girl with the banner as she struggled for a second and the struggling stopped. Anna could see her hair hanging down, light against the dark multicoloured mud.

'Let the woman go!' called Anna.

'She'll be fine,' they shouted back. 'The Ataman has six daughters of his own. Just a little conversation about what she was doing. Ask for her tomorrow.'

The hussars and Anna started on the roads from the river into town. They rode past a tiny chapel, not much more than a small barn with a tower and a crooked dome. There was a gilded cross on top of the dome. The rest was bleached, unpainted planks, like a missionary church on an Arctic shore, built of driftwood. Alone of the horsemen, the hussar who had come between her and the cossack, who now rode beside her, bobbed his head and crossed himself, moving his lips in prayer. He crossed himself twice.

'Why do you do that, and none of your comrades do it?' she said.

'Their souls are blind. For the seeing soul, the world is a dark place, but it sees other good souls, moving across the city like lanterns in the night, and it sees the light shining from the houses of God, like this one, the light of God and his son and his angels and saints and martyrs washing out into the street, and the obedient soul' – he crossed himself again – 'can drink a little of this light, and when it moves on into the darkness, it carries that light, and shines for others.'

'You don't talk like a hussar.'

He laughed. 'All the hussars are drinkers and gamblers and – and none of the girls have cameras. Why do you take pictures?'

'Because I'm not good at telling people what I see.'

When they reached Anna's house Anna asked if she could take his picture. He called his comrades to join him and she looked over her shoulder at them, and shook her head. Just him. He dismounted and stood by his horse and she took his picture. She was lucky to be there, because he was the only man in the world. The others were clay models with bad joints, and needleholes for eyes, and hearts of meat. He was the only one who was alive. She had seen a man slaughtered and left dead on the ground that day. The others were dead too, even standing up and moving. Only this one was living. He bowed and spoke words and mounted his horse and rode away, taking with him something greater in value than all her joys before, and every atom of the world was cowled again when he had gone. She had a little of him in her camera. She ran inside to show it to herself.

A heavy man in a heavy coat and heavy boots was in the hall. Her mother and another shape talked at her. They were excited and loud and explaining. It was the heavy man who was closer and dangerous to the camera. Anna wrapped it in her arms and bent her head over it and backed out towards the door. The heavy man was fast, he put his heavy hands on the camera and pulled. His strength was invincible and he tore the camera out of her, still warm from her body. Anna cried 'No,' her throat cracked and her ears rang with her own screaming, her mother and the shape held her while she would have left the ground, rageflung, and torn the heavy man's head off with her teeth. He took her camera to the back yard, laid it on the ground, and smashed it into pieces with one blow of a sledgehammer.

'Sweetest darling, what have you been doing? Where have you been with that apparatus? They wanted to arrest you.' Anna's mother was terrified beyond tears by her daughter's anger.

The shape was a policeman. He asked her why she thought a young girl could walk the town alone with a camera, visiting all the lowest, least decent, least loyal vermin and taking their pictures without the authorities noticing, and she should know that only superhuman efforts on his part had allowed the destruction of the camera to be substituted for her imprisonment, trial and likely exile.

Later, after everyone had gone to bed, Anna went out in the dark yard with a lantern. She spent four hours looking for the plate with the cavalryman's image. She did not find it. She found the mechanism controlling the camera's aperture and took it with her to bed where she lay for a while, holding the metal iris up to the moon and making its leaves expand and contract so that one moment she was holding a tiny, intense dot of light between her fingers, the next seeing the pattern on the surface of the satellite in all its detail.

Three years later, Anna and the hussar were married. The wedding banquet was held in a meadow at the edge of town and the regiment's officers performed feats of skill before the guests, snatching scarves from the ground at full gallop, riding standing on the saddle and splicing melons mounted on poles with their sabres.

In the early evening, the colonel of the regiment said to Anna: 'Madam, your husband is a born horseman. He rides like one of those Tartars who were strapped astride the backs of ponies before they could walk. He handles his sabre better than any guardsman. The enlisted men will follow him. All the same I wonder whether you might not be able to persuade him to take up some other line of work. A woman as beautiful as you shouldn't find that difficult. I don't want to have to take him to war.'

'I don't want him to go to war,' said Anna. 'But he is a lieutenant of the hussars. He is a soldier.'

'A man can be the perfect soldier, and be tested in his first battle, and fail,' said the colonel.

'Do you think my husband is a coward?'

No,' said the colonel. 'He is not that. He is brave to be so pious among the hussars. Believing is one thing, we all believe, but to be pious is brave. He's been mocked for it. When he won't join a card game for stakes, not because he hasn't the money but because it's a sin, he's been mocked, and he's not stood for it. He put a man in hospital. Did you know that? No.'

'What is it, then?'

The colonel gazed at her without saying anything for a few seconds. Then he shrieked in her face: 'BANG!!!' and laughed at how she jumped.

'Forgive me, Anna Petrovna,' he said. 'It's the noise. Your husband joined the army too late to be in the war with the Japanese. He doesn't know. Have you ever heard a howitzer firing close by, or a shell exploding fifty metres away? It's not that it's loud. It's like a blow. It's an offence. It's shock. The sound fills your head, pressing against your skull from the inside. If we were fighting the Turcomans, or some peasant rabble, God forbid, it'd be good old blade work, and your husband would win glory for it. But if it's Turkey, or Austria, or Germany, my God, it'll be a thousand heavy guns on each side, all firing at once, two thousand shells a minute, loud enough to scare the devil. I can talk about it, but words tell you nothing about what that noise does to a man's mind, even if he's never grazed by so much as a gramme of shrapnel.'

'But men must get used to it.'

'We do. We're soldiers. We've got thick heads, full of cotton wadding and kasha.' He knocked his knuckle on his forehead. 'But not all of us do. You know we have field exercises, don't you? With the big guns. Just a few. Exercises. Yes. The thing is – I wish you and your husband every happiness. I love to see my best horsemen win the prettiest brides. There is just this to think about, Anna Petrovna. When the big guns fire, your husband flinches. Flinches every time! So use your charms!'

'Is there going to be a war?'

'Not till after the honeymoon! Not soon! Never, perhaps!' said the colonel, laughing. 'Damn you!' he shouted to the wider company, striking the table with his hand. 'Whose turn to toast?'

Anna's husband returned to the table.

'Damn you!' said the Colonel again, glancing for a moment at Anna. Anna looked at her husband. The colonel banged the table harder. Anna's saw her husband flinch.

In the evening husband and wife boarded the express to

Crimea. They had a two-berth first class coupé, and the journey was to last twenty five hours. The conductor was tipped well. He made up the beds, and placed a vase of white chrysanthemums on the table under the window, and a bottle of champagne on the table. The compartment had electric lights. It was May 15, 1910.

At half past nine the villages passing outside the window, north of Kharkov, turned blue and dark, the old men left their porches, and only lovers, thieves and vagrants stirred the dust of the road. Anna saw a fox crossing a field stop and raise its head, and a moonstruck gelding cantering in circles in a paddock by a river. Anna's husband went to wash and she pulled down the blind, undressed, put on her nightgown, and let down her hair. When her husband came back he asked if she would like some champagne. She shook her head. Her husband locked the door and they sat down facing each other across the narrow aisle separating the two beds.

'So,' said Anna's husband.

'So,' said Anna. They laughed. Anna was trembling. She was afraid of such power. When it seemed there was no limit to happiness, her lover's face, his limbs, his breathing, his eyes, the gentlest movement of his mouth, or a blink, told her with a stronger dose of joy that the universe was theirs to play with, that all the world was crouched in listening and waiting, that time had stopped its jagged progress and smoothed down a place for them to love on as they chose, that there would be no more history until Anna and her lover said it should begin again.

Anna's husband put out his hand to touch Anna's, and she pulled her hand away.

'What's the matter?' said Anna's husband.

'Nothing,' said Anna, out of breath, her heart kicking at her ribs, trying to crash its way out. 'I was afraid that if we touched each other, the world would die.'

Anna's husband got up and sat beside her, putting his arms around her, and the world did not die.

'Do you believe me?' he said.

'What?'

'Do you believe me when I say I love you?'

'Yes.'

'I do. If only you could see inside my heart, you'd know how true it is.'

'I can. I do. I believe.'

'We touched before.'

'Yes.'

'We kissed. We danced. Nobody died.'

Anna smiled and kissed him on the lips and the eyes. 'I didn't mean what you think I meant,' she said. 'It was better than you think.'

Her husband blushed. 'Before, I only touched you where I could,' he said.

'And no one else? Nowhere else? Really?'

'No one.'

'All the girls say, "Ah, hussars, hussars!" I found the only one who's a monk.'

Anna's husband smiled and was anxious. 'Do you know what to do?' he said.

Anna shook her head and laughed. 'Do you?'

'It seems to me I do,' said her husband, as if surprised. 'But I can't remember anyone sitting down and telling me.'

They were both laughing. 'Shall I turn out the light?' said Anna's husband.

'Why?'

'I don't know.'

'Don't.' Anna frowned. 'I've seen horses,' she said.

'No,' said her husband. 'One thing I'm sure of is that it's not like horses.'

'But you're a cavalryman.'

'No!' said her husband, over her laughter.

'Are men like horses in other ways?' said Anna.

'I like sugar.'

'Other ways.'

'Do you want me to be?'

'Show me.'

'You won't be disappointed if it's not like a horse?'

'Show me.'

'Will you close your eyes?'

Anna shook her head. She let him turn his back on her while he took off his clothes and folded them in a trim pile. He turned round, naked except for a gold crucifix on a chain around his neck, and sat next to her, putting an arm round her shoulders and a hand on her knee. The first man's penis she had seen budded at the end like a tightly coiled rose no more than an hour away from blooming. She knew where it would go, where it would fit, and wondered if it would bloom inside her, if she would feel the petals unfurl against her tender inner flesh. She asked him and he smiled and said no, there'd be no petals.

'Pity,' she said.

'Seed,' said her husband.

'Yes? Ah yes, of course.' Anna couldn't take her eyes off it, not that it was beautiful, not that it was ugly, but it was curious, and alive, and part of the only man in the world, and made of that element which had made her afraid to touch him for a reason she couldn't explain to him, which was that she carried the element, too, and theirs combined might be too strong for the rest of the world. The moment of fear had passed but she still knew that when people talked about good and evil, darkness and light, they were lying, because they kept the third extreme a secret, the extreme for which love was too weak and silly a word.

'Can you wait a while?' Anna asked, laying her cheek on his thigh.

'If you like,' he said.

Anna saw how it beat a little, how strong the blood pulsed in it, and stroked the stalk with the tips of her fingers.

'Does it always stand like that?' she said.

'No,' said her husband. 'Only for you.'

'Only for me!' she laughed, and kissed the bud. 'Can you make it lie down?'

'Not now.'

'Oh. But it's just for me? It's mine?'

'Yes. It's yours.'

'That's very generous,' she whispered, absently stroking his gift with her fingers and looking into his eyes. 'I don't know what I can give you in return.'

'I know,' he said. 'I'll show you.' He crossed himself, kissed his crucifix, murmured a prayer, and opened her nightdress.

'I want everything you have,' he said. 'I want you all, all that you were, all that you are, and all that you will be.'

'Take it,' said Anna. 'I'll take what's mine.' And she took.

Not long after their honeymoon, the regiment was posted to Kiev. Anna gave birth to a son, Alexei, Alyosha, Lyosha, Lyosh. It seemed safe for her to buy a camera, and she began to make portraits, sometimes for a little money, sometimes for nothing, because a face interested her. She never spent less than a day with those she photographed, sometimes weeks. She persuaded her husband to let her photograph him nude, and made self-portraits. She and her husband fought, over his insistence on church attendance and observing the fasts and holy days, and her absences with her camera in a village or a stranger's house, but they were among the happiest couples. Neither cared what other officers or other artists thought of them, and Anna never lost her curiosity, or her husband his desire and sureness, when they exchanged gifts.

When the Austrians attacked Serbia, and the Tsar mobilised the army, Anna told her husband that she would not let him go to war. She warned him that she would hire men to bind him, lock him in a trunk, and ship him to a neutral country. He laughed, and then stopped laughing, and then began to believe that she meant it. The war would be too loud, she said. One night he kissed Alyosha many times, while Anna wasn't looking, and told him to be a good man, and take care of his mother when his father wasn't home, and to fear God. He couldn't lie, so he told Anna he was afraid his comrades would think he was a coward if he asked for a posting in the rear, and Anna believed his anxiety that night was over that. He left the house when she was still asleep, and by the time she reached the station, the regiment's train had left. Three weeks later, a telegram came to say that her husband was missing in action.

Anna put her camera away, dressed in black, and sat in a room with the shutters closed, not speaking or crying until they brought Alyosha to her, when she began to weep for the world, losing the only man in it. Her mind was empty. She wept for days and then stopped, wondering why she was still alive when there was nothing inside her any more. Her husband had been right: there was a hell, and she and, for some reason, her son, had slipped into it, and all she could do was to try to protect him while he was there. She began a kind of life without colour, except Alyosha, and few words, except for Alyosha.

Four months after the telegram, a thick envelope arrived for Anna, with many pages folded inside. She sat in a locked room reading it alone, until there was a short scream and after a few minutes she walked into the kitchen, where the cook was talking to a soldier. Anna was smiling. She asked for a large, sharp knife, and the cook gave her one. The soldier managed to take it from her before she did herself serious injury, but there was blood. The cook went into hysterics; Anna was unconscious on the floor, bleeding. The soldier ran for a doctor. Being drunk, he took a long time, and by the time he came back with the doctor, Anna and Alyosha had disappeared, together with some of their things. There were fears for the lives of mother and son. Anna was thought to have gone insane, although there was ridicule for the soldier's claim that rather than trying to cut her wrists, or plunge the knife into her heart, she had begun to cut off one of her breasts. The alarm ended one day when it became known that both Anna and Alyosha were alive and well. In a letter to the family lawyer, Anna apologised for the distress she had caused, and gave assurances that her wound had been treated and was not serious. She gave instructions regarding property and goods and seemed to be in full possession of her wits. She did not explain why she had chosen to settle with her son several thousand miles away to the east, in Siberia, near the river Yenisey, in a small town called Yazyk.

The Widow

Mutz walked east off the square towards the little bridge that led to Anna Petrovna's and, further on, to the rail depot. There were lights on in some of the houses he passed, blotches of buttermilk brightness behind double glass and window boxes. He wondered where the Russians got the kerosene from. Not from the Legion. They shared, no doubt. They were good at sharing, these ones. It wasn't so much even that they shared their goods, their kerosene and their axeheads and their potatoes, but that they shared their time, as well. The square was a swamp, but here on one of Yazyk's four streets, he was walking on a pavement of logs solidly bedded and up off the mud level. That wasn't the work of one man, or of convicts. And what were they reading now, by the light of their lamps, behind those thick black log walls and tiny white-framed windows? The Bible, of course. Perhaps they were pickling, perhaps embalming, towers of cucumbers in brine and dill, or perhaps they were patching elbows and knees by that light, but no, most likely they were too excited after the service not to read the Word, to reach for it, open it up and gorge on it. Mutz, who was not religious, had once tried to read the whole book from beginning to end, Apocrypha and all. He stalled; he skimmed, he skipped. The Old Testament had some good stories but seemed like a forgery contrived to make Jews look absurd, ranting, cranky warriors with a vaudeville God on squeaky wheels, while the New kept slipping back from humility and simplicity into some machination involving cash, or ecclesiastical administration, or miracles in exchange for faith. He had apprehended all the same that its contradictions and ambiguities and vastness might attract those who were dissatisfied with the world as it was, in particular, its most tiring feature, that it kept changing. Here was a whole world that never changed, and could be compared against the real one. For such, the Bible was bottomless; that which you did not understand, demanded to be read and reread for that very reason; that which you understood, you kept coming back to, for there was an unchanging truth, when out there in the darkness all was chaos. Mutz wondered if the shaman had ever read the Bible, then remembered he was illiterate.

He crossed the bridge and saw Anna Petrovna's house. He stopped. There was nothing to force him to go in. There was much to encourage him to turn back and go to bed. It was late, ten o'clock perhaps, although who knew? The time signal from Irkutsk only came as often as the telegraph line was up. Tomorrow he would have to account to Matula for the death of the shaman, and the captain would still be looking for the missing horses. Anna Petrovna didn't care if he came or not. Did she? The doubt hurt and intimidated him. Less painful than approaching her house before she'd yielded to him, but then it had been a pain of being alive, and this was not that. He'd shared her bed seven times, four times until first light, three creeping away while it was still dark, feeling the walls and the furniture with his fingertips, trying not to wake Alyosha, hearing Anna smothering laughter when he made a floorboard creak, and then making the board creak on purpose just to hear her laugh. After the seventh time she told him she wouldn't let him stay any more. No, couldn't, that was what she said, and never explained.

A dog barked. Mutz began to count to ten. If the dog barked again before he finished, he'd go forward. He reached ten. The dog didn't bark. He walked forward, as he'd known he would. He was prisoner enough already without being a prisoner of dogs.

He walked to the back of the house, went through the gate and across the yard and entered by the unlocked back door, into the warm, bright kitchen. Broucek sat at the head of the small table, hands clasped around a cup of tea, his rifle leaning in the corner like a broom. Anna was sitting facing the door in a dark blue dress. She smiled and greeted Mutz and didn't unfold her arms. Broucek put the cup down and got to his feet. Mutz closed the door behind him. He shouldn't have come.

Anna got up, came round the table to him and kissed him on both cheeks. 'Broucek was telling me about the visitor,' she said.

Mutz looked at Broucek. 'Since when did you speak Russian so well?' he asked.

Broucek grinned and shrugged, picked up his rifle and slung it over his shoulder.

'Don't fuss,' said Anna to Mutz. 'People find ways to talk. Sit down.'

Mutz sat down in Broucek's place. The wooden chair was warm. Broucek drained his cup, thanked Anna Petrovna, touched his cap to Mutz, who nodded, and left.

'I wouldn't call him a visitor,' said Mutz. Anna put a cup in front of him and he raised it to his mouth with both hands. He realised he was mimicking Broucek and lowered it without drinking.

'Well, tell me,' said Anna, sitting back down and leaning forward. Mutz tried to concentrate. How strange that the more time you spent thinking about a face, the more you were shocked to see it.

'His name is Samarin. Kyrill Ivanovich.'

'From?'

'Somewhere west of the Urals, originally. Black earth country. Near Penza, I think.'

'Age?'

'About thirty, I'd guess.'

'How hopeless you are at finding things out. What does he look like? Is he clever? He must be starving after wandering in the forest. No wonder the ones who made a revolution were prisoners. I would've been a revolutionary if they'd put me in prison.'

'If you mean the Bolsheviks, the ones who made a revolution weren't prisoners,' said Mutz. 'They were exiles. It's not the same. As far as his looks are concerned, he looks like a matinee idol.'

Anna hit his knuckles with a teaspoon. 'Don't make fun of me,' she said.

'He's tall, and thin,' said Mutz. 'I saw him change. I saw him as a convict, beaten and exhausted. And then he was something else. In a moment. A persuader. Someone who takes action, who makes others do it.'

'Go on,' said Anna. Mutz had paused. He felt reluctant to say any more about Samarin, and regretted what he'd already said.

'How do we know which was the true Samarin, and which was him performing?' he said.

'Maybe both of them were really him.'

'Maybe neither of them were.'

'You don't like him,' said Anna.

Mutz recognised it was true, but didn't want to admit it.

'You can go and see him tomorrow if you like,' he said. 'There'll be a hearing in front of Matula. Samarin will have to account for himself. You'll have to get Matula's permission.'

'Fu!'

'It's up to you.'

Anna fidgeted with her ring. 'I'll come,' she said. 'I'll take him some food.'

Mutz buried his face in the cup and felt a pleasant inner surge which he couldn't identify but which was related to the photograph in his pocket.

'So you don't know Samarin?' he said.

Anna looked at him without understanding. He felt helplessly, remotely tender towards her, like someone at a conjuring show who sees another member of the audience, who has been enjoying herself, made fearful when the conjuror calls her up on stage. He recognised the surge now, when it was too late: malice. Now she could only ask why, and he would have to tell her.

'He was carrying a photograph of you.' Mutz took it out and gave it to Anna. She went pale when she saw it and put her hand to her mouth.

'Where did the convict get this?'

'He said he found it in the street. You didn't lose it, did you?'

'Not in Siberia. Have you seen Gleb Alexeyevich tonight?'

'Balashov? Yes. He was worried about you, for some reason.'

'Did you see him before or after this Samarin was arrested?'

'After. Yes, after. Why?'

Anna put the picture down, planted her elbows on the table and ran her fingers through her hair, staring ahead of her without focusing.

'Anna, I'm sorry – I feel as if I've done you some wrong,' said Mutz. He reached out to touch her shoulder.

'Don't,' she said, moving his hand away gently.

'Perhaps there's no need to tell me.'

'This photograph was my husband's. He always carried it. I thought it'd been lost when he died, in his last battle. It's the only print. I broke the negative. I haven't seen it for five years.'

'Anna, please – if you say you don't know Samarin, I believe you. I don't want to make you think about your husband.'

Anna was nodding, not listening to him. He'd grown so used to her refusal to talk about what had happened between the death of her husband and the Czechs' arrival in Yazyk that to see her now, brooding on an old photograph and events in her life that he knew nothing about, made him feel just partly loved once, that all their night whisperings and jokes and confidences and shared memories, even the sounds and movements she made with him in bed, were abridged, altered for an uninitiated lover.

'But whatever you can tell me,' said Mutz, hopelessly. The more distracted she was the more he wanted her to desire him again.

Anna looked up, smiled in an empty way, and took Mutz to the parlour. The enclosure of her warm palm and fingers, the remote pull of her body, replaced the present for him. Leading him by the hand, sitting him down in the divan, darting forward, kissing him on the mouth, darting back, laughing, then him finding her mouth and running his hand under her skirt and between her thighs, that was how it had begun, under that ugly painting of her husband in full hussar's uniform, with the black mourning band across the corner. Now this was like a clumsy rehearsal long after the final performance. He found himself alone on the divan, watching Anna sitting at the writing desk on the other side of the room, laying the photograph on her lap, then lifting it to her face, fascinated. Her mouth opened a little and she frowned as she held the picture at a distance, brought it slowly closer, moved it away again.

Anna remembered how hot the light had been. A friend had arranged for her to use one of the new electric spotlights at Kiev Opera before it had been fitted. An enormous, focused, burning lamp shining on her face in a tiny, stuffy room. She'd kept switching it on and off to stop her skin being scorched and to stop the room becoming intolerably close. Of all the exposures and poses, this had been the only one which worked. That was why she'd been smiling: she knew she'd got it, the moment when of all the many possible truths of light and shade and skin and eyes, she'd found the one that humbled the others. She'd given the picture to her husband just before the war began. She wondered if it was only tonight that other men had seen it.

'What do you think?' she asked Mutz, knowing he would praise her skill.

'A brilliant work of art,' said Mutz, eagerly.

'What did the convict say? Samarin? What did he make of it?'

Mutz paused, wondering why Anna cared. Anna noticed that he paused. Mutz said: 'Beauty.'

'"Beauty"? He said that?'

'He said it as if it was your job. As if you were the village beauty, going about your rounds.'

'Hm. Arrogance! D'you think I'm the village beauty, Josef?'

Mutz feared invitations for easy praise from the women he loved. Anna listened while he hestitated. She wondered if Mutz had represented the convict accurately; if not, why not? An educated young Russian man come among them, like a messenger from a more normal world.

'Was that all he said?' she asked. Again, Mutz hesitated, for longer this time. Not all, then.

'He asked me to pass on his compliments, and said that your picture will outlive us,' said Mutz.

Anna nodded and tried not to let Mutz see how delighted this made her. She failed. She was surprised herself that she cared so much. She was surprised she found it so difficult, so inconvenient, that Mutz still yearned for her. She looked down again at the five-year-old photograph of herself lying on the writing desk, the picture her husband had carried, and like a reflex her thumb touched her teeth. That was the instant she realised that inside the desk she held a terrible power to resolve this. It hadn't occurred to her to use it before: it hadn't occurred to her it was something she could use, that it was anything other than a curse.

Mutz saw. He saw the quick little movement of her touching her teeth with the tip of her thumb, held there for a few seconds, then the thumb slowly lowered as the thought settled in her, and she turned to look at him, as if to make sure he was still there. Mutz felt foolish – his mind volunteered a recording of him imploring Anna to come to Prague with him – then grief, then dread. Something fearful was about to happen. He was ready to do anything to delay it, but he had no idea what to do. Tell a story? Run from the house? Stride over to Anna and kiss her, even if she struggled? Beg?

'Josef,' said Anna. 'I never told you what you wanted to know, why I was here, and why I stopped seeing you in the old way.'

She was taking out a key. She was unlocking a drawer in the desk. Mutz knew that she was planning to introduce some evil into his life that she had protected him from before and that he would never be able to get rid of. He got up. 'Anna,' he said. He took a few steps forward, and stopped. 'Anna. My darling. Please. Whatever it is, it doesn't have to be now.'

Anna paid no attention. She was reaching into the drawer and pulling out a thick bundle of paper. She turned to Mutz.

'When you read this, you'll see why I came here, but perhaps not why I stayed,' she said. She gave a sob, and shook her head, smiled and went on. 'He built this secret, but it was me who locked myself in, as if I could ever live there, as if I could *change* it. What a fool! As for you, Josef, of course it makes what we did a disgrace, but hardly compared to his own. At times I've pitied him and despised him, at times felt shame at myself, and our affair was in one of the despising times, but it wasn't just the pity coming back which made me stop with you.' She paused. 'Listen to me. I sound so earnest. Like him. But that isn't a bad thing, is it? Is it?'

'No,' said Mutz. Every cell in his body felt misaligned.

'The most important thing,' said Anna, 'is that Alyosha doesn't know. If possible, I don't want him ever to know. Is that clear? Do you promise?'

'Yes.'

'He likes you. I think you like him, don't you? But you never talk to him. Anyway. Take it. I don't want to be here while you're reading it. Will you read it?'

Mutz nodded. He couldn't speak.

'I'll be in the kitchen,' said Anna, and went out.

Mutz took the papers and began to read the neat lines of handwriting.

The Husband

My dearest Anna, my star,

I have burned dozens of pages – nothing can be left for others to see – trying to find a way to tell you about the way I have changed, and at last, here is the telling I have settled on. It will seem confused and perhaps there will be parts you cannot understand. In the beginning I thought I would not tell you everything, but I have decided not to hide anything from you, no matter how hard it is for me to write and how hard it will be for you to read. The words are for you, and they are for me, too. Even now when so much is written and read and forgotten, in the writing of a thing, it becomes in some way sacred.

Did you think I was dead? I am sorry. Yes, for that, I am sorry, and I beg you to forgive me. I can see your beloved face all twisted up in crying for me being dead, and I want to be there and show you that I am alive, more than alive, far more! So I am sorry for that. When I tell you how I have changed, I understand that you may wish I had died. (Don't be frightened.) What you must understand is that I cannot ask your forgiveness for what I have done, because I can only ask your forgiveness for sins, and what I have done is not a sin before God. On the contrary it is an escape from sin. My regret is not for the way I have changed but that it took so long before I found out how I should change. And I regret that I have had to leave you and Alyosha behind. Now I understand how it must feel to be saved from a shipwreck when your loved ones have not been saved, when you know they are still treading the cold water out there, shouting for help but not knowing from where it might come. I should tell you that we, those among whom I live now, call our community a 'ship'. Anna, I live among angels here. It seems natural for me to write that, and to tell you that I am an angel, too, but when I read the words I have just written, I remember that you might think I have gone out of my mind. So I must tell you everything, without shame or fear.

It was never a secret to you that I was a strong believer, that I believed in the truth of every word of the Gospels, that when the words of apostles and prophets seemed to contradict each other, it was my own lack of wisdom which made me fail to understand them. I think you knew how I believed in Paradise, the state of Heaven and of Earth, too, before Adam and Eve tasted the Forbidden Fruit. That was the Paradise I imagined, Eden, not Heaven, where you and I and God would walk together in the forest, talking, and you and I would ride alongside angels across a boundless meadow. I do not think you knew how much it troubled me how unlike Eden our world is, and how unlike angels you and I were. I hated to see how so many of the peasants expected they would live so badly forever; how they drank and beat each other and went hungry, how their babies would stop breathing at their mothers' breasts from disease or famine, and how they could travel hundreds of miles through black mud to kiss a famous icon. I hated to see how our factories were taking peasants and turning them into parts in a machine. I hated the way everyone lied; the lawyers lied as their profession, the bureaucrats lied about how honest they were, the priests lied about being good, the doctors lied about being able to heal the sick, the journalists lied about all the other liars. I hated the way people hurt their horses. They seem more dignified than us, closer to the horses of Eden than we are to the man and woman of Eden. They manage to be what we cannot be, proud and humble at the same time. The Colonel loved horses. He treated them well and made his men treat them well. He was killed, by the way, did you know? When I saw the Hussars for the first time I wanted to be one of them. Their horses and their clothes were so beautiful, and even their faces – they seemed more made for love than for war. Fierce love, a love that wanted to conquer, but love all the same, and I was only seventeen, it was the kind of love I wanted to carry to the world sewn on a banner. I was very ignorant and foolish. I really thought there would be no more wars, and if there were, somehow, those beautiful Hussars and their beautiful horses would be too fine to spoil with bullets. And it was only later that I found out how many of the Hussars were drunkards and gamblers and brutes to women. Anyway at that time I believed the Tsar to be especially close to God, in a way none of the priests I met were, and to serve the Tsar seemed to be a way to serve God as becoming a monk was not. Besides, if I had become a monk, I would never have been able to be with you.

You knew the officer I spent most time with, of course, Chernetsky, the one who was always trying to prove he had Mongol blood, even though he was blond, with blue eyes. We went on picnics together, didn't we? There was a meadow by the river with rushes and flowers. He spilled wine on your dress and pretended he was going to shoot himself. We laughed a lot, I remember. I should say you and Chernetsky and someone I once was laughed a lot. I suppose I don't laugh so much now I'm an angel. Only for joy, not for mockery.

There was another man in the regiment I did not tell you about. His name was Chanov. He was the farrier. He was short, thin and strong, with a tanned face and high cheekbones and a moustache that never grew beyond a few curly hairs. You could not say how old he was, or whether the wrinkles that radiated out across his face from the bridge of his nose were caused by age or the sun or both. He was from Siberia. He worked at the forge from first light to dusk and sometimes into the night, and that, together with the fact that he knew everything there was to know about horses, saved him from punishment for his caprices. He would never salute an officer, so they kept him hidden when a general came to visit, and he refused to go to delousing with the rest of the men, when everyone would strip in a hut and be sprayed and showered. He'd leave the barracks and come back a few hours later with some spravka from a private bathhouse in town, saying that he'd been sprayed and showered there. He seldom spoke. I had heard rumours about him before I met him, that he was a former convict who had served ten years' hard labour for murder, that he had lost his whole family in the famine, and that he was not Orthodox, or Jewish, or Catholic, or a Muslim, but a member of one of those queer mystical sects you read about. They said he was a khlyst, a flagellant, that he beat himself and whirled around like a top in secret ceremonies which ended in orgies. I knew he was a vegetarian, and didn't drink, which is a mark of these non-conformists, but he was also to be seen at every Orthodox church service.

I first saw him from a distance, when I was leading Hijaz for an early morning walk with the rest of the squadron around a paddock next to his forge. The forge and anvil were in a covered yard out front and we could hear and see him banging away at a shoe there. It was a frosty morning and it was hard to make him out through the mist of men and horses' breath but I was watching him and the red glow of the forge. The hammering stopped and I saw him stand up and look directly at me, following me with his eyes as I walked on. I felt as if some concealment had been taken off me by the silencing of the hammer, as if the sound of Hijaz's hooves on the hard turf and his breathing and the clink of his harness had drawn Chanov's attention, even though all of us were making the same sounds. When a crow cawed, and other men and horses passed between me and the blacksmith's line of sight, I felt grateful for the concealment. A few seconds later, however, I came into view from the smithy again and he was still watching me. He didn't take up his hammer again until I led Hijaz out of the paddock. Do you remember, Anna, when we first met, I talked about seeing good souls from far away, like lights in the darkness? I know now that this is what Chanov was looking for. At the time, I was afraid of him. I avoided any dealings with him until one day when all my troopers were busy and Hijaz shed a shoe and I had to go to him myself.

He put the horse into the care of his underlings, took off his apron and asked whether I would do him the honour of taking tea. He spoke formally to me, as a sergeant to an officer, and sincerely, but there was an expression on his face, and a tone in his voice, which was not subordinate. He was leading me, and I was following on tamely, as me leading Hijaz out of his stall in the morning.

We went to a workroom with a work bench running down the middle, a single slab of oak notched and scored, and a tangle of black iron hanging from the walls, with some shine of steel and brass. There was a stove at the back and plank benches on ammunition crates and a nicely-wrought iron table. It had been made by one of the apprentices, Chanov said. He poured tea into glasses fitted inside cupholders fashioned from thin sheets of brass cut and filed into patterns, then rolled into shape to fit the glasses. More detail was engraved onto the brass and the etched lines had tarnished, making them stand out against the gleam of the polished metal. I asked Chanov if they were made by the apprentices too, and he said no, he had made them. I held them up to look more closely. There were human figures. They had a lumpy, pagan look to them, with big heads and small bodies. There was a tree, with fruit. I understood what it was. It was the Garden of Eden, and God was there under the Tree, talking to Adam and Eve! I was so stricken with the passions that I started to turn the cup round quickly, as if I was reading a book, and spilled the tea on the floor, with the glass after it, which smashed.

Chanov cleaned it up, shushed away my apologies, and gave me a fresh glass. He told me not to worry, and not to be afraid. He had heard that I was pious, and loyal to the Gospels, and had wanted to meet me. He came from a town called Yazyk, in Siberia, between Omsk and Irkutsk. He had never been a convict, and he had no family; he was an orphan, had been adopted by the Yazyk blacksmith, and had inherited his trade on his death. He was not a flagellant, but like all the inhabitants of Yazyk, he did belong to a sect. He would not tell me about it, except that he, and the other members of the congregation, were already living in Heaven, in Paradise, here on Earth.

Anna, my dearest, I am a plain writer, I do not have the power of a St John or a St Paul to tell you how true and convincing the farrier seemed to me about such fantastic happenings. I have always listened patiently to holy fools and the kind of ranting preacher you meet in crowded cities, but I would not stop to hear a man declare that Heaven had already been made on Earth. Yet Chanov made me stop. He spoke with such certainty, looking into my eyes and smiling in such a sweet, warm, joyful way, beating out the rhythm of his speech with graceful movements of his hands so unlike the flailing of his limbs at the anvil. His voice was calm, yet with a rhythm to it, as if he was singing.

Of course I asked him how we could enter Paradise in this way, without dying, and he grew more serious, and said everyone had to make the journey alone. The only way was to burn the Keys of Hell, he said. He picked up a piece of coal, opened the stove, and threw the coal into the red embers, where it instantly began to burn. He ran hot water from the samovar over his fingers to clean the coal dust off.

I asked what the Keys of Hell were, and he said we would talk on another day, and returned to his anvil. I stayed by the stove for a time, turning the empty cupholder round in my hands. I had hoped he would give it to me, as a solid token of a promise that there was more than I knew.

As it happened, I did not see the farrier for many months after that. There were manoeuvres, I had leave – we went to visit your mother, you remember – and, when I went to speak to him, the apprentices told me he was busy in the workshop. I began to wonder if the apprentices were not also dwelling in Paradise. They had something of another world about them; smooth skin and soft voices and ageless faces. As you can imagine, I spent a lot of time wondering how men could live in Paradise and at the same time appear to be dwelling among us, among the lies and the dirt and the cruelty, the disappointments and the ugliness. I was tormented by questions, and I said nothing to you. I do not know why. Perhaps I had been given foreknowledge of what was to happen, that it would separate us. Perhaps it was the word 'alone' which made me afraid to even mention the farrier to you. But I was very eager.

You may have sensed it. I felt I was about to be entrusted with a secret power.

One night in midsummer, when the regiment was on field exercises near Poltava, I was dozing in my tent. One of my troopers came in and said there was someone to see me. I put on my boots and went out. One of the apprentices was there. Instead of saluting he put his hand on my shoulder and started to whisper something in my ear about Hijaz, who I had sent to be shoed earlier. Before he could finish the trooper grabbed him and knocked him unconscious with a blow to the face, saying that he would teach him respect for his betters. I asked the trooper if he knew what he had done, and the trooper looked at me as if I was mad. I realised that while to me it seemed the trooper had sent himself directly to Hell by striking an angel, or an inhabitant of Paradise at least, in the life of the army the trooper's action was normal, and I could not go against them now. I told the trooper to take the apprentice to the doctor. I think he knocked a tooth out. I went off towards the encampment of the farriers.

Their tents and carts were some distance away, on the edge of a wood. The field forge and anvil were set out under an awning to protect the farriers from the sun and one of the other apprentices was working there. I asked about Hijaz. He pointed to a stockade where a number of horses were penned and said Hijaz was ready and I could collect him after I had seen Chanov, if that suited me. I nodded, not able to speak with my heart beating so fast, and the apprentice put down his tools and led me through to the back of his workplace.

The awning was pitched right up against the first of the trees. They were beeches, slim and grey and tall. I followed the apprentice a little way into the forest. It was about ten o'clock. The sun had just gone down but it was still light. The apprentice led me towards a tent which had been pitched over a stream; the canvas was held firm on either bank, but the water flowed straight down the centre line of the tent, and the poles were set in the gravel bed of the brook. The apprentice asked if I would like to take off my boots and I took them off and unwrapped the footcloths and stepped into the cold water, which ran round my ankles. The apprentice left and I walked upstream into the tent.

Chanov sat in front of me on a canvas stool. The legs of the stool, and his own bare feet, were in the water, which spurted round him with a pleasant rushing sound. I had thought so much about this meeting, and prepared so many questions and answers, yet his first remark to me was quite unexpected. He asked why Hijaz was an entire. You know what an entire is, do you not, Anna? A stallion which has not been castrated. I hesitated and stammered that he was a good horse, obedient, strong, willing, fast when I asked for it. He had been wilful sometimes as a youngster, but I had coaxed him out of it with discipline, fairness and love, as a master of horsemanship does. Besides, the Hussars disapproved of geldings. They thought they lacked fire in the charge.

I hoped the blacksmith would start to say something I could understand, but instead he nodded and asked something even more strange, about whether I thought a horse could sin. I said I had never thought about it before, but no, I supposed a horse could not, no animal could.

Chanov smiled and nodded again. He said I was right, no beast could sin. Only man could. The man was master to the horse, he said, but no-one was master to the man except man himself, as God willed it. God was waiting for man to master himself, to understand the way to bring himself back to obedience and innocence and love, to be an angel in Paradise. What could be tolerated in a stallion could not be tolerated in man, because man's wilfulness was fearsome and cruel, and his desires and ambitions wicked.

Chanov stood up, unbuttoned his braces and began taking off his shirt. 'I am going to bathe,' he said, and told me to wait and listen. It occurred to me much later that if anyone had heard him talking to an officer in this way he would have been flogged and stripped of his rank, but at the time, it never crossed my mind to question his authority. He asked me, in a way that didn't call for me to answer, what it was that made men so cruel and greedy. What drove them on to steal from and exploit each other, to make war, to rape and abuse women and children, to lie and cheat and strut like peacocks, to torture animals, to maim Nature? What burden did they carry with them, placed on them by God after tasting the Forbidden Fruit, which made them despise themselves, live in guilt and shame and terror of old age and death?

He turned his back to me then and let his breeches fall into the water. He was naked in the stream except for the gold chain around his neck.

He said: 'I do not have this burden any more.' He turned round to face me. He said: 'I have been made an angel.'

It was dim inside the tent, but I could see that between his legs there was nothing, a gap. He had been castrated. The genitals had been completely severed.

Chanov squatted down and began to splash water over himself. He told me that he had burned the Keys to Hell, that he had Mounted the White Horse. He said that when war came, he would be there for my salvation. He said many other things I have forgotten. I could not listen any more. I left the tent, took my boots, and began to run. I think I may have fallen in the stream, I do not remember. I found Hijaz and rode for hours, until I could see the glow of Poltava.

For weeks, I was in anguish. It is hard for me to admit now, harder than you can imagine, but I truly thought Chanov was insane, sick-souled. I was so disappointed! That it should come down to the stroke of a knife. I felt I had been cheated. I had imagined, in my faith, that he would reveal to me some secret radiance, some long, profound prayer, even some course of fasting and self-denial. This, castration, was ridiculous. Yet if I look back honestly, even then, in my doubt, part of me wondered at his courage, that he should believe so strongly in the Word that he would sacrifice that. It is strange how many people we can divide ourselves into when we are uncertain about something. Inside our minds it is as if there is a group of men sitting around arguing, and another part of us is standing to one side with his hands over his ears, not wanting to listen to any of it.

I thought of you, of course, and of Alyosha, how Alyosha would never have been if I had been one of the farrier's castrates, how you would hardly have found enough in me worth loving, let alone marrying, if I'd been some docile gelding. And the strange thing was that last summer, before the war, the world did seem more like Paradise than Hell. Perhaps it was chance. Perhaps, after seeing Chanov, it was what I wanted to see. On the ride back to the camp from Poltava everyone I passed seemed to greet me gladly. I saw a peasant watering his old carthorse in the river and stroking its neck and whispering in its ear. I saw children running in and out of the rows of a sunflower field. They were chasing each other in pure play. They were laughing.

You were surprised, I think, when I came home a few days later, and dragged you upstairs. You were not very willing. You were hot and tired and you wanted to wash, but I would not let you, and you came round. Would God have made these

Keys to Hell so cruelly, to give us so much pleasure, I thought then? I thought you liked the way I used them. I wondered if Chanov was not an agent of the Prince of Darkness, the Enemy. I was in a fever that day. Do you remember? I spent so long with my lips and my tongue between your legs, and I burst my seed inside you, and spilled it a second time, on your tongue and your lips. I wanted you to feel me penetrate every opening in your body. I wanted to press it into your ears, your eyes, your belly, your backside. And how I loved the taste of you, the salty juice at the top of your legs.

And then the war came, and Chanov disappeared. Not just him, but the apprentices. There was a terrible scandal. It got back to the staff that the Colonel had turned a blind eye to Chanov's lack of respect for regulations, and had it not been for the urgency of the situation, he would have been punished. As it was they found some Ukrainian smith to do the job, and we were put on trains west towards the Austrian border.

Everything was unfamiliar in those first days of the war, but I did not feel a sense of dread, as I had expected. Sitting in the compartment of the train – it was a regular coupé, the kind you take to Crimea or Petersburg, the troopers and horses were in wagons – it felt as if we were going on holiday. We were in khaki, of course, but everyone told all the jokes they could remember. We had no idea what was going to happen, or how far we would go, or how quickly. We thought we might end up riding into Vienna. Or even Berlin. 'Paris!' somebody said, and then everyone pitched in with their ideas, till our heads were filled with visions of a column of Russian Hussars trotting through the streets of New York, Rio de Janeiro or Baghdad. And yet we had swords and pistols weighing down our belts, and they had trained us to use them.

When we reached our destination, a halt about twenty miles from the front, we were given some bad news. The Colonel, who had gone on ahead to see about fodder and billets, had been in a staff car which had come off the road when an Austrian aircraft dropped bombs. The bombs had not fallen close, but the driver had panicked. Everyone in the car was killed.

We camped at the halt. The Colonel was replaced by his second in command, who was less popular. He was a higher-ranking noble than the Colonel, and he had always felt he should command the regiment, but really he was a lazy man who had never learned much except to punish juniors of lesser blood. You probably remember him, a big man with a pale face, black beard and bloodshot eyes. Rumlyan-Pechersky, that was his name. He told us that we would move forward at dawn, possibly to attack.

On the train, I thought about you. I promised to be honest, Anna, and in the camp, as it got dark, I thought more about Chanov. For the first time I heard the sound of artillery in the distance. People always say it is like thunder and it is but thunder stops. All night there was a coming and going of slow, heavy trains, full of men and shells and animals, I supposed: I could not see them, I heard their groaning and shrieking and hooting and the sound of hooves, wagon wheels and marching. And they were using aeroplanes! Remember, Anna, we went down to the flying field with Alyosha to watch the aeroplanes take off and disappear into the heavens. I thought they were marvellous things. I thought when I saw the sun reflect white off their wings so high up in the blue that man was getting somewhere, that a new kind of time was beginning. Now they were using them to drop bombs. Even though I had been an officer for so long, I had never seen anything like this effort all around me, this organisation, this busyness of thousands, directed towards something I had never witnessed, but expected would not be wholesome. I still did not understand what it had to do with Chanov's ideas. It was absurd.

Late that night I went looking for Chernetsky. It was dark. Some officers from his squadron were playing cards by the light of a lantern in Chernetsky's tent, but he wasn't there. I could see from the pile of paper money on the table that they were playing for high stakes. They glanced at me with that mixture of acceptance and suspicion I was used to. I had helped each of them with a horse at some time or another, but I never drank or gambled with them, or visited the public house. You know that story, anyway. You helped me with them. They liked you. So I asked where Chernetsky was and they looked at each other and one of them said he was over on the other side of the road, beyond the cooks' wagons. They offered me Chernetsky's electric torch, a present from his aunt, so I took it. I crossed the road and found the cooks' wagons and asked if they had seen an officer. They pointed into the darkness to where I could just make out of group of trees. As I walked towards it I heard a woman's voice and a hand touched my sleeve. The woman asked if I was lonely and would I like to spend time with her. I said no and pushed her away, I hope not too roughly. I got closer to the trees and I could see a figure there with a cigarette in his hands. I switched on the torch. It was Chernetsky. A little girl was kneeling on the ground in front of him. At the touch of the light she took something out of her mouth quickly and turned towards me, holding up her hand to block the glare. I saw that Chernetsky was stuffing his member into his breeches. Neither he nor the girl seemed about to move otherwise. Chernetsky put his hand on the girl's head and with his smoking hand waved at me, swearing and telling me to put the light out. He did not know it was me until I spoke, of course. I switched the torch off and said that she was only a child. I saw the cigarette end arc up towards my friend's mouth and glow as he inhaled. He said she was fourteen, meaning that she was old enough to be bought by a man, I suppose. He let the cigarette drop and I saw it glow again as the child sucked on it. She had not looked fourteen. I do not know how old she was. Twelve? Ten? A child, anyway, however experienced in that trade. I think I spoke again, I said something about him finding an older girl. I may even have offered to pay. I did not go any closer. I did not want to. Then I heard the girl speak in the darkness. She said: Who is that? Chernetsky told her to shut up and do her job. He called me by my first name and said: This is not for you.

I went back to Chernetsky's tent and left the torch and they asked if I had found him. I said I had not. Two of them said at once: He found him! I asked them why it had to be with such a young girl. They were unhappy at what I said. Lashmanov said, quite seriously, that we all might be killed the next day, and every man should take what he could, girl, woman, grandmother, boy. I said that surely if we were going to be killed we should be praying to God to forgive us our sins. They all laughed and told me I didn't have any sins. And Lashmanov said – Anna, my dearest, you know I hate to use such words, but I promised not to hide anything from you, and now we are very close to the change – he said: A Hussar drinks, fucks and fights, and then he prays. And then he drinks, fucks and fights again.

In the morning the officers got their orders. The regiment was to attack. The whole corps, the whole army, and other Russian armies, were to attack. We knew we were to be in the vanguard but we had a sense that we were part of a numberless host, cities of warriors on the move, and we felt strong.

The fact that the senior officers had detailed maps of where we were going, even though it was not Russian territory, surprised and encouraged us. What they would not tell us was whether we were to attack Germans or Austrians. We feared the Germans, but the Austrians, we thought, might simply run away. Many of them were not Austrians at all, but Czechs, Slovakians, Slovenians, Croats, Bosnians, Ruthenians, Poles. They might even come over to our side. Our pistols were loaded and our sabres were sharp. The thing I feared most was having to strike an enemy with my sabre. I was trained to do it, of course, but the thought of coming close enough to a man to kiss him or shake his hand and bringing my sabre down to try to cut him in half was terrible. I did not think I could find enough hate in me for a stranger, even if he was trying to do the same to me. I had the same fear on the day we met, outside the factory. Thinking about this, I started thinking about you. I thought about Hijaz, the beautiful animal under me, carrying me forward, and what Chanov had said, how he had asked me if a horse could sin. I wondered if I was so different from Chernetsky with the girl: even more so, since the girl was, perhaps, not completely innocent, whereas Hijaz was. I thought about Chernetsky's last words, too, over and over again. This is not for you. How I fretted while we rode out that morning. Yet that day we never saw the enemy, even though by the time it ended, almost all the men and all the horses in the regiment were dead.

It was a hot day towards the end of August. I remember the smell of cowslips growing at the roadside, stronger than the smell of dung, sometimes, from the wagon trains we overtook. We passed columns of marching soldiers miles long. Many of them were singing. The feeling that this was some kind of strange mass excursion started to come back. It did not last.

We started to pass people fleeing their homes, moving in the opposite direction. We were still in Russia, but it was a different kind of Russia, one where the people who lived there did not believe in it. In the Jewish villages those brave enough to come out and watch us pass looked at us as if they hoped we would never come back; in the Greek Catholic villages, the cheering was half-hearted. We passed the Greek Catholic shrines, with their Christs in agony on the cross, and their contented, placid Madonnas. I remember thinking how strange it was that all the armies about to fight each other believed that Christ was sent by God to be the last man tortured by other men, yet here they were, about to torture each other by the tens of thousands. The only people who did not believe it were the Jews, and they were not fighting.

At noon, we approached the artillery line. They had not begun firing, but they were preparing to. The road passed close to a battery of about two dozen howitzers. Hundreds of men were moving around them with an energy and purpose I had not seen before in the tending of machinery. You know I am not good with comparisons, Anna, I am not a poet, but I remember thinking how it looked as if the men were serving the guns, as if the guns were their masters and they were running about for their sake. It put me in mind of that film we saw about Louis XIV, the Sun King, do you remember? How the big, fat actor playing the king stood absolutely still, just yawning, while all those dozens of servants fussed over him, dressing, bathing and powdering him. And the king never acknowledged they were there, or what they were doing. Such was his power. These machines, these big black ugly tubes with their wheels and pistons and levers, were the masters of the men. Next to each gun was a pyramid of brass shells, higher than a horse, to feed them with.

When we were a few hundred metres away the artillerymen froze, like actors in a tableau vivant, and there was a bright flash from each gun, together with a puff of black smoke, and the guns jumped back and rolled forward again. For one second I was amazed at how quiet they were. Then the sound reached us, a series of terrible, cracking thuds. I suppose we were badly trained. I had never heard so many big guns so close. What you have to understand, Anna, is that this is not just a loud noise, like a shout, or a train passing, or an orchestra at full blast. It is a physical blow, it does not just deafen you but it punches your chest as well, you feel as if your heart and lungs are being shaken free of their fastenings. Most of us struggled to control our horses. A few shied; none bolted. Hijaz took it better than I did. After a few moments I realised I was bent forward in the saddle, eyes closed, breathing as if I had just come up for air after nearly drowning, and was gripping Hijaz so tightly with my knees that he was slowing down, about to stop. And the firing was finished; there was the clatter of the column on the road again, and the larks over the fields on either side. I relaxed, opened my eyes and nudged Hijaz forward before he had a chance to obstruct the squadron behind me.

As I passed the guns, they fired again. The flash, the smoke, the recoil and the blast all happened at the same time. It could not have been much louder but it seemed so. All I could think of was myself, keeping myself whole. It was so intimate. I had the feeling that a stranger had appeared in front of me and, without any reason or sign of emotion, shoved me hard in the chest. Without realising what I was doing, I dropped the reins, and my feet seemed to lift out of the stirrups of their own accord, and I hunched over with my knees drawn up against the pommel and my hands over my face. As before, the horror passed, and I became aware of what I was doing, and moved my hands slowly away from my eyes. I could not understand what was happening; I seemed to be in shade, though there were no trees; and Hijaz was walking on as if nothing had happened. I straightened up and returned my feet to the stirrups. When I had tried to hide from the noise of the guns, four of my troopers, the tallest, had ridden around me, shielding me from the view of the rest of the squadron and picking up Hijaz's reins. They did not look at me, and did not speak. Their move was so lightly and quickly made that they must have rehearsed it. I was astonished, and grateful, although I said nothing, bracing myself for the next salvo, clenching my jaw and feeling the reins slippery with sweat. That time, the salvo did not come until we were a mile away, when it was more tolerable. I do not know what happened; perhaps the troopers had seen me flinch at the sound of artillery in exercises, and were ready, or perhaps the Colonel had spoken to them. He had asked me about this before, and I had lied that I was not troubled by it. Pride, Anna. Anyway, now, I was touched and given heart by the care my troopers showed. Yet what if I had been exposed there and then, and led back down the lines in shame, accused, I suppose, of cowardice? Perhaps I would have been shot. Perhaps I would never have met Chanov again. God knows his purpose.

We rode on. The gunfire stopped after a time, and it became very peaceful, although I remember thinking how few civilians there were to be seen.

We were on the Lemberg road. The regiment was marshalled and fed and watered at an abandoned village, where the staff had made headquarters in the house of the richest peasant. They were setting up field telephones, and a despatch rider on a motorcycle came and went. Again there was a sense of order and purpose and service to a remoter, more demanding power than we had served before. At about four in the afternoon the fighting squadrons were ordered to mount up and advance in columns, cross country.

Some word came down to the junior officers about what had been said among the staff. This was not the great attack; that would be later. We were being sent to test enemy defences. Balloons, aeroplanes, spies and scouts had looked over the Austrian lines – they were Austrians, it turned out – but there were still enemy positions the staff weren't sure about. There was a wooded valley they were interested in. The plan was for the regiment to approach the valley from the low ridges on either side. Rumlyan-Pechersky was in trouble because this was to have been done the previous day, and so even though it was late, with only five hours of decent light left, and we were supposed to go, reconnoitre, and return, he insisted we move immediately. The squadron commanders did not like his plan, which involved taking the whole regiment through a five hundred metre gap between dense woods to reach the open country that led to the valley. Rumlyan-Pechersky insisted, pointing out that the staff had promised to send a rifle battalion to secure the woods on either side of the gap. So we set off, with the sun in our eyes, as if we had given it to the Austrians to use against us.

After an hour, we saw the gap ahead. The squadrons were walking in columns four abreast across the stubble of harvested wheat. The idea was to move as quickly as possible through the gap and then wheel round and dash for the ridges. Rumlyan-Pechersky's adjutant was looking through binoculars. Even without them we could see the flags waving from the edges of the woods, the signal that the infantry had secured them. The bugler sounded canter and our horses stretched their stride. We drew our sabres, although God knows, we did not expect to have to use them. It was to make us feel strong, their sharpened weight hanging from our arms. And we did feel strong, as the ground began to thunder with the sound of our hooves, and we were young, and there seemed to be so invincibly many of us, almost a thousand, a flood of horse power and khaki stretched back in the wind. You could see the teeth, horse teeth and men's teeth as their lips stretched back. The sabres were supposed to have dull, greased flats, to slide smoothly out of the scabbard and not reflect the sun, but some men's metal sparkled among the field of warriors. I saw it shine.

I was in the van of the second squadron to go through. Ahead of me I could see the first squadron slow as it entered open country and begin to turn towards the head of the valley. I heard a strange little sound in the air around me, the kind of sound a fly swatter makes before it hits anything, and sure enough, Khigrin, the lieutenant next to me, slapped his neck with the kind of grunting cry you make when an insect bites you. And then he fell off his horse! I remember thinking how embarrassed he would be, one of the best horsemen in the regiment, falling off his mount because of an insect bite. It seems to me now that I thought all this before I became aware that above the jostling, thudding, jingling sound of horsemen and that curious whishing sound of air being struck there was the sound of machine gun fire. Even then I could not comprehend that it might be directed towards us. I turned round and saw our column was shedding little black heaps which lay dark against the bright stubble like dung. Trooper Bilenko was looking at me with a face like a fighting dog at bay. I saw him bend sharply in the middle, sideways, like a puppet, something a man could not do unless his spine had been violently broken, and he started to shout something at me, I heard the first word,

'They –' when part of his neck snapped apart, like a piece of rubber pulled tight, and his mouth was stopped with a sluice of blood. I felt some warm drops of it hit my face as Bilenko's horse died under him and catapaulted the dead trooper over its head onto the ground. I turned round again and wiped my eyes clean of Bilenko's blood with the back of my hand. I could see the first squadron exploding in front of me. Its neat outline of a few seconds ago was still there, only marked by dead and crippled men and horses, while the living and wounded remnant were flying in all directions, being cut down as they moved.

I understood the squadron had to wheel into line abreast and head for the woods on one or other side. I was confused. It would have been the right thing to do if I were a good officer keeping a clear head, since the fire was coming from there and we were too close to retreat, but in the state I was in I was thinking just of how dark and sheltered the woods were, how they would make a place to hide. What is even more peculiar is that I was thinking less of myself, or the other men in the squadron, than of Hijaz. The most important thing at that moment was that Hijaz should not be harmed. I felt something vital to me depended on it.

I could see no other officers left alive, or the bugler, so I reined Hijaz in, turned, lifted my sabre and shouted the command, looking back down the column. At first I thought the men, in desperation, were trying to take cover on the ground, or behind dead horses, there were so many lying still and so few still standing. It did not seem possible that we could have lost more than half the squadron in so short a time. Yet we had. The survivors began to wheel. Even as they did, of course, they were still dropping, in such a quick, dull way. The bullets took possession of them and in a moment they ceased to be, without a hair's breadth of space between living and dying. A kind of incantation began to swell in my mind, to whom, I don't know, calling for it to slow down, to wait, to let it be done with more mercy and dignity, to let us witness, at least, each execution, even if the witnesses were then themselves to be executed. And the more blood and falling around me the louder the incantation, as if part of me felt that I could really, if not halt the killing, at least make it pass more slowly, or be done again from the beginning, in such a way that we were ready. Perhaps I was thinking of football, looking for someone to blow the whistle, impose order and fairness. But I saw Chernetsky, sound asleep in the stubble with his jacket covered in fresh blood and his head resting on the rising and falling chest of his mutilated dying horse, sound asleep, even though a trooper whose legs had been shot to bits was screaming in his ear for him to get up. Then just as we were about to charge for the woods we heard a sound like a flock of banshees settling down on us from above and the sky burst into pieces. I was inside a drum being beaten by a mad boy as big as the world, the sound and the blast together, the shells exploding just above the ground. I knew I was deaf after the first fall of shells but I still heard the explosions with my whole body. Even though I had not been hit I felt my bones were going to break with the blasts. I toppled off Hijaz and fell on a corpse, rolling off and staggering back and opening my eyes in time to see a huge spinning blade of shrapnel cut my horse open from neck to hindquarters, cut him ragged and deep, to guts and joints. He stood four square for a moment, shook his head from side to side in irritation, as he would do when the flies got too many. Then his legs folded and he fell. I drew my pistol and crawled over to him but his heart had stopped beating. I put my hands around his neck and curled myself up as tightly as I could, burying my face in the warm dark shield of my chest and his mane, and cried like a baby. Anna, I truly did, I had read the expression, but I heard myself bawling, screaming through the tears, and even when the tears stopped, till my throat was raw.

After a time, when I had stopped screaming, still in my cocoon, it occurred to me that there was no more shelling, and the nature of the shooting had changed. It seemed incomprehensible to me that men should still be capable of fighting, but as the light faded – I opened my eyes for a second now and then – I could hear them, shouting orders, shouting for help, shooting. Horses passed at speed, singly and in small groups. I heard more shelling further away, outbreaks of rifle fire and the screams of men charging, and an aeroplane overhead. Then it was dark.

I do not know what happened, whether we mistook the flags, whether the Austrians captured our men and discovered the signal. I do not know whose shells landed on us, the Austrians or ours. It does not seem to matter. It did not matter then. I uncurled myself in the darkness and raised myself on my knees. Around me I could see the lumps of dead. There was some movement, a slithering and a twitching. They were not all dead. I heard a horse's sick breathing, and then a man's voice, murmuring and wheezing. I clasped my hands together, laid them on Hijaz's stiff belly, bent my head and prayed to God to forgive us all.

I could not rid myself of the feeling I had been hit. I took off my scabbard and gun and all my straps and cast them away. I took off my jacket and discarded it, with all my documents, and, Anna, the photographs of you and Alyosha. I remembered about them later, when it was too late, and regretted it, but at this time I seemed to have crossed into another world entirely. I ran my hands over my face, my chest, my back as best I could, my legs, my middle. There was the dried blood of others on me, but I had not bled. I was untouched.

I got to my feet, crouching down, and made my way over to where the man was talking. His was a kind of prayer too, it seemed to be a list of all the people he knew. I came up to him and told him who I was and he said he was Yantaryov. It was one of the troopers who had shielded me on the ride forward. He asked me if our people had won. I could barely understand what he meant by these words. I said I did not know. He asked if our people would come for us and I told him they would. Yantaryov's stomach had been cut open. He must have been in terrible pain, but he did not show it. How are such men made? He was from the Caspian, I think. Astrakhan. He asked me where I was wounded and I did not answer. He asked if I would shoot his horse for him. I told him his horse was dead. He asked if I would shoot him. He said he would not live for more than a few hours, which was true, and it hurt. I said I could not shoot him. It would be a sin. He said I was right, he apologised, and asked me to fetch him some water. His canteen was empty so I went to get mine. As I pulled it out I heard a shot. I ran back to Yantaryov and found him dead, with his own pistol in his mouth and his hand on the trigger. A harsh light bloomed in the sky. A flare was floating down. I dropped to the ground. Machine guns sounded again. I lay there for a long time, until there were no more flares. Then, on my hands and knees, I began crawling towards the woods. I did not know what I was doing or where I was going. Perhaps I thought that if I was going to be killed I would like to be closer to the people doing the killing. And still I thought about shelter and concealment. I did not think about going back to join the regiment. I was a deserter and an outlaw, but this did not occur to me then.

There must have been soldiers of one sort or another among the trees, but without trying to I slipped between them. These were the very first days of the war. I have not followed the news closely these past months, as you can imagine, but I know the troops are very inclined to dig themselves in and make fortifications whenever they can. They move more slowly, more carefully. The cavalry have dismounted. They have become wiser. Still they are dying, of course.

I walked for hours, trying to be as quiet as possible and trying to move deeper into the forest. It was a warm night. I curled up on a bed of last year's leaves between two tree roots and went to sleep. I woke up from a nightmare just when it was getting light. I had dreamed the events of the battle – battle? to call it a battle! only killing – just as they had happened, with one or two details added. One was that you and Alyosha and the Colonel were there, somehow, but you had your backs to us: you were watching something else. The other was that as the shells began to explode I felt as if I was being bitten by some small, vicious animal, from within, as if it was just about to burst through my skin. I stood up with a shout in a pattering of falling leaves and pulled off my vest and ran my hands over my body. There was no new mark, not even a graze. I took off my boots and the rest of my clothes and sat naked on the root, trying to find the wound I was sure was there. I found nothing. In my heart I was not surprised because I did not feel as if I had lost anything, blood or flesh. It felt more as if I had gained something I should not have, which had not been there before. I had seen the best part of two hundred comrades and their horses cut down like grass in a few minutes, and I had escaped without a cut. I should have been on my knees, for days, thanking God for his mercy. But I did not feel saved. I felt filthy inside, as if my soul would never be clean again, be there ever so much fasting and prayer, and a weight which would never let my soul float free of this world of blind killing.

I heard a branch cracking and I jumped behind the root, grabbing my clothes. I saw a dark shape moving between the trees a few hundred metres away. It was a horse, without a rider. I pulled on my clothes and boots. I became aware of how thirsty I was and thought of stopping to look for water. I decided to follow the horse. It was not difficult. The animal would stop every once in a while. It seemed to be thinking, or listening. A couple of times it looked back at me. It was not concerned I was following. When I came closer I saw it was a cavalry horse. It had one of our regiment's saddlecloths. I recognised the beast: Dandy, Trooper Shtekel's mount. I could have tried to catch him, but I had no idea of my own to follow, and I felt so base for Hijaz that I was ready, even eager, to humble myself before a horse by allowing it to lead me. I did not see how I could ever presume to ride a horse again, and I felt a lump in my throat at the thought.

After about a mile there was a crashing to our right and I saw the familiar dark muzzle of the grey, Lyotchik. I couldn't remember the rider. He was dead, I supposed, and felt awkward for not remembering. Nothing seemed strange to me now and we went forward together, two horses leading a man through the forest. After about an hour I smelled woodsmoke and we came to a clearing with a charcoal burners' hut. Four men sat on logs by a small fire. Smoke came from the hut too. When we entered the clearing one of the four, a man I recognised, got up and took the bridles of the horses, nodding at me. The three others looked at me. I recognised them all. I went over and Chanov asked me if I would like to sit down opposite him. I sat and asked for a drink of water. One of the apprentices brought me a cupful, and another when I emptied the first.

I told Chanov he had been missed. He said he could not take part in that. He pointed to the direction from which I had come when he said 'That'. He asked where the regiment was and I told him they were mostly dead. He nodded and said that it would still be called a victory.

I asked him what he meant. He said they who commanded, the Tsar, his marshals, the great capitalists and financiers, did not reckon in the lives of individual men, any more than they reckoned in single roubles or single American dollars. In their affairs and at the gambling table they would lose thousands to win millions; and if they lost millions, they had millions more. So it was with spending their men. A regiment of one thousand souls was a little stake. But I must understand the truth that was hidden even from the Tsar: that he and his commanders and nobles and capitalists, and the Kaiser, and the Austrian Emperor, and the King of England, and the President of France, and all their rich and powerful courts and general staffs and bourses, they too were only stakes, laid by a greater player in a greater game. Chanov asked me if I felt the presence of that greater hand. I said I did. Chanov asked if I knew who it was. I said: 'Is it Satan?' Chanov said 'Yes, it is the Enemy.' Chanov said Satan had stirred mankind in this war as his best-worked combination to spite God. The Devil had worked on us for decades to bring it to this, and it had been easy, because he held all men on his keychain. Satan was an evil moon, and he could tug at the seed in men and turn it to his purpose as the moon turns the tides.

'But not you,' I said.

'Not me,' replied Chanov. 'I am not a man. I have remade myself into the likeness and form of an angel. I have taken the Keys of Hell which hung upon me and have thrown them into the furnace. By doing this I have returned to that Paradise God made for man in the Beginning, and I dwell there.' Chanov said that God had told him to cross the Urals before the

foretold war and join the army so as to find even a few souls there who would understand the prison they were in, and how they might release themselves. I should think of him, he said, as an angel who had journeyed into Hell, and who would send back as many pure souls as could be found there, and could recognise their own nature well enough to agree to go.

I asked him how it was possible for a man to live in Paradise and Earth at the same time, and he said the Paradise of the White Doves – that was what he called the castrates – was like a ship, of the Earth but floating free of it, touching land at certain places yet never remaining there, outside the laws and boundaries of any mortal territory.

I asked him how God spoke to them, and he said: 'We turn.' He touched one of the apprentices on the shoulder and the man got up and stood on a flat rock near the edge of the clearing. He stretched his arms out horizontally on either side and began to turn on one foot, quickly reaching such a speed that his body blurred, like a top, and he lost the appearance of a man. He looked to be of a lighter substance than the still world around him. I thought he might rise from the rock and begin to float up into the trees. A second apprentice walked over to him and, after some minutes spinning, the figure slowed, returned to its Earthly substance, and fell, sodden with sweat and with eyes closed, mumbling and smiling, into the arms of his fellow.

Chanov asked if I would tell him about the killing and although it was hard for me I told him everything in as much detail as I could. He asked if I had been injured and I said no, I had not, and I could not understand why God had chosen me out of all my comrades to leave the field unharmed. Yet, as I told Chanov, I felt as if I was carrying a burden with me from the field of the dead, which would keep me chained to the moments of the killing forever.

And Chanov asked: 'Do you know the name and the place of that burden?' I looked at him and I understood what the burden was, and I put my hand on it, and I felt it hung there like a tumour. There was fear in me, but it was a fear that I believe came from my body, while in my soul I felt the dawning of a great joy, and a clear vision came to me of myself standing on a vessel tied to a burning land, and a sword cutting the rope that moored the vessel, and me floating free onto the peace of the waters. I thought of you, too, and Alyosha. You were not in that vision. It was as if you were in some other world altogether, some Russia that lay on the other side of the killing, somewhere I could not cross back to. The joy was rising in me, and the fear too, but the joy always greater. God had saved me for this, I understood; a trial. How else would I have found Chanov?

And Chanov said that to those who were not White Doves, the crows, he called them, it seemed that the misery and wickedness of the world was divided into a million parts, that they were not linked. That anger, and greed, and lust, and warlikeness, and the ambition that tramples others, and lying for gain, and selfishness, and the sadness that comes even to the rich in the evening, were not all part of that same Devil's urge. They were blind. Why did man make war and heap up riches and lust after women if not for the same itching of his seed, urging him on? Had I not seen in the faces of the Hussars as they rode to war, driving their innocent beasts to destruction, that same insatiable hunger which I had seen in them at the gaming table and as they coveted the goods and women of others? The Devil's keychain was too strong for the Lord's Commandments to hold. The very form of the Keys to Hell showed that they were of the Curse of the Serpent and the Fruit of the Tree of Knowledge; a trunk and two fruit. Only by destroying them could a man escape, and the Enemy had made them so dear to us. Had I not thought, when he showed me his angel's body in the stream, that he had made a greater sacrifice than if he had cut off his hands, or cut his throat? Had I not thought that?

I told him I had, and told him I was ready. He told me I was not ready. We repeated these words many times to each other until I asked what the Book said. Chanov recited the words of Matthew: 'And if thy right eye offend thee, pluck it out, and cast it from thee: for it is profitable for thee that one of thy members should perish, and not that thy whole body should be cast into hell.' And he recited from John: 'Love not the world, neither the things that are in the world. If any man loves the world, the love of the Father is not in him. For all that is in the world, the lust of the flesh, and the lust of the eyes, and the pride of life, is not of the Father, but is of the world.'

I stood up and begged him to take me with him to Paradise. He stood, and put his hand on my shoulder, and shook his head, and said he could not. I asked him again. After I had asked him many times he asked me if I truly wanted this and I said I did, the joy and fear still growing in me. He led me to the charcoal burner's hut, stopping every pace to ask again if I was certain.

Inside the hut it was very hot. An open furnace glowed red, and there was a wooden chair on the dirt floor. Chanov told me to remove my clothes. He told me that at any time I could stop before the cutting by shouting: 'I refuse!'

I heard a knife being sharpened outside. For a moment the fear surged and then I thought that compared to what I had seen in the killing, what my comrades had suffered and would suffer, this was little. Chanov sat me in the chair and bade me open my legs. He told me that for now, he would only cut the fruit, and not the trunk. This was called the First Seal, and Mounting the Skewbald Horse; Mounting the White Horse came later. He said that when he had done, I must take them and throw them in the fire.

The apprentices came in. The one who had turned was still smiling and looked a little glassy-eyed. One of them was carrying a short, sharp knife, which he gave to Chanov, a white towel, and an open bottle of spirit, which he placed on the ground.

The four men kneeled in front of me and began to pray. At intervals I was given responses to make. Anna, these I cannot tell you; they are the most secret words. The men stood. One of the apprentices held my arms behind my back; the other two held the ankles of my open legs. Chanov bent over me, lifted my member with his left hand, and brought the knife down quickly with the other. In that one moment, it seemed God turned his face away, and the fear smothered the joy. I thought about Alyosha, and I was glad I had helped bring him into the world, and I thought about you and I on the train to Crimea after we were married, and how you had laid claim to a part of me, and I had given it to you, and how I was breaking faith with that. The knife was very sharp. It cut through the skin and tubes to the wood of the chair in less than a second, long before I began to feel pain. I do not think I screamed. I tried not to, for some reason. Perhaps I had done my screaming against Hijaz's dead neck. I felt the apprentices release me, the warm gush of blood between my thighs, the shock of spirit poured over the wound, and the towel handed me to press against it. Then Chanov put the sac he had just amputated into the palm of my free hand, a warm familiar part of me that was no longer part of me. I walked to the furnace and threw it in, where it crackled and disappeared in the flames. I fell.

Anna, it is done, and it cannot be undone. I have much more to tell you and will write again soon. I wanted you to know, although I was not supposed to tell you anything. I wanted you to know. Do not tell Alyosha yet. But I wanted you to know I am a deserter, and an angel, I have been castrated and I am happy.

With the pure remains of my love for you,
Do not be angry for ever,
Your legal husband
Former lieutenant Gleb Alexeyevich Balashov

Yazyk
20 December 1914

Mutz finished reading and put down the letter on the divan. He looked up at the portrait of the man he now knew to be Balashov, Anna's father's wedding present. It bore no resemblance to the storekeeper of Yazyk, of course, but that had been the father's talent. Something to show Alyosha. Mutz had never felt so soiled as after reading Balashov's confession. He shuddered with the sense of the blade, which it was impossible not to feel severing that same thin tie of flesh between his own legs. He stood up, flexed his fingers, looked around without knowing what for. He was sweating and he swallowed several times, wondering if he was about to vomit. He should go in to speak to Anna Petrovna, but he couldn't bear to look on the bitch's face. The cold sweat rolled over him in a wave as he heard his mind come up with that phrase, as if from some unknown country inside himself: the bitch's face. It was the first flame of an anger that began to burn into him from different directions, knocking him back on the divan, immobilising him, while his skin, his whole body, went hot with it. Anger towards himself for not seeing that this was a community of skoptsy, of castrates, was the least of it. The rage flamed in from the beast-stupid, ignorant, blind literal-mindedness of Balashov, the petulant tantrum of the action, the impossibility of a sane mind like Mutz's ever spanning the distance between the two extremes, between the greatest harm and pain, and the silliest joke, a man could execute with his own body. The rage flamed in from the self-delusion and naiveté of Anna Petrovna, trusting in the sanity of a hussar obsessed with God, and letting him go to war. It burned hottest from her selfishness in following the madman here to the edge of the world, as if they could in any sense still be husband and wife, letting her son languish in an unnecessary exile, and, after allowing him, Mutz, to believe she was in love with him, revealing her eunuch jester as if he could be even a partial reason for her sudden coldness.

Mutz felt he needed to hit something. There was no reason for him to stay. He strode out through the front door of the house, slamming it behind him, out onto the road and towards the bridge. Just before the bridge was a cluster of rowan trees and he seized the trunk of one and shook it, yelling, till the berries pattered into the wet weeds around him. One of the branches cracked and the violence of the sound made him stop and try to remember why he had gone to Anna Petrovna's. Samarin's murderous thief. The cannibal.

Mutz began walking back. The same dog barked and he remembered his hesitation, the fear and the hope of walking to Anna Petrovna's only an hour before, and how Samarin's cannibal had faded from his mind. Why? His insides turned to stone. Because he had been thinking with that which Balashov had removed. If you did not believe in God or the Devil, was it worse to be led by that? Whose keychain was he on?

Mutz, docile and tender now, crept in through the front door, removed the key from the inside lock, locked the door from the outside, and pushed the key under the door. He passed round to the back of the house. He looked in through the kitchen window. Anna Petrovna was sleeping, head on the kitchen table. He did not think of waking her. Perhaps he loved her, in a way that had nothing to do with what his loins told him to do. How could you ever be sure?

He went down to the yard gate and bolted it, then lay down on the straw in the warm stink of the little cowshed. It was Balashov, of course, who had been concerned about Anna Petrovna. About his wife, curse him. He had cared. Was care love? What use was Anna Petrovna's love to her husband now? He had divorced her with the knife quicker than any lawyer. And more cheaply. Mutz found he was smiling. For a moment he felt wretched, then managed to persuade himself it was a sign that his disgust and anger with Balashov was turning to pity. All Balashov wanted, all his damaged congregation of amputated angels wanted, was to be left alone. There must still be a few islands of human feeling left sticking up above the surface of Anna Petrovna's husband's insanity; a sense of duty, perhaps. Mutz could reach those islands and work on them. Was it so ridiculous after all to believe that Balashov was what was preventing Anna Petrovna and Alyosha leaving Yazyk with him? He had to speak to Balashov and explain why he must persuade his wife and son to leave and never see him again. He would understand. It would fit within the logic of his madness. Then what would remain would be to get Matula to release the Czechs from *his* madness and begin the great journey to Vladivostok. It was hard, but it was simple. He could not leave the Czechs behind. They were his people, even if they did not think so. Mutz fell asleep.

Matula

Viktor Timofeyovich Skachkov, Land Captain of Yazyk, was eating breakfast alone in the dining room when his wife shrieked the name of God three times upstairs, each time louder than the last, then let out a long howl which rolled from high to low, ending in a gurgle of pure foundedness, like a baby laughing. The sounds were clear throughout the house. The Land Captain's lips slipped rissole off his fork smoothly and swiftly. When Elizaveta Timurovna fell silent it was light and tranquil in the dining room, with windows on two sides, dust spinning in sunbeams, the ticking of a clock and the swish of cloth as the maid, Pelageya Fedotovna Pilipenko, poured tea.

'Disgrace,' she whispered.

The Land Captain did not slurp in drinking hot water, nor did he open his mouth while chewing, or chink his cutlery against the porcelain of his plate. He was at an altar of silence.

'Good morning, Viktor Timofeyovich,' said Mutz, in the doorway. 'Good morning, Pelageya Fedotovna. Captain Matula asked us to join him at breakfast.'

The Land Captain went on eating as if he had not heard, looking at a spot midway down the long table.

'Well, sit down,' said Pelageya Fedotovna.

Mutz thanked her and entered with the two other Czech lieutenants, Kliment and Dezort.

'Could you fry us some potatoes, with a little bacon, and some smoked cheese?' said Kliment to Pelageya Fedotovna, leaning back in his chair.

'Arrogance!' said Pelageya Fedotovna. 'There's rissoles and kasha, bread and tea. You're not in Karlsbad now.'

'I wish I could take you there,' said Kliment, breaking off a piece of bread and putting it in his mouth. 'I'd buy you a blue dress. You'd look lovely.'

'Why blue?' muttered Pelageya Fedotovna, laying out plates for the officers.

'And diamonds,' said Kliment.

'What would I be wanting in Karlsbad, in your mad Europe, I don't know.'

'In a blue dress, with diamonds, coming down the stairs at the Hotel Bristol, and all the gentlemen and ladies of fashion would say: who is that fascinating Russian beauty? Surely some princess of an ancient house, or Diaghilev's new protegé?'

'Nonsense,' said Pelageya Fedotovna. 'Complete idiotism. And why blue? Why not yellow, for example?'

Kliment and Dezort laughed and Pelageya Fedotovna blushed and told them to stop, it was indecent, it was boldness, pure boldness, unforgiveable.

'I went to Karlsbad,' said the Land Captain.

Everyone had forgotten he was not part of the furniture, that his movements and consumption of food were something more inminded than the ticking of the clock.

The Land Captain said: 'I remember in one of the theatres they had a negro woman dressed in white who claimed she could talk to Satan, but it was all a trick, we weren't deceived by it, when she was talking in those two voices, one very high, one low like a bear. She tried to scare us, but we weren't scared, though like all Africans she was acquainted with the Enemy, of course, and I had my hand on my pocket pistol. The food was very bad, I remember. Their trout was insipid, nothing like the fish you can catch here. Great red fish, the size of this table, rich as venison.'

'Yes, your Excellency, the fish here is good,' said Mutz. The officers were staring at their plates while Pelageya Fedotovna spooned grey food into them. Dezort cleared his throat. Kliment began to hum very quietly, looking up at Pelageya Fedotovna when she bent over him. He blinked and made a sad mouth and his eyes flicked from her eyes to her bosom.

The Land Captain spoke again, slowly, without intonation, not looking up.

'We went to the casino, and bet on the wheel till I'd spent all the money I had with me. I put my two gold cufflinks on the red, and it came up, and the croupier reached into a box and added two cufflinks, so I had four. They were in the shape of acorns. The croupier said it was the Russian box. I said to my wife if she put her ring on a number, and the number came up, they'd give her 36 rings. But she wouldn't play. She kept her ring, the one I bought on Nevsky Prospekt for 500 roubles, with five diamonds in a cluster round an emerald. She kept the ring. Then I lost the cufflinks.'

'That's very funny, your Excellency,' said Mutz.

Soft acknowledging heh hehs came from the throats of Kliment and Dezort. The Land Captain did not smile or laugh or look up. Had it even been a funny story? Mutz and Dezort tightened in over their plates. Kliment leaned back in his chair, an elbow resting on it. He raked kasha gently with the fork in his other hand.

'I need some mustard,' he said.

'We don't have any. There hasn't been mustard since before Lent,' said Pelageya Fedotovna.

'I saw some in your kitchen,' said Lieutenant Kliment. 'I saw a big pot marked "Mustard", with yellow stains running down the sides.'

'Rubbish.'

'A huge pot of mustard. It smelled good and hot. You must have seen it. Didn't you see it? You like that hot taste on your tongue, don't you? I know you do. I know I do. Come on, I'll show you.'

'Out of your minds,' said Pelageya Fedotovna. 'Aren't you ashamed of yourselves, acting like pigs?' She licked her lips, smoothed her apron and glanced at Kliment. He got up, stretched, and strolled past her towards the door, whistling. He stopped and turned to bow to the Land Captain. He went out, with Pelageya Fedotovna behind, and the kitchen door closed.

Dezort shoved a rissole into his mouth, put down his fork, folded his hands in front of his plate and leaned forwards to Mutz, who was opposite him. He spoke quietly, switching from Russian to Czech.

'D'you think Kliment's going to give her one in the kitchen?' he said.

'I don't know,' said Mutz. 'Do you think he's going to find any mustard?'

'You must be shitting yourself thinking what Matula's going to say when he hears about the shaman.'

'He knows,' said Mutz. 'I sent a message to him last night.'

'D'you suppose it was the convict who slipped him the booze?'

'Perhaps. You'll be hearing his story later, won't you, unless you've got larch needles to count.' Mutz wondered how long Samarin would take to testify, whether Matula would judge him guilty and shoot him, and how bad he, Mutz, would feel about not trying to stop him. He was trying to work out how he could get away to see Balashov, and he was weighed down by the feeling which had been with him since he got up at dawn and left Anna Petrovna's house that he had made a terrible mistake by not waking her up and talking to her about the letter.

'I wonder what the meat is in these rissoles,' he said.

'Any meat, as long as it's not you know what.'

Mutz rolled a morsel around in his mouth, frowned, wrinkled his nose, swallowed, put down his knife and fork and took a gulp of tea.

'It's cat,' he said.

'Thank God for that,' said Dezort. 'If it'd been horse. I was out all night, trying to find the missing. Lajkurg was one of them, Matula's mount when we were in Chelyabinsk. Big evil white stallion, put a groom in hospital with his ribs staved in. That was why the train never arrived last night. The commander was so terrified of Matula that he halted short of Yazyk to check everything was still in place. He found the horses were gone, and a man with them. They broke out, or he stole them, somehow. Anyway, the train commander panicked and went back to Verkhny Luk. They sent a telegram about the horses from there.'

'I thought the telegraph was down.'

Dezort's eyes widened, as they did instinctively whenever he was about to lie, one of the reasons he would never be a successful officer. 'It was fixed,' he said. 'Now it's broken again. Matula was talking about the horse yesterday as if we were looking for his only son. What with that and the shaman he's going to be like the devil.'

'Someone's trying to make him happy,' said Mutz.

'Oh,' said Dozent. He sneaked another look at the Land Captain, who had stopped eating, and sat with his head bowed as if asleep, hands flat on the table in front of him.

Mutz leaned closer to Dezort. 'You know why the commander never brought his train to Yazyk,' he said. 'It wasn't because he was afraid of Matula. Even Matula wouldn't dare take on a train, yet. It was because everyone down the line from here hates him.'

'He's a good soldier.'

'Are you ready to die for him?'

'I want to go home, of course. But there's time, isn't there?'

'Are you ready to shoot the men when they tell you they're not going to fight any more, they want to go home?'

'It won't come to that. The Legion is strong. The Whites are strong. The English and French and Americans and Japanese, they're with us, aren't they? They are. I know they are.'

'The Legion isn't an army,' said Mutz. 'It's fifty thousand travellers waiting on a platform for a delayed train home.'

'You shouldn't be so unpatriotic, Mutz. You know I don't hold with that talk about how you're a filthy Yid but you make it easy for the people who talk that way. Some of the men believe you speak with a German accent.'

'Dezort, you do understand the Whites are doomed, don't you? They've lost their Tsar, the only cause they care about is revenge, and what they want most of all is to curl up by the fire, have servants bring them a hot meal, have a good long sleep, and wake up to find everything the way it was before. The trouble is that all the servants can think about is killing them.'

Dezort's eyes shifted. He pressed the corner of his moustache into his mouth with his finger. He bit on a bristle and uprooted it.

'That's all a long way from here,' he said.

'The Reds have already broken through the Urals. Once they take Omsk, they'll be here in days. They remember us. They know who we are and all the things Matula made us do. They've already made a film about what we did at Staraya Krepost.'

'How do you know that?'

'I don't know how you put up with this. Don't you have a wife in Ceske Budujovice?'

'Yes,' said Dezort. 'I don't think about her as much as I used to. I can't really remember what she looks like, to be honest. You know it's funny you should be so keen to leave when you've been seeing that widow at the crossroads.'

'There's nothing between us,' said Mutz. 'Except common courtesy.'

Dezort pursed his lips, regarded Mutz, and laughed. 'You're such a pompous arse,' he said.

There was a yelp from the kitchen, a crashing of pans and swearing from Pelageya Fedotovna and Kliment. Kliment came back to the dining room, buttoning his tunic, and sat down. He was out of breath. He smoothed his hair with his hand.

'What's funny?' he said, shovelling kasha into his mouth.

'Mutz is having trouble with the widow,' said Dezort.

'What made him think she'd be interested in a Jew?'

'Did you find the mustard?' said Dezort.

'Yes,' said Kliment, smacking his lips. 'It was hotter than I expected. And just when I'm about to' – he glanced at the Land Captain, motionless with bowed head at the end of the table – 'when I'm about to finish the matter, she screams and kicks out, and I think she's really liking it, and I see this flash of black and orange fur and blood. A sable! Can you believe it? A sable got into the kitchen and bit her on the thigh while we were, you know. What a place. Even the small beasts are vicious. Tiny little teeth, but sharp. Like a damn wolf. I thought they ate, you know, pine cones. Mutz, you should write something about it for *Czechoslovakian Daily*.'

'Maybe it was rabid,' said Mutz.

Kliment blinked, opened his mouth, dropped his fork and tore at the fastenings on his tunic. The cloth bulged and strained as the crazed creature inside slithered around Kliment's torso. Kliment jumped up, one hand down the back of his neck, the other up under the front of the tunic, twisting and arching and baring his teeth. A length of fur and urchin muscle streaked out and dived under the dresser behind Kliment.

Mutz stopped laughing, stood to attention and called out the command. Dezort snapped up and Kliment clicked his heels together, holding his tunic closed with one hand and his thumb on the seam of his breeches with the other. Red-haired Matula stood gazing at them from the doorway, the Land Captain's wife behind his shoulder.

Matula's dark eyes were set deep in his face. The skin around his eyes was lined and the flesh coarsely flayed by heat and cold and fevers and jaundices and scurvies gone by. He had a crooked, cross-marked scar from a badly stitched wound slanting across his chin. Only his mouth had been immune to all the frosts and bloodshed of five years' campaigning. His lips were soft and full, red like a boy's, as if he'd put them away for safekeeping when he went into battle or in winter, as if they'd never been stretched in a yell in a charge, as if they'd never been pressed or bitten when his tongue had told men to kill captives, as if he kept them for feasts, games and kisses. His eyes had seen it all. He was 24 years old.

'All my Siberian princes are here,' he said, and sat down at the head of the table, at the far end from the Land Captain. 'All my knights of the taiga. What territories should I give you? I've decided that you should all marry Russian women, and raise dynasties. Except Lieutenant Mutz. He should marry a Jewish woman, and raise money.'

Kliment and Dezort laughed. Elizaveta Timurovna smiled and lost her smile and smiled again. She fidgeted with her hair and sucked her lip and looked at Matula. She had on a white summer dress she'd once worn to picnics. It still had the creases and the odour of being kept in a trunk for years. There was blood in her cheeks and the newly polished-up gleam of sexual desire in her look. She'd tied a white satin ribbon round her neck. She sat next to Matula and didn't turn to her husband.

'There's a rat under the dresser,' said Matula.

'It's a sable, sir,' said Dezort. 'Mutz thinks it might be mad. It bit Pelageya Fedotovna on the leg.'

'I must be mad, then,' said Matula. 'I bit a woman this morning. I'd bite her again.' He grinned at Elizaveta Timurovna and brushed his fingers over her thigh under the table. She squirmed away and giggled. Pelageya Fedotovna came into the room, limping, and served Matula. Everyone watched her.

'Can I have some more tea?' said Kliment.

Pelageya Fedotovna gave him a look like murder and limped over to fetch his cup.

'Does it hurt?' said Kliment, looking up at her with his mouth twitching.

She pressed her lips together, put the cup down, put her hands on her hips, then spat at him and hobbled from the room, crying. A small gob sank into Kliment's tunic. Dezort laughed and Kliment started to get up. Matula pushed him back in his seat.

'Sit down,' said Matula. 'You deserved it. Didn't he, Mutz?'

'Why are you asking me, sir?'

'You're always passing judgement on people. That's what you are, isn't it, a judge? I mean we know you were only an engraver in Prague but with us you're a judge. You're here to tell us when we do right and wrong. It's funny, I don't know who appointed you, it wasn't me, but you've been very busy judging us, making lists of all our sins and crimes.'

'I've made no lists, sir.'

'Oh, I know, it's all in your head. And you don't pass any judgements, either, do you, it's in the way you look at us. It's the strangest thing, when I'm trying to keep us alive, and your comrades in arms are trying to keep themselves happy, we're always turning round and seeing you looking at us with that expression of disgust. You're thinking about what punishment, aren't you, like a judge. Do you know what I mean, Lieutenant Kliment?'

'Yes. Or like a policeman. As if he's not on our side at all. As if he's on the side of some law he's carrying with him from another country.'

'You passed a judgement on Lieutenant Kliment there, Mutz,' said Matula. 'I saw you. Your judgement was: guilty of taking advantage of a serving girl. You never heard his defence, either.'

Matula had his fists resting on the edge of the table. He lifted them, opened them up, and shook them for emphasis as he smiled with his boy's mouth and watched Mutz with his old eyes.

'You've been judging us for a few years now, Lieutenant Mutz,' he said. 'When are you going to pass sentence? Isn't it time?'

'We're in Siberia,' said Mutz. 'I think that's sentence enough, sir.'

'Ah! You don't deny you're judging us. Mmm. But what do we think, gentlemen, madam, shouldn't a judge be more virtuous than the people he's judging?'

'The captain's right,' said Kliment, rocking back on his chair. The sable scrabbled under the dresser, testing the walnut with its claws.

'Is it right you should be judging comrades who're courting Russian women, paying them compliments, bringing them presents, and touching their innermost, tenderest, softest' – he looked at Elizaveta Timurovna – 'most moist and delectable . . . hearts . . . ?'

'Oh! My heart!' breathed Elizaveta Timurovna.

'. . . when you're trying to seduce a widow, what's her name, Lutova, yourself?'

'That's what I said!' shouted Dezort.

'I'm not seducing anyone,' said Mutz.

'You're trying your double-damnedest Hebraic-cabalistic best,' said Matula. 'You're ready to send poor old Kliment to the gallows for the maid, and there you are singing Yid love songs in your widow's ear, telling her you love her, and all the time planning how to escape to Vladivostok.'

'That's what I told him!' shouted Dezort.

'Anna Petrovna knows the men want to leave, sir,' said Mutz.

'She's a horrible snob, Anna Petrovna, with no taste,' said Elizaveta Timurovna, folding her arms and leaning forward. She wrinkled her nose and showed her two front teeth. 'It's not as if she's from Petersburg. Poor woman. She thought she'd come to Siberia to lord it over folk even more provincial than she is, but she's hardly equipped for that, is she, with those tight drab clothes and those ridiculous hems almost up to her knees. You'd think she was proud of how skinny and flat chested she is. The way the bones stick out of her cheeks. She acts like she's an intellectual and she doesn't even have a piano in the house, let alone a gramophone. I don't suppose she can play anything except that guitar she has, and I know she can't paint as well as me. We used to have her round to play cards, and for dances, I mean she's not a peasant, after all, and she was always yawning and looking out of the window when someone was telling a story. She has such an infuriating manner. The way she moved, and turned her head when you talked to her, so slowly, as if what we were saying wasn't important and she had all the time.'

'She looks like that actress from the Charlie Chaplin film we saw in Kiev,' said Dezort.

'I believe it's pronounced Shaplá,' said Elizaveta Timurovna, who had never seen a film. 'Sharlí Shaplá.'

'*The Immigrant*?' said Mutz.

'Maybe . . .' said Dezort, frowning.

'She looks nothing like Edna Purviance, if that's who you mean.'

'Purviance! She does!'

'Come on, Dezort,' said Kliment. 'You can't even remember what your wife looks like.'

'I was hoping she looked like someone,' said Dezort. 'Someone I did remember.'

Elizaveta Timurovna screamed and pointed at a cocking, nervy set of fangs and glittering eyes and damp nostrils which keeked out from under the dresser behind Kliment and Dezort. Kliment drew his Mauser, turned, balanced his chair on a single leg, and with his arm held straight fired twice at the sable's face. The rounds penetrated the floor and a bitter incendiary smell hazed out from the gun. For seconds the room was half-deaf.

'Did you kill it?' said Elizaveta Timurovna with her eyes closed and her hands over her ears.

'No,' said Kliment, laying the gun on the table. 'It's sly. But I will. And then I'll eat it.'

'Leave the beast alone,' said Matula.

Without a word Kliment put the gun in his holster, buttoned it and sat the chair down on four legs.

There was silence for a time while Matula ate. Mutz and Kliment looked at each other and looked away. Dezort watched Elizaveta Timurovna, who was manicuring her nails with a file and her teeth.

'Lieutenant Mutz,' said Matula, 'Do you believe that a shaman's soul lives in a tree in the forest, and that when the shaman dies, wherever he is, the tree falls?'

'No, but when a shaman gets drunk, I'm sure all the trees start swaying.'

'Heh,' said Matula. He picked up crumbs from his plate and put them onto his tongue with the tip of his finger. 'Good. Mutzie. You could have tried to keep the booze away from him, couldn't you?'

'I was working on the new money, as you ordered, sir.'

'Oh yes. Money. For some people, I suppose, it's money. Mutz, you don't understand – your people don't understand, you don't feel what we Slavs do, what the shaman does. The sense of the forest. We Slavs all have part of our soul lodged in the forest. Did you know that the Tungus make their fighting bows out of mammoth ivory?'

'We're eating cat, sir,' said Mutz. 'There are only a hundred of us and no one is going to help. The Bolsheviks are coming. They'll kill us. We have to leave.'

'The forest will protect us,' said Matula. 'Our destiny makes us invincible here. It's a coming together of our European learning and our Asiatic forest souls. Why didn't you take better care of the shaman, Mutz? Eh? He was my guide, he was going to rally the clans.'

'He was very fond of alcohol.'

'He saw into the underworld and overworld!' said Matula, raising his voice, his lips like angel's and his eyes void. He bent down, swept his hand under the dresser and pulled out the sable by the throat. The beast danced from his fist, lips so far drawn back there seemed more teeth than head. It yanked itself into a c-shape, trying to get purchase on Matula's wrist with all and any clawing limbs. Matula stretched his arm out towards Mutz and jabbed towards Mutz's head with the sable's mouth. The animal's jaws were sticky with foam.

'What was his final prophecy?' shouted Matula.

'He was murdered, I believe, sir,' said Mutz, moving his head to dodge the snapping little fangs and claws. 'The political convict, Samarin, warned us that a killer had come among us from the north.'

'What was the last thing the shaman said, I asked you?'

'He said: "Everyone will have a horse."'

'Ah!' said Matula, grinning and settling back in his seat. 'You see?' He scratched the fur on the sable's head as if it was a favourite old dog. 'You see? He knew the horses were arriving. He saw it. He had all three eyes still working, whatever he said. He would have told you if he was going to be murdered, Mutz. He would have known. He must have hidden the alcohol in his kennel. That was careless of you, Lieutenant. There'll have to be some kind of disciplinary action taken. Kliment, go and tell your Pelageya Fedotovna to sharpen my sabre. I'll be riding today.'

'Am I going to meet your famous horse at last?' said Elizaveta Timurovna.

'It wouldn't be interesting,' said Matula.

'But I'd love to.'

'I mean it wouldn't be interesting for the horse.'

In the kitchen a blade scraped on a sharpening stone. Kliment came back.

'Hanak's coming,' he said. He glanced at Mutz, out of view of Matula, and shook his head. The sable squeaked and gurgled as Matula stroked it, he was nodding and smiling, the innocent happiness of scarlet lips and the eyes dead, basalt.

'Sounds like she's putting a beautiful edge on that blade, Kliment. This is going to be a good day.'

Sergeant Hanak knocked, saluted in the doorway, came forward, kneeled down by Matula and began whispering in his ear. At the same time he put a tin caddy of Chinese tea on the table in front of the captain. Matula did not appear to move while Hanak spoke. His hand stopped stroking the sable's head, though he still held it fast by the throat with his other hand, and it still kicked and swung, now with less force. Matula stared forward, a partner statue to the silent unmoving Land Captain at the opposite end of the table. As Hanak whispered on, tears formed in Matula's eyes and trickled out like dew condensing on granite. His boy's lips wrinkled and trembled and he pressed them tight. Hanak finished his report and stood up. Matula breathed in deeply and exhaled over his body's attempts to cry.

'They're all gone,' he said. 'Lajkurg is dead. All the mounts but one are dead, and the fifth is missing. They found them in the river. Someone's cut a strip of flesh from my horse, a strip to chew on, and strolled on. Who could be so wicked? Lajkurg. Meat for human vermin with a knife.'

'We'll find them and kill them,' said Kliment.

'What happened to the missing man?' said Mutz.

Elizaveta put her hand on Matula's shoulder. Matula pushed it off, stood up with his teeth clenched and with a groan of rage and pain dashed the sable's skull against the white tablecloth. It splintered like a crabshell and flecks of blood and brain landed on Elizaveta Timurovna and Kliment. Matula dropped the ragged corpse on the floor and pressed his fists into his eyes, muttering. Pelageya Fedotovna came in with the sabre, carried in a dishcloth. Matula saw her and took the sabre, seized Pelageya Fedotovna by the collar and held her close, staring into her face.

'Oh God,' she said, and closed her eyes and turned her face away. Matula held the sharpened blade six inches from her cheek, then let her go and sat down. He dismissed Hanak, lifted the bloody tablecloth, opened the tea caddy and shook out a little of the white powder it contained onto the dark polished tabletop. Delicately holding the sabre, he used it to rake the powder into lines. He laid the weapon across his knees, took out a handkerchief, blew his nose, put the handkerchief away, produced a silver straw, snorted a couple of lines and passed the straw to Elizaveta Timurovna.

'What happened to the missing man?' said Mutz.

'Dead. In the river,' said Matula. 'Somebody cut off his hand. There are some queer vermin in the woods.'

Elizaveta Timurovna blinked rapidly, giggled, ran her finger under her nose and passed the straw to Kliment. 'Music!' she said. 'I'll wind the gramophone. I love music at breakfast in autumn when the trees are falling asleep. Why don't we all stay indoors and sing? Everyone should sing.' She began to sing *Black Eyes*. A congealing bead of sable blood and brain stood on her forehead.

'Mutz,' said Matula, taking the straw back from Kliment as he seemed about to offer it to Dezort. 'You like to judge. I'm putting you in charge of the investigation. When you can tell me who tried to eat my horse, and we've skewered him from arsehole to eyeball, we can leave. I give you my word.'

'I'll hold you to it.'

'Of course you will. That's your way. Be careful, Mutz. We worry about you. You seem alone. You seem like a man in the crowd in Vienna, but without the crowd, and without Vienna.'

Mutz had done nothing to stop what happened at Staraya Krepost. Like others among the Czechs, he'd stood back, watched or turned away, listened to the screams and wanted so much for them to stop that it was almost as if they already had, when really they had only begun. He'd divided the events of two hours into hundreds of tiny pieces and squeezed them into niches spread across the whole sprawl of his memory, so he never had to put them together. Afterwards he'd saved Matula's life, which was one of the reasons Matula hated him. But every time Matula referred to him as a judge he was daring him to remember everything the captain had done and said that day. Matula wanted to know who'd mutilated his horse and how the shaman had died but for now they were only shadow investigations for the one into Matula himself, the one he couldn't order Mutz to open but believed he was fated to, the one he desperately wanted Mutz to begin because he couldn't allow him to finish it and would thus have the reason he craved to kill him.

'It's time to listen to the convict's account, sir,' said Mutz. Matula said nothing. The sun had disappeared. The sky had thickened and lowered. A smell of woodsmoke made Dezort shiver. The remains of the food were beginning to stink. Elizaveta Timurovna was sitting on the floor next to the gramophone, winding the handle and singing the opening bars of *Black Eyes* over and over again. Kliment put his head down on the table, stroking his flared nostrils across the surface, feeling for grains of cocaine. Matula sat back with his sabre across his knees, mouth twitching like a child's dreaming of sideless laughter in the days of play before knowing, his eyes as untelling as any two stones.

Without moving or drawing breath, not looking up, the Land Captain, who had been still and quiet for an hour, started to speak.

'We were too forgiving,' he said. 'We were too gentle. We were too fearful of the rankless when they should have been afraid of us. When this chaos is finished and we drive out the foreigners we'll know what to do. It doesn't matter who rules, whether it's a prince of the blood or a Marxist, as long as they're Russian, and as long as the peasants fear them as they should have feared us. Fear should shine on them like light, a sun of fear rising in the morning and fear warming their backs in the afternoon and an electric fear shining on them at night, a clear bright fear, so that even if the new ruler dies and is replaced by another weakling, the terror will stay with them and their children for generations, and even when the source of the fear is gone, they'll still be looking for it, like people who cannot live without it.'

The Tribunal

Anna Petrovna woke up. It was light outside. The sun was on the cowshed roof. She felt with her fingers at the red indentations in her cheeks where they had rested on her knuckles. It was cold. The stove had gone out. She combed her hair with her fingers and walked through to the parlour. There was a grey light there from the small windows and she could see her husband's letter lying on the divan. She breathed in sharply, snatched it up, folded it and returned it to the desk drawer. Mutz had gone. Could he have so misunderstood her that he'd gone upstairs and sneaked into her bed? She went to look. No. She found the key to the front door on the floor, went out squinting into the chilly brightness, and found the yard gate open. He really had left. She hadn't intended to drive him away by showing him the letter, but it must have frightened him.

She went into the kitchen, raked the ashes from the stove grate, shovelled them into the bucket, took a curly handful of birch bark kindling, heaped it on the grate, topped them with twigs, put a couple of logs on top, and lit the closest frayed tongue of parchment. It seized the flame, spat and wriggled hot and yellow into the centre of the pyre. Anna Petrovna half-closed the stove door and listened to the roar as it drew. She found her dislike of Mutz, which up till then she had denied, or at least tried to pretend wasn't there, taking on a shape and a name: Order. Too great a concern that things should be in one place rather than another. Too wonderful a passion for categories and analysis. Even when he told her he loved her, tra-la-la, it was neither love nor even a desire he couldn't control to put it inside her. It was a love that measured, stood back with its hands on its hips and shook its head, marvelled, and went off to write it up for a thick journal.

Anna went to the pump, filled two pails with water and hauled them to the kitchen, wincing at the discord of the muscles across her shoulderblades. She filled four saucepans with water and set them on the stove. She put on more logs. The iron of the stove was ticking with the heat. It had been more than his splendid, enlightened, rational Jewish–German mind could cope with that her husband had gone from tasselled hussar to holy castrate by an act of will. All he'd been able to do was run. When he could have asked her. And she would have told him yes, how deep and true and pure was her hate for Gleb Alexeyevich Balashov, and how contemptible the castrate cult, and what a good man he was, and what a desiring, devoted lover he'd been. It was beyond Mutz's understanding that a woman could hold all these in her mind at once. Let him run. They'd all be gone, the Czechs, and seeing the photograph had woken her up, at least: it was long past time for her and Alyosha to go back to European Russia, whatever the Reds were up to there. Going with Mutz had been a substitute for leaving Yazyk, and sharing with him her reason for staying now made it easier to get away.

Kristina Pankofska, a Polish exile whom Anna Petrovna paid a gold rouble a month to clean and help, arrived with a pail of hot kasha and two new eggs. She'd lived in Yazyk for fifty years. Her great achievement had been to force herself to forget that a place called Poland had ever really existed. She smelled of tobacco and cologne and always wore a string of old fake pearls, no matter what else she had on. She predated the arrival of the first castrates and so, unlike most of the women in Yazyk, hadn't secretly had her breasts mutilated to make her resemble an angel more closely. When she entered the kitchen, she uttered a long, low note of complaint. Anna shouldn't have carried the water herself. She slipped the eggs into one of the simmering saucepans.

'I'm washing with that,' said Anna.

'I know, golubchik,' said Kristina. 'Who for?' She was short, and when she looked up at Anna like that, almost toothless as she was, her eyes were fourteen years old.

Anna took the biggest pan and carried it upstairs. She set it down on the floor in her room and went through to wake Alyosha.

'Hey,' she said. 'Little barbarian. It's time.'

Alyosha opened his eyes, swung out from under the quilt and stood swaying on the rug, rubbing his eyes. He looked exhausted, even though he'd slept for nine hours, as if he could sleep for nine hundred. If only she could hold him in that state and he could sleep till the spring of 1920; the zero made it fresh. She could put him in a furlined box and when he woke up they'd be in a place with trains and mail and schools and other boys.

'I dreamed about politicians,' Alyosha mumbled. He yawned.

'Politicians? What politicians?'

'Striped ones.'

'Ah. Striped.'

'With long hair, and long fingernails, and red eyes, like Germans.'

'Why do you think the Germans have red eyes?'

'And then papa came with his horse and the other hussars and they chopped off their heads.'

'You need fresh dreams. Come on, beauty. Mama needs your help. Wash your face.'

Anna brought the other saucepans upstairs, taking out the eggs, and set a basin down among them. She took off her clothes and squatted naked in the basin. Alyosha stood over her and scooped water out of the saucepans with a jug. He poured water over her in a thick dribble, making it stream down on either side of her backbone.

'Aim for the mole,' she said.

'I *know,*' said Alyosha.

'Mutiny?'

'Why do I have to?'

'Good sailors . . . ?'

'. . . aren't *wailers*!' huffed the boy.

Anna stood up and Alyosha handed her the soap. He watched until she slid her hand into the dark fuzz between her legs, when he turned away, took a wooden hussar out of the pocket of his nightgown and made it gallop through the air. After a while, she called in a whisper for him to rinse her. He filled the jug and moved towards her. She looked at him, shapes of lather shifting down her skin, and she was thin. She sank down again at his approach and lowered her eyes, waiting for the water.

'What do you think of Lieutenant Mutz?' she said as the water came down.

'Don't know,' he said.

'But . . .' Anna didn't know but what. Mutz couldn't talk to Alyosha. Shy with children.

'I asked him to show me his gun,' said Alyosha. 'He said he couldn't. He said it was forbidden.'

'Thank you, Lyosha. Go down and get your breakfast.'

Anna dried herself, shivering in the cold of the upper storey, and put on a clean petticoat and drawers and black stockings. She looked in the wardrobe without hope. It wasn't that things were old, or unfashionable, she had no idea what fashionable was or where it was being decided these days, only that things couldn't change. She put on a dark green calico dress and a brown cardigan and tied up her hair. If a coat of feathers and a white jockey's cap had materialised in the wardrobe, she would have put them on. She brushed her hair. She should have washed it, but there wasn't time. She forced herself to look in the mirror. Pale. She liked her eyes still. A mark, a blotch: too bad. Only to see how much she cared, whether she cared at all, she sharply pulled out the little drawer where she kept her old cosmetics case. The drawer came free and fell on the floor. The kohl brush was stuck fast in the time-baked hardness of black in there, the last lipstick had dried to a pumice nub, and there would have been enough grains of powder fast against the rim of the compact to dab a single spot on her forehead. She did care, it turned out, but not for long. The house was full of short treats of self-pity she could console herself with if she wanted.

She licked her forefinger and smoothed her eyebrows. An alternative past formed in her head, without her bidding it, of her running after the Communists, instead of staying to photograph the strikers, twelve years before. Never meeting the sweet cavalryman who would turn into a Siberian eunuch. At the time, the Communists had seemed like cowards. Now the memory, clearer than it had ever been, of their young, quick, wise feet on the mud made her sick with regret. Their goal meant nothing to her and their journey had no clarity. Yet she could feel the heat of their purpose now in a way she had not then, their sense of tearing through a barrier into a new world. Anna did not believe in new worlds, but knew she could not help wanting to be with men and women who did. Hidden in among the fleeing Communists of her memory was a false shadow, a man who had not been there and whom she had never seen, Samarin, turned up like a misplaced token of the choice she had not made.

She went downstairs, took a few mouthfuls of kasha and tea, put a loaf and a tin of sprats in a string bag, kissed Lyosha goodbye, put on her boots and a black hat, and left. Just before she closed the door, she caught sight of Kristina's face, gazing at her as if struck by the peculiarity of a stranger. 'You'll catch your death,' said Kristina, absent, like a medium.

Scraps of ragged yellow-bottomed clouds were breaking up the sunlight over Yazyk. Standing water flashed and slunk into shade in the cart ruts on the road to the square. Anna wrapped the cardigan round her against the breeze. The road was broad but the black log houses shouldered each other as if they were crowded onto an island, as if the infinite space of Siberia was an ocean that might engulf them, or at least drive them mad, if they did not stay within armlinking distance of each other to brace. And yet they were mad; that was why they had come. The castrates had no heirs.

She passed four castrates sweating together to raise a heavy new starlinghouse on the open patch of grass and goose-grazing in front of Mikhail Antonovich's house. She knew them all by name. They nodded and greeted her soberly as she went past. Bogomil Nikonovich, driving a lean cow, last of his herd, raised his hat and uncovered a head hairless as a pumpkin. He said good morning, and glanced at Anna Petrovna's legs.

She was the crazy one. She could barely remember the fable her husband had spun for his fellow castrates about why she had come. It had mentioned photography, and widowhood, and a hysterical yearning for tranquillity, and could only have sounded to the community like the generous defence of a woman who'd lost her wits. She was Satan's niece, yet they tolerated her. She smoked; she drank; she ate meat; she never prayed; she was a fornicator; she didn't believe amputating and mutilating sex organs would turn the amputees into angels. She cared more about her son than about her neighbour. She was greedy and selfish with her time. She didn't seek perfection or paradise. She loved the world more than she yearned for heaven or feared hell. She wouldn't look to the Bible for life rules any more than she would to *Nicholas Nickleby*. She was out of control. She was no devil's family, she was the Enemy herself. And how courteous they were to this mad, evil woman who lived in their midst. To the castrates, she was as sick in her soul as the poor ranters in the cities, who could be brought to all fours and a bloody face by any group of small boys; yet here they could not give her even the ranters' pleasure of martyrdom. How they could teach the cities to pity their outcasts with dignity.

As she approached the square, she saw a man coming out of Timofei Semyonovich's house with an empty wicker basket. He wore a flat black cap and a black jacket over a peasant smock and breeches. It was Gleb Alexeyevich Balashov. Meeting her husband always began badly and ended badly. He saw her and came to meet her. They stood two yards apart, greeted each other formally, and did not kiss. The rules had been clear from the day she arrived in Yazyk, in the late spring of 1915.

'The Czechs told me I had to go to the hearing,' he said. 'As the leader of the congregation.'

'I'm going too,' she said. 'It's a kind of distraction.'

Balashov looked at her with real sorrow for her soul. It was sincere and troubled. It disgusted her. 'Captain Matula might shoot him at the end,' he said.

'Then he'd go to heaven.'

'He's an atheist. I suppose.'

'Then he's in for a lovely surprise when he gets there.'

They began walking towards the square. Balashov asked about Alyosha.

'He dreams about his gallant dead father,' said Anna.

'His father is not dead,' said Balashov humbly. 'Only changed.'

'Pretty word, that,' said Anna. She could never capture, in advance, the simplicity with which he could sour her thoughts. It was the simplicity itself. Her husband's affected manner of using a chaste little flock of words for each wild lurch of his broken mind. 'You say "changed" as if it was a leaf changing colour. Not a knife hacking at your body. It bleeds. It scars. It hurts.'

'Life hurts. The more you live, the more it hurts.'

'That isn't true.' Anna couldn't concentrate on what he was saying. The thought of the leaf changing shifted to the railway carriage on their wedding night and the bud that didn't open, and that sprang to the night a year after her arrival in Yazyk when she'd drunk half a bottle of cognac by herself and run out of the house, along this same road, to the room where her husband slept, snatched the covers off him and tried to rape him, fumbling to pull his remnant sappy stick into her sex, and not the scars or the absence or that it wouldn't harden which had driven her out of there tearily screaming but the submissiveness of his body and the low monotonous indistinct mumble of his prayers.

'Go ahead,' she said, stopping. 'Go on. I'll ignore you there.'

Balashov nodded and walked on without a word. It was impossible to believe that he didn't know what would anger her most.

'I told Mutz about you,' she called after him. 'I broke my promise.'

Balashov faltered without stopping, looked at her over his shoulder, said: 'I'm very sorry,' and continued on his way.

'Why did you lie to me about the photograph?' she shouted. 'You said in your letter you left them all behind on the battlefield. Why did you lie to me?'

Gleb halted, turned round and said, not raising his voice: 'I was ashamed of myself for keeping it.'

'Ashamed? To be carrying a photograph of your wife? Is that why you left it lying in the street?'

'I'm sorry. May I have the picture back?'

Anna looked around for a stone to throw at him. She failed to see one and when she looked back Gleb had continued on his way. She couldn't tolerate watching him. She stood on the log pavement by the mud road, nowhere to sit and nothing to lean against and nothing to see that she hadn't seen, and felt abominably lonely.

After a few minutes she walked to the administrative building and into the courtyard, where the shaman's hut looked as forlorn and cursed as a dead man's boots. She had seen him a few times, tried to talk to him once with the thought of using one of her last remaining plates to photograph him. He had kept his legs crossed, chained ankle over unchained, and his arms folded, shaken his head, and refused to look at her. Perhaps he'd thought she would be intimidated by the distance and untouchability of a man of esoteric religion. Some states even Siberian shamans could not dream themselves into; these demanded black earth peasants, or nice, well brought-up, bourgeois boys from the European provinces.

A cluster of people stood a little distance from the hut, chatting with their hands in their pockets and smoking, as if they were about to go into the theatre after an interval. They turned to look at Anna. There were the Czechs, in their little factions. Mutz looked as if he had been about to speak to her husband when she arrived and he saw her. If she thought of Mutz, and she did quite often, it was with that just disturbed look on his face, and her occasional marriage fantasies always ended with her trying to call him away from some finicky labour he was engaged in under a big lamp in a faraway room. He was shadowed by Sergeant Nekovar, the clever craftsman who had fixed Anna's heating, asked her some odd questions about whether a woman's heart was like a stove, and saw in Mutz both a fellow-artisan and the only officer as determined as most of the soldiers to leave Siberia as soon as possible. Sergeant Bublik, who called himself a communist yet had never dared desert to join the Reds, stood apart in a corner. Skachkov, the Land Captain, still the civil authority of Yazyk on a piece of paper somewhere in the White chancellery in Omsk, but in no other way; the destruction of the old order, the death of the Tsar and the seizure of the town by the Czechs had struck him like a stroke, after he had spent so long successfully denying to himself and to external inquiries that the town was, as rumour had it, almost exclusively inhabited by apostate monsters, executors of a sin too grotesque to name. He could still walk, talk, eat and drink without assistance, but every day he would sit behind his desk in his office, the big desk with the little desk in front of it at right angles for the visitors who never called, and stare into space, trembling, clearing his throat sometimes, adjusting a stack of old documents in front of him so that their edges were exactly in line.

At the centre of the group was Matula. The town was so much his toy that Anna was surprised he hadn't become bored with it. Was there really enough fate in Yazyk for him? He seemed to feed off the sense of accumulated darkness under the millions of trees in the forest around, counting shadows as others counted gold. He had his retinue, Sergeant Hanak, whose jaw and nose came forward together, like a dog's, the helpless Lieutenant Dezort, and Skachkov's wife, Elizaveta Timurovna, Matula's mistress, who could never forgive Anna for failing to take offence when she snubbed her. The only one missing was the odious Kliment. Matula and Elizaveta Timurovna were giggling together. They seemed drunk, in a strange, speeded up way. Matula asked Anna Petrovna if she'd brought her lunch.

'I didn't know if you were feeding the prisoner properly,' she said. 'You didn't take care of the last one.'

Elizaveta Timurovna tutted and whooshed. In the corner Bublik studied the tin of sprats and muttered: 'Bourgeois.'

'I thought you carried only kosher food, Anna Petrovna,' said Matula, speaking very fast. 'Did we lose a shaman? Yes we did. Mutz's department. Keeps losing things. Shamans, horses, trust o' the men. Don't know if the prisoner will get time to eat. Maybe find him guilty in a minute. Ping! That way we'll all share Anna Petrovna's lunch. Loaves and fishes.'

'Sir,' said Mutz. 'We should go in.'

The ten of them filed into Yazyk's old courtroom, a small chamber with a dock, two rows of chairs, and a larger, padded chair, with armrests, set on a dais raised a few inches off the floor. Matula went up to the big chair, prodded it, sprawled in it, took out his pistol, closed an eye, sighted on the dock, laid the pistol on his lap, and waved to Mutz. Mutz nodded to Nekovar to fetch the prisoner. The others sat down. After a minute of silent shifting and coughing, double footsteps were heard and Samarin walked into the room, trailed by Nekovar covering his back with a rifle. Samarin looked around, nodded to the assembled company, wished them good morning, to which Anna answered with a smile and Bublik with a formal greeting, brother. Samarin seemed about to take an empty seat in the front row opposite Matula but Mutz stepped over, took his elbow, and led him to the dock. Samarin appeared surprised but walked amiably to his place and stood there, looking around without blinking. His eyes fixed on Anna's for a moment and he smiled at her. She felt the blood burn in her cheeks like a girl's.

'In the –' began Mutz. Matula interrupted him.

'Is there something wrong with you?' said Matula.

'It's my hair,' said Samarin.

'You don't have any hair.'

'That's the problem,' said Samarin. Anna, Nekovar and Dezort laughed. Twice Samarin had tossed his head like a horse bothered by flies, or a man with a severe twitch. 'They shaved my head this morning. It's hard to get used to not having long hair after nine months. It's hard to get used to being clean. I'm grateful to Sergeant Bublik' – he nodded to Bublik, who grunted – 'and Private Racansky, who provided me with hot water and clothes and put my hair on the fire.'

Matula nodded and Mutz began again. 'In the name of the provisional administration of Yazyk, on behalf of Captain Matula, I open this hearing into the circumstances of Mr Samarin's arrival in town last night, without any documents, at approximately the same time as the death of a shaman. Sir, would you please tell us your full name, your date of birth, your place of permanent residence, and your occupation?'

'Am I entitled to a lawyer?' asked Samarin.

'No,' said Matula.

'Am I on trial? Am I accused of something?'

'You're accused of having an undefined personality,' said Matula. He ballooned his cheeks, exhaled, leaned his forehead forward on the muzzle of his pistol and scratched with his eyes closed. He was slowing down. He straightened up and looked lazily at Samarin. 'Look, old boy,' he said. 'The woods are full of Red spies, and we haven't the foggiest who you are. Mutz here thinks you slipped the shaman a litre of alcohol –'

'Sir, I'm just –'

'Don't interrupt, y'damn Yid! And Mr Mutz thinks you're a menace to society. There's also the matter of my beautiful brave horse, who is dead, and whom somebody tried to . . .' Matula began to breathe heavily. The breaths became louder and louder until Matula burst out: 'EAT!' He let his head loll back and ran the muzzle of his pistol to and fro along his lower lip. 'I'm the law in this part of Siberia,' he said quietly. 'We want to hear your story. If I like it – I don't say believe it, I say like it – I'll probably let you go. If I don't, you'll have long enough to regret not making up a better one before you get to try your act on the crows.'

The River

'My name is Kyrill Ivanovich Samarin,' the convict began. 'I was born on the third of February, 1889, in Karelia, and after the death of my parents went to live with my uncle in Raduga, near Penza. I was a student there until I was arrested in 1914. I have no other profession. I don't know what has happened to my family and our house. There have been many changes, I believe.'

Bublik and Racansky had found him a peasant smock and breeches, but they hadn't been able to help him with boots, or a coat. He wore the same broken boots he'd arrived in, and a blanket over his shoulders. As he talked he took it off, folded it and hung it on the edge of the dock. His head and face were shaven. He quickly lost the habit of tossing his non-existent hair out of his eyes, but it seemed to Anna that he was humbled and made wary by the stripping of the hair. While he spoke, he had a way of turning to each of the people in the room in turn, and widening his eyes at them. 'You, at least, will know what I'm talking about.' He left no-one out, even Skachkov the Land Captain, who didn't look in his direction once and showed no sign of listening. He let his eyes linger longer on Anna, and she was happy to let her eyes meet his, until it became a contest, and she lost, or rather didn't want it to be a contest; she looked away first.

'You told me last night that you'd been arrested on suspicion of being a terrorist. That you had a bomb,' said Mutz. 'I'd like –'

'Mutz, Mutz, Mutz,' said Matula, with his free hand over his eyes. He massaged the bridge of his nose and his pistol hand twitched. 'Let the man tell his story. Don't interrupt again. My spirits are very turbulent now.'

Mutz, who had been standing between Matula and the dock, pressed his lips together and stepped back to lean against the far wall. Samarin began to look from face to face. 'With your permission, respected ladies and gentlemen, officers and men of the Czech Legion, Your Excellency, Comrade Bublik,' he said. 'In a few admirably concise words, Lieutenant Mutz has recounted the reasons for my arrest, and mentioned the bomb which I stole in order to protect a young friend from the consequences of her naivety. I propose to explain to you something of what I suffered in the prison camp to which I was sent, the White Garden, and the reasons for, and manner of, the escape which brought me here. Before I begin, I must repeat the warning I gave the lieutenant last night. I'm certain that the man who facilitated my escape, the thief I know only by his klichka, the Mohican, has pursued me to this first place of sanctuary from the wilderness. I'm certain that he is here, now, in Yazyk. I'm certain that he was responsible for the death of the shaman, and the mutilation – Captain Matula, I cannot tell you how sorry I am to hear of this despicable act – of your horse. Whatever my fate, you must all see to your locks and your weapons. The Mohican . . . no. Everything is not where it should be. Friends. Let me start with the river, the great middle river, the Yenisey.'

As Samarin told his story, making his careful rounds of the listeners, Anna wondered at how alive and guileless his pleading eyes seemed against the ugliness of the events he described.

She became aware that she had already decided he was innocent, and wouldn't change her mind; innocent, that is, of what Mutz was trying to chip out of him. She was surprised that she had reached a judgement so quickly, and realised there was nothing so convincing as a man who could feel all the richness of the world – its worst, so, presumably, if it could happen, its best as well – without losing his soul to any one part of it, and becoming attached to that part. Convincing was wrong. Perhaps what she had in mind was endearing. Sometimes, as he talked, when he parted with his listeners for a moment and seemed to dive within himself to fetch up memories, or when his voice changed and out of his mouth came the argot and pitch of the other convicts, she felt it was for her; that this was a man not only bargaining for his life but taking her with him, to show her what it was like to be him.

'When I reached the railhead at Yeniseysk with my escorts, I still thought I was going to be exiled to a village in the hinterland,' said Samarin. 'I could imagine the kind of place they were sending politicals, somewhere a couple of days' journey downriver, and you could probably make it to the railhead by cart, or by sledge in winter. There'd be a row of houses along the water's edge, with a jetty and grazing land and the forest behind. There'd be a store where aboriginals and trappers would come for drink and supplies. I'd be given a room in a peasant's house, next door to the cowshed, and light chores, chopping wood, teaching people to read, drinking tea with whoever fancied himself as the local liberal, keeping them company over samogon in winter, arguing over reports from Europe in old newspapers, going for walks in the forest, making notes for articles about the flora and fauna. They'd expect me to try to escape. It wouldn't be difficult. I'd just walk out. But I wasn't going to escape. I was glad not to have been hanged. I didn't want to touch a bomb again. The empires were destroying themselves in the war in the west. They were tearing each other apart better than a lone terrorist could, and they were far away, on the other side of the Urals, with three wide rivers between them and me. I'd wait it out. Sitting on my box on the wharf, while my escorts were comparing papers with the local police, I dreamed I was going to be like the young Tolstoy, and Siberia was going to be my Caucasus. Some old dyadya would take me hunting in the forest, I'd have an affair with a local girl, my skin would get so tough in the heat and the cold I wouldn't feel the mosquitoes any more except to help me know I was alive. This was five years ago, a little later in the year than now, but the sun was still out, the Yenisey was flowing in front of me, it was wide and slow. I saw fish snapping at the surface. There was time.

'I heard the badly oiled door of the steamship company office open and not close. Someone had come out and was standing in the doorway, watching me, a fat man in a steamship uniform, wrinkling his eyes and fiddling with beads. He studied me for a minute and without lifting his feet he turned round into the darkness of the office and called to someone I couldn't see: "We could send them the political."

'Nobody answered for a while. Then I heard a voice, but I couldn't make out what it was saying. The fat man looked at me and said: "What does your father do?"

'I told him he'd been an architect before he died.

'"No rank," said the man to the inside of the office, and he spat. He said to me: "They must think you're a great threat to society to have exiled you when they're so short of cannon fodder for the Germans. I doubt anyone cares what we do with you."

'They put me on a steam launch with my guards. The launch

was carrying a geologist and a crew of three: the captain, the engineer and the deck hand. They chained me by my ankle to a rail and left me and the guards to sleep on the deck overnight. In the morning we headed north with the current. I asked where they were taking me. The crew wouldn't say. The geologist said it was a state secret. For the first few nights we stopped at settlements on the riverbank. Each time I thought they'd let me off and leave me, but the same thing always happened. A crowd with their dogs and cows waiting for us beyond the jetty, watching the boat being moored as if they were seeing a lost child come back, and hardly believing it. Then the geologist, the crew and the guards got off, and I stayed where I was, chained up like a dog, with a blanket and some dried fish and water, and only the stars and the frost for company. I could see the lamps shining in the windows of the cabins of the settlement, and hear them singing and toasting while they welcomed the guests with vodka. Sometimes the guards brought me extra food. Sometimes a villager would bring me tea or kasha or a piece of sausage, usually the old ones who'd been exiled themselves, or young ones whose parents had. They asked me about myself, and about politics, and about the war. They all had sons and brothers at the front. They'd end up shaking their heads, muttering "Lord My God" and wandering away, and I'd try to sleep in the cold, with the sound of the water on the hull, and no other sound once the singers and their beasts had fallen asleep.

'The settlements thinned out and disappeared as we got further north. The trees and the nights became shorter and ice on the deck wouldn't melt till the afternoon. The geologist, Bodrov, became excited. He was always in the prow of the boat. Whenever there were cliffs he would beg the captain to stop. He had his little hammer in his hand, he wanted to take samples. The captain shook his head. The closer we got to the Arctic, the quieter the captain grew, except to call down to the engineer for more power. He was afraid the river would freeze over and the boat would be trapped before it could return south. The quieter the captain became, the more Bodrov would talk. He shouted out one night when the northern lights appeared, like a shower of dust falling through a gap in the field of stars, and put his arms round the shoulders of my guards when they ran to see what was happening. He told them what makes the aurora, and counted off the names of the stars making up the constellations. One day we saw a Tungus mounted on a deer the size of a horse, watching us from the edge of the forest, holding a fish spear, and Bodrov began waving and shouting at him. The man turned his mount round and disappeared into the darkness between the trees. When we crossed the Arctic circle, Bodrov brought out a bottle of French brandy and got us all to drink a toast to the honour of the north star, and he sang student songs about how "our goal's the pole, boys, those Tungus girls make lovely wives, we'll live in a tent, we won't pay any rent and we'll eat snow all our lives."

'The captain drank his brandy, went to the water bucket, chucked it over the side, brought it up full and threw it over Bodrov. We all felt the sting of the cold on our cheeks. The captain said: "That's the being of this river. It flows north. It's cold like death and it is death. This is the desert where nothing grows. No-one should be made to live here."

'Bodrov wiped the water from his eyes, and was confused for a moment, but then he laughed and rubbed his face till it was red. "Look at your river!" he said. "Full of fish! The air's full of birds and the forest of elk and sable. A few thousand Tungus with spears and axes, living in wigwams, they live well here, and you civilised men go running south at the first sign of frost. The rocks are full of gold, diamonds, platinum, rubies, there's copper and nickel, there's seas of coal and lakes of oil. Lakes of oil to light the world!" He was taking off his clothes while he said this, and he dived into the river and surfaced grinning, shaking his fists above his head. The captain swore, stopped the boat and threw him a rope. If they'd left him in he would have been dead in a couple of minutes. They took him below with a blanket round him, shivering. The captain looked at me and said again: "No-one should be made to live here."

'The captain had the chain taken off me and let me sleep in the boiler room, where it smelled of smoke and sulphur. Before that time I'd never in my life been so happy as when they brought me in from the cold and let me sleep there. There was nothing soft to lie on, and the deck was covered in ash and cinders and crumbs of coal, but it was warm. The warmth was so good, it was like a friend who'd missed me, and was going to miss me when I went away again.

'The deck hand shook me awake, handed me a broom and told me to go up and clear the snow. It was morning, and the boat was moving against a blizzard. You could hardly see either bank of the river for the rolling clouds of it. The captain's face in the wheelhouse was angry and frightened. He'd never come this far north so late in the year before. I cleared snow for hours, working my way up and down the boat till my back hurt. The blizzard lifted, the wind dropped and the snow fell in big, heavy flakes. At the water's edge I could see what the captain was afraid of. There were delicate, curving blades of ice crystallising out from the freezing mud, half transparent, fragile and powerful. There were fewer trees now, they were further apart, and they were stunted.

'Next day we turned east off the Yenisey onto a tributary.

It meant steaming against the current, which slowed us down. The current was strong, though, the river was black and deep, which kept the ice back. The sky turned the colour of leather and the blizzards returned. When they cleared we saw steep mountains of grey rock patched with snow. Bodrov, in a wolf hat and a black lambskin coat, was in ecstasy. He said it was Putorana, and that the story of the world was written there.

'They put him ashore to a log hut and promised to be back within four days to pick him up. He wasn't listening to anyone. He wanted to get ashore with his hammer and his instruments and his snowshoes. Before we moved out of sight we could see him walking steadily up the slopes behind the cabin, making a trail between the trees.

'I asked the captain what would happen to Bodrov if the steamer got frozen in upriver. The captain looked at me like a man seeing a dog juggling. He said: "He hunts, or he dies. But where you're going you won't be worrying about him." Just after dawn two days later, we reached the White Garden.'

The White Garden

'The White Garden is in the tundra, between the river and cone-shaped hills of rock, the foothills of the Putorana mountains. The hills have deep grooves, and the grooves are serrated; have you seen limpet shells? They're like that. They're only a few hundred metres high, but even in August there's snow between the grooves. To the north of the hills are the mountains, glaciers, Taimyr, and the Arctic sea. The river bends, and the White Garden is on the promontory, so the river binds it east, south and west. There's no human settlement except Tungus chumas for a thousand miles in any direction. In the summer you get moss and berries and flowers on the ground, and there are bushes, hard bushes. When they turn green for a few weeks it's like barbed wire sprouting leaves. No trees. No grass. The earth's always frozen under your feet. Out on the ice on the river in January you'll get 70 degrees of frost. That's when it's still. When the black purga blows it can pile the snow higher than a ship's mast overnight. It's not our world. When I was a student we used to talk about how it might be possible to build a ramp high enough and long enough for a train to fly off the end into space, to the Moon, or Venus. The White Garden was a place like that, at the terminus of a journey from the sum of all our homes. In deep winter the air is another air, it hurts to breathe. The sun isn't seen for weeks. You have to kick the pilings of the jetty to believe there's any connection between the place you are and the place you were, and even when you see the boats hauled up on the shore, they seem like craft fallen by mistake from the astral plane, when the river's frozen so solid it might be harder and older than the rocks themselves, and to believe it could melt and be water again takes an act of faith harder than any godbeliever's. When the summer comes with its everlasting light it's like the final passage into madness, the sun never going away. The barracks sat on a stretch of white quartz gravel. It used to reflect the sun for a few days in midsummer, sparkling like a dragon's hoard, burning a pattern into your eyes that you'd see when you closed them. Up by the hills there was a waterfall, and when it wasn't frozen it left minerals on the rocks where it fell, big white crystals shaped into trunks and branches like Christmas trees. The first time you saw them you thought they were pretty but later you got to hate them, as exiles do when souvenirs of their old lives turn out to be fakes. The first Europeans to see it saw the quartz twinkling and the mineral trees and called it the White Garden and thought there would be gold there. They kept us looking, digging into the hillsides with picks, spikes and hammers, trying to find veins of precious metal, or any metal, iron, nickel. We found nothing. We only turned solid rock into fields of broken rock, and every rock broken made you stronger or weaker, but either way it made you older.

'When I arrived I was given a bunk in a barrack hut with forty others, and assigned a foreman for a work detail which began the next day. Twelve hours a day, six days a week. Sunday was a rest day. I wasn't ready for the White Garden. I came into the hut with a valise and a box of books, with my head shaven like a convict, but still wearing my student's uniform. The other convicts looked at me as if I was a fat wallet someone had dropped, and it was only a question of making sure the owner was far enough away. I was there under the criminal code like them but not like them. It wasn't that they hated me. There was no hate. It's nothing to do with hate, except the hate you need to take like a drink before hitting someone. Here's how little I understood: I thought the commandant, an aristocrat called Prince Apraksin-Aprakov, ran the camp, and I thought the guards were his means of controlling us. Of course he didn't run the camp; he owned it. The guards were there to protect him and to make sure nobody escaped. The running of the camp was left to the most senior prisoners, mainly three criminal authorities, Avraam the Matchstick, Sergei the Machinegun, and the Mohican.

'I began to doubt Prince Apraksin-Aprakov existed. For years, I never saw him, although he was said to be there. He had a house on the edge of the camp, up against the barbed wire. At night you saw lamps burning, and you could hear a gramophone. The only evidence of his presence was his warped decrees. Once Pchelentsev, the head of the guards, got us together at the autumn equinox and said the prince had been pleased to give us the honour of sculpting an ice replica of the Royal Pavilion at Brighton, England. Pchelentsev asked if any of us had ever been to England. Nobody said anything. Tolik Redhead, a recidivist chicken-thief from Kiev, said he hadn't been to England but he knew a girl in Brovary whose underwear came from Manchester. The lieutenant gave him twenty strokes of the knout and stuck him in a cage for a few days till the snow was ankle deep. He lost a couple of toes. They turned black and the surgeon cut them off like a cook trimming a potato. Tolik said it was nothing terrible, he still had eight left, and the doctor gave him a swig of spirit before each one, so he asked him to take them all off, slowly, in return for 100 grammes of alcohol for each one and he'd settle for the pain to wash it down with, but the doctor said he hardly had enough spirit left for himself till the thaw came, and what would he do with eight healthy toes now that the ground was hard and he couldn't bury them, he'd have to burn them. He was afraid they'd come back to haunt him, eight ghostly Christian toes pattering up to his mattress in the moonlight. The ice sculpture was never made.

'I was robbed, cuffed, and mocked by some of the convicts, helped by others, left alone by most. For the first year, when there was a tolerable amount of food, steamers ran through the summer and deer teams made the winter run from the south to the White Garden, I could endure the labour. The Prince set quotas, but the foremen of the work gangs didn't enforce them tightly. They cared that when they walked by your spot, your pick was striking rock, and they cared that their gang had altered a stretch of hillside by shift's end, and because they cared, your neighbours cared and kept their eye on you.

'It would have been in 1916 that it started to change. A military barge came and took the strongest and most generous convicts away to be slaughtered in uniform. The Prince was ordered to seek war metals, whatever that meant, and he doubled our quotas, with fewer men to work. At the same time our rations were cut.

'In the beginning, when I arrived at the camp, they had a kitchen hut. A group of prisoners who'd got in with the guards cooked the food, baked the bread, and doled it out inside. They fed us twice a day, bread, kasha, soup and tea, sometimes a bit of sausage on the Prince's birthday or some saint's day. The guards ate there too, but they sat down inside, and we took ours back to our barracks to eat. When the shortages began the first thing was that the soup got thinner and there wasn't so much kasha on your plate. They put sawdust, ashes and bits of dried moss into the bread flour to make the bread go further. The bread was grey and the loaves didn't hold together properly. When they tried to cut them they'd crumble like rotten wood. Sometimes you wouldn't get a slice of bread so much as a handful of flakes and crumbs.

'I began to be an object of trade. I belonged to Matchstick, and he began to sell me. Either he'd sell me as a slave, to work an extra half-shift for a buyer, or he'd sell my ration. One day he sold both. It nearly killed me. Sixteen hours with the pick in the snow, and nothing but hot water at the end of it. I put straw from my mattress in the water. I know it sounds absurd, but there was nothing else to thicken it with. The next day I ate and worked a normal shift but I carried the deficit with me for months. I can still feel the missing meal now. My salvation was Machinegun, or so it seemed. Authorities like him never felt the shortages; they were always looking for amusements. I heard he couldn't read and I offered to teach him, to read to him, if he would buy me from Matchstick. He made the purchase. I still had to work my twelve hours but no more, and I had a better chance of eating. Machinegun liked to have the books on a shelf by his bed and I'd read to him. He liked Pushkin and the Book of Revelation. He was sentimental. He was from the Caucasus, Svanetia, he wore the grey skullcap. He robbed banks. He stole a machine gun from a unit in Kutaisi and fixed it to the back of a four-horse hearse. He called ammunition caviar, and the gun the mother-fish, the sturgeon. He'd come riding into dusty Mengrelian squares, pull the tarpaulin off and cock the gun, screaming "She's going to spawn!", and everyone would run out of the bank, they'd throw the money out of the windows, but it was no good, once he'd announced it, he couldn't stop until he'd emptied every last bullet he had into the bank. When they caught him he was bathing naked with the gun in an earthenware tub full of olive oil. He offered to go to the war with it, to kill Germans. He said: "Only I can make the mother fish spawn." They separated them, sent him to the White Garden and took the gun to the war without him. And it never did work, though they said it was because it was the wrong kind of oil. I wanted to read to him from Bakunin. I thought he'd like Bakunin. But he only wanted to hear about the last trumpet and *The Prisoner*. You know, Pushkin.

We are birds, we are dying; time, brother, time!
There, beyond clouds, where the white mountains climb
There, where the land takes the blue of the sea
There, where only the wind walks, and me.

'The first couple of times I read it to him he shed a few tears, hugged me, kissed me and went to sleep. The third time the flesh on his face seemed to harden to stone while I read it. He lay on the bunk without moving, his eyes wide open, for a long time after I finished. He got up and began walking up and down the barracks. He put his fists together and shook them and started making noises as if he was firing the machine gun. He paced from one end to another, the noises getting louder, and each time when he reached me he looked at me. He stopped, screamed "She's going to spawn!" and hit me in the face with his two fists together. He was a big man, I went down straight away, he sat astride me and was battering his knuckles against my face, my neck, my chest, making this sound in his throat akh-akh-akh-akh-akh-akh-akh-akh-akh, foam and phlegm dripping off his lip. I think he . . . well, he stopped suddenly and fell forward on top of me, his stubble combing the bloody curls of my beard. He had never had a wife, and he was missing his gun very badly.

'I believed in God less than any of them but I was the only

one who believed I deserved to live. Not just wanted, but deserved, as if there was someone else to make the choice. They felt that. They were curious. It provoked them. They wondered who the someone else was. They wanted to take me to pieces. They wanted to feel inside me. Machinegun said: "What makes you think you're better than us?" I said "I don't, all men are the same." He looked into my eyes for a long time and told me to undress. He said "We'll see if all men are the same." Two days later I woke up on the floor of the barracks. I could hardly see but he was there, I could make out his boots and his fat knees bulging out over the toecaps as he squatted there, looking at what he'd done to me. He said what was that you were saying, it was interesting, about the proletariat. He said: "Under socialism, will I get to have my own machine gun?" I told him that, according to my understanding of socialist dogma, all workers would have full and equal access to the means to defend their homes and workplaces. He said: "Yes, but will I get to rob banks?" I told him there'd be no need to rob banks in future. He spat and said I didn't know what he did and didn't need and left me there.

'After that Machinegun didn't beat me so often but he still stole my food. At night when he couldn't sleep he'd kneel by my bed, put his hand under the blanket and stroke my ribs, running his fingertips in the troughs between them, rubbing the pit where my stomach'd been with the palm of his hand, kneading the hollow from hipbone to hipbone like a baker smearing dough. He said: "Do you want to know what I'm doing?" I said "No." He said: "I'm feeling for your heart." I lay still on my back and let him do it. I wanted to ask him for bread. I was afraid to. His fingers were rough and warm and down through the bones and flesh I could feel him shaking as he wept. Sometimes his tears fell on my face and I opened my mouth. He couldn't see in the darkness that I was drinking them. In the morning he'd take half my ration. He took food from the others too, not so much. He said to me: "Who is it that looks after you, Intelligent?" and I said: "No-one." He said: "You're not a saint, are you, God wouldn't have saints who don't believe in him." "No," I said. "Why d'you think you deserve to live, then?" he said. "It must be the proletariat." I said I couldn't eat the proletariat. He said: "Well you wouldn't have to eat it all," and he laughed. I tried to laugh too, thinking he might leave me more bread. I noticed how much quieter Machinegun had become, part of the general murderous quietness over the camp as the food ran out and the guards began to disappear. The convicts and the garrison were starving. You could see the bird of hunger roosting on them, waiting for the hunger to hatch out, a mildewed mother bird waiting for a brood of white skulls to peck their way blindly out of these shrivelled heads.

'We heard about the revolutions, and the peace with Germany, and how there was fighting across the country. Usually when there's a revolution they empty the prisons, don't they? Not the White Garden. We were too far away to be remembered. The Prince decided he would wait. Perhaps he thought he'd be safer there. He tailored the news for us. He took delivery of a box of news in midsummer and doled it out through the cold season, bulking it out with lies to keep his prisoners down and his guards loyal. Somewhere, in some chancery in Petrograd, some minister or revolutionary or minister-revolutionary must have signed orders dissolving the camp, setting the political prisoner, me, free at least. And the minister went out to dinner, because the White Garden is very far away from Petrograd, over the Urals and along the Trans-Siberian and up, up, up to the very edge of the world, and he wasn't going to deliver the order himself. So maybe it got lost. Maybe it came down the telegraph wire and got stopped where the wire was cut by partisans, or got incinerated in a battle in a city along the way, or was used by a looter to roll a cigarette in, or was just blown away by the wind, and went flying through the trees in the taiga and got stuck in the branches of a stunted larch and made into the lining for a squirrel's nest. So two years ago we heard there'd been a revolution but the revolutionaries were loyal to the Tsar and to the war, so we were still prisoners. Then last year we heard the revolutionaries weren't loyal to the Tsar and the war, but they were about to be destroyed by the Whites, who were, so we were still prisoners. And because Russia was now at war with itself, rather than Germany, there would be even less food.

'There were many days I thought would be my last, and on one, I was stopped by Machinegun and Redhead outside the kitchens. I had their bread and mine: one full ration altogether, and that adulterated with whalebone meal from skeleton parts the Tungus had hauled down from the northern ocean and flogged the camp for a crate of rifles and ammunition a month before.

'The only advantage of starvation was that it had taken all pride from me. I kneeled in the snow in front of them, holding the bread to my chest, and bowed so that my forehead was touching Machinegun's boot. I bowed again and again, hitting his boot with my forehead, as I'd seen the peasants do to the tax collector, and begged him to let me keep my bread. I called him nice, lord, your excellency, the bravest and most honourable man in all the Caucasus, the finest machinegunner in the world, I said I was a stinking turd who wished only to serve him, who'd give him my life, unworthy as I was, I wasn't fit for him to walk on, I was the poorest, weakest sinner in Creation, who deserved to crawl with worms and snakes and beetles for the rest of my days, dragging myself along with my hands, praying for forgiveness and for the everlasting glory of the great Sergei Machinegun Gobechia, a hero and a saint, if only he'd grace me with a drop of his infinite mercy, if with one simple act he'd earn the final adoration of a man who already loved and worshipped him as a god among men, if he'd allow me to keep a few crumbs of the bread I humbly brought him from the kitchen, to be repaid a thousand times over in gold and blood and any other measure when the war and his unjust imprisonment had run their course.

'While I was saying this Redhead was pulling my head back by the hair and Machinegun, not saying anything, was prising the bread from my fingers. They took it all and walked away. I saw a couple of crumbs on the ground, picked them up and set them to rest on my tongue. I raised my tongue gently to the roof of my mouth and let the crumbs melt there. I began to look for other crumbs on the ground. I became aware of a change.

'A man was looking at me from about twenty yards away. He was standing next to the space between two huts from where Machinegun's boots stuck out, horizontal. He had a grey face. We all had grey faces but his was the grey of a veil blowing across the outlines of wisdom carved in stone, not the grey of starved hopeless flesh. His smile was like a beckoning finger, like pity. He looked fed, thoughtful and gentle. I went over and looked down at Machinegun lying there with his throat cut. The Mohican said: "He stole your bread," and gave me a full bread ration and a piece of sausage. As I stuffed it in my mouth and felt the world and my pain again I grieved for Machinegun. He'd shot and beaten people because he couldn't talk to them. Violence was the only language nobody could understand. There were no translators. And he'd spoken to me for longer, and more painfully, than anyone.

'The Mohican said to me: "I understand. Because I understand

and I understand you understand, I have to look after you. Everyone has their place, and you weren't supposed to die here."

'The Mohican said: "I spoke to him in his own language."

'The great thieves think of themselves as a people apart, like aristocrats, living and breathing honour, obsessed with fashion, their own fashion and nobody else's. They see the non-thieves as a kind of game animal whose only honour is to be hunted by thieves. They divide women into five kinds. Their mothers; grandmothers; child-bearers; concubines; and whores. They're vain, brave, pitiless and sentimental. They love to spend the money they steal on roses, perfume and gold for women they don't know. They'll bet everything they have on anything they can, their lives on which icicle'll drop first. Their clothes are worth more than their houses, they hate progress, they think the world was always the way it is, and should stay that way. They'd rather die than swallow an insult. I learned this in the White Garden. I thought the Mohican was one of these. I was wrong.

'He was a thief, and they honoured him for that. He'd robbed a gold barge, and killed soldiers. He was handy with a gun and a knife. There was a story that he'd broken out of jail in Bukhara and killed all the guards, every one, and a story that he'd dynamited the home of a businessman in Taganrog, burying the whole family, and they even said he'd done a bank in Alaska and crossed to Chukotka with an Eskimo dog team. He was more dangerous than the other thieves because he didn't have their sentimentality and their longing for a court to flatter them. He felt the human passions. No, he didn't feel them. He handled them. He felt their quality and sniffed them and tasted them and rubbed them against his cheek, but they didn't lodge in him. He was like someone who could feel the agony of poison but couldn't be killed by it no matter how much he drank. So he could feel pity flood through his body watching a child looking at him out of the window of a house he had wired with explosive, and still close the circuit, because the pity left no mark as it passed through. What was most terrible about him was his certainty. For such a man, you'd think, life would be a game. When there's nothing to strive for, no irresistible human desires, you play. He wasn't playing. With him, it was like the difference between writing and drawing. We live our lives like writing. The pen moves over the paper in regular lines. The past is written and can be read, the future is blank, and the pen must stay in the word that is being written now. The Mohican lives like drawing. He draws one stroke after the other, but the strokes can be anywhere on the paper. When you watch, the strokes look disjointed and meaningless, but in his mind he sees the whole picture, complete. Complete until his death. He's just filling it in. That's what you are to the Mohican. A stroke in his picture. You could be on the edge or in the middle, you could be a cut throat and a tiny detail or a single look that fills the whole foreground. Only he knows, but he does know. He knows his own order of things.

'In January, not long after the Mohican started feeding me, the White Garden came apart. The last boats had left five months earlier with the guards who'd been able to buy a place on them. We'd been cut off since then, and the river ice wouldn't break up till the end of May at the earliest. In the camp, for most of the year, the guards and the commandant were just as much prisoners as we were. Where could they go? The mountains and glaciers were a wall to the north, and even if they could have been crossed, there was nothing on the other side except more tundra and the Arctic ocean. Sure, you could walk across the river ice and head south, or even walk along the river to the first settlement. But you'd freeze to death, or starve, before you got there. The camp didn't have horses or trucks. There were the Tungus. They might sell you deer to ride on. But they didn't come to Putorana till spring, and you couldn't be sure of finding them if you went looking for them, or of them finding you, or even of reaching the tree line. A couple of guards had set out in November to try their luck. We watched them walking across the river, climbing up the far bank and wading through the snowfields on the other side. There was a tilt to the land there, and in the few hours of light we could see them moving slowly through the snow, up to their waists. Nobody had expected the snow to be so soft and deep in that place. When the light went they still hadn't reached the ridge, and then a blizzard came down, and the next day the track they'd made was covered, and perhaps they were too. I don't know that the Tungus would have helped them. They were losing a lot of deer to Russian marauders, Cossacks, Red partisans, whatever, people who didn't expect to have to pay.

'The chaos was outside. I was protected. I'd never felt so safe and comfortable. The Mohican had a screened-off area to himself in one of the barrack blocks, with four bunks, a table and chairs, a dresser and some crockery. He had his own stove, and sheets hung across the window. He'd sit there and smoke and play cards with other thieves and guards, while I sat on the top bunk, reading or writing. They ignored me. They brought the Mohican food. He'd put it to one side and they'd play. When they left he'd divide everything up and give me half.

'"Eat every crumb, Intelligent," he said, as if I needed to be told. I stopped working; he told me not to go. "Keep the stove going," he said. "You're not going to die here." For weeks, that was all I did. Read, slept, put logs on the stove, listened to the sound of the wind outside and to their talk as they played cards. My ribs faded into a solid covering of flesh and my stomach swelled, my thighs became wider than my knees for the first time in months. For a short time it was bliss. Later it wasn't so good. When you're tired and cold and hungry, you've got nothing to think about except how to appear to be doing the most work while doing the least, how to get food and how to steal warmth. When the weariness and the cold and the hunger go away you begin to think about other things. You have time to dream, and the dreams become a torture. All the useless passions come dribbling back into your heart, fear of dying, hatred of the authorities who imprisoned you, loneliness, even pride.

'The Mohican and I didn't talk. We had nothing to share with each other. He slept, but he never rested. His mind was always working, but he never stopped to think. He was always active and all I had was free time. I watched him sometimes, trying to catch him in a moment between cards or sleep or sharpening his knife, believing there had to be instants when he'd be so disturbed by a memory that he'd have to stop, or frown, or when a thought he hadn't provided for nudged his mind and it showed on his face. I never caught him. He never did a superfluous thing. How many men can you say that about? No scratching, finger-drumming, whistling, yawning, chin-rubbing, lip-biting, hesitation in his speech. When he used his eyes, it was to a purpose, he never stared out of the window or at the wall or the ceiling to settle his mind while he dreamed awake and worked things out in his head. I decided he was a great man. Yes, his eyes. A fish looking up through clear ice at the afternoon sky would see that light and that mystery. At cards it took him a second to scan his hand and he was done with looking at the cards, what would he do with his eyes then? All that interested him was watching the other men round the table. He found a lot to see in their faces. He wasn't thinking about anything else when he was studying them, just them.

'I don't know how long this life went on. The camp outside

was a murmur with shouts and the sound of axes on wood. One of the last pieces to come back to me when I was fully fed was the sense of how far I was from the world, but I was dealing with that by letting myself go a little mad, imagining I was an Arctic explorer, trapped in a ship in the ice, waiting for the relief expedition to come. The whole camp had been mad for years, a deeper madness and getting deeper with the hunger, but I'd forgotten that, otherwise I might have realised that when the sun flashed over the horizon for the first time since November, the light would cut straight to the convicts' brain stems, crack their nerves like a chisel, and bring the White Garden to an end.

'On the morning the sun came back, I sat by the window eating bread and cheese and reading Edward Bellamy. Something came through the window, a clenched fist, all bloody torn knuckle and shrivelled veins and tendons, the arm behind trailing rags and freezing air. The skin was alive, blue grey, transparent, covering wasted muscle. The noise of breaking glass and the punch of cold and the sight of the red rips in the grey skin came in a moment, I threw the book away, stood up and stepped back. The human talon closed around the food and snatched, severing an artery in the arm as it pulled back through the jagged hole in the window which I saw because I lifted the sheet and saw the camp outside in the first light for the first time in so long. I saw the man who'd broken the window to snatch my food, the blood dripping out of his sleeve and turning to red ice when it hit the ground, him not noticing and pushing the food into his mouth, which had shrunken over his teeth so there were no lips, only a hole and teeth. The cheeks had shrunk, too, his cheekbones jutted out over his cheeks and the skin had become thin and tight over his forehead, his eyes were dead and deep in dark pits, it was a skull with the unupholstered skin of a dead man sewn onto it. While I was staring at him another convict, another moving skeleton, tried to take the food from him. They fell fighting onto the snow, labouring at killing each other with the last strength they had, going for each other's eyes with their thumbs, legs pedalling away for advantage though they were hardly thicker than the bones inside them. They didn't speak or scream while they fought, I could just hear them breathing.

'About twenty metres from our block, I could see a naked corpse, another skeleton in skin, face down in the snow with hair and blood mangled and frozen together round an axe wound in the head. A guard in a sheepskin coat ran past with his revolver drawn. I heard a whistle, and shooting.

'I heard raised voices in the other part of our barracks. The other authorities, Matchstick and the Gypsy, Gypsy who'd spread into the niche left when Machinegun was murdered, were after something from the Mohican. Matchstick said: "You've got to share. He's too much for one." The Gypsy said: "It's the end, finished. Time to do the town, brother. Just a little piece, a tiny little piece. I'll have the heart, me. Raw heart, still hot, that's what I like."

'The Mohican says: "It's the end. What I have I keep. What I keep goes with me. You go do the Prince and his people. They've got enough champagne and caviar in there to keep you all high till spring."

'And the Gypsy says: "Oh no, brother. That's not the way. You want to do the Prince, you line up with us and you cross the open ground in front of their lovely Mauserkins, my dear. Ekh, you know his house, concrete walls, that thick! The rats've found a good place, and we, what, what are we, sixty dogs too weak to catch them."

'And Matchstick says: "You've got to share. Where are you

going with him? Run in midwinter? You won't get five miles, you and your pig."

'And the Mohican says: "I told you not to use that word here."

'"Ah, the beautiful man and his little knife," says Matchstick.

'"No need, brothers, eh," says the Gypsy. "So nobody has to put their knife away without using it, let's do the fattened-up one, let's have a drink and some nice meat, do the town a bit, and then we'll go and have the Prince."

'"I'm going to have this one," says Matchstick. "I'll cut him like an artist and then I'll kill him."

'"You'll not be an artist," says the Mohican. "You haven't got the imagination."

'Listening by the stove, I heard the Gypsy shout. I never heard the sound of the Mohican killing Matchstick. Knives are quiet things, in themselves. I heard the Mohican telling the Gypsy to take the body, and the Gypsy running away, and the Mohican coming to me. He pushed through the screen of blankets, still holding the bloody knife. He said it was time to leave, that they had stopped handing out rations that morning. I asked him what Gypsy and Matchstick had wanted, and he said: "They wanted something I couldn't give them."

'For a moment, I thought I knew why animals don't speak – not because they can't, but because the terror stops them at the very moment they need to beg for their life, the fear and the hopelessness hits them when a two-legged creature comes at them with a sharp shiny blade in its coiled white fingers, and they understand how much they've been fed and how slow and weak they are, and how greedy and stupid they've been, and how their hooves and paws can't do what fingers can do, and they're outclassed, already dead, already meat. For a moment I was an animal. I was a pig, ready to squirm under the butcher's hands, and squeal, only not to speak. Then I started grabbing words. I said: "Was that something me?" I said: "Am I the pig?"

'And the Mohican said: "Listen, intellectual. It's four months till the river melts and we find out which pricks are running the country, and whether they remember there was a place such as this. Four months, and the only food is in the Prince's bunkhouse. If you stay here, the Prince and his dogs'll kill you and all the rest to stop them taking what he has. Or else you'll be taking your chances with the Gypsy and his friends. They're hungry, and you're not a fighting man. Now here's another way. We leave together, this hour, two of us." He said: "Is it a hard choice, intelligent? You can stay and be shot. You can stay and be eaten. Or we can walk into the wilderness together."

'He licked one side of his knife clean and held it out to me. I shook my head. He licked the other side, wiped it on a rag and stowed it in his belt. Gunfire began to clap and patter on the far side of the camp, where the Prince's house was. I had no choice except to leave with the Mohican, even though I knew there could only be one reason for him to take me. In the White Garden, all I could look forward to was a quick death. Death was most likely in the tundra and the taiga too, but for as long as we moved south, hope was more than a symptom of madness.

'The Mohican had made preparations. From different hiding places he took sheepskin coats and mittens, fur hats and felt boots. He unwrapped a long black Colt and put it in his coat pocket. Inside his coat he stowed an axe. He produced two bags of food and a bottle of spirits, and told me to take two books. We dressed and left. We walked out of the gate. It was already dark, but there was a moon, and we knew the way down to the river. There were no guards. They were fighting, some with the convicts, some against them according to hierarchies and deals. Even if they hadn't been, even if keeping us prisoner had any meaning, there was no need for barbed wire and gate-houses and watchtowers. If you escaped, you ran in May. In winter the tundra was wall enough to hold anyone.

'We passed between the hulls of the boats, down the bank and onto the river ice. The Mohican said we'd have to put ten miles between us and the camp before we could make a fire and rest. I remembered talk at the card table I'd heard while the Mohican had been out of the room and I was lying on my bunk, pretending to sleep. Someone, I think it was Petya, the one they called Fireman because he set fires, asked if I was sleeping, and the Gypsy said "Oh, that one always sleeps, except to eat. He's a lovely one, lullabies and cakes, that's all." Petya said it was a dark business and the Gypsy said "Hush, my dear, darkness is good for business," and the others laughed, and for a moment all I could hear was old cards slithering and the clinking of small stakes, and then someone said: "Kyesha from Rostov, he was in a work gang north of Baikal, he took a cow with him when he ran, him and a couple of folk he knew. The cow was a young one, knew nothing, soft-skinned. Kyesha and the others killed it even before the rest of their food ran out. They didn't make a fire for fear they'd be seen; they cut the throat, drank the blood, cut out the kidneys and ate them, still warm."

'I followed in the steps the Mohican made in the snow on the river. The wind had driven the snow up against the bank and out on the ice it was a few inches deep, a foot at most. The moonlight showed us the sweep of the river flat through the frozen boglands of the tundra. I knew no-one had ever escaped from the White Garden and I knew no-one ever would in midwinter, when it was a good ten or twenty days' walk to the beginnings of a tree line, and much further to human habitation; at this time even the Tungus pitched their chumas with their herds far to the south. I knew it, and I knew that having fattened me up the Mohican intended to kill me, butcher me and carry me onwards as meat, dropping my bones days apart in the wilderness. But I could still hear shooting in the camp behind us, and to be moving again and shortening the distance to the warmer side of the Arctic circle was almost like finding a sanctuary in itself. It was no colder than twenty degrees of frost, and marching in the sheepskin and felt boots only my face felt the cold. No matter how long it was, for the first hours the river seemed like a glorious road home, generous and easy, half a mile wide, the snow blown into ripples with sharp edges that stood out black under the moon. The Mohican hardly spoke, but when I watched his feet drawing their mark across the untouched wasteland, and put my feet in the hollows after him, my fear of him and my trust in him went their separate ways. There was terror, the thought of waking up to find him with one hand gripping my chin and the other pulling a blade across my throat, and at the same time there was love, a son's love for a father who shows the way, who can lead him out of a place of death towards the world of the living.

'We made our ten miles. The Mohican's first good intelligence was a place where a boat from an early expedition had run aground. It had been stripped and most of what was left was embedded in ice but there was enough wood for a fire with half of my Bellamy for kindling. We ate and lay together to sleep in a close embrace against the cold. I could hear his breathing in my ear and I said we could fish, or hunt, when the food ran out. He didn't answer for a long time and I thought he was asleep. Then he said: "When the food runs out, intellectual, I'll show you what to do. And now you sleep."

'When we woke in the dark we were frozen together, my mittens to his back, his to mine, sealed at the chest and the legs, the hairs of our beards twisted into one. We pulled ourselves apart, piled wood on the embers of the fire, squatted down on either side with our toes in the ashes, leaning so close to the flames that we almost fell in. We ate and moved on upriver.

'The second day was colder than the first. It got light but the sky and the earth were a grey enclosure, the riverbanks were smudged with haze, the rocks and ice and horizon and all the lines of the hardest things were dissolving in air as harsh as acid. My hands and feet burned and then the burning began to fade. All the ecstasy of movement away from the White Garden died, and all the fear of the Mohican, and I only wanted to lie down in the soft foggy snow. The sound of our footfalls was a lullaby and my breathing was troubling me, keeping me awake. I watched the banks, picking out a hummock or rocks, hauling myself onward with the reward of seeing them approached, passed and left behind me, meaning I was still moving. That became an effort and I watched the back of the Mohican, learning by heart the patterns in the rime marking the stiff folds of the sack over his shoulder. After a time that was too much and I lowered my head to watch the footprints in the snow in front of me, white within white, the only substantial colour in the mist. The footprints didn't change, a perfect white oval, a face blind of features, serene, happy, without nose or ears or mouth. I stared at the face, and heard the sound of my breathing and the lullaby of footfalls fade away, and decided I would kiss the face, and I would lose all sensations too. I was lying in the snow, face down, nuzzling the footprint, and dying, savouring the joy of sleep.

'The Mohican brought me back from death by cold. I opened

my eyes and saw a tree. It was very beautiful. I hadn't seen a tree for more than two years. It was a pitiful larch, there were a few of them somehow hunched in a sheltered inlet far above the tree line, but the trunk and branches seemed like living gold to me. The Mohican had carried me there, put down a lattice of branches to lie on, built a fire and made a shelter. I screamed from the pain when the feeling came back to my hands and feet. I don't know why I didn't lose fingers. The Mohican sprinkled snow on bread, held it up to the fire so the snow melted and put pieces of it into my mouth. He said: "You need to want to live more than you do."

'I asked him why. Was it so he could have a hot meal?

'He said: "Intellectual. You use your imagination too much. When a thief meets a civilian, the thief always wins, because the civilian can only imagine what his throat'll be like after it's been cut, and while he's busy doing that, the thief is cutting his throat. Think less, intellectual, breathe more. Breathe. Your heart has to beat harder. The blood has to circulate. Winter. Frost. That's what wants to eat you this minute."

'I was lying on my side, facing the fire. The Mohican lay behind me and pressed his body close. He told me the story of the Alaska raid, how he'd planned it with a group of Eskimo outlaws from Russia and America, how they'd crossed the straits from Chukotka by boat, laid up for months in a cabin on the American side while the weather turned and the straits froze over, then walked into a gold town on Christmas Day, blown a hole in the wall of the bank, blown the safe inside, chalked "GELLO AMERIKA" on the wall, stuffed their furs with plunder, and crossed back across the ice on dog teams.

'When I woke the moon was up, full. The fire had burned down to embers. The Mohican was locked around my body, his chest hard against my back, his legs against mine, arms crossing over my chest. The feeling in my hands and feet was fading again. I was shivering. The landscape had altered. We were more protected by trees than when we lay down, but in the trees there was watching and wakefulness. On the far side of the fire was a stump, which hadn't been there before, crowned by tangled strands of frost that reflected the moon back at it. And the stump blinked! It was a Tungus boy with white hair and cracked lips, wrapped in deerskin and a bear pelt, staring at us over the last glow of the fire.

'I shouted and pulled free of the Mohican with the strength of all my fear. The albino ran behind the trees, away from the river. He ran through the snow like a bear, using his arms like a second pair of legs. The snow was knee deep. I tried to run and fell and got up with wads of snow falling from my coat and face. I knew the Mohican was behind me. I was his beast, his stray lamb, needing to be brought back and tended till slaughter. One hour he'd stun me with a stave, lay me out on a rock, cut my throat, bleed me into a vessel, drink it, and butcher me, without any hurry or hating, sawing off my head, cutting me open from neck to navel, gutting me, setting the heart and lungs and kidneys aside, eating the liver while it was still warm, jointing the legs and arms at the knees and elbows and hips and shoulders, jointing the rest of the carcass into chops and bagging the meat, frozen, for his journey to the railhead. I saw myself made food and my head naked in the snow, one eye and one ear and half a mouth and nose and half a raw neck stump poking above it. I felt so sorry for my head, left over by a man maneater in the Arctic, left alone in the dark, with nothing to cover it. I saw the albino's trail after he was out of sight, weird shallow marks, as if he trod the snow like waterfowl tread the waves in the first moments of flight. I couldn't move so lightly and the eviscerator was behind me.

I raised my legs with the power that the soon to be eaten have just before slaughter and made a kind of prancing freakish canter and saw a light ahead. It was a yellow light in the opening of a chuma. I ran towards it. There were reindeer tethered outside, two big riding does and pack animals. I looked over my shoulder. I couldn't see the Mohican behind me. I passed inside the tent.

'There were skins spread on the snow and an oil lamp with a steady flame hung from the roof poles. The albino sat cross-legged on a grubby fox pelt. Opposite him was a shaman with iron horses sewn to his deerskins and an eye tattooed on a lump on his forehead. This is the unfortunate man whom you all know and whom, I believe, was the Mohican's first victim in this town last night.

'Around them they had deerskin panniers and horn tools and bunches of bark and grasses and ivory divining sticks and deer bridles and an old empty bottle of Church wine and a drum. It stank but it was as warm as summer in there and I was glad enough to cry out loud. I squatted down close to the lamp and asked them if they spoke Russian.

'The shaman asked: "Do you have the avakhi drink?" I told him I didn't. 'Avakhi' is the Tungus word for 'demon', which is everyone who isn't Tungus. The shaman asked if I came from the White Garden, and whether they had strong drink there. I told him it wasn't safe to go, that men were killing each other for food. The shaman said: "I've seen it. First the old get eaten by the weak, then the weak get eaten by the strong, and then the strong get eaten by the clever."'

Samarin stopped speaking. A bad human sound was coming from outside the room, a mixture of sobbing and retching. Mutz stepped over and opened the small frosted glass window which looked out to the rear of the shtab. The people in the courtroom could hear him having a murmured conversation with someone outside. He turned back into the room. His first attempt at words was unsuccessful; his mouth was dry. He ran his tongue around his gums and tried again. He said: 'It's Racansky. He was looking for Lieutenant Kliment. He found him. Kliment is dead. He appears to have been killed. Murdered, I mean. I . . . he isn't very far away. I suppose we should . . . adjourn.'

'I feel sorry for you all, now that we know he is among us,' said Samarin.

'Adjourn! You ridiculous man,' said Matula to Mutz, getting up. 'Everyone can see we should have adjourned this before it started.'

Mutz hurried out of the room after Matula and Dezort. As he passed Anna Petrovna, she heard him ordering Nekovar to take Samarin back to the cells.

'Wait!' she shouted after them, but the striding cacophony of important boots was already out of hearing. Hanak and Balashov were following the officers. Nekovar was prodding Samarin out of the room with his rifle. Anna grabbed his elbow and asked him what he was doing. Nekovar shook her off and told her she had to leave the building.

'But he's not guilty of anything,' said Anna. 'This isn't your country.'

'Russia isn't our country, correct, Anna Petrovna,' said Nekovar politely, grabbing his prisoner by the collar and halting for a moment. 'But you've got to remember we've only just made one of our own. It hasn't been trimmed down yet.'

'I won't allow you to keep him another night in that cell,' said Anna Petrovna. Nekovar ignored her and marched Samarin forward. Anna heard Samarin call over his shoulder, thanking her by name.

The Fields

The group of men, Mutz, Matula, Dezort, Hanak and Balashov, followed Racansky down the southern road that led to the grazing land of the castrates' herd. The forest fell away and there were only stands of birches breaking the flatness. With the slaughter of the cattle by the occupiers the pastures had grown scraggy and neglected. Crow calls measured the emptiness under a thickening sky. A dank wind moved the yellow grass by the roadside. The men's boots sounded unnaturally loud on the road, as if, despite the great space of clear wide land, the splash, scrabble and grind of their soles on the dirt was being reflected against invisible walls moving in around them.

Racansky set a troubled pace, spurting forward at a run for a few yards, then slowing down to a hesitant walk. He began to talk over his shoulder as he moved. Mutz was glad someone had broken the wordlessness of their progress.

'He said one of the farmers told him about an outsider, a great savage man with his skin shrunken down over a big skull, that he'd seen running through the fields. Like a wolf after an elk, he said.'

'Who said? Kliment?' said Mutz.

'Kliment, yes, of course,' said Racansky. 'He told me this morning. We left the shtab at the same time, I was coming off duty after guarding the prisoner overnight, Kliment was on his way to the station to see if the telegraph was working, and I told him about the killer the prisoner said was coming. The Mohican. Here. He's here.'

A cart track led off the road into a ploughed field. Kliment's body lay face up on the crest of a deep rut, one arm trailed in water to the elbow. A blood stain spread across his chest, black at the edges and still sticky and crimson in the centre.

'I turned him over,' said Racansky, hanging back. 'I have some of his blood on my coat.' His voice has become a whisper. Balashov fell to his knees, clasped his hands, closed his eyes and began to pray out loud.

'My God, what's that on his forehead?' said Dezort.

Mutz, Matula and Hanak leaned over Kliment's face, which looked more lovable in its dreamless, breathless serenity than it ever had in life or sleep. Four quick shallow cuts had been made in his forehead to make a letter M.

'The Mohican!' said Dezort.

'Or Marx, or Madman, or Murder, or Mother,' said Mutz.

'Or Matula, eh Mutz?' said Matula. 'Poor Klim. Get his arm out of the water, Hanak. Still warm, is he? He wasn't already dead when he died, was he? A hot breakfast, a fuck, a toot of snow, and a knife in the ribs. He had a full morning, I'd say. D'you remember when he stopped in the middle of no-man's-land to light a cigarette, with the men falling around him, bash, bash, bash? I swear if I catch this Mohican, I'll flay him.'

'For Thine is the Kingdom,' intoned Balashov.

Mutz saw how Matula was looking round, distracted, already impatient with the uselessness of the dead. He was irritated by the shrinking of his tiny army, and offended to be reminded of his own mortality. Mutz had seen before how Matula cared little for the dead but hated to lose an officer. It shrank the empire of his mind; he cast around for new men to commission. It was how Mutz had become a lieutenant.

'Racansky,' said Mutz. 'How did you know he was here?'

'I told you. We walked away from the shtab together. When I told him about the Mohican, he told me about this stranger someone had seen down here, and he said he was going to look. I woke up an hour ago and I realised I shouldn't have let him go by himself, and I came down the road to look. I saw him lying on his face with a wound in his back.'

Mutz nodded. He remembered Kliment shying pebbles at Bublik and Racansky a few weeks earlier after they had organised a political meeting, and calling them 'the guard's van of the revolution.' One of the stones had hit Racansky just above the eye. 'Here,' said Mutz to Racansky. 'Help me turn him over.'

Racansky shook his head and took a step backwards. Dezort was staring at the corpse with his arms hanging by his sides, chewing the corner of his mouth. Balashov had reached the beginning of the third recital of the Lord's Prayer. 'Thy kingdom come,' he said.

'Hey! You! Local man!' said Matula. 'That's enough of that. We've got our own chaplain.'

'He died of typhus last year, sir,' said Mutz.

'Hanak! Turn Kliment over,' said Matula. 'There you are. Big nasty stab wound. Autopsy over. Hanak, you're a Lutheran, aren't you?'

'Used to drink with them all the time, sir.'

'If you can get Kliment's stars off him, you're a lieutenant, and acting chaplain. Come on, you and Racansky carry him out of here. Dezort, go with them. See about a box. And a flag! We have flags. Local man, clear off. Me and Mr Mutz have some matters to discuss.'

'Balashov,' said Balashov. 'Gleb Alexeyevich.' He bowed to Matula. In that moment, Mutz saw and understood the previous Balashov, the horseman and swordsman who was proud before all men and an abject slave before God, and saw that this could have been more terrible in war than Matula's humility to no-one. It was no more than a moment. Balashov went meekly away, Hanak and Racansky shouldered the not yet stiff bag of flesh that had contained Kliment, Hanak starting to work the lieutenant's stars loose with one hand, and Mutz and Matula were left alone.

'Look at this, Josef,' said Matula. 'All this fine land going to waste. Think what Czech farmers could do here.' He only called Mutz by his first name when they were alone together and when he was about to bully him with special viciousness.

'It wasn't going to waste before the wars, sir,' said Mutz. 'They were sending butter to England.'

'You think you're a fair man, but fairness is just your way of getting what you want,' said Matula. He stuck his hands in his pockets and kicked a clod of earth with the toe of his boot. Mutz knew that if the clod flew like a stone, serenity might prevail. If it shattered into dust, it would mean a change of state.

The clod crumbled into lumps of mud, staining the toe of Matula's boots, which had been cleaned overnight by Pelageya Fedotovna. Mutz looked down at his feet and tapped his toes gently together. 'Why are you such a hopeless failure, Mutz?' he said. 'Eh? I told you to arrange transport of the horses. You were in charge last night when the shaman drank himself to death. You interrogated Samarin, he warned you about the Mohican, and instead of having our boys sweep the town, you had us in a courtroom all morning listening to convict Gothic. You're supposed to be clever. I don't think it's clever to get a stablehand, an aboriginal and one of your brother officers killed in the space of less than twenty four hours. Damn you,

Jew boy, no wonder the Austrian empire fell apart, taking your kind into its army. The only thing I can't understand is whether your filthy tribe is mentally defective or whether this is part of your conspiracy, like that bunch of Yids waving the red banner in Petrograd. Which is it? Eh?' He marched over to Mutz, took his chin in his hand, and roughly moved it from side to side to study his profile. He pushed the head away. 'You're degenerate,' he said, and spat on the ground. 'It's as if some other man promoted you. I can barely believe it, but I'm going to let you try to clean this up.'

Matula's fingers had pressed hard into Mutz's jaw. There were three Matula-worlds here, nested inside each other, the innermost the most secret, and so far Matula had spoken only of the outer. Now he had opened a door through which Mutz could descend to the second, more dangerous level, if he dared.

'Clean it up, sir?' He swallowed and passed in. 'Do you mean clean it up as in bury everything and cover it with earth? Or do you mean clean it up as in find out who is responsible?'

'What's the matter?' said Matula. His breathing was audible. 'Decided you don't mind if I kill you?'

Anna Petrovna's coldness at the hearing, where she hadn't looked at him, and had made eyes at the convict, made Mutz more careless. But he doubted Matula would be happy losing two officers in a single day. Matula could try to mash his face to pulp, it was true.

'We still don't know who Samarin is,' Mutz said. 'We don't know who killed Kliment, or the shaman, or what happened to the horses.'

'You greasy viper,' said Matula. 'I know your Israelite wet dreams, I see them before you do, you leading my Czech boys home out of the wilderness with me buried here.'

'There's nothing to keep us here, except you.'

'I've got orders from Prague.'

'No-one's seen them. It's pleasant to be king of Siberia, sir, I understand, even a small part of it. No-one's surprised you don't want to go back to being a sales representative for a light bulb manufacturer in southern Bohemia. You're a much larger man here. It's wonderful for you to be able to imagine you rule the forests, to imagine you're the Czech Pizarro, making a new empire with a handful of soldiers, to be chaining up women, gold and land. But sir, here the Aztecs have artillery of their own, and machine guns, more than we do, and better missionaries than us. I can take out my pistol as quickly as you, sir.'

Matula had begun to move his hand towards his holster. He opened his mouth, bared his teeth, gave a shrill cry, part bellow, part shriek, and charged towards Mutz. Mutz began to run backwards, tripped and fell over into the mud. As he scrambled to get up and take out his pistol Matula stopped.

'Like two cowboys. Some time it'll be real,' he said. He reached out his hand and helped Mutz up. 'I was going to kill you, but one more time for giving me my life back on the ice. Listen, people die. We'll find this Mohican. Only do one thing for me, will you? Go out there, to the bridge, and bury my horse, and the Czech fellow who snuffed it. Put some crosses up, get a Christian to say some words for them. I want it to be a place I can visit, put a monument up later. Just do that.'

'Sir,' said Mutz. He felt the damp seeping through the clothes to his skin. 'Can I ask, sir, you will keep Samarin locked up until I get back? Of course he couldn't have killed Kliment, but his testimony had inconsistencies.'

'"Inconsistencies." "Inconsistencies." That's a real Mutz word, isn't it? Whatever you want. You're a hard man after what he's been through. Come out into the road with me.' Mutz followed Matula out onto the deserted road. Matula stood facing him a few yards away. 'Now,' said Matula. 'We both take out our pistols, very slowly.' The two men took out their guns. Matula began walking backwards. 'Just so there won't be any inconsistencies,' said Matula. 'You see, Josef? I can walk backwards without any in-con-sis-ten-cies. Follow me when you can't see me any more.'

Mutz watched Matula walk backwards for two hundred yards, stumbling twice, before turning about. Mutz put his gun away. The mud was caking on his clothes and he could brush most of it off. He went to sit on a fallen tree-trunk close to where Kliment's body had lain. Kliment had left no mark there distinguishable from the effect of cartwheels, hooves, feet and rain. The clouds on the horizon had a gregarious look. It wasn't too early for snow. This was what civil war must always look like, the untended fields, uncropped grass and weeds hiding old furrows, lumps in the distance where folk had made a bit of hay for their yard-cows. Neglect, rather than wounds; a country gone bald, wrinkled, lame and unwashed. Mutz had a flash of taste memory and ached for a glass of dark red wine. He took a sheaf of papers out of his shirt pocket and read through a draft report of the actions of Captain Matula's company in the town of Staraya Krepost six months earlier, the inmost fear which neither man had dared mention, although that was what they had been talking about. The greatest number of crossings-out and insertions in the draft were in the same places as in previous drafts, where Mutz attempted to *explain*, or rather *justify*, or rather *excuse*, or, yes, *account for*, the killing of civilians, with reference to *prior incidents* in which Czech prisoners had been executed; where he attempted to *characterise* the *political views* of the townspeople – *a broad range of Red and White sympathisers, sympathisers* changed to *activists* – and where he described what he had been doing. *Attempted to restrain, restrain* crossed out and replaced with *reason with,* the whole phrase crossed out and *fearing for my own safety, I made no significant attempt to intervene* written in. *Significant* crossed out.

Three heavy bumps sounded to the west, sharp blows on the hollow world. Artillery was being fired about fifteen miles away. Nobody had heard the sound here before. Mutz crumpled the papers he held in his hand into a ball, dropped the ball on the ground, lit a match, and squatted down to see that the papers burned through to black flakes which he trod into the mud.

Mutz began walking back to Yazyk, stupefied by the variety of menace and idiotism he had met since yesterday. In one quiet attic of his mind a man was trying to think while all around him the neighbours were jumping out of windows, setting themselves on fire and garrotting each other. He didn't trust Matula; trust, with the captain, was something which only applied retrospectively. You trusted that he had not killed you, rather than that he would not.

Halfway down the road Mutz came across Balashov foraging on the border of a copse. Balashov stepped out to meet him and shook his hand.

'I wanted to speak with you,' he said. 'I pretended to be looking for mushrooms. I was afraid of Matula. I'm sorry about your friend.'

'Kliment? He wasn't a friend, but thank you.'

'What should I tell my congregation? A murder like this seems more terrible in the midst of a war. Did you hear the guns?'

'Yes,' said Mutz, looking into his face for echoes, sneaking a peek into his eyes, as if the key to his deed of harm was to be found floating there in formaldehyde. 'The Reds must have taken Verkhny Luk and shunted up some heavy ordnance to frighten us.' He paused. They were shy men. Mutz had found lust and fear of shrapnel were helpful against shyness, and he found them helpful now. He said: 'You've heard the big guns before, Gleb Alexeyevich. Anna Petrovna told me.'

'I know.'

'She let me read your letter. Does that make you angry?'

'No.'

'Does anything make you angry?'

Balashov made the small laugh that some people do when they are remembering the worst things that have happened to them. 'When you ask questions like that, I feel as if I'm on a stage in front of an audience of professors.'

'I'm sorry.'

'Do you have patronymics?'

'Patronymics?'

'Like I'm Gleb Alexeyevich, Gleb the son of Alexei. I feel more comfortable – you speak Russian very well, I'd like to be able to use your first name and patronymic. Your titles sound unholy. Pan this and lieutenant that.'

'My father's name is Josef.'

'May I call you Josef Josefovich?'

'If you like,' said Mutz, feeling outmanoeuvred in a gentle way.

'Josef Josefovich, I wanted to speak to you about promises. Hear me through. It is not a market, where promises are weighed and some are worth more than others, and the promise breaker can be taken to court. Not in this world, at least. You can only ask and hope. I broke a promise made before God to my wife, but we have made promises since. I promised her that I would not help others do what I was helped to do. I promised that I would not wield the knife. I promised that I would never go to her home without her invitation, and to do everything I could to prevent Alyosha finding out who I was. She promised that she would never tell anyone what I had done. I am hurt that she has broken this promise, whether or not you or she feel I have any right to be hurt. But I do not believe a promise broken once is useless. It becomes a promise in two parts, held by two people, and I do not see that either of you have any reason to break it further.'

Mutz blushed and felt a tenderness for Balashov in that, beyond his concern for his secret, there was a deeper fear that he would be laughed at.

'Anna Petrovna made another promise, Josef Josefovich,' said Balashov, folding his hands behind his back and looking Mutz in the eye. Mutz wished he had not told him his father's name, at least not the real one. Regret made Balashov colder. 'About men.'

'She promised she would not see other men?'

'She promised she would.'

'Ah.'

'There is nothing I can do about it. About you, or any other man. I do not want it to happen, I know it is happening, and there is nothing I can do.'

Mutz had foreseen a humble man, still shocked from the knife five years before, gone simple, and had foreseen his own abhorrence after reading Balashov's letter carrying on into the daylight to make his persuasion of the castrate more perfect. He had expected to be able to dominate him. It was not going well. Without any right on his side, Balashov was shaming him. Mutz was even beginning to be sorry that he had not known him better earlier. But the roaring of events in Mutz's ears was becoming so loud that only by clinging to his plans could he remain sane. He was obliged to make his request.

'I'm sorry you feel that way,' he said. 'I see you know about me and Anna Petrovna. That makes what I'm about to ask you easier.'

'What?'

'You have to tell your wife to leave, and to take your son with her.'

'Easier?'

'It's not enough to tell her that she's free. You've got to beg her to leave you if she refuses to go.'

'Anna is my wife, and Alyosha is my son,' said Balashov steadily. 'Why should I beg them to leave if they don't want to go?' He lifted his chin up and Mutz saw a light come on in his eyes. Where was the humility?

'I don't want to hurt your feelings, but haven't you been ridiculous enough already?' said Mutz. He heard his voice thin and heighten as he lost his temper. 'The only reason for them to stay here is you, and you've done all you can to fail as a husband and a father. You ran away from your family, and you mutilated yourself so you could never love or make love to a woman again. Can you really not understand that nothing except Anna Petrovna's pity keeps her here? Why do you need that? Why do you need her, now? Why do you need a child? You're not a man any more, and a wife and child are man's things. You've got to tell them to leave and you've got to tell them never to come back.'

'I shall not! I shall not. I didn't make Anna come here, and I shan't tell her to go. You men,' Balashov said, his body tightening with pride and anger, 'You men, you have that burden between your legs, that heavy sour fruit and that little poisonous tree-trunk, and you think that without it, there's no love.'

His voice grew calmer. His face grew placid and he looked into Mutz's eyes, almost smiling, severe and sure. 'Do you truly believe that this world is such an awful place that love can be taken out of it with a knife? D'you think surgeons could remove it? I disgust you. But do you not disgust yourself if you believe you need to be led by a stiffness in a stick in your loins, and a fever, to love your son, or your friends, or a woman?'

'This is sophistry,' said Mutz, blushing, humiliated in a way he couldn't name. 'There are kinds of love . . .'

'Your kisses will always have teeth in them.'

Why had Mutz thought a man who carried ideas to such extremes of execution would ever be persuaded by rational argument? He said: 'They're not safe here. You heard the Red guns. I don't see Matula surrendering Yazyk without fighting. The town will be destroyed. Anna and Alyosha will be caught here and killed.'

Balashov wasn't listening. He was waiting for Mutz to finish, his eyes shining now, righteous. 'If you loved my wife,' he said, 'instead of trying to steal her, perhaps you could protect her. If I were a man, that's what I would do.'

The Legion

Anna Petrovna stood by the salt fish kiosk in the square, waiting for Matula to finish holding his parade so that she could ask for Samarin to be released. She was cold. Kira Amvrosevna, the fish lady, had lent her a shawl.

'That's how they'll look on Judgement Day,' said Kira, resting her full self on her forearm and judging fish with the point of her knife, bobbing from flank to flank. The scaly grey fish-skin was rough with salt. The fish were thin as parchment and tough as green wood. 'All the sinners. All the fornicators and deceivers, all the great liars. All these unkinlike halfwit outsiders with guns. Christ'll thread string through their skulls and hang 'em up in racks like fish, with their mouths hung open and their eyes wide and not believing. And then there'll be such a judging. You'd better make sure you're clean inside, Anna Petrovna, cause Christ's going to gut you with his gutting knife, and judge you on what he finds in there.'

'Leave me in peace,' said Anna.

They heard the sound of the guns beating at the world. 'Lord,' said Kira. 'The end time's nigh. That's how it sounds.'

Anna fetched a cigarette and matches out of her purse. Supposing Alyosha had inherited his father's terror at the sound? So much the better if he learned now never to go for a soldier. Her hands shook as she lit the cigarette. In her imagination she had already put Samarin in their house as a shield. He couldn't protect them against all the warriors but he could be an envoy of the lights of cities beyond the forest, the noise and chatter and thinking there. She didn't think of touching him. She didn't think of them touching. Well, perhaps she did, if thinking of stroking his cheek with her fingertips was touching, while he looked into her eyes.

'You'll not be smoking that filth here,' said Kira.

'Let me smoke quietly.'

'You'll end up like this,' said Kira, waving one of the fish in her face.

A bugle sounded from the roof of the shtab. Metal parts clinked with purpose up above and the barrel of the Maxim gun poked out over the edge of the guttering. Smutny and Buchar were preparing to cover the parade. Czech soldiers began to drift towards the shtab from all corners of the square. One of them walked slowly past Anna, watching her cigarette. She thought he had a limp, but it wasn't that. He only had one boot.

'You've lost a boot,' she said.

'No,' said the soldier. 'I found one.'

She held out her cigarette to him and he took it and walked on.

When the Czechs were assembled they formed a curved, notched line outside the shtab. At the time they left Prague in 1914 there had been 171 of them. They had lost Hruby, Broz, Krejci, Makovicka, Kladivo and Kral in Galicia in 1916, when they were still taking orders from the Austrians, and the Russians attacked. The Russians shot Navratil when they captured the company, because they thought he was going to throw a grenade, though he was just reaching for his water bottle. Slezak and Bures died of their wounds on the way to the prison camp. The company buried them in a little cemetery near the Dnieper.

The company was put to work on a farm outside Moscow and Hlavacek was murdered when the foreman found him in bed with his wife. The three Kriz brothers, acrobats, were taken off to a Turkoman circus, and Ruzicka, a carpenter, got a job in the city. The Russians cut the rations, and Chalupnik was executed for stealing a cow. There was some fever in the barracks, and the company lost Stojespal and Kolinsky. The company left for Kiev to join the Czech Legion, but Tesarik, Rohlicek, Zaba, Boehm and Kaspar said they didn't want to fight with the Russians against their own people, and they stayed behind as prisoners of war. In February 1917, when the Russians had their first revolution, and nobody knew who was in charge, there wasn't much bread to be had. The younger Cerny died of the fever, followed by Lanik and Zito. Dragoun and Najman froze to death on the second night, they'd hidden a bottle of brandy and went onto the roof to drink it so they wouldn't have to share it, they fell asleep up there and there was a bad frost. The company had to lever them off with crowbars when they stopped near Chernigov. Kratochvil, Jedlicka, Safar, Kubes and Vasata, who always took an interest in politics, set up a soviet in the last wagon and uncoupled it from the rest of the train in the night. When the company reached Kiev and joined a new regiment things got better for a while, the Ukrainians were good to them. Bilovsky made a girl from Brovary pregnant and was given an honourable discharge when her father gave Matula his best horse, and Vrzala started sneaking out to the casinos at night and became a cocaine dealer. By the time they reached the front they were fatter and not so ill. The Russians put the company into their offensive. The older Cerny took a bullet as they came out of the trenches and went down without a sound. Matula was calling out to the company that it could fight its way back to Bohemia, and every time he looked at someone they would fall down dead, and he ran forward, and the company followed him, and Matula told Mutz not to crouch, he was setting a bad example, and Mutz stood up straight. Everyone stood up straight, and Strnad took so many bullets in the neck that his head popped back like the stopper on a beer bottle. Besides Cerny and Strnad the company buried Vavra, Urban, Mohelnicky, Vlcek, Repa, Precechtel, Ruzicka, Prochazka, Zahradnik, Vavrus and Svobodnik. Knedlik and Kolar died later of their wounds. Then the Bolshevik revolution occurred, and the Russians in Kiev asked the company if it would help them fight the Bolsheviks, and Kadlec was shot by a woman in a leather coat. The Ukrainians took over, and the company helped them get food from villages on the left bank of the Dnieper. After the company shot some peasants, Buchta and Lanik said their comrades were dirty reactionary sons of bitches, and went over to the Bolsheviks. Biskup and Pokorny, who kept complaining that they weren't being paid, went off to rob a bank in Odessa, and it was said they became rich and crossed the Black Sea, and ended up in Batumi, with three Adzharian girls each, and a big house by the sea, and little black pigs running about among the palm trees in their yard. It was also said they were hanged.

Then the Czechs in the west said the Legion had to move to fight the Germans on the western front, and the only way to do that was to go round the world, to travel along the Trans-Siberian railway to Vladivostok and across the Pacific and across America and across the Atlantic to France, so the Legion started moving east. When Trotsky tried to take the Legion's weapons, Matula and the other officers thought they were going to hand them over to the Germans, and started to fight them, and the Legion took over the whole of the Trans-Siberian, and for a while the only free Czechoslovakia was six thousand miles long and two metres wide and stretched from the

Urals to the Pacific. The company was in Irkutsk when the fighting started, and the railway workers were very Red. The company spent the summer fighting them in the railway tunnels and on Lake Baikal. Skounic, Marek and Zaba died when a train was derailed by partisans, and Brada was wounded in the fighting in the forest and died of gangrene. Myska went over to the Reds. When the company captured him later, Matula shot him in the head. In autumn Red partisans ambushed the company on the Baikal shore and killed Vasata and Martinek. Matula became angry and the company went to a town called Staraya Krepost. Matula ordered all the factory workers and their families out into the square and the company shot dozens of the men. After that Kubec and Koupil deserted. The Reds put up posters saying Matula was a bloodthirsty butcher and an enemy of the people. They raided the company's billets and Benisek was killed, but the Socialist Revolutionaries turned up and helped it drive the Reds away. By that time Baikal had frozen over and the company heard that the partisans were crossing the ice. It went after them but couldn't find them in the darkness and the ice began to break up because it had frozen early. At dawn the company found that Hajek had drowned, and while it was counting the frostbite cases the Reds opened up from the shore, killing Zikan and Noha and Smid. Matula was hit in the chest and his throat and windpipe was filling up with blood and he couldn't breathe and Mutz punched a hole in his throat with the point of his knife, saving him. Jahoda led the men off the ice, and he went down when they reached the shore, and Mutz carried Matula. The second bullet seemed to have passed directly through Matula's heart, but somehow failed to kill him. It was after that the company was posted to Yazyk. With Kliment's murder, there were 101 left.

When they marched to the station in Prague in 1914 they

had worn new uniforms of stormcloud-coloured cotton and new boots, their badges and buckles had been bright, and even though they hadn't believed in the sense of what they were doing, they had bothered to keep in formation, both because mutiny was too big a single step then from where they were and because, in summer, fresh, unblooded, in the streets with girls watching, marching had seemed a kind of dancing.

In a Siberian rail halt in autumn, five years later, mutiny hung from the branches, too ripe even to need to pick, it was falling. The soldiers' uniforms were cut with loot and patches, darned with stolen string, a Cossack's breeches under an English khaki tunic, American shirts stained with blood, wine and the yolk of raw eggs sucked warm from the straw they'd been grabbed from two years before and their ends finely punched with bayonet tips, a belt buckle made in Khiva and carried to the snows of the north by a railwayman who died at the controls of his locomotive as it ground from Central Asian spring to still winter in the months between revolutions, one entire Czech uniform, as handed out by the quartermaster in Bohemia when its wearer was still a citizen of the now dead Austro-Hungarian Empire, but a deception, since every sleeve and hem and quarter had been replaced since it was new, and nothing remained of the original but the idea of its old identity. A hundred men carried fragments of two dozen armies, some ancient and vanished, some formed and dissipated in a month in the edgeless continent of grass, snow and stones between Europe and Manchuria, when a charismatic gambler, generous and violent and ambitious in an occasional way, would walk into a store in some town without paved roads, dump a sagging bag of assorted gold on the counter, and request scarlet-trimmed billowing horsemen's gear and lance pennants and mane-ribbons for a cohort of arbitrary warriors and their mounts, and within a month, after a single raid or vodka-bout or quarrel, the finery would be sold on or lying bloodied and frozen in mud, only ready to be taken. Some of Matula's men's rifles had the first orange lines of rust; all had places where the varnish had worn off the wood. Their hats were a bestiary of hide, wool and fur. One soldier, Private Habadil, had swapped his watch – his own, not booty – in Omsk for a cap resembling the scalp of a balding old man with long red hair which, the vendor swore, was from a kind of man-beast which lived in the mountains of Altai. The boots they wore reported years on the move and dread of a sixth winter, leather wrinkled like great-grandfathers, makeshift re-solings of wood, truck tyre, bark, all trailing straw and rags and scraps of felt or fur stuffed inside for warmth, though it was not yet cold in Yazyk. A hundred men with 945 toes between them, the balance lost to frostbite, and 980 fingers; 199 eyes; 198 feet; 196 hands; stomachs scored by microbes; one in ten syphilitic, one in ten consumptive, and most tasting the first foul tang of scurvy.

Matula came towards them, his sabre stuffed bare into his belt, Dezort a few paces behind. Sergeant Ferko called the men to attention. They spat, sneezed, sniffed, coughed, scraped their feet together and humped their rifles over their shoulders so they leaned every way. Ferko and Matula exchanged salutes and Matula spoke, looking the men in the eye one by one. In turn each looked away, or down at their feet. Some even closed their eyes rather than contemplate the druggy charm of the captain's lips and the carcass soul in his eyes.

'Men,' said Matula. 'Comrades. Friends. We have fought together for five years. We have fought for the Emperor of the Austrians against the Emperor of the Russians. We have fought for the Emperor of the Russians against the Emperor of the Austrians. We have fought for the White Terror of the monarchists against the Red Terror of the Bolsheviks. We have fought with Socialist Revolutionaries and Cossacks against Cossacks and Socialist Revolutionaries. I can say to you, with pride, that not once have we compromised our ideals.

'We have fought together for five years. We have fought for others. It is time we fought for ourselves. I know you are tired. I know you do not feel like fighting any more. I know you want to go home.'

The men had been silent throughout, but when Matula said the word "home", the quality of their quietness changed, it stiffened and tightened. It braced. It became important not to let it break.

'I could suggest to you that instead of going home to Europe, we make a home here,' said Matula. 'I could remind you of what opportunities there are for enterprising men in this empty land, so little colonised and so carelessly looked after by our fellow Slavs, the Russians. I could persuade you that our own new country in crowded Europe, the country named Czechoslovakia, will need to have its empire and its colonies, as other great, civilised, modern white European nations do. But you want to go home. You want to return to that small, safe, green homeland. I am your commander, and I say: I shall not stop you. Even though no order has come from President Masaryk to leave, even though it would be shameful to desert this rich virgin land where we have spilled so much blood, I shall not stop you going home.

'My men, there is, however, one obstacle to your departure. It is an officer of this company, Lieutenant Josef Mutz. He is not here. He has set off towards Verkhny Luk on an errand, and we can only pray that no harm comes to him along the way. Lieutenant Mutz is of the opinion that on no account must we leave Yazyk until we receive an explicit order to evacuate.

I have tried to reason with him: I pointed out how eager you were to leave. He looked at me with an expression – I would not say cold, I would not say bureaucratic, I would not say officious – evil would be putting it strongly, heartless, likewise – anyway, he warned me that he would personally denounce to the general staff in Omsk and Vladivostok any attempt by any soldier or officer to leave Yazyk until the order came to do so. I was surprised at his harshness. True, he is not like us; his first language was German, not Czech; he is of that race which killed Christ our Lord upon the cross, and persists in carrying out its mysterious private rituals; in the hardest hours of our campaigns he has hung back and watched from a distance, as if secretly preparing a dossier for use against us at a future tribunal; but I had never thought badly of him before. No doubt, according to the letter of our new military code, which he seems, strangely, to know better than us, he is correct, even if his stubbornness violates every rule of natural justice. Men, the fact exists: we cannot leave Yazyk while Lieutenant Mutz is alive, that is, while he thinks the way he does. Therefore, in the meantime, let us carry out our duties here a little longer. In the first place, that means defending this place against the Red menace, whose artillery you may have heard. Do not be concerned: I can assure you that the local reds only have three shells, and they have used them all. Perhaps, in defending Yazyk, we'll learn to love the forest and its bounty.

'Men, I know you are disappointed. I know you are frustrated. I must warn you not to turn your anger against Lieutenant Mutz. He may have cut himself off from his comrades. It is true that should one or more of you catch him in some isolated spot, such as the railway line, it would be impossible, despite a full inquiry, to identify who fired the fatal shot. Do not yield to temptation. That is all.'

Ferko dismissed the men. Anna Petrovna went over to Matula, who was talking to Dezort and Hanak. The three of them formed a triangle of backs. They knew she was there and ignored her. Hanak's eyes flicked over to hers and flicked away. He had already sewn Kliment's torn-off stars onto his shoulders. Anna could see broken threads from the dead man's coat poking free.

Anna stood behind Matula and said loudly: 'I want you to release Mr Samarin.'

Matula turned round slowly, still talking in Czech to the lieutenants. He nodded, and went back to his conversation. He made her wait ten minutes then came to her, the boy's mouth smiling falsely and the eyes true to their lack of symptoms of affection, and put his hand heavily on her shoulder. She shrugged it off and pushed it away.

'Will you let him go?' she said. 'You can see now that he's not a killer.'

'But I promised your Jewish friend to keep him locked up till he got back.'

'Lieutenant Mutz is wrong about all sorts of things.'

'Anna Petrovna!' said Matula, clasping one of her hands in his, and holding it tight when she tried to pull it away. His hands were hot. 'That's what I've always said! How wonderful that you agree with me.'

'It's not that I agree with you about anything,' said Anna, blushing. She managed to snatch her hand away and took a step back. 'You've got to let him go.'

'And have him wander off into the forest? Leave him in the wilderness?'

Anna looked at the ground. 'He can stay with me,' she said. She looked into Matula's face. 'I'll take responsibility for him.'

Matula licked his lips and nodded, smiling more broadly.

'This is interesting,' he said. 'If I understand correctly, you wish to sever your relationship with the Jew, and replace him with the convict? Are you quite certain? Perhaps you'd rather choose one of my men? I think I can find one who's never been in jail, and none of them are Yids. There's a few Catholics in there, mind you, perhaps that'd be more to your taste.'

Anna's heart was beating hard and she considered striking Matula. She anticipated the feel of his rough skin and the scar under her hand. She thought of spitting but that took skill. 'You won't provoke me,' she said. 'I know you already. Mock me all day if you like, but let the man go.'

'I can't do that,' said Matula. His smile went. 'That's called "bail." What guarantee do I have that he's not going to run away before I decide what to do with him?'

'I promise he won't run.'

'You guarantee it?'

'I'll make sure.'

'How about this? If he runs, I'll shoot you.'

Anna shrugged. 'Do you think I feel safe as it is?'

Matula's smile returned, and his eyes moved, like a machine shifting to the next seam.

'Lieutenant Mutz will be disappointed when he returns today and finds his friend Anna Petrovna living with a convict he doesn't trust. Or perhaps you're hoping he won't come back.'

'If he finds a way to get home to Prague, I hope he doesn't. D'you think he doesn't know you've been inciting your men to kill him?'

'Cold!' said Matula. 'Such busy eyes you have, such blood in your cheeks, and so cold to old Mutzie. Go on, take possession of the unfortunate, and keep him interested, if you don't want your boy to be an orphan.'

In

Anna was made to wait outside the shtab while they brought Samarin out. He didn't seem surprised that she had obtained his release. He shook her hand and told her he was grateful. She didn't tell him the terms of his bail, only that he couldn't leave Yazyk, otherwise there would be unpleasant consequences for her. They walked to her house. The road seemed short and the air less cold. Anna felt clean and light, as if some heavy, sticky stain had been washed off her. She talked in short, cautious phrases about her home town. It was only a night by train from where Samarin had grown up. Samarin's language was close to her own, closer than the Czechs with their accents, closer than the castrates with their Bible talk, or than the Land Captain and his household with their concerns of class and rank. They were the same age. Samarin asked her why she'd moved to Yazyk after her husband's death. Anna was frightened and angry for a moment before she understood it was a question that was fair and bound to be asked, and would be asked as often as other strangers came. She told a story about a house which belonged to a dead great uncle, a need for peace and solitude, and a wish to sit out European Russia's times of trouble.

Samarin said nothing to suggest he disbelieved her and they walked on in silence. Anna Petrovna turned to him, watched him for a second, and turned away. He asked her what it was.

'Nothing. I'll tell you later,' she said.

'You'll forget.'

'It's foolish.'

'Well?'

'I expected you to be more impatient to be free. To make me understand how much you want to be away from here. To be more angry.'

'I could be angry. Do you want me to be?'

'No.'

'As far as I understand, your house is to be my new jail, and you're to be my new jailer. Is that right?'

'I suppose,' said Anna Petrovna, and laughed.

'An experienced convict, when he's moved to a new prison, will say and do as little as possible until he's explored the new surroundings and found out how tough the guards are. That's any convict, including the dangerous ones.'

'Are you dangerous?'

'Yes,' said Samarin. Anna glanced at him to see if he was smiling, but if he was it was hidden.

A wet, icy presence touched the back of Anna's neck, in among the soft down between the tendons, where the spine begins. It was snowing. A flake landed on her eye and she blinked and kept her eyes open though it stung. She lifted her head to watch the grey bits come spinning out of the white sky towards them. A piece of snow rested on her mouth. She licked it off and tasted the grainy, rainy, travelled taste of cloud.

They went into the yard through the back gate. Alyosha was striking poses and mimicking the clash of steel with a wooden sabre in his hand, a peeled stick with a crosspiece he had lashed on himself. Anna called to him and he ignored her. She called again more sharply. He turned, ran towards them, and with his arm stretched out touched Samarin's breastbone with the tip of his sabre.

'Surrender!' he said.

Samarin put his hands in the air.

'Coward!' said Alyosha.

Anna took him by the shoulders and pushed him away, scolding him for being rude.

'This is Kyrill Ivanovich, a student,' she said. 'He'll be staying with us for a time. He's walked here from the Arctic. He escaped from a very cruel prison camp. So behave yourself. Be nice to him.'

Alyosha looked into Samarin's face. His pride didn't know what to do with this information. 'My father fought in the cavalry,' he informed Samarin. 'He died near Ternopol. They sent us a telegram. He killed seven Germans before they cut him down. There should've been a medal but it never came. Some of the Czechs have medals. Do you have a medal?'

'Here,' said Samarin, squatting down so his head was at Alyosha's level and tapping a small scar on one knuckle. 'This was awarded to convict first rank Samarin, Kyrill Ivanovich, for meritorious conduct on the march from prison, when he fought off hunger, thirst, cold and wild beasts with nothing but his wits and his faithful knife. Despite having to walk one thousand miles through the tundra and the taiga to reach the nearest settlement, convict Samarin remained cheerful, often stopping to share a joke or a friendly word with a passing elk or deer. Each morning, after a vigorous routine of exercise, he'd sing national songs and recite the catechism. He bathed in running water twice a day, breaking the ice as necessary with rocks and a system of levers of his own devising. In the early days of the march he'd pass the coldest days, when the birds fell dead from the trees, by wrapping his clothes in a bundle, fastening them to his head and running naked through the snow, performing elementary Greek gymnastics as he went.'

'What're Greek gymnastics?' said Aloyosha. A snowflake landed on the end of his nose and he blew it off with a puff of breath from his pushed-out lower jaw, not taking his eyes off the newcomer.

'Like this,' said Samarin, and he straightened up, bent forward, planted his hands on the ground, kicked his legs into the air and balanced on his hands for a moment, head down, feet up, before flexing his elbows and springing upright again.

'I can do that!' said Alyosha, dropping his sword and preparing to hurl himself at the snowy mud.

'Don't!' said Anna and 'Wait!' said Samarin, at the same time. While Anna laughed Samarin put his hand on Alyosha's shoulder and said: 'First you have to learn to tame wolves so they run alongside you in the moonlight and protect you from the blizzards with their bodies, and train bears to bring you fish and berries. You should be able to make beavers fell trees when you make a clicking sound in your throat, like this.' Samarin's Adam's apple bobbed as he clicked in his throat.

'You're lying,' said Alyosha doubtfully. 'You can't make them do that.'

'You can. You can make shoes and clothes from birch bark, sewn with braided reeds and a needle fashioned from a splinter of mammoth ivory. You can drink liquor distilled from birch sap and the juice of rowanberries. And you know how you can make light at night in the taiga?'

Alyosha shook his head. Samarin leaned forward to whisper in his ear: 'Capture an owl and make it fart.'

Alyosha giggled. 'Where do you get the flame from?'

'Pine resin, young fir cones, and marten-skulls,' said Samarin, counting them off on his fingers. 'I could show you.'

'You couldn't light our stove that way. It's hard. You need matches.'

'It's easier with matches, of course,' said Samarin.

Alyosha poked in the dirt with the point of the stick. 'Come onto the roof of the byre,' he said. Samarin and Anna followed him. With their help the boy dragged the ladder out past the cow Marusya and set it up by the door. Alyosha led the way to the roof, where the fuzz of moss on the boards was already slippery with melted snow. They saw the sky was falling on Yazyk, the grey scourings turning white when they reached the ground and flying across the face of the forest, dimming the perimeters of the world with rushing grains. As the blizzard thickened, the world shrank, and the bell tower of the derelict church, the common grazing and the trees disappeared.

Anna left them there and went indoors to the warmth, the stuffy smell of heated wood, cloth and down. It would be dark soon. She heard Alyosha shouting in the yard and Samarin moaning like a bear that he'd been hit. She went to the kitchen, took a stool and opened the larder. She took a squat half-litre jar down from a high shelf and wiped the dust and cobwebs off. The jar had the dark lustre of a lake on a clear night. She took off the lid and spooned blueberry jam into three dishes. The berries subsided comfortably into the sweet ooze. She glanced over her shoulder and licked the spoon clean, shivering from the tartness of the acid.

Alyosha brought Samarin back, the boy stomping in, bright with cold, shedding straws of packed snow, throwing his hat on a chair, the convict behind him, tall and wary. Anna had lit the lamp in the parlour, and the three of them sat down without speaking. Anna poured tea and handed the man and the boy jam spoons as if she was giving out ten-kopeck prizes.

Out

The rail track from Yazyk to the bridge ran level through the trees for seven miles before beginning to climb towards the heights through which the gorge ran. For the first part of the journey Nekovar and Broucek worked the pumping handles on the hand trolley by themselves. Mutz sat in the front between coils of rope, his feet dangling over the edge, one hand on the brake. When they hit the gradient the labour of working the trolley slowed them down. Mutz took off his greatcoat and joined Broucek on the handle, facing the way they were going. Nekovar stood facing them, working the other handle.

'Broucek, what about these muscles? The shoulder muscles?' asked Nekovar. 'Are they important? Do women like them?' Broucek didn't answer. 'Has a woman ever stroked your shoulder muscles before agreeing to sleep with you? Did she become aroused? Did her pupils dilate? Did her breathing become more rapid?'

'It's going to snow,' said Broucek.

'Maybe,' said Mutz.

'Tell me, Broucek,' said Nekovar. 'What if the female erotic machinery was wound tight by the pressure of the man's muscles, so tight that her soft outer hide began to palpitate and heat up with the tension as it strained against the unreleased mechanism, causing the nipples to harden and lubrication to be released into the mouth of her lower valve, which the rigid male member would then slide easily into, triggering the release of her coiled sexual spring and causing her body and limbs to shake and move with violent energy, which in turn –'

'Stop,' said Mutz. 'Stop the poetry.'

'No, brother,' said Nekovar. 'Just trying to understand from a master how they work.'

'They're not alarm clocks,' said Mutz.

'I know women are not alarm clocks,' said Nekovar. 'I understand how alarm clocks work. I can use alarm clocks. I can repair them. I could even make one. I'm a practical man and I'm trying to improve myself. Do you understand how women work, brother?'

'No.'

'Well, brother, not all of us have given up trying.'

'You frighten the girls in the public houses,' said Broucek, without malice. 'Men who wear glasses take them off before they start fondling the girls. But you put a pair of glasses *on*, you roll up your sleeves, and you kneel over them and start turning them this way and that and testing their insides with your finger and seeing how they jump and squeal like you were repairing a broken motorcycle engine.'

'How else can I understand the mechanism?'

'It's not a mechanism!' said Broucek, beginning, after years of acquiring patience, to lose it.

'Lads,' said Mutz. 'Lads. The tunnel.'

The tunnel leading to the bridge was on a long shallow incline and the trolley built up speed with Nekovar and Broucek resting at the pumping bar. They came out onto the bridge, Mutz pulled on the brake lever and the trolley stopped with a spray of sparks. A cold wind blew down the gorge and the clouds were yellowing. At the mouth of the tunnel were the remains of a horse. Scavengers had been. Its bones had been stripped clean overnight and the mane and tail left as blood-dirty black tassels on a grinning empty rack.

Nekovar fastened a rope to one of the girders and let the free end fall through the hatch, pulling the coils after it. Mutz went first, leaning back against the rope to slow himself and kicking off the rockface. Halfway down he stopped, stretched his neck to look more closely at the rock, reached out a finger to touch it, nearly lost the rope, regained control and descended to the riverbank. Where the banks steepened and narrowed under the bridge the noise of the river was as loud as the breathing of a million souls together and the currents were chopped and broken into sharp stubby waves.

The bodies lay at the water's edge near where the trees began. A strip had been cut from Lajkurg's right foreleg and flies were laying eggs on the carcass. Otherwise the horse was whole and untouched, its very eyes unpecked. Nor had Lukac, the dead soldier, been gnawed by scavengers overnight. He didn't lie where he'd fallen. His greyed, swelling body lay at right angles to the river, boots touching the water's edge, arms by his sides. His right hand had been severed, then placed next to the stump, knuckles upwards. On the corpse's stomach was something wrapped in a rag. Mutz looked back at the bridge. Broucek had come off the end of the rope and Nekovar was halfway down. Mutz signalled to Broucek to unshoulder his gun and watch the forest.

Mutz leaned down and picked up the package. It was damp. He heard Broucek pull back the bolt of his rifle and push a cartridge into the breech. The package was stiff and weighty. Mutz squeezed it. A stench of old meat breathed outwards and the package resisted under his fingers. Mutz opened the cloth. A human thumbnail set in a grey darkening stinking human thumb pointed at him. Mutz said 'Fick!' in his throat and dropped the package. He rubbed his palms furiously on his breeches and washed his hands in the river.

It was a third hand, a putrid half-crab with incurled fingers and the tendons standing out pale under the taut knuckleskin like the yellow core of chicken feet. What had once been the plumpest parts of the hand, what palm readers call the Mount of Venus beneath the thumb and the Mount of Luna on the opposite edge, had been gnawed, the hardened hems of skin patterned ragged by teeth.

Broucek came over and looked down at the half-eaten hand, lying on the shingle, palm up.

'Look at the palm,' he said. 'Look at the length of the life line.'

'What does that mean?' said Mutz.

'It means long life and happiness.'

Mutz squatted down by the body of Lukac and studied the original severed hand, the one placed next to Lukac's wrist. The night's rain had wettened it yet it was grimier than the arm to which it belonged.

'Watch the trees,' said Mutz.

'What for?' said Broucek.

'I don't know.'

Nekovar came and stood back to back with Broucek. They turned their heads east and west and east and west, sweeping the forest tiered on the escarpments on either bank. The colour and geometry and motion outdetailed all their eyes together, the rowan berries plump scarlet on the branch, the yellow birch leaves flittering their pale and rich sides quickly in the wind, and the clumps of larch needles nodding. Between the colours the darkness did not stir.

'Did you hear something?' said Nekovar.

'No,' said Mutz. How did you bury a hand?

'I thought I heard a sound,' said Broucek. He was afraid. They all were.

A ragged scurf of crystal settled on Nekovar's sleeve and he said: 'Son of a bitch.' The first snow came dark and sparse and barely frozen out of the yellow sky yet soon they were all blotched with it like a quick lichen on their woollen tunics.

'Someone has been watching this place,' said Mutz. 'Lukac didn't fall standing to attention.'

'It could have been whoever cut off his hand who laid him out, then left,' said Nekovar. 'Hell, I hate to see snow falling on the lately departed.'

'Someone's been keeping the wolves from his body, and the crows from his eyes, right up to now,' said Mutz. 'Someone's close.'

'They didn't keep scavengers from chewing on that extra hand there, now did they?' said Nekovar.

'Wolves don't wrap their food,' said Broucek.

'The most dangerous scavenger here is the same as the most dangerous predator,' said Mutz, 'and it's got teeth enough, and it walks on two legs.'

Mutz and Nekovar fell silent. The snow touched their faces. Broucek whispered the Lord's Prayer to himself. Their muscles prickled at the sense of being meat for another man. In a dark place in the infinite taiga a cross-legged butcher bowed his crusted jaws to a flayed thigh, fist round separated white kneejoint, fist round separated white hipjoint. And so along more tangled needle-muffled paths through the larch labyrinth until all the choice cuts and soft parts were eaten and only a hand was left for nourishment.

'God forgive me if I'm showing disrespect for the dead,' said Nekovar, 'but if I was a cannibal, and down to the last hand,

and I came across a fresh corpse, and an entire horse, I'd make more of a feast than's been made here.'

Mutz nodded. Broucek raised his rifle, stopped back, sighted and said: 'There!'

Mutz and Nekovar followed the line of the gun into the trees above them. They couldn't see it.

'A white creature,' said Broucek. 'Merciful God, like the devil's own ghost.'

'What? A hare? A fox?' said Mutz.

'A man, in the shape of a man! Not a hundred metres away. White, with red eyes.'

'How could you see his eyes?'

'I can see,' said Broucek. 'I can't help but see well, I was born to it.'

They all saw the movement then. It was a quick paleness from shadow to shadow, large and lightmoving.

'Don't shoot,' said Mutz. 'Not until we know what it is.'

'What if there are ten of them?' said Nekovar.

A chip of stone snapped out of a rock close to where Mutz was standing and the air gasped with the passage of a bullet. After a moment they heard the shot. Mutz, Nekovar and Broucek ran for the cover of the trees. Two more shots followed them to the birches.

'On the bridge,' said Broucek. 'Reds.'

Mutz could see two or three figures moving along the bridge, but they were just faint black motions through the thickening snow.

'Can you tell?'

'I can see their pointed hats. Red stars,' said Broucek. 'I could take one out at least.' He lifted his gun.

'Don't,' said Mutz.

'They're taking the trolley.'

Mutz watched the trolley creep away from them towards the far end of the bridge, as if under its own power. The Reds were at most fifteen minutes from Yazyk by train, an hour by horse. Who knew what they wanted from the town? How easily he had come to think of Bolshevism as an invincible force whose plans were unknowable to its enemies, but which knew its own will perfectly. It was about will, the desire to struggle which migrated from cause to cause, leader to leader, people to people, without anyone being able to hold it. In the Reds, though, will had found a long resting place, able to lift up a giant made of millions of people which would walk the earth, shedding dead like hairs as it advanced, and sprouting new believers to replace them.

'We have to get back to Yazyk, and we can't go by the bridge,' said Mutz. 'The Reds aren't likely to move till tomorrow. We need to find a way up through the trees here, up the side of the gorge and over to the other side, and reach the railway line from there.'

'It's getting dark,' said Broucek. 'There's something terrible in among the trees.'

'We don't have a choice,' said Mutz. He took out his pistol and began to lead them further into the forest, away from the river.

Some snow reached the ground as snow and filled the margins between the rocks and the ground. The rest was caught in the trees above their heads and began to melt, casting heavy drops onto their uniforms, which were soon sodden. The forest hissed and pattered with falling water. Their boots sank into the floor of moss and rotten twigs and leafmould and made tiny cracking sounds as they broke old larch needles. The rocks were black and shiny with damp. Mutz had never felt so cold. He had left his greatcoat on the trolley. All he had besides his tunic, breeches, boots and hat was his pistol, which he hadn't cleaned for days. It was getting dark; he had no idea where they were going, except up.

The rocks began to thicken, and their vertical faces became higher, with fewer spaces between them. The trees themselves had to balance on thin crazed roots to grow. Mutz, Broucek and Nekovar began to use their hands as much as their feet. They climbed in short spurts; Broucek would cover them, while Mutz climbed with his gun in its holster and Nekovar with his rifle slung over his back. Then Broucek would climb while the others watched the woods and rocks around.

'Take my coat, brother,' said Nekovar to Mutz.

'I'm fine,' said Mutz.

'You're shivering, brother.'

'Shivering is good, it keeps you warm.'

His cold wet clothes chafed at his cold wet skin. Water had leaked into his boots through cracks in the leather. His hands burned as if the water in them was acid. He pressed his teeth together to stop them chattering. The spongy patch of ground under his feet, chill and damp as it was, would be comfortable to lie on. He wondered if Nekovar had brought food with him.

Broucek hissed from above that it was time for them to climb.

'I can't see anything,' whispered Mutz. The snow had stopped but it was completely dark.

'In front of you. Between the rocks, a space, and stones like steps. That's it. Climb. Damn! I can see him.'

'Don't shoot!' said Mutz. 'What do you see?'

'The white creature. He's been shadowing us.'

'Wait till we get up.' Mutz climbed up through the narrow space, his shoulders squeezed by rock on either side. A trickle of icy water ran down Broucek's steps, which seemed to end in a blank wall. Mutz flapped his dead arms in front of him and found that the wall ended some way above his head. With an effort he grasped the ledge and squirmed his way up the chimney of rock, bracing his feet and shoulders against the sides. When his elbows were in the dirt and gravel he felt Broucek grasp him and help him up. They reached down together to drag Nekovar up after them.

'Let's go on,' said Mutz.

'I can't find a way,' said Broucek.

The ledge where they stood, about the size of a large room, had enough earth on it to be muddy and for a couple of spindly larches to grow. It was enclosed by sheer walls of rock, with no safe footholds for night. In the distance below they could hear the sound of the river. A light shining briefly out of cover showed where the Reds had made their position on the bridge. They couldn't go up; they couldn't go down.

'We're here till first light,' said Mutz. Saying it, he began to shiver again, squatted down and wrapped his arms round his knees.

'You won't last the night without shelter,' said Nekovar. 'Take my coat.'

'I won't take it.'

'Take it. I'm going to do some exercise.' Mutz let him drape the soaking heavy coat over his trembling shoulders and wondered if his body was too cool for it to help. He heard Nekovar begin to work at the larches with his hatchet.

'Our white friend?' said Mutz.

'Gone,' said Broucek. 'Can't see him.'

'Do you have any food?'

'No.' Broucek squatted down beside him. 'I wish I was in the shtab at Yazyk.'

'Aim higher,' said Mutz. 'You'll be home next year, drinking beer and eating pork knuckle and dumplings with mustard sauce.'

'It hurts when you say that.'

Mutz tried to focus on the sound of Nekovar's hatchet, the only report from any of his senses which contradicted his urge to sleep. If he slept, like Samarin on the frozen river, he wouldn't wake up. Broucek was asking him something irritating, in the way that it required thought. Broucek was asking about the hands.

'What do you think?' said Broucek. 'The cannibal arrives at the bridge at the same moment a train comes across, and the accident with the horses.'

'He arrives at the bridge,' muttered Mutz. 'Carrying his victim's hand. Not the choicest cut. It's the last of his supply.'

'But if he sees the train, and the horses, he understands he's reached civilisation. Why doesn't he throw the hand away, pretend he never had it?'

Mutz struggled to keep his eyelids open. The darkness danced for him and his bones ached. He was moving in and out of a dream. Thinking about the cannibal he found himself watching as he walked along the riverbank towards the bridge, then he was the cannibal, the Mohican, presumably, watching the train. Then Broucek was shaking his shoulder, telling him not to sleep, and the hacking of Nekovar's hatchet.

'I do – he does throw it away,' said Mutz. 'It's the only thing keeping him from starvation in the wilderness, his hard-won piece of meat. He earned it honourably: one of two had to die, and it wasn't him. And then he sees the bridge. He sees the train. And the package he's carrying becomes, in that moment, the most vile, hideous, evil burden that any unfortunate ever came to possess. A murdered man's hand, with his own teethmarks in it. Of course he throws it away. Too soon.'

Broucek began to speak. Mutz, awake now, interrupted him. 'Wait. He becomes afraid that the hand will be found. Perhaps he throws it in the river. What if it's washed up? What if it could be linked to him? He can't find the hand he threw away. But there's another hand there. The dead man, Lukac. He cuts one of Lukac's hands off and buries it in the forest where it will never be found. Then, if his original victim's hand is found, it won't appear that some monster in the forest has eaten an entire human being.'

'Why –'

'He was being watched. Not from the bridge, from the forest. The white creature, perhaps. Another man of some kind. We don't believe in ghosts, or Siberian gorillas, do we? The watcher recovered both hands, placed them there on Lukac's body, and kept watch over Lajkurg. Why did he, or they, do that? They knew someone like us would come. They thought we might end up in the forest. And here we are.'

Nekovar came over with bundles of larch twigs which he spread on the ground, under the rockface. He leaned stretches of trunk against the rockface and spread branches across and between them to form a roof. They crawled inside and huddled together. Freezing rain began to fall and Nekovar cursed. More snow might have settled on the roof but the rain leaked through, soaking them again, and gusts of wind began to tear at the shelter. Mutz decided he would not fall asleep. It seemed to him it was getting easier to stay awake, which was good, because if he closed his eyes, he was unlikely ever to open them again. He felt light and alert. He was already asleep. He was already dreaming.

Causes

Anna made soup and potatoes for Samarin and Alyosha while they brought logs in from the pile outside and stacked them by the stove. Anna heard few words from Samarin while Alyosha talked on about his dead teacher, the Czechs, the cow, how he'd tasted pineapple once, and how in Mexico, the dogs were bald. Samarin restarted him with a question every so often. During the meal Samarin hardly spoke, not to thank her, or to ask why she'd agreed to let him be a guest in her house. He ate quickly, but not greedily. When she asked if he would like more, he said yes, and held out his bowl. While they were eating, she watched him. He would catch her eyes and hold them for a second or two before he looked down at his food again. He seemed more at peace than a man from such a prison camp would be, yet he kept arrogance out of his face. Nor was there humility. When he looked at her it was expectant. It was an opportunity for her to say or ask anything she liked, whenever she was ready, which was more delicate a courtesy than thanks, and more intimidating. The more so because he knew, without impatience, that she would ask. His eyes didn't show curiosity so much as a readiness to devote all of him inside which thought, breathed and felt to whatever she said now. At other times, with other men, she would have found this waiting silence tiresome, and she didn't understand why it was different now, unless there was something fascinating to her in his face, something which promised, not that she could see it but she would be able to see it if only she caught it at the right angle, which she was bound to soon.

'Would you like a cigarette?' said Anna. Samarin said he would and they lit up. Anna took Alyosha to bed, made him take a big draw on her cigarette to keep his lungs clear of infections, read him a page of *Tsar Sultana*, kissed him good-night, blew out the candle and went down to Samarin, who was turning the pages of a St Petersburg weekly.

'That's two years old,' said Anna, nodding at the magazine. 'Would you like some cognac?'

'Yes,' said Samarin.

'It's all I have,' said Anna. 'There's nothing sweet to go with it.'

'I don't like sweets.'

Anna poured two tumblers and sat opposite him at the kitchen table. Anna hesitated, then, seeing Samarin wasn't going to make a toast, raised her drink and said: 'To liberation!'

'Liberation,' said Samarin, and touched his tumbler against hers. He didn't knock the drink back. He drank half the tumbler and placed it down.

'When you talked about the Mohican today,' said Anna, 'you spoke as if you admired him, even though he was a murderer. Even though he was making ready to eat you.'

'Is it worse to know somebody is planning to kill you, or to know they're going to kill you and eat you afterwards? Does what happen afterwards matter?'

Anna thought about it for a while. 'Yes, of course,' she said. 'It's worse to believe that your companion thinks of you as nothing but food. That's worse than being his enemy. Then you would know, at least, that he still thought of you as a man.'

'As far as food is concerned,' said Samarin, 'I say this not out of any disrespect for your late husband, but I'm sure you've heard the expression "cannon fodder." I believe it's worse to feed hundreds of thousands of men you don't know to the guns than to feed one man you know to yourself.'

'That can't be right!' said Anna. For some reason, she felt like laughing, not at Samarin, but at the world and the absurdity of reasoning in it.

'Wait,' said Samarin, raising his hands a little. He didn't gesture much. 'Of course I was afraid of the Mohican. I did long to believe that we'd become too close for him to use me in that way, and the more close it seemed to me we were, the more terrifying my imagining the moment when he would turn on me. But out there on the river, when we ran and the whole of nature was trying to kill us with cold, and even before, in the camp, where he was protecting me and fattening me up, the comfort I drew from thinking of him as a father was greater than the horror I felt at the thought of him as my butcher. Don't you think it would have been the same for Isaac? Abraham's son?' There was a new edge to Samarin's voice, as if, now, he was trying to persuade her of something, although she couldn't think what it might be. 'Isaac knew his father was going to kill him, yet he trusted him, and believed him, and loved him to the last.'

'That was different,' said Anna. 'Abraham was listening to God, and Isaac knew that, as far as I can remember. The Mohican was just a criminal, a thief. He didn't have a greater cause. Only staying alive.'

'*Is* just a criminal,' said Samarin. 'You said "was". Remember, I believe he's in Yazyk. He might be listening. Outside.'

'Good, now tell me how the Mohican can be like Abraham.'

'Do you believe in God?'

'If there is one then he's a fool.' Anna spoke more sharply than she'd meant to. Now it would be obvious to Samarin that she had a personal grudge. But he made no comment.

'So, you don't really believe in God, yet you believe Abraham believed, and that made it right for him to sacrifice his son? That gave him a cause?'

'No,' said Anna. 'A God which demands such sacrifices is a God not worth listening to. I – I know people who have . . . shed their own flesh and blood for God and it hurts so much, so much more and further than the pain of the wound. But I don't see what this had to do with the Mohican. You never said he was religious. You never said he was sick in the soul.'

'Perhaps,' said Samarin slowly. 'Perhaps a time will come when you'll hear more about all the things he's done.'

'What do you mean?' said Anna.

Samarin said nothing, he sat back in his seat with his eyes a little wide and his lips pressed together. Looking at him Anna's insides hollowed, her scalp prickled and she had an unpleasant feeling that he was holding himself prisoner. She wanted it to stop. She drank back the rest of her cognac, got up, filled their tumblers, drank a little more of hers, left the bottle on the table, and it did stop. She left her right hand resting on the table too, close to her tumbler. Samarin had regained control of himself. The sense of horror was fading and she wondered if she'd imagined it. Samarin leaned forward, put his hand on hers, and asked if he could address her with the familiar 'ty'. She nodded and flexed her fingers so they wove in between his.

'You're right,' said Samarin. 'The Mohican had no cause except his own. I said so this morning. What I wonder is this. If not thieving, if not God, is there any cause which would justify a man butchering and eating his companion in the wilderness? We're not talking about lots here, about those stories of shipwrecked or Arctic explorers who decide by chance among themselves who has to die in order that the others live. We're talking of a man who not only uses his own brute fighting strength to overpower his companion in order to eat him, but who raises the companion for that purpose, like a farmer fattening a hog.'

'I can't think of a cause that would justify that. Drink up.'

Samarin swallowed his drink, gently unlocking his fingers from Anna's. Anna filled their glasses again. His taking away his hand had startled her and his putting his hand on hers had not.

Samarin said: 'Supposing a man, the cannibal, knew that the fate of the world rested on whether he escaped from prison or not. Suppose this. He's a man so dedicated to the happiness of the future world that he sets himself to destroy all the corrupt and cruel functionaries he can, and break the offices they fester in, till he's destroyed himself. Suppose he's realised that politics, even revolution, is too gentle, it only shuffles people and offices a little. It isn't that he *sees* the whole ugly torturing tribe of bureaucrats and aristocrats and moneygrubbers who make the people suffer. It's that they fall to him and his kind like a town falls to a mudslide. He's not a destroyer, he is destruction, leaving those good people who remain to build a better world on the ruins. To say he's the embodiment of the will of the people is feeble, a joke, as if they elected him. He *is* the will of the people. He's the hundred thousand curses they utter every day against their enslavement. To hold such a man to the same standards as ordinary men would be strange, like putting wolves on trial for killing elk, or trying to shoot the wind. You can pity the innocent man he butchers, if he is innocent. But the fact the food comes in the form of a man is accidental damage. It's without malice. What looks like an act of evil to a single person is the people's act of love to its future self. Even to call him a cannibal is mistaken. He's the storm the people summoned, against which not all good people find shelter in time.'

'Was the Mohican like this?' said Anna.

'I only ask you to imagine the existence of such a man,' said Samarin. Anna was a little tipsy. She knew that. Her imagination was blurred. Samarin's imaginary terrorist–revolutionary–cannibal didn't frighten her as it might have done had she been sober and she'd been able to see him sharp and daylit in her mind, blood around his mouth, looking up. As he spoke to her Samarin's voice grew warm and quick and his eyes made her important, which she liked more than she disliked the words he spoke.

'Your imaginary cannibal sounds terribly vain,' she said. She ran the tip of her index finger over Samarin's knuckles. There was no price to be paid by anyone for such a small act of touch. She began to play with his fingers. 'Men shouldn't be making blood sacrifices for things they can't know, like God, or the people,' she said.

'Are there to be no ideals?'

'I thought you were the cynical one. Let's talk about something else. Come through to the parlour.'

Samarin followed Anna. He asked her: 'Tell me about Lieutenant Mutz. Is he a friend of yours?'

The Avakhi

Mutz woke up from a shallow intricate dream. He was on a hard dirt floor and a fire at his feet was down to embers. He was in an enclosed space; the air was still, there was a faint reflected glow above his head and from either side, and there was a smell of woodsmoke and drying wool.

'He's awake,' said Broucek. Mutz put his hands on the ground and pushed himself into a sitting position, with his back to rock and his boots still pointed to the fire. They were in a cave. The fire glowed at the cave mouth. Sitting cross-legged by the fire and staring into it was a man Mutz could not see clearly, but it was not Broucek or Nekovar, who seemed to be on either side of him.

'Who's that?' he said.

'The white creature,' said Broucek. 'We couldn't wake you.'

'An aboriginal?'

'Tungus,' said Nekovar. 'A boy with pale skin and white hair.'

'Does he speak Russian?'

'Yes,' said the man by the fire. Now that Mutz could see him more clearly he could see he was as Samarin had described him, between a boy and a man, and hair as white as the moon. A pair of home-made goggles, the eyepieces covered in some dark woven filament, was pushed up on his forehead, and he wore a deerskin coat, leggings and boots. He held an old muzzle-loading rifle across his knees.

'We were trying to rouse you,' murmured Nekovar in Mutz's

ear. 'And somebody started dropping larch cones on us. We look up, and see the aboriginal's head, poking out of the rocks. Broucek was all for shooting him but I stopped him. I could see it was a Tungus, not some forest monster, and just a lad, and excuse me for saying so, but you weren't going to last without warmth and shelter, brother. So I asked him if he had a fire. He reached down his hand and pulled me up into an opening in the rocks above that ledge where we got stuck. Even Broucek hadn't seen it in the dark. Between the three of us we managed to haul you up there and then it was an easy hundred-metre climb to his cave.'

'The Reds will see the fire,' said Mutz. He felt weak, but clear-headed and grievously hungry. His bones ached as the warmth returned. That was foolish, forgetting his coat. He wasn't built as solidly as Broucek and Nekovar to begin with, and there was nothing to be done about that, except to be cleverer. He was grateful to them but the gratitude was a burden, too.

'The cave faces the other way,' said Nekovar.

'We're grateful,' said Mutz, raising his voice to speak to the albino. 'Do you have any food?'

The albino reached down and passed over a dirty cotton drawstring pouch with dried reindeer meat in. Mutz chewed some. It was too hard to chew; it might as well have been cow hide. He let it sit in his mouth and soften and sucked it every so often. It was a reminder of food.

'Your shaman's dead,' said Mutz.

'I know,' said the albino.

'How do you know?'

'You just told me.'

Broucek laughed.

'Wait,' said Mutz, putting his hand on Broucek's shoulder and continuing to speak to the albino. 'You travel with him, don't you? I don't want to trouble you with questions, but there's something here about another man which is important to us. Why were you and the shaman travelling so far south, separately?'

'Our Man leaves me in the forest. He goes ahead, to the town. One month, he tells me.'

'Yazyk?'

'Yes.'

'For drink?'

'Not only. He wants a horse. He says: "Come in a month."'

'What did he mean, he wanted a horse?'

'He sees them, and he wants one. He wants to reach the Upper World. The deer, he says, are too slow for me. I'm too big, he says. I need a horse to ride to the Upper World, me and the drink together. He says: "If I haven't returned in a month, come and get my body."'

'But you could have gone together.'

'Yes.'

'Why didn't you?'

'I'm afraid.'

'Afraid of what?'

'Of the avakhi.'

'All Europeans are avakhi to you, aren't they?'

'No!' The albino looked up from the fire, and the red of his eyes took the glow of the embers. 'This is not a name like for all of you. This one *is* avakhi. This one is a demon. He is from the Lower World. We see him. We see him, and he hunts us.'

'You saw him?'

'In the forest.'

'What was he doing?'

'He kills his friend. He kills him, and bleeds him. He hangs him up on the tree. He takes off his friend's clothes. He cuts him open from here to here, takes out his liver, and eats it while it is still warm, like he kills a deer.'

Nekovar and Broucek shifted in the back of the cave and invoked the protection of God and all the saints.

'Was there a fight?' said Mutz.

'No. We follow them and see it all. But he sees us.'

'What did you see?'

'The two are walking together downstream, by the river. They eat all the food they carry on their backs. They are hungry. They don't know how to hunt. The avakhi falls behind. Both of them walk slowly. They are tired. The avakhi lifts his head. The other European does not see it. The avakhi pulls out a knife. The other does not see it. The avakhi is not tired. He makes it seem he is. He jumps forward, once, like a dog, again, like a bear. The sound of his feet on the ground makes the other look round. He sees the avakhi. He raises his hands. The avakhi is on him. One arm pulls his head back. The other arm draws the knife across his throat. All the blood is let out. The weight of the avakhi's body throws the other to the ground. The avakhi licks his knife. He hangs the corpse of his friend against a tree trunk. He butchers him. He cuts up every part. He hangs it all high in a birch tree to dry, the jointed legs and arms and the meat cut from the ribs. While it dries he lives off the innards of his friend. He buries the head and ribs. We watch him for days. He is not afraid. He thinks no people are near him. He lights fires.'

'Why didn't you stop him?' said Mutz.

'Why should we?'

'Then why did you watch him?'

'The shaman didn't see a creature from the Lower World before. Not without mushrooms. Maybe he'll drop something we can use. It's not our business when a man eats his friend.

If he wants to eat one of us, it's different. Then we offer him to buy a deer instead. There are many deer nearby. The avakhi can't smell them. This is strange, for an avakhi.'

Mutz felt the stillness of the Czechs on either side of him. They had been surprised and properly nauseated at the revelation of an act of cannibalism in their boundless, temporary Siberian parish, but they were used to it already. It was like a story in the yellow press, always lit up as something that had never happened before, and being modern, progressive men, Nekovar and Broucek had enjoyed that lighting for a moment, and now they were ready for something else, because the novelties of this age of wonders came with the assurance that just as such things had never happened before, they were certain to happen again. What made him ask more questions, when he was so feverish, dizzy and hungry, aching like a rheumatic? So perhaps it wasn't the Mohican who had tried to eat Samarin, but Samarin who had successfully escaped the penal colony with the Mohican in his belly. Deep within himself Mutz turned in shame from the discovery that he considered it a tiny increment of advantage for his class, the intellectual eating the criminal, rather than the other way round. Still he yearned to prove Samarin's guilt. The structures of Russia had altered, fractured and collapsed, but not so far that they could not rig up a tribunal to try a cannibal, at least. Where three gathered together, be they a rabbi, a Cossack and a Bolshevik, be they a castrate, a widow and a Czech Jewish officer, they could agree that nothing justified that. Could they not? Samarin was safely under lock and key until Mutz returned but now he might be able to persuade Matula he should remain imprisoned. If the Reds held off. What was attractive was the opportunity to show Anna Petrovna what kind of a man the student convict was: a liar, a murderer, and a maneater. The lying would hurt her most. Again, he recognised the malice in himself, and the endless reckoning of scores and balances, and recoiled from it. Was a man to be admired because he recognised the wickedness latent in himself, and knew to keep it hidden, and mainly contained, or did right conduct demand that the wickedness should not even be there? Burn it out. Like Balashov. Not that. That was not the place where it rested. Not there.

'How did he find you were watching him?' said Mutz.

'One morning he's not there, at his camp where he sleeps, where he feeds on human guts. Sometimes at night we see him waving fire at wolves. Now he's not moving. We don't see him. We see his friends' limbs and chest meat hanging. The meat is dry now. When the wind blows the pieces move. Our Man says he'll eat mushrooms. When he eats the mushrooms he sees the avakhi clearly. He eats mushrooms and we wait. It's morning. Our Man is singing. I'm listening to his song. I eat a mushroom. We're travelling together, Our Man and me, down the road that leads to the Lower World. We meet the avakhi's friend. He's angry, because he's cut into pieces. "Look!" he says. "My arms are here, my legs are there, my head and chest are buried, my heart, liver, lungs, kidneys and other guts are all eaten. All I have is being eaten, and what's left is food for the wolves and crows. My spirit goes naked into the Lower World." Just then there's a sound like the sky breaking open and the avakhi is standing over us.'

'Was it a dream?' said Mutz. 'I want to understand. You took hallucinogenic mushroom and dreamed that you were in your hell, seeing the ghost of the dead man. Was Samarin – was the avakhi in your dream, or was he real?'

The albino nodded. 'Yes. He is with us there in the Lower World. He's angry. He is real. Eating his companion's guts has made him blind in the Lower World and he cannot see his companion's spirit there. He shouts at us. He waves his knife. His jaws are stained with blood. His teeth are sharp and black. His breath stinks of meat. He is as high as the sky. His knife is the size of a tree. It cuts the sun when he lifts it. Red clouds bleed from the sun. He says he'll kill us. He cannot see what we can see. He listens while Our Man tells the journey of his companion's spirit into the Lower World. He listens to Our Man tell how sad his companion's spirit is to be in the Lower World without a body. Our Man says to the avakhi: "Your friend is standing next to you. He is asking if he can have his body back. He says: "Take my arms and legs and chest meat off the tree, dig up my head and my ribs, and sew them together."

'The avakhi becomes more angry. His nails are like rusty picks. His teeth are like icicles. He takes Our Man. He pushes him to the ground. He kneels on his chest. He cuts in his forehead with his knife. He cuts the word LIAR in your language. Our Man cries. His third eye is blinded. The avakhi says that he kills us both if he sees us again. We leave the Lower World by separate paths. "Come for me in a month," Our Man says. "If I haven't returned. Now I need a horse to reach the Upper World." When I leave the Lower World, when the mushroom is finished, the avakhi is gone. He takes his meat with him. Our Man is gone. He cannot find the Upper World, you see. He's blind to it now. He cannot get there without a horse.'

'Did you see the avakhi by the river here?' said Mutz.

'I see him throw the last of his friend into the water. His hand. He cuts the hand off a dead soldier and buries it. He eats some of the horse. He climbs the bridge. He meets a man on the bridge. They leave. I fetch the hands –'

'What was he like, this man the avakhi met on the bridge?'

'Too far to see.'

'Does he have a name, a name in Russian, the avakhi?'

'Yes.'

'What is it?'

'I can't tell you. He kills me. He promises.'

Mutz reached inside his tunic to his shirt pocket and took out a small leather-bound notebook and a pencil. The edges of the pages were damp but the main part of the paper was dry.

'Can you make the fire brighter?' he said.

The albino blew on the embers and put some spiny green twigs on. There was a smell of resin and a crown of small flames poked out of the fire. Mutz got up. His head spun and he almost fell. He recovered and squatted by the fire. He held the open notebook on his knee, steadied it with one hand, and began to sketch with the other. He drew like an engraver, making series of parallel lines, cross-hatching them to make dark areas. Nekovar and Broucek came over to watch. Their mouths were slightly open. The flames reflected from their faces and cast more light on the paper. The albino did not look. He turned away to watch the darkness outside. For a quarter hour nobody spoke. There was the hissing and creaking of boiling resin from the fire, the scurrying sound of Mutz's pencil and the noise of the men's breathing.

Mutz finished and buffed the sketch with the edge of his hand.

'Good,' said Broucek. 'It's good. It's him.'

Mutz had drawn two heads of Samarin, each three-quarter face, one with his shaven head and no beard, the other with a full growth. He showed it to the albino, who did not look. Mutz touched him on the shoulder. The albino glanced at it and turned his head away as far as it would go.

'Please look,' said Mutz. 'Is this him? Is this the avakhi?'

The albino looked again. He sniffed. 'Yes,' he said.

Songs

Anna sat on the divan, leaving room for another. She put her tumbler and the bottle on the dresser and lit another cigarette. There weren't many left but she didn't smoke often. Samarin followed, took the cigarette she offered, bent his body to the match, and sat in an armchair on the other side of the room. A single lamp burned in the corner. It lit them equally but, it seemed to Anna, the play of shadows and surfaces made the light shine more brightly and obliquely on Samarin, emphasising the hollows of his cheeks and eyes. He had chosen to sit apart. Well, there was time. He was her captive. She would take his picture tomorrow. She took a sip of cognac and laughed.

'What's it like to be my prisoner?' she said.

'Comfortable,' said Samarin.

What had he asked about? 'You were asking me about Mutz. Did he say anything about me?'

'He was upset that I found a photograph of you someone dropped.'

'He used to visit me. He'd stay overnight.' Anna held her breath, trying to see if Samarin reacted to this. He didn't. 'It's lonely here for a woman. Do you think I'm a slut?'

'No.'

'I like a drink. I like company, sometimes. I like to like myself when I look in the mirror. I sing. So Mutz – he liked me, and that's the most attractive thing in anyone. He's kind. He has a good face. I don't mean handsome, though he is almost that, and I don't mean his face expresses good intentions, though it does. You can't separate the two; perhaps he'd be ugly without the good intentions, and look like an idiot without the well-made features. Perhaps what it means to be civilised is not to force yourself to like people however they look, but to force yourself to stop wondering whether the way they look makes any difference to whether you like them. He's clever. He knows so much about so many things. Yes, he's Jewish. Yes, a Jewish soldier in Russia is like a penguin in the desert. You know here, it matters less? Siberia. Any live human being is exotic here. Would I have had the strength to take a Jewish husband to Europe, to deal with the slanders and suspicions of his people and my people and, what, bricks through the window, I suppose? I don't know. Perhaps that would have made me love him. But I didn't, not here. I'm not sure why. It's not that he's Jewish. He's not religious. He's an outsider among the Czechs, but it's more that he seems German, to them, than Jewish. It doesn't matter to some of them that he speaks Czech better than they do. They think of him as German. And in some sense, perhaps, they're right. Even now, even here, he inhabits a place that doesn't exist any more, an empire of all sorts of languages and nationalities, but where the rules were in German, and they spoke German in the offices, where the trains ran in German. He worked as an engraver in a firm in Prague which printed share certificates in that empire. All in German. I don't mean there's anything wrong with German, I mean he was attached to that world of a certain order. Attached in a way we mustn't be to organisations, but men so often are. His empire was kind to him and he was unhappy that it died. I think he was disappointed that the Austrian empire hadn't become an Austrian United States. It unsettled me that behind his sense of order, of the right way of doing things, his need to put everything in its place and understand who was doing what to whom, was this set of laws and manners from a world which no longer existed. I was angry when the Czechs shot the teacher. We called him the teacher, he was an exile who taught Alyosha to read and write and count. Of course Josef was angry too, but he said something I could never forgive him for. He said: "We have such stupid rules." As if the rules were the point, and not the shooting. Do you see?'

'Yes, I see,' said Samarin.

'He was nice, though. He is nice. He could never talk to Alyosha like you. He lost his whole family when he was a child, in the strangest way. I don't mean lost as in they died. Lost. Mislaid. His parents and brothers and sisters emigrated to the States when he was very young, and at the last minute he fell ill. His family had their passage booked, they had very little money, they left Josef behind with an uncle and went, with the plan that he would join them later. And the family arrived in America, and disappeared. Who knows what happened to them? Perhaps they died in a fire, or a railway accident. Perhaps letters were mislaid; a misunderstanding of the American way of writing addresses. Ten years after they left, when he was twenty, Josef went to America to look for them. He spent three months searching around Chicago. He didn't find them. Even so everyone was surprised that he came back to Prague.'

Anna stopped, taken by a feeling she'd been talking too much. She was on the way to being drunk and Samarin was sitting there with deep listening eyes, which seemed to get deeper the more she filled them with her rambling thoughts. She would have another drink, and so would he. He would sort her many stories into one. He had that power. She got up and refilled his glass and her own, and sat back down. She crossed her legs and uncrossed them to make him look at her legs, and he did.

She wondered if he was really clean. She wondered if she cared.

'It was strange you finding that photograph,' she said. 'I made a present of it to one of the local men. Gleb Alexeyevich Balashov. He runs the store on the square. He pestered me for a picture for so long, and then he went and lost it.'

Samarin nodded. 'You were generous to let him have such a photograph.'

Anna blushed and said quickly: 'Balashov's sweet, but very devout. You do know they're not really Orthodox in this town, don't you?'

'I didn't know.'

'I'm sorry I don't have a gramophone. We should have some music.'

'You have a guitar over there.'

'It's out of tune.'

'We could tune it.'

'I play very badly.'

Samarin rose, picked up the guitar by the neck, swung the body into the crook of his arm, and ran his thumb across the strings. He came over and handed it to Anna.

'It's perfectly in tune,' he said. 'When you mentioned music, you must have wanted me to bring it to you. Play.'

'Well, sit down,' said Anna, nodding at the empty place in the divan beside her and setting the instrument on her lap. She played the open strings one by one and fiddled with the tuning keys. She felt his weight settling into the divan and blushed.

'I play very badly,' she said again.

'Everyone plays badly,' he said. She glanced at him. He sat leaning against the corner of the back of the divan with his hands behind his head, watching her and smiling. A small silver fish swam ticklishly up from her womb to her breast, leaving a trail of effervescence. She tried to hide from him the light of permission in her eyes and pressed her teeth gently into her lower lip to stop herself smiling too much.

She began to pluck the strings. It was a man's song she played for Alyosha and now she tried to sing it more gently, without the heavy marching rhythm.

The Most Honourable
Leavetaking, Esquire
We've been brothers long enough
To know which one's a liar
Letter in an envelope
No, wait, don't pull it out
Death'll give me longer
To see what love's about

The Most Honourable
Dearest Lady Luck
Sometimes you arrive in time,
Sometimes you get stuck.
An ounce of lead in your heart?
Hear your trigger finger's doubt:
Death'll give me longer
To see what love's about.

The Most Honourable
Your Majesty, Abroad
When you hug them tight like that
I know that you're a fraud
I see your nets of finest silk
Wait, just hear me out:
Death'll give me longer
To see what love's about.

Anna stopped and bowed her head and laughed. 'There are more verses, but I can't remember,' she said, while Samarin smiled and clapped. Anna presented the guitar to him.

'Now you play,' she said.

'I only know one song,' said Samarin.

'Well, it must be good.' Anna grinned. 'Play!'

Samarin rested the guitar on his knees and began to play, without any delaying business of tuning or strumming or fingers wandering up and down the fretboard. Samarin's song wasn't major or minor. She didn't know which key it was in. The key of earnest came into her head and she smiled.

Samarin sang:

To say the name of one star is enough
Among the worlds where night allows no spark
It's not because this star's the one I love
Because to me, all other stars are dark
It's not because this star's the one I love
Because to me, all other stars are dark

And if my heart is heavy in the night
I have another praise of her to give
It's not because with her there is more light
But that with her, I don't need light to live
It's not because with her there is more light
But that with her, I don't need light to live.

Anna jumped up and clapped, sat down and ran her hand quickly over the side of Samarin's head and his shoulder.

'Another one!' she said.

'I told you, I only know that one.'

'Play it again!'

The Reds

The Czechs slept in shifts around the fire for two hours each. When Nekovar woke him Mutz tried to curl up and turn away from the shaking hand. His head and his body felt as if they were falling apart from each other through surfaceless space. Nekovar persisted and Mutz sat upright. His eyes seemed to have been salted and he was nauseous. The cold from outside the cave touched his neck insolently and the dizziness subsided. He told Nekovar to sleep and moved closer to the fire. The albino had brought more wood. Mutz piled it on. Outside it had begun to snow again. Broucek slept under his coat, resting his head on a rock for a pillow, and looked content. The albino cushioned his head with his clasped hands. Even asleep, he seemed to be awaiting a blow. Had the shaman ill-treated him? Mutz studied his own heart, the only instrument at his disposal for divining the morals of the dead, and concluded that the shaman had not. He wondered at how they, the Czechs, had treated the shaman so badly, and cared so little that he'd died, as if it had been his weakness for drink that had killed him, as if he had killed himself. You looked at the faces of the shaman and the albino, you knew their stories, how they sometimes feasted and were sheltered in furs, no doubt, but were sometimes cold and hungry and hunted and were hunted in the Siberian forest. And you thought: they're used to it. But that was how those who suffered less always thought about those who suffered more, that they were used to it, that they no longer felt it as you did. Nobody ever got used to it. All they learned to do was to stop letting it show.

Once inflamed, the conscience puts out a steady heat, and guilt spreads. Mutz thought of Balashov, and felt another wave of nausea at how he had demanded he persuade his wife and child to leave his town forever. If he got back to Yazyk he would ask Balashov's forgiveness. He would do more. He would ask Balashov's advice. Who better to ask about Anna than her husband, who had loved her as a man, and now, as he claimed, loved her still, as a not-man? He would go to Balashov, humbly, and ask about love. They laughed at Nekovar, searching for the secret which would set women's sexual machinery in motion, but in his way, Nekovar was ahead of Mutz; at least he was asking.

He would make friends with Balashov. His enemies were Matula and Samarin, the twin poles of madness in Yazyk. Nothing could move forward while Matula prevented the Czechs going home and Anna remained infatuated with Samarin. It did not seem possible that a woman whose husband had castrated himself for God's sake would tolerate a lover who had murdered and eaten a fellow-convict. Mutz realised he was smiling. Those who commit the most extreme acts always laid themselves open not only to the most extreme punishments but also to the most extreme ridicule. The war was hardly over in Europe and already jokes about demobilised men whose balls had been blown to bits by bullets and shrapnel were flying round the northern hemisphere. What would the wives of such men do? In some ways, they were in a worse position than Anna Petrovna. No, it was not really very funny. And was it not possible that her husband's self-mutilation had inoculated her, in some sense, to the terrors that would grasp the imaginations of others at the story of cannibalism in the forest? Samarin might argue that, compared to Balashov's brutality to himself and his family in the name of a high ideal, his killing and eating of the Mohican was self-preservation. A criminal such as the Mohican could have been hanged. Somewhere west of Vladivostok and east of San Francisco a subscription society would exist of enthusiasts campaigning for criminals to be eaten. More modern, and less wasteful. In America they grilled them with electricity. No. It was not the cannibalism itself. It was what Samarin did afterwards, as described through the drug state of the albino, when he saw him standing over them in the daylit forest in the form of a demon on the fields of ash and clinker in the Tungus underworld. He carved letters onto a man's forehead. Mutz had seen them himself. Mutz had seen how Samarin was able to alter his front, how he had all his moods on a dial and hid the mood of the dialler. Still it was hard to credit him with such savagery. And if Samarin had killed and consumed the Mohican to secure his escape from the White Garden, who had murdered Kliment, and carved the letter on his forehead? Could there have been a third man in the forest?

All such questions of men and women known to Mutz now lay on the far side of an element which had altered since he had last encountered it, the Reds. Back in 1918 the Reds had been men who possessed an Idea. Now the Idea itself possessed men, and armoured trains, and land. From the little Mutz knew, men who had once possessed the Idea were still arguing about what the Idea was; and that was something the Idea, now that it possessed men and armoured trains and land of its own, was unlikely to tolerate for long.

He was awake. He shook Nekovar, Broucek and the albino. He asked the albino if he would come with them to Yazyk to collect the body of the shaman. The albino nodded sleepily.

'There's something we have to do first,' said Mutz. He looked at Broucek and Nekovar. The trust in their faces was terrifying. 'We have to go down to the Reds.'

'They'll string you up,' said Broucek. 'Shouldn't we go back to Yazyk first?'

'You'll do what Lieutenant Mutz tells you,' said Nekovar.

Mutz said: 'We can slip past them now, and back to Yazyk, but we can't escape from Yazyk without them. They hold the bridge.'

Broucek was thinking about it, still trusting, not avoiding Mutz's eyes, but waiting for more.

'They could attack Yazyk when they like, and kill us all,' said Mutz. 'We haven't the means to stop them, except to talk to them.'

'Let's go, brother,' said Nekovar. 'Only let's be sure we know why we're going. The Reds aren't all that's stopping us leaving.'

'No,' said Mutz. 'I'm glad you understand that. Do you understand, Broucek?'

Broucek was silent for a long time. Then he said: 'I'll kill him for you. I don't mind. It'd be like shooting a mad dog.'

'You're not doing this for me,' said Mutz. 'Don't ever think it's for me.' Even though it was. How easy treachery was when more than one man was already thinking of the same way of betrayal, and they opened their hearts at the same moment. Now he was seeing into Matula's soul because he was acquiring one like it. The convenience of a time and place between war and law, when a gun and a word was all it took to make a problem go away. How natural it had seemed to save Matula's life on the ice. How natural it seemed now to sell his carcass to the Reds. Mutz had a screaming urge to jump back inside the borders of a sensible nation, or an empire, such as he had once lived in, and slam the door on anarchy like this. But he could only do that now by making the anarchy wilder. Moses! The last thing you needed in the wilderness was ten commandments. That was for later.

The snow was falling in sparse, heavy, damp flakes. Mutz still had Nekovar's coat. It was unpleasant to leave the cave but the snow was not deep and the white ground made for easier navigation. They followed the albino down a shallow slope for a mile till they came to an outcrop above the railway line, a few hundred yards from the mouth of the tunnel. They could look down from the rocks to the line without being easily seen. The Red train stretched in dark rest from the tunnel. A squat dense apparatus poked up off a flat car coupled to the front of the locomotive: their artillery piece. Behind the locomotive tender were freight cars, flat cars with machine guns behind sandbags, and passenger wagons with windows, some dark, some showing lamplight. Mutz could smell coal smoke from the stoves in each wagon. Sentries in groups of three sat in greatcoats around small fires, rifles across their knees. The closest was a hundred yards away.

Mutz beckoned the others up.

'They're not ready to move,' whispered Nekovar. 'They're just keeping the locomotive from freezing, but it's not fired up. It'd take them two hours. They'll probably move at first light.'

'What are the wires for?' said Broucek. 'There are wires leading from the train to the telegraph line.'

'They must have a telegraph aboard the train,' said Nekovar.

'Maybe they have a restaurant too,' said Broucek.

'I'll bet they've got Red tarts on board,' murmured Nekovar. 'Communism's all about equal shares for all, isn't it, lieutenant, brother?'

'Yes,' said Mutz. 'Or they could just shoot you.'

They divided the party. Broucek and the albino would stay back, hidden, while Mutz and Nekovar went to parley. If the negotiators were well met, Broucek and the albino would leave and wait for them in a derelict railwayman's hut up the line, halfway to Yazyk. Mutz looked down at the train a last time. The snow had stopped falling and it was colder. Perforated clouds wound over the moon. The snow on the ground and on the branches of the trees was beginning to crust and glitter. The solid riveted bulk of the train and the circle of bright fires around it stretched out from the tunnel, out from the planetary web of rails and telegraph wires, like the feeler of the world's intelligence, groping in the darkness and chaos of Samarin's and Balashov's and Matula's void for something it might have lost. It was reaching for Mutz. In London and Paris and New York they saw the Reds as an anarchic, destructive, turbulent menace which demanded to be controlled. Here in the dark forest, looking into the circle of lights, Mutz saw only a new order, a new empire, coming to take its place among the old, and how he wanted to be inside the circle, and not outside, with the maneaters, handmade angels, narcophilic visionaries and Bohemian warlords. And how it was tearing him apart to know that Anna was outside that circle, and though she would hate this desolate place of madness as much as her wisdom told her, she found a source in it she couldn't do without. Even when the order of the new state flowed around her, as it was bound to, she would never tolerate for long a man who fled from the extremes they had encountered here so eagerly, who sought, even worse, to explain the extreme, and to cure it.

A wolf howled from far off in the forest behind them. Another joined, and a third. Some of the sentries turned. None got up. Mutz put his hand on Nekovar's shoulder. They looked at each other and nodded. Mutz took off his belt and holster with his pistol and gave them to the albino, who strapped them on with unexpected swiftness, and looked like a ghostly buccaneer. Nekovar gave his gun to Broucek and shyly embraced him. Mutz took out his once-white handkerchief. Nekovar produced and unfolded a piece of paper with what looked like a design sketch of an electrically-driven artificial woman on it. Raising these surrender flags above their heads, they climbed round the outcrop and out into the open snowfield, in full view of the sentries. The moon shone down bright.

No-one noticed them. Mutz drew a deep breath of freezing air and shouted: 'Don't shoot! We want to talk! Don't shoot!'

As his voice rolled across the snow, echoing slightly off the flank of the train, the sentries rose black and indignant. Mutz heard a snickering of rifle bolts froing and toing and the Red soldiers were running towards them, coat skirts billowing, rifles held out in front of them as if they were farmers running the devil to ground with pitchforks. Mutz suppressed the instinct to run and duck. He shouted 'Don't shoot!' again, and Nekovar added his voice.

A dozen Russians hemmed them in. They wore assorted civilian caps and shapkas and had red armbands over the sleeves of their greatcoats, which were British issue. Swollen and grim with entitlement, several were shouting at the Czechs to stretch their hands up even higher. Others were demanding to know who they were. Numerous hands were searching them, reaching into their pockets, removing documents, Matula money, photographs. One of the Reds grabbed Nekovar's paper and a sub-crowd formed around it, frowning deeply. Among them all, one wearing a sheepskin jacket, a leather cap and military boots began to push the mob back. He called the soldiers comrades, requested order, and asked Mutz and Nekovar if they were unarmed.

He led Mutz and Nekovar to the open door of one of the passenger cars. The mob of sentries followed them while their chief climbed up and went inside the car. The soldiers kept their distance from the Czechs. Some had bayonets fixed to their rifles. Their faces showed suspicion and curiosity. They were as eager to kill as they were to talk. Either would serve. There were women among them.

'We're Czechs,' said Mutz. 'From Yazyk, up at the end of the line.'

'Interventionists,' said one of the Reds.

'White filth.'

'Counter-revolutionaries.'

'Are they bourgeois?'

'Factionalists!'

'How can they be factionalists?' said a lanky Red in a squirrel-skin shapka, shoving a rival in the shoulder. Some of the Reds laughed. Vapour rose from their mouths.

'Are you communists?' asked Nekovar.

'Communists!' said several and deep 'Yeses,' rumbled round the semicircle.

'We're railways workers,' said one.

'That's a military secret!'

'Yes, shut up, you fool.'

'I'm proud to be a communist, and a railway worker,' said a white-bearded man with a well-oiled rifle, addressing them all, as if it were a meeting, and it was his turn to speak. None of the younger Reds was inclined to shut him up. 'I worked thirty years in the railway, and they gave me nothing, and the boss talked to me like a child, and they took my son to the war, and he never came back. They gave me a bad house. Small. Damp. They hated to part with their money, parasites. My wife caught cold and died. It was a shame.'

'Right, Styopa 'Xandrovich. Speak it.'

Styopa Alexandrovich crept forward towards Mutz and Nekovar, pushed his face into theirs, and jabbed at them with his finger. He had no teeth. 'This is a People's train,' he said. 'This,' – he slapped his rifle – 'this is a People's gunbarrel. The People – that's us. It's been published so.'

'We shot our bosses. They were swine.'

'Shut up, Fedya.'

'God save Red Lenin!' A brawl broke out when the lanky one heard this.

A man jumped down from the train. The crunch of his boots in the snow and the track bedding silenced the other Reds and they stepped back several paces. The brawling ceased.

The chairman of the Verkhny Luk Railway Workers' Soviet was in his early twenties, with a full, neat blonde moustache. Even in the moonlight Mutz could see he was looking at him with an extraordinary degree of hope in his eyes; not hope that Mutz was going to provide something he needed, but immense hope that every new man and woman he met would turn out to be an early messenger of the new society he was expecting, no matter how many times he was disappointed.

He was Comrade Bondarenko, in a black leather coat, with a pistol, loving being young in a revolution, and knowing it, hence some newsreel gestures. The other Reds liked him for seeming young and good-looking and unsullied, even though he had led them in an enterprise which ended in the execution of rail administrators loyal to the Whites, or loyal to the old order of property, at least. Mutz saw the Reds looking at Bondarenko as if he was the repository of their virtue, their guarantee that their honour would be returned to them, intact, when the killing days were over.

Bondarenko ordered Mutz's and Nekovar's hands to be tied behind their backs, which was done eagerly and without viciousness. Bondarenko climbed back inside the train, and Mutz and Nekovar were pushed up after him, with an armed man each behind them. This group shuffled through the passenger car down the corridor leading past the coupé compartments. The sliding doors of the compartments were open. The wagon was overheated. It smelled of bad tobacco, men's feet, thin soup and old wound dressings. In the compartments men could be seen smoking, playing cards, reading newspapers, arguing about politics, and sleeping the enviable sleep of the exhausted, limbs cast about as they first stopped. One compartment held sick and wounded. Two bare-chested men, one with a bandaged skull, the other with a bandaged arm, lay in blankets to their waists, one hand behind their heads, staring out at those passing by with the particular beady attentiveness of the wounded irregular.

Mutz and Nekovar were led into a room fashioned from half a car. There were beige blinds over the windows and a thin green carpet which had been new recently. It was rucked up and tracked with black mud and crumbs of snow. Technical maps of the central Siberian rail network were pinned to blackboards and there was an empty draughtsman's table. In the far corner, by a door marked NO ENTRY, was a desk with a green baize surface. A lamp on the desk was reflected in the captured turmoil of varnished walnut. There were dirty tea glasses and a half-eaten apple on a crumpled piece of newspaper on the desk, and more newspapers in stacks, some freshly printed by the look of them, on the floor near the desk, alongside an open crate containing hand grenades wrapped in straw. A clock on the wall showed 8.45. Bondarenko's takeover of the old railway bosses' staff car was deliberately careless. He wanted to show how little he cared for the bourgeois trappings of the old bureaucracy, without ruling out the possibility he might need them in future. It was not, Mutz sensed as the chairman sat in the padded swivel chair behind the desk, that Bondarenko was cynical; more that he was humble and trusting enough before the wisdom of the People to know that he did not know what, exactly, they would expect a new order to look like once their war was won. Mutz was reminded of Balashov, but perhaps the pious warrior whom Anna had first met in Europe before the war.

'I have a proposal,' said Mutz. Bondarenko smiled and looked interested but shook his head and interrupted Mutz when he tried to go on. He began to tell them about the fall of Omsk, two days earlier. Did they know? Comrade Trotsky's Red Army was triumphant, the Whites were in shameful retreat west towards Irkutsk, and the Revolution had won. Admiral Kolchak's train, full of drunks, cocaine and loot, was jammed in the middle of a rout spread out over hundreds of miles west into Siberia, with Cossacks sealing off villages to use as their blood playgrounds and leaving with no-one alive, and the rich paying in jewellery by the boxful for a place in a hard car to Vladivostok or China. White officer cadets, whores, impresarios, waiters, spivs, music hall singers, moneychangers, dealers – thousands lay dead of typhus by the rails, and scavengers were stripping them of gold and furs and boots.

'We understand the Whites are finished and the Reds are winning,' said Mutz. 'The Czechs in Yazyk only want to go home. That's the substance of my proposal.'

'The Czechs in Yazyk,' said Bondarenko, with a sadness Mutz didn't like. The chairman met Mutz's eyes again and looked away. Still there was the boundless hope in his eyes. It occurred to Mutz that this hope, which had seemed so seductive, might be no more than the hope he and Nekovar would be men enough to understand why their life or death was the Idea's to decide, and not his, mere Bondarenko's.

'I would like to read you a telegram our Soviet received one month – one month – ago from the Red Army shtab in the Urals,' he said, taking a piece of paper out of a drawer in the desk. 'I would like you to tell me if you think this leaves me with any room for doubt. One moment.' He laid the paper face down on the table, took out his pistol, popped the clip, checked the number of bullets, snapped the clip back in, placed the gun carefully on the baize, its muzzle pointing towards the Czechs, and picked up the piece of paper. Some bitter substance manifested itself in Mutz's saliva and he swallowed. He tried to read the characters on the telegram as the light shone through it but he could only see the strips of telegraph tape stuck to the paper.

Bondarenko said, very slowly, repeating some words, 'It reads: "To Bondarenko, chairman, Soviet of the Railway Workers of Verkhny Luk. Concerning Matula's Czechs in Yazyk. The Yazyk railway spur is of no immediate military importance. However. *However*. Bearing in mind the bestial acts – *bestial acts* – committed by this unit in Staraya Krepost, it is ordered that, at the earliest opportunity, you will liberate Yazyk by force of arms, regardless of the cost in blood to military or civilian persons there. It is further ordered that any Czechs – *any Czechs* – taken prisoner in Yazyk should receive, from you, swift and merciless revolutionary justice, in the form of the death penalty – *death penalty*. Any of Matula's Czechs attempting to flee or surrender – *flee or surrender* – before you attack are to be dealt with in the same manner. *The – same – manner*. Signed Trotsky. *Trotsky*!'

'This is –' Mutz began. Bondarenko cut him off. 'Wait.' He turned the telegram round. 'There. You both read Russian, don't you? Read it. Could there be a clearer order? Come along.' He picked up the pistol and stood up. Mutz and Nekovar were lifted from behind to try to get them to their feet. Both men resisted and had the chairs pulled out from under them so that they fell to the floor.

'I can't believe a loyal servant of the people would commit such an act,' said Mutz.

'Why?' said Bondarenko. He sounded offended, disappointed in Mutz's lack of understanding. 'Comrade Trotsky is the People's commissar.' Mutz heard him reaching into the desk drawers again. He kneeled down by Mutz's head, which rested on the carpet. His boots creaked. He held something in front of Mutz's eyes. It was Bublik and Racansky's Legion identity papers.

'We shot these ones today already,' said Bondarenko. 'We picked them up this afternoon, on our way to the bridge. They told us they were communists, deserters, and they wanted to join us. We had to execute them, though. It's extraordinary to see the power of the People at work. Your comrades seemed to be good men, yet the Revolution had no use for them. One of them, Racansky I think, told us he'd killed one of his own officers this morning.'

'Kliment?'

'Perhaps. I don't remember. That's enough talking. Let's take them outside.'

The Czechs were hoisted to their feet. This time they didn't struggle. Again Bondarenko led the way and they followed.

'It looks bad, brother,' said Nekovar.

Mutz found his mind was having difficulty accommodating what was taking place. It was used to counting imaginary paces forward into possible futures and returning with the news of what it had seen. Now his imagination sent messenger after messenger forward down the only possible road and none of them came back. How was it possible to prepare for death if you couldn't imagine it? Now that his life was measured in minutes he wished Anna could know what had happened to him. To his surprise, no prayer was budding in him, no god. He was very frightened of his consciousness dripping into death's ocean and being not. It wasn't like sleep. Mutz didn't feel brave, or proud, but the chairman was so amiable that he knew there was no point in begging for his life. What he found most unexpected was the anger he felt towards himself for not returning to Yazyk to warn Anna and the Czechs and the castrates. That was a place his imagination could go, too easily, Anna's precious life, the life in her that was so much greater than an ordinary person's life, being ended, in pain and fear. He wouldn't die peacefully.

'How long before you attack Yazyk, Comrade Bondarenko?' he asked.

'A couple of hours,' said Bondarenko, without turning round. 'It'll be quick.'

Cannibals

Samarin played his song twice more, at Anna's insistence, and refused to play it a fourth time. He put the guitar down carefully so that it leaned against the dresser and wasn't between them. Anna had heard the song before but Samarin had made it a part of his life.

They sat and looked at each other for moments. Anna's heart beat hard. She longed to put out her hand, clasp the back of his head and kiss him, stroking him with her other hand, and wondered why he couldn't see the longing and readiness in her face, and act. Had the good looks walked away one recent night, even an hour ago? Was she old? Was she foolish? A change came over Samarin's face. He smiled and it was a younger, more eager Samarin, a liberation, Anna saw at once, more real than any he had experienced in escaping from the White Garden or being let out of Matula's jail. An inner prison had set him free, and he was astonished by it, and the world outside looked the brighter for coming to him so unexpectedly.

'Why are you smiling?' she asked.

'You,' he said. 'I'm falling into your curiosity. Such a great demand to be satisfied.'

Anna shrugged. 'So fall,' she said hoarsely.

He leaned forward and kissed her on the lips, putting his hands on her waist. Their heads tilted and their tongue tips touched. Anna put her hands on the sides of Samarin's head and held it a few inches away from hers. Her eyes moved across his face. So much at once. His head was warm and she felt his pulse beating. His eyes stayed fixed on hers.

'What are you doing?' she whispered.

'What you want me to do,' he said.

'Can you know that?'

'Yes.'

'So simple.'

'You know, it's been a very long time,' he said. 'Perhaps I've forgotten. Perhaps all women are like you. But I don't think I have. I don't think they are.'

'You kept looking at me in the courtroom today,' said Anna. 'You were looking at me all the time. I felt you knew me.'

'I know you,' said Samarin. 'I'll know you more.'

Anna kissed him again. She heard feet on the stairs and Alyosha crying for her.

'Wait,' she said, and went up the stairs to meet her boy.

'I'm cold,' said Alyosha. 'Can I sleep with you?'

'Of course you're cold, running around out of bed without any slippers on,' said Anna. 'Mama's not going to bed yet. Don't tell me the stove's gone out already?' But it had. The little stove in the corner of Alyosha's room, which Anna lit when the sun went down, to give out its warmth slowly while the boy slept, had to be brought back to life, and Alyosha tucked in again. Anna laid the kindling hastily and at first the logs didn't catch. She scolded Alyosha for a pest.

'Stay with me,' said Alyosha. 'The stove downstairs will be out by now.'

'Your head's full of nonsense,' said Anna, more harshly than she'd meant. She got up from the stove, which had finally caught, and leaned over him. He was fast asleep, his cheek squashed on his hand. He must have spoken in his sleep. Would he dream of a sharp-tongued mother, turning her back on him? Well, let him. He would hear worse things in his life. Still, it troubled her. She kissed him and went downstairs.

Samarin was standing, looking at the photographs which hung on the wall on either side of her father's painting of Balashov. Some she had taken in her home town as a girl; others were from Ukraine.

'Did you make these?' said Samarin.

'Yes.' For a moment, she hoped for praise. But that wasn't Samarin's manner. He felt his interest was praise enough, and she found that it was.

'Who are these people?' He was looking at a photograph of a peasant family at a railway station in 1912. It was winter. The father and mother, wrapped in ragged layers, were bowed like hills over a baby lying in among bundles, their thick fingers tightening the baby's swaddling. In the foreground, a girl, sitting on another bundle, turned away from the baby and stared into the camera lens, her face hopeless and proud, her eyes wide and uninterested and rimmed with a circle of dirt. She looked hungry.

'I don't know,' said Anna. 'I took their picture. I don't know what happened to them. There were a lot of peasants passing through the station that year. The harvests failed in the new lands. I don't know where they were going.'

'No-one should have to run when harvests fail, should they?' said Samarin. 'They should be able to call on a scourge to destroy those who have money but don't feed them.' Anna saw the old Samarin re-emerging and felt a jump of fear. It was Samarin who changed the subject. 'There's no photograph of your husband,' he said.

'The painting,' said Anna quickly. 'It's a poor likeness. My father was a bad artist. Besides, my husband met me when I was taking pictures of a demonstration. He stopped a Cossack from beating me, or killing me. The photographs have him in them in that way.'

'And no pictures of the people of Yazyk.'

'I have some. But they don't care to have their picture taken.'

'They are very devout, you said, like Balashov, and not Orthodox. Wasn't that what you said? And the other thing you said was that you knew people who had shed their own flesh and blood for God. I thought that was a very unusual expression. Is Balashov one of these men?'

'What do you mean?' said Anna hopelessly. He knew but she was obliged to pretend. The comfort was that he wasn't using his knowledge to torment her, and that he didn't know Balashov was her husband. There was a tenderness in his inquiries; it wasn't a greed for prurient details or a stroke for advantage. He was trying to gently slide open her mind and climb inside. Part of her was aware that she felt so well about his questioning because she wanted to touch him, to kiss him again and begin to play with his body, but she wouldn't pay attention to that part of her.

Samarin said: 'Is Balashov a castrate?'

Anna nodded, hating to hear the word in Samarin's mouth. It wasn't the way he said it, but the word spoken out loud by a man, in particular this man at this moment. It struck her like a fist in her belly, and she remembered how much the whole Gleb had meant to her once and how much she had seemed to mean to him, and how it hadn't been only an act against her, how it hadn't been only a preference for God over her, mocking their lovemaking and their child as young sinners' follies like cards and duelling; but how it had been an act which almost killed in her the hope that there existed men worthy of the love women gave them, a hope already crippled by her realisation that her father was a fool.

'What does it matter to you whether he's a castrate or not?' she said. 'Let the man rue it in peace.' She sat on the divan, lips pressed together, and watched her fingers on her lap, playing with her ring.

'I don't ask for intimate knowledge of Balashov or any of those folk,' said Samarin, sitting down next to her and leaning towards her. His animation excited her and his desire to keep talking about the castrates made her dislike him. 'But you can't be surprised that I wonder. You live here. You forget how many people west of the Urals think there never were castrates, or that they died out a century ago. It shows there's hope.'

'Hope?' said Anna, looking up. She laughed. She hadn't heard anything so funny for a long time.

'Hope to think that modern man will make such sacrifices for something they believe in, for more than something they can reach out and touch. That not everything is a transaction.'

For a moment Anna felt all the weight drain out of her, leaving her as light and empty and sad as a single Chinese lantern, rocking in the wind. She began to speak and with the first sound from her mouth her face reddened and she began to cry, and as she raised her voice against the tears she became angry.

'Hope,' she said. 'Hope! Some clown ends his manhood in the forest with a knife when he gets the word from God. Yes, he thinks he's a fine man, standing there with a cupful of blood draining out through his fingers, he thinks he's done a bold thing. He's made his covenant with that thirsty old swine in Heaven. But Heaven is such a long way away, so far, d'you know, Kyrill Ivanovich? It's such a long way to go, and by the time you get there, the blood's not hot any more, it's all dried up, and you can't put them back, and you say to God, "Look!

Look what I did for you!" And God says: "Thank you." And you look round and you see all the heads bowed around him, all the millions who've brought him their blood sacrifices, and you know what? God doesn't have the time. And you think, "What if I hadn't?" What if I'd stayed with the people I know, what if I'd stayed with the people I'd loved, instead of going all that way with my mean little sacrifice for God, who doesn't need it? Would that not have been a better and a harder sacrifice? Too late! Your cannibal. Too late! To build a shining future on the meat of his companion? Do you really think a man can eat another and it not leave its mark on every act he does thereafter, and in every consequence of every act? Do you really think the stink of that one betrayal isn't going to spread to all the acts of all the anarchists he inspires?'

'It's not that way,' said Samarin calmly.

Anna wiped her eyes with the back of her hand and spoke more gently. 'When I hear a man talk like that,' she said, 'I think of a spoiled child, who'd kill his mother if she wouldn't let him go and try to catch the rainbow.'

Samarin put out his hand and touched Anna's moist red cheek. 'Well,' he said. 'What if this imaginary cannibal wasn't an anarchist revolutionary after all?' He moved his face closer to Anna's so that his eyes were looking into hers only a few inches away. 'Would you like it better if he killed and ate a man for love?'

Anna was still dizzy from speaking so loudly and so fast and so carelessly when she was crying. Yet she could see a change in Samarin. As he came closer, his liberated self was fading, as if his harder, colder self was drawing the young open Samarin back into an inner cell. She didn't want that to happen.

'Would I like it better?' she repeated.

'If he killed and ate a man for love. If he slaughtered his

companion, butchered and ate him, so he could live long enough to see the woman he loved again. Would that be better for you?'

Samarin, the Samarin Anna liked, was disappearing, and Anna wanted him to come back, and was prepared to pursue him. 'Yes,' she said. 'I would like that better.' She put her lips to his mouth and it opened and she pushed her body forward so that her breasts pressed against his chest. She put her hand between his legs and felt the blessed reassurance of his hardness there and, as if hoping were a form of magnetism, his left hand slipped under her skirt.

'Are you thinking? Don't think,' she said. 'You like me.' She stroked him and bunched her skirt and petticoat up around her hips and pulled off her drawers. With both of her hands she lifted his hand, the hand that had moved between her legs, and folded it so that his forefinger and finger were sticking out. She drew it down and slipped the fingers into her slit, which had been moist long since. She looked into Samarin's eyes as she teased herself with his fingertips. 'Let's follow each other,' she said. 'Don't think.' Samarin smiled and nodded. Anna could see he was trying not to think, even though he was being pulled back inside himself. Anna had paid a young castrate lad to do this to her one night when she was a little drunk and lonely and he'd been chopping her wood all day. He'd lent her his fingers but how he'd giggled, like a girl.

In Dark Heaven

In the meeting hall of the castrates, Drozdova cried Balashov's return from Heaven to the congregation, and the castrates greeted him. Balashov tried to stand still. He'd never spun for so long before. Sweat drops pattered on the floor. He staggered and fell to the ground. Drozdova and Skripach pulled him up and stood close. He was shivering.

'How far he has travelled!' cried Drozdova. 'Far, far,' echoed the congregation. 'Truth!' They looked hungry. There was such an expectation of being fed on their round smooth faces.

'Yes,' whispered Balashov. 'Yes.' There was a rustling as the castrates leaned in to hear him. Now he spoke more loudly. 'Sometimes the journey is harder. Even angels, even God's favourites, must be tested. I have been tested. On the journey to Heaven from which I have returned, Jesus Christ our Saviour hid the light from me, and I had to find my way in the dark. I had to find my way.

'In this dark Paradise, it is peaceful still, and there is singing, and running water, and grass underfoot. But there is no light. You hear voices around you, and you hear the beating of angels' wings above and around you, but you cannot recognise anyone. In the dark, Paradise is crowded with souls. Each voice could be the Lord's.'

'The Enemy!' said one of the congregation.

'No, friend Kruglov, the Enemy is not in that place. It is a test, not a trick. Listen: I walked through the darkness of Paradise for hours, which seemed like days, until I found the Saviour, sitting alone by a waterfall. There was a phosphorescence from the waterfall, and I saw the outline of his face against it. I had heard many voices, and was not sure if they were Christ, or not: but when I saw him, I knew it was him. He turned to me and by the light of the waterfall I could see that he was full of sorrow. He did not speak, but held up to me something he held in his hands, across his knees. It was a sword. The sword began to glow. It glowed red hot, as if it had come straight from the forge. I could tell it was burning his hands, and that he must be enduring great pain, and I knew I was to take it from him, but I was afraid, and did not take it. And I returned to you.'

The congregation was silent.

'Brothers and sisters, forgive me,' said Balashov. 'I cannot tell you what this means.'

'It's good, brother,' said Skripach. 'It's God's own best commission, the fiery sword, like the guarding weapon with which the angel wardened Eden.'

'Perhaps, brother,' said Drozdova. 'Perhaps it's a sign of your great power to convert, that there'll be a host of doubting souls in the lands around who'll mount the white horse by the offices of your holy scalpel.'

'It resembled a sword I once carried,' said Balashov. 'When I was a soldier.'

'God protect us,' murmured voices in the congregation.

'That was not you,' said Drozdova. 'That was the body of a man you left behind when you became an angel.' She began to sing. Skripach and the congregation joined in. After an hour, the worshippers dispersed. Balashov heard their petitions and told them to lock their doors, for there was a killer abroad.

Later, Drozdova sat reading out passages from Job while Balashov swept the floor and Skripach copied items between a series of ledgers spread out on a trestle table.

'Kruglov's short of kerosene for his lamp,' said Skripach.

'Everyone is,' said Drozdova.

'He lives next door to the Darov twins,' said Balashov. 'How are they for light?'

'They have more, but only two months' worth.'

'Let them share it,' said Balashov. 'They can read and write and cobble their boots at the same table.'

'The Darovs reckon Kruglov is a slacker.'

'Let him help them caulk their roof. If he doesn't I'll talk to him.'

Skripach said: 'We lost a cow to wolves.'

'How many does that leave?'

Skripach ran his finger down a column. 'According to the Czechs, ninety.' He opened another book. 'According to my list, we have two thousand, four hundred and eighty-seven hidden in the forest.'

Balashov leaned on his broom, bowed his head and spoke to the floor. 'I'm afraid they'll be found.'

'They never were till now, by God's mercy.'

'Heaven was never dark for me till now. Could it be a sign that I am to be cast out?'

Drozdova got up quickly and embraced him. 'How could you be cast out? You're the best among us, an angel among angels. It was a good sign, even though you couldn't read it.'

'I spoke with the Jewish lieutenant, with Mutz,' said Balashov. 'I shamed him because he asked me to do something I could not do, and I refused, and he left thinking he had made no mark on me. But he was wrong.'

'What did he ask you to do?' said Drozdova.

'Persuade the widow and her son to leave.'

'I knew the widow stood in this. Gleb Alexeyevich, what kind of strange affection can you have for her? You're not a man now.'

'She is a good woman.'

'She's a painted harlot! She exults in the chains of lust as if they were garlands! You know that. Gleb Alexeyevich, how can you say such things to me? Not to belittle your own acts of purification but you know what pain, what long, grievous hurt it is for a woman to have the knife taken to her breasts.' She began to cry and went back to her chair and hugged the Bible, rocking back and forth. Skripach looked up and bowed his head deeper into the books. Balashov put the broom down and came and put his hands on Drozdova's shoulders.

'Olga Vladimirovna,' he said. 'I know. But it's just as I said to Lieutenant Mutz. If we say that love dies with a stroke of the knife, what kind of angels are we? My love for Anna Petrovna is no different from my love for you, or for Skripach, or for friend Kruglov.'

'It should be different,' said Drozdova. 'She isn't one of us. You should love me more than her. And how did this affection begin? Did you know her from your old life?'

'A little.'

'I knew it. The Jew was right. You must tell her to leave. She is on the other side from us. She's left behind. Let her burn.'

'Perhaps I'm the one who is to burn,' said Balashov. 'The sword that burns the one who holds it: perhaps I'm to go back.'

Drozdova was shaken out of tears. 'You can't go back,' she said. 'You carried out the act. You purified yourself.'

'An angel who commits a mortal sin must still burn in hell forever,' said Balashov. 'After we have thrown all the Keys to Hell into the fire, are we to turn our backs on all those who haven't, for fear of spoiling our purity? Are the rituals and rules and habits of the life in common enough?'

'Yes! They are enough! We are so close to Heaven already. Why go back?'

'God would rejoice at an angel electing himself for damnation to stop a sinner suffering.'

'Rubbish! Blasphemy! Where are you going? To see her?'

'No. I have other errands.'

'Gleb Alexeyevich!' Drozdova stood up with her hands clasped together and called after him. 'Take your hat!'

Balashov took a path that led from the back of his store south towards the grazing lands. The snow which had fallen earlier had frozen and his feet left light prints and a faint scent of earth, the last loose earth of autumn, quickly lost in the woodsmoke of the town stoves. He dropped down to avoid a Czech sentry who was rocking from foot to foot to keep warm, twists of paper hanging over the tops of his boots, his face wrapped in a scarf against the first baby frost. Balashov met the road to the fields and began to run. The ruts showed up deep and sharp with the moon on the shading of snow and his feet smashed ice like a drunk keeling home through an arcade. He turned off the road along a line of birches and walked for a mile to a field which lay in a slight hollow, circled by tall old scraggy pines. Backed up against the pines so it would be hard to see from any direction outside the field was a hut, a well, and a larger building without windows.

Balashov went to the well and let down the bucket. He carried full buckets to a barrel which stood by the paddock fence and poured them in, breaking the thin ice that skinned it, until the barrel was two thirds full. He took off his boots and his clothes, hanging them on the fence, and eased his lean white body up onto the top bar. His flesh shone smooth in the moonlight, the sharp light that gave the old pines the look of attendants. At the top of his legs there was nothing left; after his wife had tried to force him, he had taken the knife to himself a second time for a further act of purification. He slid into the barrel, roaring through clenched teeth and quivering for a second as he went down into the black water, bracing his hands against the sides to pull his head under and holding himself still there for a short time while the remaining fragments of ice tickled him. Then he crouched and jumped up, catching the rim of the barrel in his hands and swinging himself over and out onto the ground. He took his clothes and boots and ran into the hut.

In the sooty, resinous dark he found a coarse blanket and wrapped himself in it, carefully closed the door and made sure the window was shuttered. By touch and practice he found the lamp and the match beside it, made light, and lit the stove. The room contained a hard, narrow bunk, two chests, the stove and a table. Balashov folded the blanket and clothes and placed them in a pile on one of the chests. From the other he took a clean white blouse and white trousers and foot-wrappings and put them on, and his boots. He combed his hair and his beard. He took a small pair of scissors from the table and cut his fingernails. When he had collected a heap of nail shavings he threw them into the stove.

Balashov took a key from the table, extinguished the light and left the hut. He stepped over the hard ground to the other building, unlocked a padlock, and went inside. He closed the door behind him. In the darkness a large warm beast shifted its hooves and snorted.

'Hello Omar,' said Balashov. He lit another lamp. Omar was of an Arab bloodline and Russian breeding. His black hide shone. He had a stall in the corner of the building. The walls of the stable were thick and partly lined with bales of straw and the warmth of the horse took the chill out of the air. Omar looked steadily at Balashov, took a few steps forward and rubbed his nose against the struts of the stall. Balashov asked him gently to be patient and went to prepare food for him. While Omar was eating, Balashov stood in the stall with him, leaning against his flank with his arm up over the horse's back, stroking him.

'Eat, fine one,' he said. 'How glad I am you can't talk. I know you listen. I don't think you understand. That is, I think you understand that talking is what people do instead of getting on with things. But you do listen. It makes you like a mirror for me, Omar. When I speak to you your silence means I can hear how my words must sound to others. You know, I've been talking to the congregation, my congregation. We are angels, you see. We're free from sin. It's wonderful. We are very good. We help each other. We don't eat meat, we don't drink or smoke, and of course, of course, we don't kill. Killing is a mortal sin, whether you are a soldier or not. And there can be no question of fornication, Omar, or procreation, because, like angels, unlike you, I don't have anything to do that with. I cut it all off. So everything is lovely. We live in Paradise. There's one thing, though, Omar, that troubles me. This is what it is: I keep lying all the time. You won't know what lying is. Horses can't lie. It would be funny if they did. What would they lie about? That it isn't your foal? That you never touched that mare?' Balashov laughed. 'That wasn't the laughter of an angel, was it, Omar? There was mockery in it, not joy. And I do not think it is an angelic thing to be a liar. Let me see. Lies. Yes, I wrote a letter to my wife, telling her I had become an angel, and telling her I was confessing everything, yet somehow I could not tell her that like my friend Chernetsky I went with a ten-rouble whore on the night before my regiment and my horse – Hijaz, Omar, you would have loved him – before they were slaughtered. God sees the end as well as the beginning of things, remember, Omar, and I think it is more likely God punished me for the lie by letting my comrades be slaughtered than that he punished me for going with the girl. You know, Omar, the wonderful thing about lies is the way they give birth to other lies. So I lie to my wife and to the Jewish lieutenant, saying that I have kept my promise to her not to purify any other men or women, when two nights ago I castrated a young man in Verkhny Luk and brought him to God. My own hand on the scalpel. And to protect that lie, I had to tell another one. I had to lie about the convict Samarin murdering the shaman. I do not think I am a good angel, and an angel must be perfect. Omar, I have begun to find it so easy to lie, even to protect my pride, and I must not have any pride. I returned from the vision of a dark Heaven this evening saying that Christ had offered me a red hot sword. This was true. But I said his face was full of sorrow, and it was a lie, Omar! Christ was laughing! He was holding out the sword with his burned hands and he was laughing at me!'

At Mutz's Execution

From the way the railway workers arranged themselves in the snow Mutz could tell that Bondarenko himself would shoot them and that less than a minute was given to him to live. The sound of his feet in the snow was dear to him; it seemed to him that he owned it, that every particle of ice belonged to him. He was stricken with the urge to taste it.

'Wait,' he said. 'Before you shoot.'

'We don't do that,' said Bondarenko, stopping and turning round. 'We don't do last requests.'

Mutz foresaw his quickness. It was a man who'd shoot immediately once he'd drawn his pistol. There'd be no words. Brisk.

'I'm thirsty,' said Mutz. 'Let me put some snow on my tongue.' Bondarenko didn't say anything and his hand didn't move towards his gun and Mutz kneeled down and cupped a light heap of snow in his palm. He stood up and put his tongue into the cold powder. The ice crystals hurt and their taste went deep. Mutz the boy and Mutz the man recognised each other and for an instant he was engulfed by a joy so intense that he could hardly stand.

He heard Nekovar speak. Nekovar was questioning the age of the telegram. Nekovar was right. Nekovar would bring them back to the cold darkness of war and a railway and to the possibilities of living further. And Mutz knew it was right but he'd seen on the threshold for a moment a way to take the certainty of death and the great wonder of life and hold them in balance, neither denying the other and each casting light on the other, death and life as both the rim and the core. Death gave life the beauty of finity, the beauty of the edge line, and life, even a second of it, made death small. And Mutz knew that while he could see this only in this moment, later, he would bat at it clumsily and either not believe it or not remember what it was, and though Anna and Balashov and Samarin would never see it, they lived on that threshold already.

'Why not wire for new orders?' said Nekovar to Bondarenko. The sergeant looked uneasily at Mutz for support.

'The telegraph's broken,' said Bondarenko.

'What make is it?'

'Siemens.'

Nekovar shook his head, struck his thigh and turned from Bondarenko to Mutz and back. 'I could fix that in half an hour.'

'He could, comrade Commissar,' said Mutz.

'For what?' said Bondarenko. It was not that he wanted to kill them, Mutz saw, but he was tired and wanted to sleep and them being alive was keeping him awake. Besides, he didn't want to hesitate in front of the collective.

'Comrade Bondarenko,' said Mutz. 'Your revolution needs bullets and shells. Some of your men are wounded. Of course if you attack Yazyk you will beat the Czechs, but more of the collective will be hurt, peaceful citizens will be killed, there will be destruction and you will spend munitions. We only want to be allowed to leave Russia through Vladivostok and see our new homeland. I understand a wicked act was committed at Staraya Krepost. The orders were given by our commander, Captain Matula. He is a tyrant, a murderer, and a madman. If we can bring him to you as a prisoner, you must let us go west through the east in peace. My comrade Nekovar will mend your telegraph, and you can ask your commanders.'

Bondarenko raised his eyebrows, pursed his lips, and scratched the back of his head with the butt of his pistol. He waved the gun at Mutz, looking at Nekovar. 'I could shoot the lieutenant, and you could still fix the telegraph.'

'I could, but I wouldn't,' said Nekovar.

'Ladno,' said Bondarenko abruptly, putting his gun away and clapping his hands together, waking himself up with a suffusion of decisiveness. 'We'll have a meeting of the organisational committee.' He walked some distance away and came to be at the centre of a semicircle of communists who spoke in turn. Nekovar and Mutz were guarded meantime by short, bearded men in badly-fitting coats who did not say anything, but stared them out. After a while Bondarenko came back, the other members of the committee straggling behind.

'We have discussed your case and reached a conclusion,' said Bondarenko. All the members of the committee had seen the Red Cinema film *Savagery,* depicting the massacres at Staraya Krepost. Comrade Stepanov argued that, on the basis of their behaviour in the film, all the Czechs must be executed, without mercy. Comrade Zhemchuzhin said that some of the Czechs, and the Jewish lieutenant, Mutz, had tried to stop the massacre. Comrade Stepanov had said that the film was an artistic work, and that the actor's portrayal of the lieutenant was a false representation of reality, in that it was not possible a Jewish officer could be so different from his men, and set himself against them, without them trying to kill him. Comrade Zhemchuzhin had said that if the portrayal of the lieutenant was false, perhaps the actors playing the other parts could not be relied on to tell the truth about what the Czechs had done. Comrade Stepanov had said that Comrade Zhemchuzhin was a counter-revolutionary and that it was a slander against Red Film. Comrade Titov had wondered about Captain Matula; did he not seem like a character in a cheap melodrama, with his mad cruelty? Why had the Czechs not rebelled against him? Comrade Bondarenko had said that the point was, the telegraph was broken, and it would be useful to have it working again. If it couldn't be repaired, they could just as easily shoot the prisoners in the morning, before they attacked Yazyk. His motion was carried.

Bondarenko led them back to his staff wagon. Mutz became aware that Nekovar continually turned to stare at him as they walked. It was uncomfortable. Mutz had received respect and solidarity from Nekovar before, never awe.

'What is it?' he said. 'Thank you for saving my life. Why are you looking at me like that?'

'They put you in a film!'

'Not me,' said Mutz. 'I never tried to stop the killing.'

'The film shows you did, brother, and that's good for us.'

On board the train, Nekovar was sent, with an armed guard of two, into the telegraph room, through the door marked NO ENTRY, with the warning that if he so much as touched any of the code books, he would be shot.

'Good luck, brother,' said Mutz, the last word pungent in his mouth, like untried medicine.

'Half an hour, brother!' said Nekovar, as he passed through into the dim light beyond. Bondarenko brought Mutz a chair and placed it some yards from his desk, up against a far window. A railwayman came in with two glasses of tea, and left them. Mutz wrapped his chilled hands around the embossed metal of the glassholder. What would Balashov be doing now? Were eunuchs potent in their dreams? Bondarenko was bent over the desk, mouth reaching for the glass, as if he was too tired to raise it. The tea bubbled between his lips. He looked not only weary as he leaned back in the chair, but deprived of fulfilment. To Mutz's surprise, he spoke: and curiosity emerged from the commissar, although he seemed ashamed of it.

'Czechs,' he said. 'Always ready to kill each other. Why? You're not a Czech, of course.'

'I'm a citizen of the Czechoslovakian republic.'

'I couldn't understand why your soldier Racansky killed your comrade, the officer. He was very excited, and your sergeant, Bublik, was even more excited, and kept interrupting him. They didn't expect us to shoot them.'

'They were communists, like you.'

'So they kept pointing out. Some of what they said sounded sensible. But they were Czechs, and we had this order. And with their accents, it was so hard to understand what they were saying.'

'Did you bury them?'

'They're on a flat car down the train.'

'They have families in Bohemia.'

'We all have families.'

'I have to write to them.'

'We all have to write those letters. The soldier, Racansky, he kept talking about killing the officer. It seemed to me he expected a commendation from us, or a post of some kind. And he kept talking about a great revolutionary in Yazyk. The blade of the will of the people, he called him. Elegant speech for a private soldier, a foreigner. Like he was quoting. Do you have a great revolutionary there in Yazyk?'

'There's an escaped prisoner, an intelligent, a student. That's who he meant.'

'An exile?'

'He says he escaped from a prison camp in the Arctic called the White Garden. His name is Samarin.'

Bondarenko did not seem to find this interesting. He leaned his chair back on two legs, clasped his hands behind his head, and yawned, staring ahead of him unfocused. Through the door they could hear the sound of tools on metal.

'Why prison camp?' said Bondarenko, not looking at Mutz. 'That's grandly put. There was just one prisoner there, and she's dead. It's all in *Red Banner*.' He picked up a newspaper from the floor beside his chair, waved it at Mutz, and laid it on the desk. Mutz felt a weight drop inside his chest and a terrible, proximate menace, incomprehensible, tiny as a needle and heavy as a mountain.

'Perhaps he lied to you,' said Bondarenko. 'Our scientist, Academic Frolov, visited the White Garden in his airship a few months ago. You must know about the Frolov expedition. No?' Bondarenko leaned forward, more awake. 'It's a marvellous journey around the Arctic by air, dedicated to the October Revolution and carried out in the name of the people. The whole world has been following it. Academic Frolov was always one of us. Not like that dog at the White Garden, Apraksin-Aprakov. Prince Apraksin-Aprakov, the geologist. The White Garden was his camp, his expedition to the Taimyr Peninsula. He believed there was gold there, and nickel. He had huts up there, and servants from his household, and other geologists.'

'Who was the prisoner?'

'A young revolutionary, a bomber. The Tsar's people gave her to Apraksin-Aprakov to use.'

'To use?'

'Yes, to use. Those were their morals. Anyway, it seems their supplies never arrived, with the revolution, and they starved. That was how Academic Frolov found them. Starved, frozen, dead, dried, like mummies there.'

Mutz asked what the prisoner's name was. He heard Bondarenko lift the paper, then, after a moment, turn a page.

'Orlova,' said Bondarenko. 'Yekaterina Mikhailovna.'

'Comrade,' said the guard. 'He's fixed it.'

Mutz got up as Bondarenko moved towards the telegraph room. Over shoulders he caught a glimpse of Nekovar's face, staring into the apparatus with joy and affection. It began to click and he heard the Russians murmuring and laughing. Bondarenko came back with a strip of printed paper tape in his hands and waved it at Mutz. He came over. Mutz flinched and Bondarenko embraced him.

'Victory!' said the commissar, and shook his hand. Over his shoulder he shouted: 'Get the Czech out of there!' Nekovar and his guards emerged. Nekovar was grinning and Mutz clapped him on the shoulder and shook his hand. Hugging was not his way.

'You're a genius,' he said.

Nekovar shrugged and scratched his nose. 'Siemens,' he said.

'Comrade Bondarenko,' said Mutz. 'Please send the message to your commanders.'

Bondarenko's face took on the same expression of hope that they had seen on their first meeting, as if Nekovar's triumph over German technology had reassured him that the movement of which he was part could not be defeated. Yet Mutz knew now how doom was the dark background which gave hope its shape.

'Our telegraph operator is sick,' said Bondarenko. 'Raving.'

'Sergeant Nekovar can transmit,' said Mutz.

'This message has to be encrypted,' said Bondarenko. 'I can't let you see the code book. I'm the only one who can send it. It'll be slower. The people of Russia are grateful to you for your work, but it's most likely that we will have had to shoot you, and Yazyk will be taken, long before we get an answer. We only have until dawn to hear from them, and then we have to move.'

Mutz looked at the clock. It read 9.30. 'That gives you at least nine hours,' he said.

Bondarenko looked at him earnestly, willing him to understand.

'We're railwaymen,' he said. 'Our clocks are set to Petrograd time. Local time is four hours later. If I don't hear from the people's representatives in Trotsky's shtab in five hours, you will have to be shot, and your comrades liquidated.'

'Can it be so hard for you to encrypt and send one short telegram?' said Mutz.

'But then it has to find its destination. There are twenty telegraph circuits for the telegram to cross between here and the shtab, and they pass through all the shades of Red and White. What are the chances that each of those circuits is intact? Our partisans are supposed to cut the telegraph wires across the White retreat, and the Whites should be cutting them to their rear as they flee. Even if the wires are intact, how likely is it that each of those twenty telegraph stations is going to relay a message in our code? Most of the telegraph operators are for us in their hearts, even in the White areas, but not all. I know one telegraph centre on the Urals way where the day shift puts up a black, white and gold flag for the memory of Bloody Nicholas, and the night shift puts up the red banner in its place. And if the message arrives, in the small hours of the morning, somebody has to read it, and draft a reply. And then that has to make it all the way back.'

Mutz looked at Nekovar.

'Don't worry, brother,' said Nekovar. That was all he could manage by way of reassurance, and Mutz could see he had known what Bondarenko was saying already, and had resigned himself to death. Fixing the telegraph was a gesture of defiance towards a process which even Nekovar could not reduce to mechanics and electricity.

Bondarenko pulled the chair closer to the desk and bent his body over a pad of telegram forms, awkward and boyish in composition. He began to scribble, speaking as he wrote: 'I'm saying you're offering to deliver Matula to us, dead or alive, by nightfall, in exchange for our delaying our attack, and the lives and safe passage east of the rest of the Czechs. It sounds generous.' He tore off the page, got up and walked towards the telegraph room. Mutz thanked him and Bondarenko did not reply. He went into the telegraph room and closed the door behind him. After a time they heard clicking; a few clicks, then a long pause while Bondarenko looked up code words. Nekovar and Mutz were left in charge of two guards who stood watching them, rifles lowered, one at each door. The grime on their faces made their eyes look brighter. Nekovar asked the name of the near one. He was Comrade Filonov. He shifted his weight when he spoke as if he found the gun an awkward burden. Behind his beard his face worked anxiously. He gave the impression of one who was bullied.

'Did you see the film about us, then, Filonov?' said Nekovar, sitting on the floor next to Mutz.

'Well?'

'Do you remember if there was an actor who played a Czech sergeant? Was he handsome?'

'You weren't even there,' said Mutz. 'You were left at the station that day.'

'I don't remember,' said Filonov.

Nekovar was disappointed. 'They might have put me in there, brother,' he said to Mutz. 'Then I could have seen myself from the outside, and repaired myself.'

'Repaired yourself?'

'Yes, brother. A man who doesn't please ladies is a machine that knows it's broken, but it can't fix itself, because it can't see itself from the outside. I can fix anything, brother, any machine, any device you give me, but I need to look at it from the outside, turn it round in my hands, understand how it works by examining it. I can't do that with myself. I've tried examining ladies, as Broucek said, tried to understand how they work, but I've come to think maybe it's not the ladies that are broken, it's me. And I know I could fix myself, me of all people, I could do it, but I'm the one thing I can't fix.'

Mutz felt the obscure impatient anger rising in him again.

'Yes, brother. It's a shame,' said Nekovar. 'I'd like to see myself on film.'

'It looks likely enough in five hours you'll be broken beyond any sort of fixing,' said Mutz, and as he said it, felt he'd only added to their curse by speaking out loud. It was hard again after that moment of ease at the point of execution. His thoughts ran forward and this time did not vanish into the vast anticipation of death. They ran into an impenetrable wall, black, soft to the touch but unyielding, like velvet glued to a granite cliff face. And at the same time there were other thoughts which flew easily over the obstacle, reaching to Anna in the days ahead, and Alyosha, and Broucek, and even Dezort, surviving the Red onslaught, perhaps, but these were strange, pale, through-the-window thoughts, because they were thoughts about what would be after he was gone, and those he had touched would, incredibly, be carrying on without him. Was that what ghosts were? Thoughts about the living in the future, thought about the living by the dead when they were still alive?

A paunchy man in his fifties with a silver beard, hair coming out of his ears and head in tufts, and a crumpled white coat with dried purple bloodstains over a black suit, entered the wagon carrying a bottle of vodka and three glasses. His face had a bloated, sleepy, refolded look, sulky, like a new-born child's, as if no amount of indulgence could compensate him for the suffering inflicted on him by the act of his birth. He sat in Bondarenko's chair, began to fill the glasses, and said: 'Czechs?'

'Czechs,' said Mutz.

'I thought they'd shot you already. Dr Samsonov.' He gave them glasses, and raised his.

'I need a hundred grammes too,' said Filonov.

'Soldiers don't drink when they're on duty, don't you know that?' said the doctor. 'Now. Czechs. Here's to our acquaintance. I feel very warmly towards you, because I am certain that I will know you for the rest of your lives, short as that is likely to be. To lifelong friendship!' They raised their glasses and drained them.

'You're on duty too,' said Filonov.

'This is prescribed medicine,' said Samsonov, refilling the three glasses.

'I need medicine,' said Filonov. 'I ache all over. I have the fever.'

'Just wind,' said Samsonov. He raised his glass again and looked expectantly at Mutz.

'Here's to the Russian telegraph system,' said Mutz, and they drank to that.

'I'm sorry there's no food,' said Samsonov. 'Was it the hunger that caused the revolution, or the revolution that caused the hunger? I could never work it out.'

'It's because bloodsuckers like you won't share what they have that folk go hungry,' said Filonov.

Samsonov sighed. 'I'm a liberal, you know,' he said. 'I spent all my life talking to my friends about liberty, about the day the Tsar would be gone, the aristocrats would be gone, the priests would be gone. I longed for it to happen. And now it's come, I don't like it.' He poured fresh glasses and handed them out. Nekovar stood up slowly and offered his glass to Filonov, who took it.

'Oh!' said the doctor. 'The condemned man grants the executioner's request. That's something I haven't seen before.'

'TO THE VICTORY OF THE WORLD REVOLUTION!' yelled Filonov, and drained his glass. The doctor hesitated, then knocked his back. Mutz followed. The doctor's mouth stretched into a frog shape and he wrinkled his nose. 'That didn't go down as well as the other ones,' he said.

The door to the telegraph room opened and Bondarenko came back. He pushed gently past Filonov and looked at the doctor, who began to rise from the chair. There was something deliberately guilty about the doctor's movements, as if he was trying to mimic a servant caught in his master's library.

'Sit down,' said Bondarenko. 'You work here too.' The doctor sat down and Bondarenko lay on the floor opposite Nekovar and Mutz, head resting on the wall of the wagon. He closed his eyes.

'Did you send it?' asked Mutz. 'Comrade Bondarenko?'

The doctor, still acting his caricature of a doltish retainer, poured another glass of vodka, emptying the bottle, and walked on exaggerated tiptoe, like a marsh bird, to where Bondarenko lay. Bondarenko opened his eyes, looked up, shook his head, and closed his eyes. The doctor tiptoed back, draining the glass as he moved.

Mutz tried again. 'Comrade –'

'Yes, I sent it. Sleep, Czechs. Should they not sleep, comrade Doctor?'

'Yes,' said the doctor, nodding, trying to shake a last drop from the bottle into his glass. 'If they sleep soundly, they'll know their fate in a moment. And if they dream, their dream minutes'll pass like years, and it'll seem to them that they lived whole lives in the hours till dawn. That's where I live, anyway.'

Mutz turned to Nekovar. 'Brother,' he said, and frowned, and smiled. 'Now I know what brother means. Please don't look at me like that.'

'Like what, brother?'

'Like you're more worried about me than yourself. What's your first name?'

'Best not to remind you, brother. When we go back to the others, you'll have to be calling me by my family name again, and you'll feel bad.'

'You can't think we'll leave here alive.'

'I do, brother. I've got faith in that spark that's travelling down the wire. It's a thin wire, brother, and it's long, but that spark, she goes fast, like light. She's a wonderful messenger. She doesn't feel the cold, she doesn't get tired, and she doesn't get hungry. She's here and she's there, fifty miles away, almost at the same time. Don't worry, brother. The message is already there.'

'But the operators have to pass it on.'

'I can't answer for them, brother. But they're only there to serve the spark, the messenger. Who are they to stop it?'

Mutz was nauseous from the drink and lack of food, his temples beat with blood, his eyes hurt and his limbs ached. He was falling asleep. He could have tried to stay awake, to savour the last hours. Only there was nothing to savour in this stinking, stuffy carriage. He could tell from the sound of Bondarenko's breathing that the chairman had already drifted off. The doctor was hunched over the table, his face nestled in his folded arms. Filonov was still awake, but now he leaned against the carriage wall, resting the butt of his rifle on the floor. It was 10.15 in Moscow, 2.15 in the morning here. Anna would be in her deepest sleep.

'Nekovar,' said Mutz. He saw the sparks flashing between the hills, darting from horizon to horizon in the darkness of Siberia. 'I know how women work. I can explain. Are you listening? They need to believe you're sending them a message. It doesn't matter if it's in a code they don't understand. They need to believe it's important, and that you depend on them to pass it on. Do you understand, Nekovar?' Nekovar, far away on an ice floe, did not answer.

Mutz woke up. The telegraph was clicking like teeth. The clock read one: five a.m. in Yazyk. Everyone except the guards was asleep, and the guards were dozing. Mutz got up. 'Comrade Bondarenko!' he shouted. 'The telegraph! A reply!' The wagon stirred. Filonov lifted his rifle and pointed it at Mutz. Bondarenko yawned, blinked, rubbed his scalp with the pads of his fingers and rose. He looked at Mutz, nodded and walked slowly towards the telegraph room. Nekovar got up. It seemed to Mutz he could smell dawn coming, and a southern wind through the larch needles.

'The spark!' said Nekovar.

Bondarenko came back with paper tendrils streaming from his fists. He looked at Mutz and shook his head. 'Local reports,' he said. 'Messages from Verkhny Luk on the local circuit. Filonov, your wife's had a boy.' Filonov blushed and grinned. 'Glory . . .' he began, and stopped and looked down at the ground. When he looked up he had mastered the grin, and looked serious. 'No church names,' he said. 'This one'll be to Marx, Engels, Lenin, the October Revolution, and Trotsky. Melort!'

'Melort,' said Bondarenko. He nodded. 'A good name, reflecting our socialist reality. Glory indeed.'

'If you have a grandson,' said the doctor, waking up and speaking through curtains of phlegm, 'He can be Melort Melortovich.'

Filonov walked over and struck the doctor hard on the ear with the back of his hand. The doctor cried out and teetered but did not fall. A glass fell from the table and rolled across the carpet without breaking. Bondarenko glanced up from reading the tapes. 'Doctor, I told you,' he said, without heat. 'Don't sneer at working people. Your class only ever sneered, up and down, and at each other. Your time's finished. If you sneer at the modern men of action, they'll hit you, because you're in the way. Comrade Filonov, perhaps Rosa would be a better name.'

Everyone looked at him.

'I misread the tape. It's a girl.'

Mutz could not sleep. The telegraph chattered without a break. The clock had no second hand. The minute hand moved wastefully on, jumping a minute at a time. It was hard not to watch it. Bondarenko was sitting on the floor, slowly, sleepily going through the tapes. Mutz looked from the clock to Bondarenko and back again. He should beg Bondarenko to go and sit by the telegraph, but hopelessness had taken over. It was as if someone else was going to be shot, and he, Mutz, was dead already, and this wagon would be his afterlife. Was that the first change in the light, the blueing of darkness? The paper tape rustled in Bondarenko's hand, the doctor snored, the telegraph chattered, and all the wonder of the world and the life of the world was squeezed into the silent two-millimetre jump of a clock hand under glass. An hour and forty five minutes remained. Without conscious effort on his part, Mutz felt a change come over him, a wakefulness and an awareness return. He no longer felt tired. The nausea had gone and his senses sharpened. He saw and smelled and felt and heard more details at once than he was used to sense in a day. The smudge of fingerprints on the vodka bottle, the bright brass jackets of Filonov's cartridges, the delicate scrape of two edges of telegraph tape rubbing together, the tiny gaps between the planking floor under the carpet he was sitting on, the smell of drying boot leather, the way Nekovar's jaw jutted out when he slept. He remembered how Samarin had described the Mohican, his control over himself and his ability to see the life that had passed and the life now and the life to come as a single whole picture, his actions strokes in that picture which no-one else could understand until it was finished.

'Doctor,' he said. 'Doctor, wake up. Doctor. Wake up, doctor. Please. Doctor. Listen. It's important. Do you think that a man can be so in control of himself, of his passions, that he can sit in secret inside himself, like a pilot inside a vessel, and steer himself in any direction he chooses, make it seem to others that he is any kind of man he wants to seem?'

'Oh God,' said the doctor. 'So many dead, and my head hurts so badly, and you talk about this.'

'Suppose,' said Mutz, 'Suppose a man appeared, at different times, as a strong, merciless, murdering cannibal, and as an intelligent, sympathetic, attractive young student? Would it mean he was a lunatic, or would it mean the very opposite, that he was in perfect control of his external appearance?'

'I was always hungry as a student,' said the doctor with difficulty. 'I could have eaten the dean of anatomy whole. He had meat on him.'

'That's not what I meant,' said Mutz.

Without looking up from his tapes, Bondarenko spoke in a quiet, optimistic voice: 'Still, why shouldn't a student be a cannibal, or a cannibal be a student?'

'A good way to study anatomy,' said the doctor.

Bondarenko looked up at Mutz. He rubbed his eyes and ran his tongue over his teeth. 'You think too much in the old way,' he said. 'Such men do exist, and one day all men will be like that, but not in the way you say. This inner pilot will not be secret. Secrets are for capitalists and bourgeois parasites. Communist man will be the master of his passions, and he'll have no reason to keep that secret. He'll be proud. He'll navigate through the life of the world exactly as he chooses, exactly as the will of the People chooses; his chosen course, and the People's course, will move closer and closer until it becomes impossible to tell them apart.'

'But why should they be eating each other?' said Mutz.

'Nobody said they would,' said Bondarenko.

'If the life of the many is more important than the life of the one,' said Mutz, 'why would they not? Why wouldn't one man make a sacrifice of another, and eat him, for the sake of the people?'

Bondarenko thought for a while. 'There would have to be a very good reason,' he said.

'Sweet reason!' said the doctor.

'And, of course, a plenary meeting of the relevant Soviet, with a vote.'

'Reason, justice and cannibalism,' said the doctor. 'Utopia!'

'These are your writing desk fantasies,' said Bondarenko, smiling in turn at Mutz and the doctor. 'They only go to show why your class is living out its last days. After the revolution, all the wealth will be shared fairly, and no-one will ever be hungry again. You're like children. You've never seen equality, so you don't believe in it. But of course it's not possible if you don't believe in it first.'

'Like God,' said Mutz. 'Or fairies.'

'He said it!' said the doctor to Bondarenko, pointing at Mutz. 'Not me!'

Bondarenko was not troubled. 'A man will never find God or the Devil outside his head, no matter where he looks,' he said. 'But he'll find the unfairness of other men everywhere. Am I right, Comrade Filonov?'

'Used to pray all the time,' said Filonov. 'Morning to night. Kiss the icon, keep all the feasts, fast like a saint. Father and grandfather the same. And the little priest, a whoring thieving drunk, give him half my wages for candles, and to say prayers for the family. Wife has a kid. Boy. Beauty, strong and fair, like a golden bear cub. Good church name for the boy, Mefody. Priest wants a rouble for the christening. Haven't got it. Winter, family need clothes. Food a bit short. Priest says no rouble, no christening. Can't have boy not christened, already owe my friends half a year's wages, get an advance in wages off the workshop boss, pay the priest, christen the boy. Boy gets ill. Need money for the doctor. Friends skint. Boss says you owe us your wages already. Try the priest. Church full of gold, face on him like a railway clock, eats for five, keeps his own cook, electric light in the house. Taken my life blood for years. Father, I say, lend us a rouble for the doctor. Can't, he says. Why not, I say, after all I've given you. It's not my money, he says, it's God's. Boy dies. Folk in the workshop knock up a small steel coffin out of corroded boiler plates. Priest's there in the churchyard at the grave. Don't worry about the money for the funeral, he says. You can pay me later.'

The doctor opened his mouth to speak. He saw Filonov raise his hand and said nothing.

The clock hand twitched forward. Mutz wondered if he could be shot in his sleep, and whether that would be better for him. He wasn't troubled about looking brave. He didn't want to die in an hour's time, and it seemed that he was going to. How much time did he need to live? He didn't need a year. He didn't even need a month. A week would be good. He could do a lot in a week. He could help many people and uncover many secrets, knowing he was going to die in seven days, and people would remember him when he was dead, and think well of him. And then, in that last hour, he would realise that he needed another week. Nobody was ever ready to die in an hour.

'Chairman Bondarenko,' he said. 'Would it be possible to send one more telegram? Not in code. A simple question. You could address it to all Russian police departments. Perhaps after I die your investigators will be able to make use of the answer to establish the true history of the marvellous revolutionary of Yazyk, Samarin. There is, or was, a thief and a robber who goes by the klichka Mohican. Could you send a telegram, asking the Russian police, White or Red, what they know about him? Somebody may answer.'

'We have no police,' said Bondarenko. 'Communists don't steal from each other.'

'Will you send the telegram?'

'No.'

Mutz nodded slowly and folded his arms across his chest. He looked down at Nekovar, who had fallen back to sleep, and seemed to be smiling. The doctor had gone quiet, head resting on the table. It seemed to Mutz that at this moment it was important to remember, yet all he could think about was who would remember him. It was six months since he had received a letter from his uncle in Prague. His family was gone. Nekovar would die with him. Anna would wonder what happened to him, but not for long. For some reason he most desired to be remembered by Alyosha. There was something deeply honourable and fine about being someone else's childhood memory. He would never be a father now, but those men who cannot be fathers can be fathers for an hour, or a minute. All of a sudden he felt, for the first time, something he had only apprehended with his intellect and prejudices before, the misery of Balashov and Anna, the husband and wife, the father and mother, living a mile apart, separated forever and by a universe by a single stroke of the knife. He felt it without condemnation of Balashov, without jealous anger towards

Anna. The wordly demons of war and guilt and religion and self-loathing which had inspired his contempt for Balashov were the same as those which had driven the gelding knife onto the cavalryman. Were he, Mutz, to live, the most important thing would be bringing together those two whom he had tried to drive apart. Not that he was going to live. He found himself staring at his corpse in the snow, amazed at its lack of movement, that this wonderful machine could be so simply stopped. He fell asleep.

A curious sound woke him, of paper fluttering close to his head. He sensed daylight before his eyes opened and his soul dived inside him. He opened his eyes. It was morning. Bondarenko was standing over him, waving a telegram in his face.

'Wake up, beauty,' said Bondarenko. 'You've got work.'

Mutz didn't understand, but it seemed like a new world. Nekovar stirred beside him. They stood up.

'Comrade Trotsky gave the good word. He never sleeps,' said Bondarenko. 'It came ten minutes ago. You've got till this time tomorrow to deliver Matula to us, dead or alive. You should leave now. You'll have to walk. Two comrades will escort you as far as our forward posts.'

Mutz could not speak. The rush of joy was poisoned by the prospect of cold treachery. It was good and bad to be alive, as it always had been, but this was a steep time of being thrown up and flung down again. He and Nekovar began to move towards the door.

'Wait,' said Bondarenko. He went to his desk and picked up a block of newspapers tied tightly with string. 'These are your propaganda sheets, I think. They might help you.'

'Yes,' said Mutz, taking the bale in his arms. Nekovar was staring at them. The top of the front page could be seen under the wrapping.

'Do you see what it says, brother?' said Nekovar. 'Good orders from Prague.'

'Yes,' said Mutz. 'Good orders from Prague.'

'They remembered us,' said Nekovar.

Bondarenko put his hand in his pocket and took out another telegram, folded in four. He gave it to Mutz. Mutz looked at it, and looked at Bondarenko. Bondarenko shone with optimism.

'I carried out your other request,' he said. 'To help you. Now you're with us. Because you will come to believe that ours is the only truth.'

Mutz unfolded the telegram and read it.

+++ EX PANOV IRKUTSK + ATT MUTZ YAZYK + RE MOHICAN + ESP DANG CRIM-POL ACTIVIST+

MOHICAN IS MEMBR REVY ORG RNS + BANK ROBS ODESSA 1911 ORENBURG 1911 ALASKA 1912

+ BOMBS PETERSBURG 1911 KIEV 1912 + MURD FAMILY GEN BODROV 1913 + BELVD RESP 10 OTH ASSNS +

SENT DEATH 1913 + ESCAPED + LAST KNOWN ORGING REVOLUTIONY CELLS PRUSS FRONT 1914 + DOB 10 AUG 1889 VOLGA REG +

REAL NAME +

SAMARIN, KYRILL IVANOVICH +

ENDS +++

The Locomotive

Alyosha was a little out of breath, trying to keep up with Samarin, who had a long, quick stride, and Samarin was holding his hand, clasping it in his rough warm palm. The man's feet crunched in the papery snow on the road and the boy's pattered in a light fast rhythm with him, two paces for each of his. They walked up the road from the house towards the station. Samarin rose above Alyosha, a mountain of swinging bones in wool. The man didn't look down. The light around them was clean and blue. The hollow scrape of crows sounded from the murk at the forest's edge and a cat did honour to the sun in the carpenter's garden, bowing and narrowing its eyes.

'Mama will be up soon,' said Alyosha.

'What, you don't want to see the locomotive?' said Samarin. He looked down for a moment, without breaking his stride.

'I do,' said Alyosha.

'We can have breakfast at any time, but they only fire the train up once a day, early in the morning.'

'Why?'

'To be sure it works, naturally.'

Alyosha didn't reply to this. It was a great revelation to him that it was possible to have breakfast at any time. He knew he really had woken up this morning. The sting of cold on his cheek wasn't to be felt dreaming. Only: he had run over Yazyk lengthways and crosswise, inch by inch, over the years, and no-one had taken him on the road he was walking down now. He had run and walked and been carried past these houses many times, but with Samarin, it was a new road, which had started when he woke up to find Samarin standing over him, watching him sleep. When Alyosha opened his eyes, Samarin had grinned at him, put his finger to his lips, bent down and lifted him out from under the quilt, and Alyosha felt like a loaf, hot and fresh from the oven. Whispering 'This isn't for girls. This is what the boys do when the girls are sleeping,' Samarin had carried him like that downstairs to the kitchen, where his clothes were waiting. When Samarin carried him downstairs the stair hadn't creaked as it had when Mutz left their house in the mornings. Mutz was clumsier, and secretive, and never wanted to play, or talk. When Alyosha had woken up the first thing he saw was another expression on Samarin's face, not the grin. It had been like looking in the mirror. Like catching himself in the mirror when he was concentrating on something important.

'Kyrill Ivanovich,' said Alyosha. 'Can you wake somebody up just by looking at them?'

'Why not?' said Samarin.

'And you didn't wake Mama, all the same.'

'No.'

'Where did you sleep last night?'

'In a safe place.'

'With Mama?'

'Oho. You'll be a prosecutor, then, not a cavalryman, or an engineer.'

'I want to be a prisoner,' said Alyosha.

'Why?'

'So I can escape.'

They came to the station. The sound of the locomotive came like an old dog breathing from the far side of the yellow station buildings. A group of three Czechs with their hands in their pockets turned from their conversation towards Samarin and Alyosha, and picked up their rifles by the muzzles from where they leaned against the wall.

'Wait here,' said Samarin, letting go Alyosha's hand. Alyosha watched as Samarin went over to talk to the Czechs. The Czechs were suspicious. They followed Samarin's hand pointing towards him, then asked Samarin more questions. Alyosha knew Samarin had spent the night in his mother's room. He had only hoped the man would share something of the strange and frightening dance which Mama and men performed there at night. Sometimes it sounded as if it might hurt, but she was kinder and happier the next day. Perhaps Samarin would tell him about it later.

Samarin beckoned to him and he walked up. The Czechs looked down at him, two smiling, one still suspicious. They asked him if he wanted to see the locomotive, in their bad Russian. Stupid! Samarin had just told them, hadn't he? There was so much repetition among the adults. He nodded. One of the Czechs put his hand on the small of Alyosha's back and was making to push him forward towards the train.

'I want to go with Uncle Kyrill,' said Alyosha, as Samarin had told him. Samarin wanted to see the locomotive too. He was interested. He knew about steam. After a few minutes' more consultation, the three of them went together, Samarin leading Alyosha by the hand, the Czech soldier alongside them, with his rifle slung over his shoulder.

The locomotive was a dark green brute hissing with possibility. It smelled of smoke and oil. Had men made such clever work? It seemed to have come out of a crack in the ground, ready to drag the station and all Yazyk back to the hell-mouth, houses and men and roads rocking and slithering with it. But this engine wasn't hitched to anything, except a tender piled above the lip with fresh quartered logs and a single bare flat car. There were two men inside the engine, Czechs again, suspicious again, but of anyone entering their domain of steam, not because it was the Russian prisoner and the widow's boy. Samarin lifted him up to the footplate and climbed up himself. The Czech soldier stood below, a few yards away, watching.

The engineer nodded at Samarin, looked down at Alyosha without changing his expression, and went back to his dials and levers. The fireman glanced up and resumed passing logs from the tender into the furnace. His bare forearms shone red when they fell into the furnace light. The heat pressed against Alyosha's skin.

'Here's the fire,' said Samarin. 'And here is the wood.'

Alyosha took a log from the tender and handed it to the fireman when he turned from the furnace. The fireman gestured to the open door of the furnace and Alyosha threw the log in. His hand felt scorched where it came closest to the heat.

Samarin started explaining how the locomotive worked, how important the temperature of the furnace was, the gauge that showed steam pressure, the regulator that sent the steam to drive the wheels, the brake, and the little glass tube that showed how much water there was in the machine's great snout, and which must never be empty. As he talked, telling Alyosha about different sorts of engines in America and Africa and England, the engineer began grunting one-syllable affirmations. After a time he joined in with the explanations.

Samarin said he was surprised the crew didn't carry weapons.

'There's a pistol!' said Alyosha, before the engineer could reply, pointing to a Mauser in an open holster hanging from a hook near the engineer's head.

'Thank you, Alyosha,' said Samarin. 'I didn't see that. Now, I wonder where the whistle is.'

'Here,' said the engineer. He bent down, picked Alyosha up and presented him to a length of chain, dull with dried oil, looped down from the roof of the cab.

'Can I pull it?' said Alyosha.

'Pull it,' said the engineer. Alyosha's hand closed round the chain and he pulled. Nothing happened and he pulled harder till he felt, within the guts of the machine, a valve opening and the power trembling through the chain against his palm. The locomotive uttered its long hoarse shriek. Alyosha felt strong, as if the engine was carrying his own cry of loneliness and longing out over the taiga.

Alyosha found that, when violent, unexpected events occur suddenly, it becomes difficult, a moment later, to remember the precise order in which they occurred, no matter how vivid the memory of each separate event. Inside the sound of the whistle came another sound, sharp, breaking out of the shriek. More than a sound, a blow to his ears, a clap, an explosion. Alyosha also saw a hand pulling the gun out of the holster. It must have been Samarin's hand, and the sound of the gun being fired must have come afterwards. The Czech soldier could only have fallen to the ground, like a suitcase bursting open, as a result of the gun being fired at him, and this could only have been before Alyosha saw the gun, held by Samarin, pointed at the engineer. Yet all these things seemed to have happened simultaneously, and they danced together like freaks in the stage of Alyosha's mind, the muzzle pointed, the dead Czech soldier, the shot that killed him, the speed of Samarin's hand reaching to take the gun, the whistle. For the next few moments time melted and Alyosha could only watch the freak show of shocks dancing in his mind, even while he was aware of other things happening, of Samarin ordering the engineer to put him down, of the engineer lowering him to the footplate floor, of

Samarin telling the fireman to stoke for his life, of Samarin telling the engineer to raise pressure. Samarin didn't shout. His eyes moved across the crew and at the yard around and back, swift and angled, like insects on a pond. He told Alyosha to jump off the locomotive. Alyosha pressed his back against the tender and wrapped his arm around a metal bracing strut.

'Jump!' said Samarin. 'Don't disobey me. I shall not turn round again.' Alyosha shook his head. He was afraid and he knew Samarin was the centre of this terrible new trouble and he found that he wanted to be there, in the centre, with the trouble, and not watching the trouble come towards him or move away.

'The devil,' said Samarin. 'Stoke!' He kicked the fireman. The furnace was roaring. 'Your pressure's good!' said Samarin. 'Poshli!'

The engineer and fireman were pale and frightened. It showed in their silence and delicate motions. The engineer took the brake off and moved the regulator. Vapour crashed on metal and the locomotive began to move.

'Jump!' said Samarin. He reached behind him without looking to take hold of Alyosha. Alyosha squeezed his body away from the clutching hand. The fireman was throwing logs into the furnace now with a broadheaded shovel and the light from the doorway shone white and hot like the summer sun. It sounded a river roar and the old greased parts of the big engine stretched and hauled and tumbled and the pistons sucked and bellowed steam.

'Where are we going?' called the engineer.

'Nowhere,' said Samarin, and with two powerful movements of his leg, one to wind the spring and one to release, he pushed the engineer off the footplate. The Czech vanished, and it was Samarin's hand on the regulator. Alyosha's instinct was to rush forward to the doorway to see what had happened to the engineer. It was far to fall without warning, and it seemed to him that they were moving fast now. But he only gripped the strut more tightly because he understood that Samarin would throw him off the train too if he saw a chance. As long as he pressed himself back in the corner, he was safe. Samarin was watching the controls, had the gun pointed at the fireman, and moved his head every few seconds to look out the window. From where he stood Alyosha could see moments of birch and larch passing in the precise autumn light. They were already beyond Yazyk. It was almost a year since he had travelled by train, and never like this. He had a growing hollow of worry in his stomach that he was getting too far beyond his mother's reach, and at the same time the wind from the open doorway, the crash of steam and the quick tall back of the fearful, clever man in front of him promised a place to be safe that consisted of always running towards a far-off destination that could not be known or seen but was good and existed. Alyosha had only ever known one centre, to which everything returned: home, roof, mother. Now there was the centre of speed, journey, leader.

Samarin looked quickly over his shoulder at Alyosha. 'Are you still here?' he said. 'Devil. I told you to jump. I'll throw you off the first bridge if you don't.'

'You killed the Czech soldier,' said Alyosha, full of wonder.

'I don't need a boy with me to count heads. Stoke, filth!' To the fireman.

'Who are you really?' said Alyosha.

'Destruction.'

'Destruction of what?'

'Of everything that stands in the way of the happiness of the people who will be born after I'm dead.'

'What about Mama?'

'She doesn't mean anything to me, Alyosha, and nor do you. Everything in the world is broken now and can't be mended.'

Dread came to Alyosha. He said: 'Did you hurt Mama?'

Samarin turned round and stared at Alyosha. His eyes were more terrible in their anger than any punishment. 'No,' he said.

There was a strange sound in the cab, as if a thin metal rod had snapped in two. Other delicate breakages sounded down the length of the engine. The fireman inexplicably sagged forward in the act of shovelling logs into the furnace, pushing the handle in up to his hands. His gloves began to blacken and smoke and Alyosha saw that his side, just under his ribs, was darkening with seeping liquid from a tear in the cloth of his coat. Except it wasn't only the cloth which was torn. It seemed impossible, but a ragged part of the fireman himself seemed to have come loose as well, and from the dark entrance under that strip of cloth and flesh his lifeblood was flowing.

Samarin pulled the fireman away from the furnace and let him lie in the back corner opposite Alyosha.

'Machine guns,' said Samarin, going back to the controls. 'Keep low.'

Alyosha crouched down onto the floor of the cab. He looked over at the fireman. His flesh seemed to be turning grey already, and his eyes were closed. The ease with which life could be taken from him was astonishing. Alyosha could hear the sound of the machine guns. They sounded far away, another thing altogether from the little clanging of metal against metal when the bullets struck the locomotive. How strange that those small sharp metal taps could stop a life of tens of years, all that talking and moving.

Samarin, looking ahead down the line, shouted something Alyosha could not hear and sounded the whistle, two or three times. The locomotive smashed into an obstacle on the line. Every bolt and plate shuddered and the train continued on. The sound of the guns grew louder. There was an explosion nearby, a blast that seemed to pass through Alyosha's head, leaving it light and empty, ears singing. The locomotive thundered on. Samarin began adding logs to the furnace. The guns were still firing.

A bullet struck the inside of the cab and something touched Alyosha on the shoulder. He felt an outrageous, unreasonable pain unfold in him and he was frightened. He knew part of him had been pierced by flying metal and he wondered if he would go still and turn grey like the fireman, and what would happen to the part of him that wasn't still. The space between his chest and his clothes was filling with something warm and wet, which must be his blood.

'Kyrill Ivanovich,' he said, and was surprised at how faint and thin his voice was. Samarin wouldn't hear it. When he spoke, his whole body glowed with pain, but now he was angry and afraid and he screamed. 'Kyrill Ivanovich!' It was loud, and he was crying, and frightened and in pain as he was, he still felt a little ashamed and babyish when he saw Samarin turn round and look down at him. Samarin was angry with him, he could see. Samarin put a hand over his eyes, struck the instrument panel with his fist, and dropped to his knees, bringing his head so low that it touched the floor. Then he lifted it and turned to Alyosha, touched him and spoke his name. Alyosha tried to answer but though his lips moved he couldn't make a sound. It was hard to keep his eyes open. Samarin kept saying his name and the guns kept firing and there were more explosions. Alyosha heard the sound of the brakes being applied, felt the locomotive slow down and stop and then, after what seemed like a long time, with bullets hammering the train from end to end, it began to move back towards Yazyk. Alyosha felt cold. Waves rolled over him, pushing him deeper under each time, until he went still.

The Nature Of The Burden

Anna woke with the wonderful feeling bad sleepers have when they know they have slept well, as if they have stolen something and got away with it. At these times, the memories of what led up to such deep sleep keep their distance for a few seconds, and those few seconds are perhaps the only time the world can ever be said to show mercy. She heard the whistle of a train in the distance and wondered if that was what had woken her. She remembered something extraordinary, dangerous and lovely had occurred. She remembered a broad hard bud had entered her and filled her. A man had kissed her with desire and she had pulled at his sex to get it inside her more quickly. What a long hunger satisfied once! She stretched and pedalled her legs under the quilt, and wondered where it was he'd gone, and what time it was. It was light outside, bright light. It was surprising Alyosha hadn't been in to see her. Could he have hauled Samarin out into the garden to play at cavalrymen already? She smiled, it was likely. A sense of being part of threeness crept into her, and she knew how perilous that was, because it couldn't last, but there would be more hours yet together. She got up and splashed her face. The noise of her hands in the water of the basin met a different silence, one that seemed cold and did not beat. It was the silence of one. Anna's mouth dried in a moment and in her dressing gown she ran into the corridor and saw that Alyosha was not in his room. She heard shooting in the distance. Aloud she spoke God's name she did not believe in, over and over, while she ran downstairs. She shouted for Alyosha in the kitchen, in the yard, and ran out across the frozen ground, out of the gate until the splash of a tear on her foot made her realise she had no shoes or stockings on. She drew in breath till her lungs hurt and let it out in a scream that tore the flesh of her throat, 'ALYOSHA!'

Snivelling, wiping her nose with the back of her hand, shaking, breathing too quickly, she put on clothes and laced her boots, dizzy from the sickening, heavy wheel that had begun to rotate in her mind, displaying the same sequence of thoughts over and over. She had killed her son for lust. She, Anna Petrovna Lutova, had killed her son for lust. She had taken the killer into her bed. She had sacrificed Alyosha because she could not bear the wanting to be touched and wanted and filled. She had lost her love, her joy, her warm tight squirming giggling pouting strutting essence of a boy, her dear pampered prince, that she bore and cared for so hard and so long, out of that sickness in her that couldn't endure. No prayer could bring him back and she was damned forever. Her husband saw the slut in her and took the quickest way out of it. It was her fault. Could Alyosha be alive still? No, she was greedy. She was cursed. She was a fool. She had killed her son for lust.

Anna ran up the road towards the station. The castrate carpenter, Grachov, said he had seen Alyosha hand in hand with the convict. He asked her what was happening and she did not answer. The wheel grated round inside Anna. She had killed her son for lust. Could he be alive still? She was a fool. There was more shooting in the distance, the thud of heavier weapons now. Czech soldiers overtook her. Chaos rippled outwards from the station. A soldier tripped and fell, picked himself up and ran on. The brilliant blue of the sky, the brightness of the puddle-ice, made this a shiny chocolate-box doomsday. The soldiers shouted at each other in Czech. They ran holding their rifles in both hands, looking from side to side, bent forward slightly, as if they thought the enemy was on either side.

At the station a corpse lay half covered in a tarpaulin by the tracks, boots lolling at their dead angle. Anna felt as if a hand had reached inside her, gripped her by the heart and shaken her whole body. She was too broken up to cry out and she held her hair in her fists. The Czech soldiers milled like a mob. She could barely understand this language but she understood a train, their only train, had been stolen. She ran towards the heart of the mob, which was a man she recognised as the Czechs' train engineer, sitting shivering in a blanket. One of the soldiers was squeezing and twisting the engineer's leg. The engineer winced.

'Who's seen my son?' said Anna. The wheel grated. The son she killed.

'You fucking bitch,' said the engineer in Russian, looking at her, and looking away said more in Czech. The other soldiers stared at Anna.

'I don't care what you call me,' said Anna. 'Where's my son?'

'The convict took him. We're all like children to him. Oh, the little lad wants to see what the train driver does! Well come up and see, and bring your uncle with you!' The engineer spat and the soldiers murmured. The engineer said: 'Your brat knew what he was about, and so do you. Don't worry about the boy. You'll both be crow's meat when Matula gets to you.'

A man was shouting and waving down the line. He had a pistol in his hand. It was Dezort, yelling at the Czechs to move. They began to run along the tracks, Anna among them, red with tears and pounding blood, hardly able to see the sleepers and rails, shivering with self-hate. In a short time, they met up with the rest of the Czechs, who had cut across town to the railway straight from the square. Smutny and Buchar had set up the Maxim gun so it pointed down the line. Hanak walked in circles, roundshouldered and skinny, hands in pockets, watching everyone while they weren't looking. Standing with his legs apart and his thumbs in his belt, straddling the line like a barricade, back to Anna, face down the line in the direction of the locomotive, was Matula. Anna ran to him and around him so that she could look at him. How could his eyes report the presence of a living mind behind them, and be so without life? The wheel grated round inside Anna. It seemed to her Matula had become part of the punishment she had earned by betraying her son, by taking a convict into her bed. Those opaque eyes of Matula's, lacking even the comfort of malice, spite or hate to assure her of his humanity, now seemed natural. It was not that his eyes were, as she had thought before, alien in their lack of feeling. It was that she had not until now committed the sin to enable her to understand how much a part of the human world his inhumanity was.

'Where's my son?' she whispered.

'The village whore wants to know where her son is,' said Matula loudly. The other Czechs hushed, stilled and listened. 'They've all left you! Your Yid Mutz has run off, and your convict friend has taken your boy away. There's nothing left for you now, is there, unless Lieutenant Hanak wants you.'

'Why don't you go after them?' whispered Anna.

'They will all fall to me,' said Matula. 'In the meantime, you forfeit the convict's bail. We agreed that would be your life.'

'I've been a fool,' said Anna. She began to sob. 'I've made

bad mistakes. Please save my son.' She went down on her knees. 'Please save my son.'

There was a shuffling of Czechs around and no-one spoke.

'Kiss my boot,' said Matula. Anna felt an instant of relief. There was to be no waiting. She'd been admitted to the place of punishment already: it could go on but it couldn't be worse. The shooting had stopped and there was an entire silence. Anna bent her body and lowered her lips to the polished leather tip of Matula's boot. It smelled of war, winter, scraped-off shit and mud. She pressed her mouth to the toe. It was hard but she wanted him to feel it. The worse the better. She straightened and wiped her mouth with the back of her hand and stood up and looked Matula in the eyes. His boy's mouth was twitching as if he was about to laugh and to look in his eyes was like scraping your knuckles on rough granite.

'Well, take her away, Hanak,' said the captain, but as Hanak stepped forward they all saw a bulging figure walking towards them from where the line disappeared between the trees, about four hundred yards away. Anna began to run towards the figure and Hanak caught her by the forearm and when she struggled and tried to bite he wrenched both arms behind her back and held them there so she could not break free. He was skinny and slight but strong. Anna screamed Alyosha's name.

'Shall I send men out?' said Dezort.

'No,' said Matula.

Samarin walked towards them between the rails, quickly for a man with a burden, held in his arms in front of him, wrapped in a bloodstained once white shirt. Anna screamed Alyosha's name again, and again. The burden didn't stir. No-one else spoke. They watched, until they could see Samarin's face clearly, and see how he was concentrating on his task. There was nothing else. Fast as he walked, he moved with great care, and that introduced into Anna the toxin, hope. Hope burned through her like acid: how it hurt, and when she cried Alyosha's name again, her voice was weaker. They could hear Samarin's feet on the gravel now, and his breathing. When he was twenty yards away Anna knew Hanak could no longer hold her and she broke away, almost tripping, and took her son from Samarin. She felt the boy's warmth. Oh, she had been forgiven a little! He was alive, and only she would be punished now, perhaps, not him? The wheel would not stop turning. All that was around her became silent and invisible. She looked into Alyosha's face. It was white and still and his eyes were closed, but he did not have the soiled, derelict look of the dead. 'Alyosha,' she whispered. 'My good, my favourite, my love, my poor one.' She put her cheek close to his slightly open mouth, then her ear. A thin breeze from lungs smaller than her hand. He was breathing. So far away as to be a rumour, on the other side of the world of her consciousness, there was a stirring of anger. One failed broken lover had returned, had brought the broken son back to his treacherous broken mother. Where were the others?

'He was hit in the shoulder,' said Samarin. 'There was a lot of bleeding but it missed the vital organs, and the bones.'

Anna glanced at him, and at Matula. She knew she had to run with Alyosha, but she didn't know how.

'Why did you take him?' she said. She had no interest in hurting Samarin, it didn't matter now, but she saw that the softness of her voice was like a blow to him: she hadn't seen him show an ounce of doubt before.

'Because it's more important to the future world that I should escape from here now than that Alyosha should live.'

'Then why did you bring him back?'

'Because I'm weak.'

Alyosha stirred in Anna's arms, frowned and made a small sound. She brought her face down to his, nuzzled his cheek and whispered in his ear that he was the bravest, the best, the most beautiful boy in the world. Alyosha whimpered again but didn't open his eyes. Anna looked up.

'He needs a doctor,' she said.

The words ended the spell of watching and listening which had fallen on the Czechs. The engineer came hobbling up to ask after his fireman and Samarin looked at him without speaking. Matula put up an arm to hold the engineer back. He drew his pistol and cocked it.

'Where's my train?' he said.

'The boiler ran dry when I reversed back away from the Reds,' said Samarin.

Matula raised the pistol and gestured at Anna and Alyosha. 'Go and stand in front of the convict with your bastard, madam. I'm going to see if I can do all three of you with one bullet. Too bad the Jew's not here or I could exterminate you all as a family.'

'Sir,' said Dezort.

'What?' said Matula, turning to him in surprise. As he turned he drew in breath and dropped the pistol, coincident with the sound of a bullet striking metal. The sound of the shot followed a second later. The Czechs threw themselves into the gravel and weeds on either side of the track. Anna dropped slowly on her knees to the ground. Her care for Alyosha, that he should not be moved roughly, tethered her panic to a solid place. The wheel in her head would not stop grinding round. The message had changed, now it only said the word No over and over again, as a prayer to space and time. She closed her eyes and put her face into the warm dark space between Alyosha's jaw and shoulder, seeking with her lips for his pulse, to hold to that as a measure. She couldn't stop herself listening to Matula speaking in a joyful growl, his battle language, his happy time.

'Find the sniper!' he was saying. 'Ten thousand hectares of forest land to the north of here in perpetuity to the man who takes the sniper down, and the title of Prince in my realm, and the widow here to breed off. She'll bear a dozen more yet if you hobble her. Dezort, take three men and work up-line to the locomotive, secure it. Gods, I've never felt so in love with this place. Every man we lose here, his blood makes this ground more sacred to us.'

A voice from far away rippled through the air, distorted and amplified and metallic, as if the person was speaking through a horn. Anna recognised the voice. It was Mutz, speaking in Czech. She heard Broucek's name. Whatever Mutz was saying caused a strange tremor to run through the Czechs, a stiffening and a pain. Matula began to shout. 'I'll flay you!' he screamed. 'You clyping kike toerag, I'll skewer you, I'll cut the senses out of you one by one, eyes, ears, nose, tongue and skin! The same goes for any scum here who listens to a sound that perjuring backstabbing Red-loving Yid pronounces.'

Anna stood up and opened her eyes. She looked round. All the Czechs were watching her. The few who watched in hatred were trying to magnify it. The others were trying to hide their shame by imitating Matula's stone eyes, but they could not imitate them. Anna moved away from them. Alyosha stirred in her arms. The marvellous boy had strength. Anna began to run. Samarin was not there: he had escaped.

Declarations

Alyosha lay delirious on his bed, raving about hussars and chocolate, while Anna cleaned and dressed his wound. The metal fragment had slipped into his small white shoulder under the collarbone, leaving a jagged slit where it had come in and a sorry gash where it had come out. The blood had stopped flowing. The boy twisted and arched when she touched the rawness deep with the hot wet cloth and Anna concentrated on that, on making the torn part clean, whispering good words to him, trying not to grip his hale shoulder too hard with her other hand as she held him still. The Tungus albino sat in the corner, watching. Anna had come across him squatting in their yard, staring at a shape he had made with pieces of straw in the snow. He had turned red eyes onto her and stood up and she had understood he was the shaman's apprentice and wanted to know only what he could do for her. She told him her boy had been hurt in a battle and asked if he had any treatment. The albino shrugged, but followed her inside and upstairs. When she told him to bring hot water from the kitchen he went to prepare it. Later he sat on Alyosha's little wicker chair, making it creak as he breathed. The way he watched Alyosha, attentive and indifferent, like a bird, gave Anna comfort.

She asked the albino to come to help her, to hold pieces of lint against the wounds while she bound a bandage tightly round Alyosha's shoulder. His peeling fingers were barely darker than Alyosha's skin. He smelled of smoke, fallen leaves and worn deerhide.

'Is he your only son?' asked the albino.

'Yes.'

'Where is the father?'

'Dead.'

'How does he die?'

'In battle.'

The albino thought about this. 'Your family's unlucky,' he said.

'The idea of bad luck used to be a great comfort. Not now. I made this happen.'

'Are you a witch?'

Anna found it in herself to laugh, an older, cloudier laugh than the laughter of the night before. 'If I were a witch, wouldn't I make him better?' A fresh wave of self-hatred rushed over her and she leaned down to kiss Alyosha's eyes, but his head moved violently from side to side, and she put her hand on his hot forehead instead.

'You must have seen your shaman treat wounded people,' said Anna.

'Yes. He sends me out to gather what he needs. Moss, plantain, honey . . . this isn't the best time of year.'

Anna looked at the albino and said harshly: 'Why are you sitting there, then? Go and find what you can for medicine.'

'No,' said the albino. 'You don't need our medicine. You need one of your doctors.'

'There's no doctor here. If I don't put something on this wound, anything, it'll be like letting go his hand while he's slipping down a steep slope. Wouldn't it be easier if I believed in those wonderful terrible forces over the horizon, like you and Mutz and Samarin and remarkable Mr Balashov, none of whom can help me now? I understand Alyosha doesn't matter, I don't matter, we're too shamefully small. But I wish my boy was more important to the world than this. Would you go, please, and see what you can find? What's your name?'

'Igor.'

'Your real name, in your language.'

'Develchen.'

She asked him again to go.

'I'm not a shaman,' said Develchen. 'I can't see into the Lower World and the Upper World, as Our Man can, learning whether a place is being kept there for a sick one.'

'I don't care about that!' shouted Anna. 'I don't care, do you understand? I don't care about heavens and hells and gods and demons and tsars and empires and communists and the people this and the people that. Don't tell me any more. I want something for my son's wound and whatever kind of forest witchery comes with it doesn't matter, d'you see?'

Develchen stood up and walked out of the room. Anna turned to Alyosha and murmured: 'Is this what happens when a foolish, greedy woman who doesn't believe is left with nothing else to lean on? When you don't believe in anything, that one day you'll end up believing anything? Oh, just be healed, little son.' Alyosha moved his head from side to side.

Develchen left the house by the front door and walked east, away from the town, the station and the fields and into the woods. He looked up once at the roof of a high barn which stood opposite Anna's house, overlooking the crossroads it stood on, with a clear view of the bridge to the west and the station road to the north. Mutz, Nekovar and Broucek were there, with other armed men Develchen had not seen before. He hurried on.

Mutz lay on a blanket on the steeply sloping roof, braced, like the others, against a length of thick rope Nekovar had slung along the roof's length. With their feet on the rope, they could keep most of their bodies covered while watching the approaches to the crossroads. The castrates were hiding in their homes. The sun thickened the woodsmoke coiling over the town streets. Mutz wondered if he would have a chance to see Anna before the fighting began in which they would all be killed. What could stop the Reds attacking Yazyk? They must have taken Samarin's attempt to escape in the train as a previously worked out plan to deceive them, even though Samarin had smashed into the trolley Mutz and the others were riding back to town on, a second after they jumped clear.

Common sense said that Matula would direct all his forces towards defending the town against the Red attack, but Matula did not have common sense, and Mutz had now absolved him of any obligation for saving his life. Most likely Matula would divide his remnant army in half, one to cover the railway against the Reds, the other to attack Anna Petrovna's house, which is where he would assume Mutz would be. The Reds would then destroy the town in order to crush Matula. It was all perfectly normal.

Against the onslaught to come there were three, Mutz, Nekovar and Broucek, perhaps the albino, and perhaps three more. Dezort lay alongside Mutz on the roof, the flag of truce he had come under wrapped round his neck as a scarf. He had brought two soldiers with him. He was reading one of the Czech newspapers Mutz had been given by Bondarenko.

'Finished?' said Mutz.

Dezort nodded.

'Do you agree it's genuine?'

Dezort nodded again. The front page of the paper was given

over to a decree from the new government of Czechoslovakia, promulgated in Prague five weeks earlier, ordering the entire Czech Legion in Siberia to disengage and move to Vladivostok for evacuation with all speed.

'Matula must have known about this for a month,' said Dezort. 'The telegraph to Irkutsk and Omsk was working until a week ago. He'd never let anyone else see the messages, just him and Hanak. We could have got out, and now we're trapped.'

'You're with us, then, brother?' said Nekovar, from the far end of the roof. He put his hand in his pocket and held out a grenade to Dezort, nodding and smiling, like a man coaxing a cat out from under a bed with a treat.

'It seems hopeless,' said Dezort. 'Matula has ninety men, and the Reds are about to attack.'

'You came, didn't you?' said Mutz. 'The lads heard what I said through Nekovar's voice trumpet about the evacuation. How can they be loyal to him now? Everyone understands he's lost his mind.'

'They're still afraid of him and his cronies. He's a madman, but he's one of your cunning madmen, you know. There's another thing, Mutzie.'

Mutz asked what, though he knew.

'Matula's been good at making everyone believe you're a kind of spy, that you're compiling a report about what happened in Staraya Krepost, the killings, you know. That you're not really one of the boys in that sense, you won't stick up for us. He tried to blame it on you that we had to stay here, and I don't think anyone will believe that, but I suppose . . . we . . . they think you've made a deal with the Reds to testify against us in exchange for your life.'

'You're full of shit, brother,' said Broucek, without taking his eyes from his rifle sights, watching the station road.

'I'm as guilty as anyone for Staraya Krepost,' said Mutz.

'Josef,' said Dezort, dropping his voice and moving his face closer to Mutz's over the damp timbers of the roof. 'You only watched. You hung back. I shot a man in the head when his hands were tied behind his back.'

'Did I try to stop you?'

'All three of you, Mutz, Broucek, Nekovar. That's what you have in common. You all hung back while we did the killing.' Dezort glanced over at Nekovar, who was staring at him steadily, mouth slightly open, about to smile yet not smiling, tossing the grenade gently up and down like a tennis ball.

'I don't like the way you're playing with that grenade, sergeant,' said Dezort. His lips rose over his dry front teeth and he licked them back.

Mutz put a hand on Dezort's shoulder. 'Have I ever betrayed anyone in this company?' he asked.

'Not yet.'

'Have I tried to stop anyone being left behind in Siberia, even Matula?'

'Up until now, yes.'

'I want us to leave this place, and I want to haul those hundred arseholes all the way to Vladivostok without any of them dying or disappearing, and I want us to sail home to Europe, and take the train to the new country, and open our old front doors, into that smell of coffee and varnish and good tobacco, into warm arms, and take this filthy khaki off. All of us except one. They don't need all of us, the Reds. They just need one. A sacrifice. They're a big organisation, a big idea, the Reds. The Reds are a bit like a god, you see, Dezort. People talk about them as if they're one big real thing with intentions and actions and needs, but you can never actually see it, just small signs of its power, in the things and people it made and destroyed. Even when it's there, you never see it all. Like a god. Like a god, it wants the occasional sacrifice.'

'Who?'

Mutz frowned at Dezort's obtuseness. The man seemed genuinely confused.

'Matula. Only Matula. The rest go free.'

'Oh.' Dezort frowned, and laughed a hiding little laugh. 'I see. Because he had a similar sort of idea. He sent me here to try to persuade you to come back. Then he was going to hand you over to the Reds as the real mastermind of the massacre at Staraya Krepost.'

'But you wouldn't have agreed to Matula's plan.'

'Of course not!' The hiding little laugh again.

'Because the Reds have seen their film about it. That was their investigation. The film. And they think Matula is the murderer in chief.'

'This film. Am I in it?'

'I don't know. Are you with us?'

'How are you going to capture Matula?'

Mutz looked at Broucek, who turned for a second to meet Dezort's eyes, before returning to his gunsights. 'Oh,' said Dezort. 'I see. That way. The thing is . . . I know Broucek is a very good shot, but Matula won't show himself now.'

'I would have hit him an hour ago if you hadn't distracted him,' said Broucek.

Mutz stepped off the rope and began sliding towards the guttering and the ladder leading to the ground. 'Lieutenant Dezort, Sergeant Nekovar, Private Broucek, please defend the crossroads while I'm away. Don't shoot at our friends unless it's really necessary.'

Mutz went down the ladder. He walked to the edge of the barn and realised with sadness he was an old soldier at the age of thirty. Like the inhabitant of a windy city, who knows by instinct that when he turns a corner he is liable to be hit by the prevailing gusts, Mutz knew without thinking that he was about to walk across a likely line of fire from Matula's troops, down the broad flat station road. It seemed to have become very quiet. Mutz glowed with a fear sweat and his heart was busy. His guts churned. He began to imagine all the ways the bullet could cripple him. He looked up to see if Dezort was watching. It was like seeing a reflection of his own face. The same pallor, the same awareness of lines of fire, that they did not know how to get out of this, that they were far away from home, that nobody cared.

Mutz ran across the street and went into Anna's house. He paused for a moment. He was dizzy. He heard Anna calling from upstairs, asking who it was.

Mutz was trembling. The fear of the bullet had given way to the fear of what would happen now with Anna. He ran upstairs, almost falling, and met Anna outside Alyosha's room. She wrapped her arms round him and pressed herself warm against him. He felt her tears trickle down his neck.

'Josef, I've been such a terrible fool,' she said. Mutz's presence, his familiarity and quietness, seemed like the beginnings of a gift of forgiveness to her. To be given such a chance now to confess, and offer herself. 'I took the convict into my home. I slept with him. I should have trusted you. He stole my son to help him steal the train, and Alyosha was wounded, and now I'm afraid he's going to die. I deserve to be hanged. I did it because I wanted him, Josef. Can you believe it? I wanted Kyrill Ivanovich so badly I forgot to guard my own beautiful son. When you'd been so good. When you'd tried to give me what it was I longed for. I'm worse than a whore, Josef.'

'Don't say such nonsense.'

'A whore takes money and I didn't take money, I let that beast have me and then steal my son.'

'How is he?'

'Sleeping. Or dying. I shouldn't say that, should I? I don't know what to do. The albino went into the forest to make some medicine. That's what I'm reduced to, Josef, isn't it low? There's Anna Petrovna, the slut, sending for the witch doctor.' She was speaking quickly. She stopped, stepped away from Mutz, looked up at him and wiped her eyes and nose with a limp handkerchief she took from her sleeve. He was looking at her with doubt, of course; she would have to convince him. 'You're going to tell me to stop feeling sorry for myself. Josef, I wonder what it is in me that stopped me from trusting you. A permanent fever. You never trusted the convict. If I were a good mother I'd have listened to you, and God, Josef, it's not as if you weren't ready to be with me at night. I'm ashamed.'

Mutz was more drained of words by Anna's self-hatred than he had been by her pride or turning away from him. To his own surprise, he asked about Balashov.

'He hasn't been here,' said Anna. 'He may not know. He may be hiding from the sound of the guns. If he came, I'd let him in. I don't believe he'll come. What difference would it make?'

'Alyosha is still his son.'

'We should go back, I want to watch over Alyosha. Come with me. I know, you have to go, Matula is coming, I know, just for a moment, come into Alyosha's room and stay and talk to me, please.' Anna took Mutz's hand, looking up at him with a tenderness and humility he hadn't seen before. He let her lead him into Alyosha's room and they sat together on the edge of the bed. Anna stroked Alyosha's forehead, and took his wrist in her hand to see that his pulse was good. She looked at Mutz, then looked at Alyosha. It seemed to Mutz as if Anna was inviting him to touch Alyosha, but he was too confused to stop staring at her.

'You can put your hand on him,' said Anna. 'Talk to him. Maybe it'll help.' How strange that she had found Mutz's awkwardness with her son irritating before. Now she was moved by it, his respect for the boy, for her, after what she had done. She would love Mutz, if he wanted; she would listen to him.

Mutz knew he should talk to Alyosha, but he couldn't. He could only watch Anna. He'd come into her house dragging with him a great prize of knowledge about Samarin, to turn her against the convict. Now he had no use for it. It was simpler than he could have hoped. Samarin had made it easy: he could not have done a worse thing to Anna. She was his, Mutz's, if they lived. She had said so. Yet all he felt was sorrow eating at him. She was sincere. When she looked at him so tenderly and humbly, she wanted to believe she could love him, that good sense and a rational mind was what she must desire now. Truly, she was sure. But he knew she would not be so sure tomorrow. Today, believing she must love Mutz was part of Anna's penance for the crime she thought she had committed. In the very moment of her offering herself to him he was most sure that he could never have her. Not knowing what to say, and knowing that he shouldn't mention Samarin, he couldn't help reaching for the news he had originally meant to bring.

'The Reds held us prisoner last night,' he said. 'I found out some things about Samarin.'

'I wish you could've sent a message. He so charmed me last night, in his distant way. We drank cognac. I was like a schoolgirl. I don't understand why I couldn't see he was a common criminal, like the thieves of the White Garden, like this Mohican who's been running around murdering people. Shouldn't it show? Am I really such a fool as that?'

'Of course not,' said Mutz. 'It's his genius, to know himself so well that he can hide or show the parts of him that make him what he wants to appear. He'd never show you himself complete. It'd be too much, even for him, to do that, to be the whole man. It's not that he pretends to be something that he isn't but that you only see the side he wants to show you, and somewhere, above and beyond, his scheming intelligence sees it all, his student self and his criminal self, the degrees of his ruthlessness, his past, present and future, and the great glow of utopia in the distance, that he believes he's cutting a path to. Anna, think what you just said! The thieves of the White Garden – who told you about that place? Samarin. The Mohican – who told you about him? Samarin. Samarin describes himself and the Mohican so well because he knows them both so well, because they're both him.'

Anna put both hands to her mouth. It muffled the shriek that burst short and shrill from inside her. Mutz was still talking but it seemed to her he was speaking much too quickly, mixing up his words, and it was hard to make out anyway against the evil whistling noise in her ears. She realised it was the effect of the blood pounding in her head. She wanted to ask Mutz to slow down, but couldn't speak. She tried to put together what he had said, about how it wasn't that the Mohican, the man who killed, robbed and destroyed without mercy, was pretending to be Samarin the anarchist revolutionary, or pretending to be Samarin the charming student, but that they were all faces of a single man, Kyrill Samarin the Mohican. About how this was the man who had killed the shaman with alcohol because the shaman was the only man in Yazyk who knew his identity, about how this was the man who had persuaded Racansky, under his spell and an enemy of Kliment, to kill the officer and carve the letter M on his forehead, to make the Czechs believe the Mohican could be on the loose while Samarin was in captivity.

'Wait,' whispered Anna. All the blood was gone from her face. 'Speak more slowly, Josef. I can't stand to think I kissed him, that I let him make love to me. I wanted him!'

'I could stop,' said Mutz. 'I'd rather not tell you any more.' It was true. If he'd thought he might have gained the tiniest pleasure from extinguishing his remaining jealousy of Samarin, he'd been wrong. Now that Samarin was gone the knowledge Mutz had gained, even having it, never mind inflicting it on Anna, made him feel unclean, like a torturer and the worst village gossip all at once.

'Is there more?' asked Anna after a while, her voice a little stronger.

'Yes.'

'Is it . . . is there nothing good?'

'Perhaps. But not before worse.'

'It's hard to understand what you're saying, Josef,' said Anna. She shuddered. 'If Samarin is the Mohican, does it mean Samarin escaped from the White Garden alone? That nobody tried to . . . that nobody took a companion as food for the journey, as Samarin said?'

'No,' said Mutz. 'No to all of those things. Samarin wasn't alone. He didn't escape from the White Garden. And there was such food.'

'Oh, Alyosha,' said Anna, lying back and resting her cheek on the pillow so she was looking into the sleeping boy's face. 'What have I done?'

'Samarin wasn't escaping,' said Mutz. 'He was travelling to the White Garden, not from it. He was never a prisoner there.

His description – it was so real, wasn't it? – was a fiction. He made it so real because he believed it himself, not that it happened in reality but that it could happen to people like him in the future. That's the span of time and of possibility over which his mind works. He really was imprisoned, in the past. He really did escape. But none of it happened there, and then, in the Arctic. And because the Tsar and old Russia is Samarin's enemy, and treats him as such, any way he imagines his enemy treating him could become the way men like him would treat their enemy, if they had the power. Samarin himself won't survive the Reds. His destructiveness is too pure. But the way he described the White Garden, it wasn't a true history, it was a prediction. It was a premonition of the righteous retribution of the Tsar's enemies.'

'I don't understand. If there was no White Garden, where was he going?'

'There was a White Garden. It was the camp of an expedition led by an aristocrat called Prince Apraksin-Aprakov, an amateur geologist who thought there were deposits of rare metals in the foothills of the Putorana mountains, by the upper reaches of the Yenisey. For some reason, Samarin made a journey there, or tried to reach it. If he left one of the river ports of south Siberia in spring, he could have travelled there and back in this time. You can imagine how hard the going would have been through the taiga and the tundra, with the rivers and swamps melting and the mosquitoes, for a man on foot. He must have known he couldn't make it without taking another man with him as food. And he did take that man, and he did eat him, down to one hand he discarded the day before yesterday by the riverbank when he came to the railway bridge.'

Anna closed her eyes. After a while, she said: 'Go on. You said there might be something good.'

Mutz felt as shy as when he had first knocked on Anna's door. They had been so intimate since and now that had been put away as memory. Every word he spoke, he knew, was pushing them further apart. It was as if he wanted to destroy what he couldn't mend. 'You hurt me when you turned me away, and you hurt me again when you fell in love with Samarin before you even met him.'

Anna got up quickly, took Mutz's hand and led him away from the bed so that they stood facing each other by the window. She looked into Mutz's eyes. It was too intense. He looked away. It was too intense, but it was not the same consuming hunger that had been. 'Josef, you're so clever, how can you speak like that, like a little boy? What do you mean fall in love? You know it wasn't that. You know it was never that with Samarin. How old are you, and you know so little of what a woman needs and feels? Do you really think only men feel lust? I know I turned you away, but I was mad, Josef, foolish, impatient, greedy. I've paid for it, don't you think? You can forgive me, surely? We can be together now, can't we?'

'Do you want me to finish telling you about Samarin?'

Anna nodded, touching the inside of Mutz's palm with her fingertips. Mutz took his hand away. He reached inside his tunic and brought out a newspaper, *Red Banner*, the copy Bondarenko had given him. 'Here's a description of what an aerial expedition to the Arctic found at the White Garden not long ago,' he said. 'It speaks of a terrorist, Yekaterina Orlova, being kept by the Prince at the White Garden in some kind of bondage, as her sentence for carrying a bomb. It was her exile. When we arrested Samarin two days ago, he was carrying a piece of bark with a message scratched on it. It said "I AM DYING HERE. K." I think the K was Katya, as in Yekaterina. I think Samarin, the Mohican, travelled to the White Garden to rescue her. I don't know why, whether he was acting as part of a strategy with his terrorist comrades, or for some other reason.'

'What other reason could there have been?' said Anna.

'I don't know. But he did bring your son back. I don't see how that could be a part of any vision of his destroying intelligence. Alyosha and you should be nothing to him. There. That's all I know. I have to go. I'm sorry about Alyosha. Don't torment yourself. The Reds have a doctor. If we can get past Matula to surrender to the Reds he'll be all right.'

'Thank you,' said Anna. 'Will you forgive me?'

'If I have anything to forgive you for, I forgive you. But to forgive you isn't going to change you.'

'Take me with you to Prague when we leave here.' Oh, yes, it was what she wanted, what Alyosha needed, a brave, careful, clever man in a neat busy little country in the far-off west. Not a punishment for her stupidity, no, no, look at the kindness and thought and coolness in Mutz's dark eyes, none of the bloody madness that her other lovers were poisoned with. Now she would love with wisdom.

'I can take you, if we live,' said Mutz. 'Do you want to go?'

'Yes!'

Mutz couldn't help smiling, even though he still didn't believe. Anna's eyes were almost back to where they had been before, eager, inquisitive, daring you to show that whatever difficult new game was to be played she had skills to play it.

'I'll ask you again at this time tomorrow,' he said.

Downstairs there was a knock at the door.

Samarin's Request

Balashov was asleep in his dark cabin next to the stable. The door opened with the kick of a stranger's boot and the latch banged off the inside wall. Sunlight arrived. Balashov opened his eyes. From what light got past the silhouette in the doorway it was late, nine o'clock at least. He sat up and swung his legs over the edge of the bed. Samarin came in and sat next to him. He put his arm round Balashov.

'Good morning, Gleb Alexeyevich,' said Samarin. He was hearty and cheerful.

'Good morning, Kyrill Ivanovich,' said Balashov. 'What do you want?'

'How unwelcoming you are for a man of God!' said Samarin. 'You're always good for some food, my dear. Let's have some breakfast.'

Balashov pointed to one of the chests. Samarin went to open the other one. It was locked.

'Secrets, secrets, secrets,' he said, lifting the lid of the chest Balashov had pointed to and rummaging. After a while he took out some dry fish, a piece of bread, some brick tea, some cups and a pan. 'May I?' he said.

'My guest,' said Balashov, standing up. 'Let me get water.'

'No,' said Samarin. 'No, you stay here. I'll get the stove going and make tea. You've been up all night, I think, you must be tired. All that shooting to the north of town and you didn't hear a thing, did you? Well, it was a small business, a few people hurt.'

'What people?'

'Be patient, Gleb Alexeyevich. All in good time.'

'I have things to do. I don't wish that you be here.'

'That's because I haven't told you why I've come! There's a small thing I want you to do for me, and then I'll be on my way.'

Samarin prepared the food in silence, except for when he sang a phrase from a song. 'Among the worlds,' he sang. Waiting for the water to boil, he stood watching it for a while with his back to Balashov, then spun round.

'Here's one,' he said. 'What do you call a vegetarian with six legs and one big cock? No? A castrate on a horse!' He laughed. Balashov didn't. 'You led your horse on quite a parade last night. Round and round the paddock, man and beast walking side by side. You can still see the foot and hoofprints out there in the snow. After a while, you stopped leading him, didn't you? No more footprints, just hoofprints! I'd like to say the hooves looked a bit heavier with you on his back but I'm not a tracker. It must be fine, if you haven't got a cock and balls of your own, to go cantering around on a stallion in the moonlight, in the snow. Bareback, perhaps? If only there were wild mares out there to mount. You must feel like a centaur. Half man, half horse. Well, half man, whole horse. And now here we are together in your cosy cabin. One and a half men. The horse is beautiful, Gleb Alexeyevich. What's he called?'

'Omar.'

'Omar. I went into the stable to look at him this morning. He's very fine. Don't look at me like that! I didn't touch him. But he is very fine. It would be so wonderful for me if I could have that horse. I haven't seen such a beautiful horse in a long time.' He paused, tapping his foot. 'No, Gleb Alexeyevich, you're supposed to say: "Please take him." It's Christian generosity. Come on. "Please take him." Say it now.'

'Is that the small thing?'

'No!' Samarin laughed. He handed Balashov a cup of tea, with flakes and stalks from the brick turning in the brown. Balashov shook his head. Samarin put it on the floor next to Balashov's feet. 'Now, the bread.' He picked up the hunk of dry rye loaf. 'A bit of luck. I've got a good sharp knife already. Not the old one. I took this one from Anna Petrovna's kitchen, see? She's a friend of yours, isn't she? Not a very likely couple.'

'What were you doing at Anna Petrovna's?'

'I asked you not to look at me in that way, Gleb Alexeyevich, anyone would think you cared more about Anna Petrovna than you do about Omar. I know you're friends but it's not as if it's going further than that, is it? You can't put it back now.'

'I don't understand,' muttered Balashov.

'I'm sorry, what?'

'I don't understand what it serves to be so cruel.'

'It doesn't serve. I don't serve. You know that. I'm a manifestation. Of the present anger and the future love. But that's all very fancily put, Gleb Alexeyevich, and I haven't answered your question, which was: "What was I doing at Anna Petrovna's?" Well, I was fucking her, for one thing. Woah! Steady there. Please don't stand up. You might accidentally run onto this knife, and that would be the end of you, before you'd eaten your fish. Since it obviously bothers you, I didn't force her. She was very eager. Her husband's been dead for a long time, you see. It was lovely, the fucking, and before the fucking. You probably don't know how nice it can be to touch with your fingertips that little soft moist place just inside the lips and see how she smiles and closes her eyes and twists her body and says something which is like a new word of delight and a breath and a heartbeat all at the same time. Do you know? Of course you don't. You probably never put it inside a woman before you lost it. Well, Gleb Alexeyevich, all I can say is that if you knew what you were missing you would know what was missing from you. So that was nice – are you all right, Gleb Alexeyevich? You look pale. Do have some tea.' Samarin took a bite of bread, tore off a piece of fish and chewed them with great effort, still talking. 'Yes, that was nice, but that wasn't why I did it. The thing was, I needed to get away from here, I needed to take a train, and to take a train, I had to get close to it, and to get close to it, I needed to borrow the widow's son. What could be more natural than a boy's curiosity about locomotives, dragging his strange convict friend off to the station early this morning while Mama's asleep to have a look at the Czechs' train? It worked very well. I stole the train. It was annoying that the boy refused to jump off and stayed on board. It was tiresome that the fireman was shot when we ran into some troops up the line. Reds, I think. It was tiresome that the boy was shot. Sit down, or I'll kill you.'

Samarin held the knifepoint an inch from Balashov's throat. His other hand held Balashov's hair.

'What happened to Alyosha?' said Balashov. His voice was breaking. 'Please let me go.' He sat back down and Samarin stepped away.

'You seem upset,' said Samarin. 'Did you have your eye on the widow's son as one for the chopping board? An heir, perhaps? I suppose you have to get other people to have your children for you.'

'Is he badly hurt? Is he alive?'

'He's alive,' said Samarin. 'It troubles me that you care. I thought you eunuch crackpots only cared about your own.'

'You're like the Jewish lieutenant,' said Balashov. 'You think love, even friendship, any human bond, fails when the Keys to

Hell are thrown in the fire. It is not true.'

'Of all the religions, yours is the funniest, Gleb Alexeyevich. When the lights go out for the last time and the world ends, somebody in their final sleep will wake up and chuckle over the men and women who mutilated their genitals because they thought it would make them into angels. Stay where you are! Listen. Will you listen? Can you? Things have happened which will not— which I will not allow to happen again. Your sect is ridiculous but it carries something which I need to take from you today, a method that is absurd in the way you carry it out and the beliefs you attach to it. Still, I need it. Things have happened which I will not allow to happen again.' Samarin was breathing heavily. His voice was uneven. 'What's your philosophy? That to enter Paradise, you have to rid yourself of even the means to commit sin? Why don't you take your eyes out and cut off your tongue? All you can think about is the forbidden fruit and carnal knowledge, which means – fffffft! The knife. It's shit, my friend. There's no other world than this, and no other life. We have to make our own Paradise here if we want one, but it'll take a long time, and many people will have to die. Do you know who I am? I'm Samarin. I'm the Mohican. I'm Samarin–Mohican. I'm thief, bomber, terrorist, anarchist, the destroyer. I'm here on earth to destroy everything which doesn't resemble Paradise. There are others like me. Understand. Every office, every rank, every service, every banker, shopkeeper, general, priest, landowner, noble, bureaucrat. In ten years we've left our mark. It has been difficult. Things have happened which I will not allow to happen again. There have been times when the mission has been hard, Gleb Alexeyevich. Hard. Too . . . hard. There have been times when the ones the destroyer needs to use, and destroy if necessary to move forward, or at least abandon, have . . .' Samarin blinked rapidly as he searched for a word '. . . *imprinted* themselves on him. Do you know, I had a clear line from here to here' – Samarin drew a careful horizontal line in the air – 'six months ago. I was never a prisoner at any White Garden. That was a necessary lie. I was at liberty and had a clear journey and means from Moscow to Georgia to affect the course of what they called a revolution there. That was what I had to do. It was agreed with my comrades, but no agreement was necessary. The lines of life and action and necessity coincided so well. Yet I never went to Georgia. I made a six-month journey to the Arctic, on foot, for no purpose except to see if I could save a woman I once knew as a student, who was being held prisoner there. Katya. Why did I go up there? Do you know how badly I wanted to find her? Do you know how much she meant to me? I took a companion with me, a nice stout young socialist revolutionary, clever, so that I could kill him and eat him when our food ran out. And that's what I did, Gleb Alexeyevich.'

'God forgive your soul.'

'God forgive, God forgive – fuck God. Are you hearing me? To plan to butcher and eat another man because you want to help one single woman who's probably dead anyway? Not for a cause, but for yourself? What does that sound like?'

'You must have loved this Katya very much.'

'Idiot! What do you think love is? Is it going to haul a man a thousand miles through the tundra and make him a cannibal?'

'Did you find her?'

'Yes. She was dead. They were all dead. She was frozen. There were tiny pieces of ice on the soft down above her mouth.'

'Kyrill Ivanovich . . .'

'Listen, damn you! Can you not listen?' Samarin kicked the cup and it shot under the bed and hit the wall, impregnating the raw floor timbers with a spreading stain. 'Again! Today. A boy takes a small piece of shrapnel in his shoulder. He bleeds. He falls down. I have no cause to turn back. I can leave him lying there, jump off the train, run into the forest, and slip past the Reds to the west. That's where I must be. That's where the destroyer has to work. And again, another one of those bitches has hold of me, and drags me back, carrying her boy. I had to go on, and I went back, for the sake of that woman. I only spent one night with her, we sang, I kissed the little scar on her breast, and she had me. You know what I'm saying, Gleb Alexeyevich. It must not happen again. You reached the moment of it must not happen again, for the sake of a better world than this miserable one. Now I've reached it. Take the knife. Take it. Castrate me.'

Balashov, who had been sitting hunched, looking at his feet with his hands clasped together, looked up and asked Samarin what he meant.

'What do you think? Take the knife. Do what you do. Castrate me.'

Balashov took the knife and threw it on the bed, shaking his head. Samarin grabbed it, prised Balashov's fingers open and pushed the handle into Balashov's hand. He threw off his coat, loosened his trousers and let them fall.

'It's not there,' said Balashov, shaking his head. 'That's not the place love is, otherwise what kind of world is the one you're trying to make?'

'Geld me,' said Samarin. 'I can't be like this. It's not love, it's a sickness, it's a power over me I can't endure.' He dropped to his knees in front of Balashov, lifted up his shirt and held his scrotum in his fist. His lips stretched and quivered and two tears made wide tracks in the soot on his cheeks. 'Castrate me, Gleb,' he sobbed, 'Or I'm no good to the future.'

Balashov dropped the knife on the bed again, stood up, pressed Samarin's head against his belly and stroked it for a few moments. He bent down to kiss it, then left Samarin crying and began walking towards Yazyk.

Tripping The Demons

Downstairs, there was a knocking at the door. Mutz went to see who was there. He took out his pistol. Anna heard him cock the gun as went down, the warning of industrial death against the bootsoles on the wood. She heard the door opening. Instead of voices, there was a moment of silence, and what might have been a word. Then the door closed and she heard feet coming up the stairs. It wasn't Mutz.

'Hello Gleb,' said Anna to Balashov. He looked different. His serenity was broken. He didn't look as if he'd been on a good trip to Heaven for a while.

'I heard about Alyosha,' said Balashov. 'I'm sorry I came, but I wanted to see him.'

'It's good that you came,' said Anna. 'He's your son, in spite of everything.'

'Mutz left,' said Balashov. 'He looked at me and shook my hand. He just said "Matula", shook my hand and left.'

'Alyosha's sleeping. He was hurt in the shoulder. It went right through. The damage isn't so terrible, it didn't touch the bone, but it'll hurt, poor one, and I'm worried about infection. He was feverish.'

Balashov went over to the bed and knelt down beside it. He was about to touch Alyosha's head when he stopped and went to wash his hands in the bowl on the dresser. Anna watched him. There was something about the way he moved that was more careless than before. He looked like something that Anna had not seen him look since she arrived in Yazyk: alone. Well, she was all cried out, empty now. Balashov returned to his post on the floor by the bed. One of Alyosha's hands was outside the covers and Balashov put it between his own. Anna wondered whether, if Alyosha woke up, he would be frightened, or if, in some deep place he would never find, he would recognise his father as his own flesh and blood.

'Do you mind?' said Balashov.

'No. But if he wakes up, don't tell him you're his father.'

'No. Do you mind if I pray? Without speaking.'

'No.'

Minutes passed in complete silence. Balashov got up and came over to Anna.

'You've changed,' said Anna.

'What we do . . . there are changes to our bodies . . .' said Balashov, blushing. 'The skin is smoother, we are heavier.'

'No. Since yesterday.'

'Do you see something?'

'Is there trouble in your fellowship?'

'I can't lead them anymore. I've begun to lie to them about my visions. I've lied to you as well, and I always meant to tell the truth to you, and to keep my promises, after I broke so many to you before. I promised you that I wouldn't help any others to purification, and a few nights ago I broke that promise.'

'You took the knife to a man?'

'Yes. He was nineteen.'

'Oh, Gleb.'

'I met the convict on the road back from Verkhny Luk and he found out what I'd done. He said he'd say nothing if I said nothing about him taking a litre of spirit from me. I knew

Samarin killed the shaman, Anna. I could have warned you all. This is my doing. I was too proud to tell you. I was too proud to let you know that I'd broken a new promise to you. So I became a liar. A liar can't be an angel in the house of God. What it means is that I care more about what you think than what God thinks.'

'That pleases me.'

'It doesn't please God.'

'Gleb, I invited Samarin to spend the night with me. We slept together. We made love.'

'I know.'

'I was the fool who itched for him and couldn't do without him, and trusted him. I let him steal our son.'

'Our son!' Balashov smiled. 'It sounds strange.'

'Whatever you do to yourself you can't make it that he isn't.'

'Why did you come to Yazyk? I never imagined you would. When I saw you at the station with Alyosha for the first time, four, five years ago? For a moment I was glad. Then it was like the knife again. I hated you. I wondered if the Devil had taken your shape, to torment me. That was easy. I prayed, I fasted, I spun. Later it was harder, when I saw it was really you. At first, I still hated you. I felt like a small child playing some wonderful game on a summer evening that never ends, who notices that an older child is watching from a distance, and though the small child still believes in the game, he can't help feeling the eyes of the older child, who thinks their castle is just a pile of sticks, and their magic robes are just sheets borrowed from the big house. Then I stopped hating you. I tried to help you. You remember that was the hardest of all. I'd left the world, I'd boarded the castrate ship, I'd burned the Devil's keys, and still you had some hold on me that was nothing to do with passion. As if you and I had once shared a great secret, and now I'd forgotten it, and I knew you had it, but I couldn't get back to you any more to find out what it was.'

Anna realised she had never for a moment thought that her husband was insane. How much easier it would have been if she'd been able to do that. He sounded as if he was asking her to stay. It made Anna understand that if they survived she would have to leave.

Alyosha called for his mother and she went and sat on the bed and fussed over him. His eyes were open and he was half-lucid. His temperature was high and his shoulder ached. He asked after Samarin and Anna told him Mr Samarin was fine and that he, Lyosh, was a brave boy. Anna looked over to the doorway where Balashov was waiting.

'Gleb,' she said. He walked over and resumed his position on the floor, his face level with Alyosha's.

'This is Gleb Alexeyevich, our good friend from the village,' said Anna. 'He's come to see what brave people – I mean, he's come to see how you are.'

'Hello, Alyosha,' said Balashov.

'Hello,' said Alyosha.

'You're going to have a fine scar. Your friends'll be jealous.'

'I'm going to be a hussar, like my father,' said Alyosha. 'He had a lot of scars.'

'Yes,' said Balashov. 'I heard that he had scars.'

'He died in the war.'

'Did he? You know I'm sure that he can see you, all the same, when you're in trouble, and put in a good word.'

Alyosha winced and drew in breath. 'Will it still hurt like this when I'm grown up, in the army?'

'The pain goes away, unless something reminds you of the wound. But that doesn't happen very often.'

From outside, they heard shouting, glass breaking, and shots.

A single explosion a few hundred yards away made the glass in the window shudder. Anna flinched and saw her husband duck and cover his head with his arms for a second.

'Don't be frightened,' said Alyosha to Balashov. 'The hussars'll come.'

Balashov let his arms fall. 'Goodbye, Alyosha,' he said. 'I'll pray for you. Get well, grow tall, be wise, love your mother.' He kissed his son on the forehead and stood up.

'What should we do?' said Anna. 'Take him downstairs? Would that be safer?' Outside the shooting intensified.

'Stay away from the window,' said Balashov. He went to the door. Anna asked him where he was going.

'If an angel falls so as to save someone, it must please God, though never so greatly that God can save the angel,' said Balashov.

'Wait,' said Anna. 'Where are you going? Let's kiss goodbye, at least.'

Balashov was gone downstairs, shouting mad words she could only half understand, of farewell, of affection, perhaps, though she wasn't sure. Develchen arrived with a fistful of moss and frostblackened leaves.

'They're shooting,' he said. 'The man coming downstairs says he's going to hell. I say to him Our Man knows how to get by in the Lower World. Take a weighted rope, he says. The big demons are easy to trip when they're running towards you.'

The Gift Horse

By mid-morning Mutz and the others on the roof could see that the Reds had begun to attack the town to the north-west. Plumes of dirty grey smoke would erupt like djinns from the houses near the railway, the crack of the blast arriving a few seconds later. Two of the houses were on fire. Machine guns pecked at the air on either side. Towards noon, single shots began to be aimed at Mutz's position. Jagged points of wood would jerk erect to invisible blows. They saw Czechs running from house corner to house corner towards the bridge, to the west, and down the station road, to the north. Dezort and his two left the roof to cover the bridge from the ground. Nekovar gave all his rifle ammunition to Broucek. Broucek let off a few rounds into the corners of houses, trying not to hit anyone, but to let them know that they were there. There was no sign of Matula.

'I thought we'd be going home before we had to fight again,' said Broucek. 'I feel like a farmer getting a drought for the fifth year straight.'

Towards noon, the attackers brought a small mortar to bear on the barn. A shell landed not far away, shattering windows in Anna's house.

'I see it,' said Nekovar. 'Behind that alder tree.' He picked up a length of plank roughly fashioned into the shape of a tennis racquet, pulled the pin out of a grenade, tossed the grenade in the air, swung and whacked it with the bat. The grenade landed in a ditch outside Anna's neighbour's house and did not go off.

'Don't do that again,' said Mutz.

'Just to scare them off, brother,' said Nekovar. 'It isn't my game. I prefer football, as you know. But I used to watch the aristos and bosses play when I worked as a groundsman at the All-Bohemian Lawn Tennis Association. That was how they would usually hit the ball, but sometimes a good player would hit it from above, with great force. It was more accurate. Like this.' He stood up, balancing awkwardly against the rope, took another grenade, depinned it, put it in the air, leaned back and smashed it downwards. It landed short of the alder tree and exploded, littering the snow with yellow leaves and twigs and sending the mortar crew running.

'That would be fifteen-love,' said Nekovar. He grinned, lost his footing, slid down the roof and fell to the ground. When they reached him he was bleeding from a long gash at the back of his skull and hardly breathing. They ran the gauntlet of fire to carry him across the street to Anna's house. Anna and Develchen had brought Alyosha downstairs to the divan in the parlour and they laid Nekovar out on the kitchen table. With difficulty, Mutz persuaded Broucek to return to the roof. Anna and Develchen were left to tend Nekovar. There was nothing they could do. Anna stood looking down at him, wondering where to begin bandaging his head, when Nekovar opened his eyes. They were surprisingly bright. He stared at Anna for a while. The sight seemed to please him. He spoke, in a quiet but clear voice.

'Pane,' he said. 'Sister, please tell me. You don't have to hide it from me now. Just tell me, what is the secret? What is the secret of the mechanism that arouses women?'

'Hm,' said Anna. 'If you promise not to tell anybody.'

'I promise,' whispered Nekovar.

Anna bent down and said quietly in Nekovar's ear: 'There's a tiny, tiny, tiny bone women have inside their vaginas, two inches in, on the left. It's very hard to find, really very hard, but if you do find it, and pinch it ever so lightly, while stroking her right ear lobe as if you were stroking the ear of a baby mouse, that woman is set in motion to love you forever. That's how we work.'

'Ah!' said Nekovar. 'I knew Broucek was hiding it from me. Thank you.' He sighed, smiled a smile of bliss and closed his eyes. Noon came. The late autumn sun had a little warmth left at its height. It flashed off meltwater across Yazyk. Mutz and Broucek felt it on their backs. More houses were burning now. They could smell the smoke. The shooting had slackened but not stopped. They did not know Nekovar was dead. They could see their former comrades setting up the mortar again. Down by the bridge, Dezort shouted up. He was shaking his head at them and making a thumbs-down sign.

'Is that singing?' said Broucek.

'I can't hear it,' said Mutz. 'Perhaps I should give myself up to Matula.'

'I wouldn't let you, brother. Besides, would it save us?'

'We could make a run for the forest.'

'I can hear singing.'

Mutz could hear it, too. A chorus of unskilled but strong voices, singing Russian words in music that sounded like the hymns the English and American missionaries sang. Broucek pointed to the procession. It was coming from the square towards the bridge. Balashov was at the head, carrying a white cloth on a pole in one hand and leading a black horse with the other. Behind him walked dozens of villagers, dressed in white and pale grey and cream under black coats and cloaks.

They were all singing, and as they walked, more villagers, mainly men but with a few women, came out of their houses to join them. They crossed the bridge and turned the corner into the station road, passing Anna's house and passing beneath Mutz and Broucek.

'What should I do?' said Broucek.

'I don't know,' said Mutz. 'Cover Balashov as far as you can see him.'

The procession had some eighty souls in it now, all singing, drowning out the sound of small arms fire continuing to the north west. Balashov sang out the loudest.

Hallowed father, our Redeemer,
A singing nightingale in the green garden,
While the Holy Ghost, the true first mover,
Sounds the heavenly bell
Calling the white sheep to him:
'You, my sheep, my white sheep,
You will go to Paradise in joy,
In your hearts, you will all be happy,
You will not be naked forever,
In the garden, you will be precious birds,
I shall protect you from all misfortune,
I shall put grace in your hearts;
He who wants to receive grace,
So must he suffer for God.
You must apprehend the works of God,
You must receive the golden cut,
That your soul will have no sins to answer for,
That your hearts will be forever pure.'
Our father, our Redeemer,
Is at his golden table always;

The fearless ones shall see him
The hard, audacious ones,
To them is Zion given.
For them, a white horse shall be brought.
Quickly mount this white horse, my friend,
And rejoice in your heart,
Hold tight to the golden reins
Travel far from here,
Walk through your country
And slay the fearful dragon.
We will plant green gardens everywhere.

Two hundred yards from the bridge crossroads a Czech sentry stepped out from behind a house and ordered the procession to halt. Balashov said he had brought a good horse for Captain Matula.

'Who are the other people?' said the soldier.

'These are my friends.'

'They should stop their singing.'

Balashov turned and nodded and the singing stopped. Matula came out from cover with Hanak, who was warning him about the sniper.

'Not with these people around,' murmured Matula, who was gazing at the horse. His eyes were as lifeless as ever but the skin around them trembled at the thought of a mount.

'How much do you want for it?' he said to Balashov.

'It's a gift, Captain.'

'I know the classics! You've got twenty Reds and Yid soldiers hiding in its belly, haven't you.' Matula stroked the horse's head. The beast shifted its feet. It was saddled. 'You were singing about a white horse.'

'We know horses of different colours.'

'I've never seen any of you God-botherers riding a horse before, let alone one like this. Where did you steal it? What do you want?'

'We hope you can prevent the destruction of the town,' said Balashov. 'Would you like to ride him?'

Matula looked up and down the road. 'Why don't you ride him, local man?' he said. 'Show me what sort of pride the beast's got. If he drops you in the dirt like a sack of flour off the back of a cart I'll know he's worthy for an officer to ride. Go on, up you get. Come on, man, there's no need to go hugging and kissing your friends, it's a horse you're mounting, not the gallows.'

Balashov began to mount the horse, but put his right foot in the stirrup. The Czechs laughed. Balashov tried again, swung into the saddle heavily and tugged the reins to try to make the horse turn round. The stallion would not budge.

'The horse should be riding you!' roared Matula, slapping his thighs. His eyes filmed with water, like rocks after rain.

Somehow Balashov made the horse turn round and the two began to amble back the way they had come, through the procession, which had fallen back a little to either side of the road. Matula was careful to keep the villagers between him and Broucek as he watched Balashov trot down the road.

'Well, he's managed to stay on, which marks down the horse,' said Matula. 'Gorgeous animal,' he muttered.

Balashov reached Anna's house and turned Omar again. He saw Anna looking at him.

'What are you doing?' she said.

'Going away.'

'Where?'

'Where I need to go. Go inside, it's not safe out. How's Alyosha?'

'The same. Gleb, whatever you're doing, I'm begging you, don't.'

The horse bowed and tossed its head and pawed the slush of the half-frozen road. 'You know,' said Balashov, 'when you're no longer a man, and no longer an angel, life can be very tiresome.'

Anna began to move towards him. 'You sound more like a man to me than you have for a long time,' she said.

'And, though you've been kind today, no longer a father.'

'I told you, you're still that,' said Anna. 'I burned all my photos of you.' She held up her camera. 'I have a couple of plates left. May I?'

'I have to go,' said Balashov.

Anna sighted and pressed the shutter. 'It's done,' she said.

'Goodbye,' said Balashov. 'We did love, didn't we?' He leaned forward, whispered in Omar's ear, and moved away.

'Yes,' said Anna, when he was already out of earshot. 'We did.'

Up the road Matula frowned as he watched Balashov canter back. 'He'll never control him at that speed. He's going to break his neck. Too bad if he takes the horse with him.' Horse and rider were approaching at a gallop. 'It's a miracle he's staying on. He must have put glue on the sides of his boots. Although . . .' Matula stroked the corner of his mouth, a gesture he had last performed under fire on the Baikal ice floe. 'I wonder if local man has been a little deceitful with us about his experience, Hanak. What's this fellow's name?'

An instant before reaching Matula, so fast that only Matula understood what was happening, Balashov took his right hand off the reins, reached into his long coat, drew a cavalry sabre, held it high above his head, drew it back across his left shoulder, braced in the stirrups, and leaned off the saddle to the left.

As he passed Matula the full force of his released arm and the full momentum of the charging horse went behind the swing of the heavy, sharpened sabre, into the gap between Matula's chin and his collar.

'Beautiful stroke!' cried Matula. His voice diminished to a crackling whisper as the upper part of the throat and the mouth from which it emerged arced, with his head, into the air and into a bunch of dock leaves on the far side of the road. A silly gush of blood fountained out of the headless man who stood there and lashed into the snow as the villagers scattered. Hanak fired his pistol twice at Balashov, shooting him in the back and killing him as he reined Omar in, before Hanak was hit himself by a single shot from Broucek.

Anna heard the shots and the cries of the villagers. She could go there. She would not. She would not leave Alyosha. She was sure she would never see her husband alive again. She caught sight of herself in one of the few uncracked panes of glass left in her house. Her face frightened her. It was like one of the faces of the railway platforms in times of famine, or of the Jewish women in times of the pogroms, when they are moving from living to enduring.

Alyosha was awake. He had heard the horse.

'Did the hussars come?' he said.

'No. That was Mr Balashov.'

'He said his name was Gleb, like papa.'

Anna lay on the bed and hugged the boy. 'It's only a name,' she said. 'Although, little son, Mr Balashov has certain things in common with your father. For some men, the closer something is, the less they care about it, and the farther away something is, the more they want it. Oh, don't listen to me. We're going to leave Yazyk. We have to find a city to live in. What do you think about Lieutenant Mutz? Do you like him?'

Among The Worlds

Anna and Mutz barely saw each other, and didn't speak, until the next day. With the death of Matula the Czechs accepted the authority of Mutz and Dezort, and their promise that they would leave Yazyk. They put Matula's corpse on a stretcher, head and body together, and went to the Reds with it, under a truce flag. Two of the Reds had been wounded in the fighting. In a meeting, eloquent proposals were seconded and voted for that all the Czechs should be put to death. Bondarenko argued for clemency, on sanitary grounds if on no other, and, when the discussion seemed to be going against him, pulled Matula's head out from under the blanket covering it and waved it at the assembled rail workers, tempering their desire for revenge. Mutz saw that Matula's eyes were open. In death, they had, at last, acquired an expression. It was little more than a dull surprise, though Mutz wondered if he saw there the echo of an instant of admiration for the sabre blow which decapitated him, and in that instant, an acknowledgement of his greater defeat, that there were others beside himself and the Tungus to contest for the rule of the taiga.

The Red train steamed into the station, shunting the Czechs' broken-down locomotive before it. The sides tended to their wounded, while the castrates extinguished fires and began repairing the damage to their homes. None of the villagers had been hurt in the fighting, but most of the houses facing the railway line were damaged or destroyed, and there were scuffles as the castrates accused Czechs or newcomers of looting. Red flags appeared over the station and the administrative building. Bondarenko led a squad through the town like a sorcerer, pointing to things and declaring them to be the property of the people. Mutz spent hours persuading; persuading the Reds' overworked, hungover doctor to go to see Alyosha, persuading Bondarenko that the Czechs should be allowed to keep their weapons and, until they reached the Pacific, their train, persuading the suspicious Czechs that the Reds were to be trusted and persuading the socialist Czechs that they weren't. There was no fraternising until the evening when Mutz, Dezort and Bondarenko came out of hours of unsuccessful negotiation on the terms of the Czechs' departure to find that the senior Czech and communist cooks had agreed on the best way to cook a heifer which had been killed by shellfire (boil it).

Next morning a troop of Red cavalry arrived, their horses painted with mud up to their knees and the riders dirty and haunted, bulked up with sheepskin vests over their greatcoats. Their commander, an Avar called Magomedov in an Astrakhan hat and a Cossack cloak, was jealous of Bondarenko for the congratulatory telegram he had received from Trotsky on capturing Yazyk, and Mutz found himself being taken by Bondarenko as an ally in the argument that began over which parts of the people's property the two commanders' people should be quartered in. Magomedov's political officer Gorbunin excused himself and went off on foot to explore the town. He came upon Anna Petrovna standing on her doorstep in a black overcoat with patched elbows. She was holding a camera.

'Good morning,' he said.

'Good morning.'

'Your windows are broken.'

'I'm waiting for the carpenter.'

'Gorbunin, Nikolai Yefimovich.' He nodded.

'Lutova, Anna Petrovna.'

'Peasant?'

'No.'

'Worker?'

'What do you think?'

'Bourgeois parasite?'

'Widowed mother.'

'Your camera?'

'Mine.'

'Take good pictures?'

'Can do.'

'What d'you think of this?' Gorbunin took out a flimsy newspaper, four pages printed on a single folded piece of paper. It was called *Hooves of the Soviets*.

Anna studied it. The frost made her cheeks pink and, since the doctor had been and reassured her about Alyosha, the shine of curiosity and hunger was in her eyes again.

'It doesn't have any pictures,' said Anna.

'It's my paper,' said Gorbunin.

'Congratulations.'

'D'you like it here?'

'No.'

'Leaving?'

'Yes.'

'Where?'

'Prague.'

'When?'

'Soon.'

'D'you like me?'

'Can't say.'

'I like you.'

'What do you want?'

'Can you ride?'

'Yes.'

'Children?'

'A boy. He was hurt, but he's going to be well soon.'

'Does he ride?'

'He could learn.'

'The paper needs pictures.'

'Yes.'

'Do you want to leave Russia?'

'No.'

'Do you want work?'

'Depends.'

'Come and work for me.'

'As what?'

'Photographer.'

'Would there be food?'

'Of course.'

'Clothes?'

'The people provide.'

'And my house?'

'Confiscated.'

'Why?'

'Bourgeois.'

'And if I stay?'

Gorbunin thought for a moment. 'Confiscated, definitely.'

Anna frowned and nodded slowly. 'Photographer.'

'Yes.'

'And school for my boy?'

'There are three teachers in my unit. Including me.'

'What do you teach?'

'Philosophy, French and elementary horsemanship.'

Anna stared at the man, well built, not tall, in his early forties, with lines around his mouth and eyes suggesting a benign impatience, a life of pondering difficult lessons, and a readiness to laugh. His eyes were black and vertiginous.

'What kind of photographer?' said Anna.

'You're the photographer.'

'What did you see last week?'

Gorbunin came inside to tell her about it and, while he drank tea in her kitchen, Anna began to see pictures between the words of his stories: a very old woman crying over hot bread. Three crows on a corpse. A horseman nailing a picture of Lenin to a church door from the saddle. Shadows of riders on bright new snow. Gorbunin's face in rusty water. Tracks in the mud around a fallen statue. Two peasants at a fire frightened by a Tartar's glass eye. A tired girl. An unwashed baby. A mad father. Gold teeth in an old palm. The entrance into hushed cities. Red banners twisting in the wind and mouths open to sing.

She asked Gorbunin: 'When would it be?'

'Soon,' said Gorbunin. 'Will you come?'

Anna nodded. 'Of course,' she said, and laughed.

The Czechs buried Matula, Nekovar, Hanak and Horak, the fireman, that morning in graves at a plot close to the station. Later that day a fifth man, Smutny, died of wounds he had received in the fighting. The castrates would not receive, never mind bury in their own graveyard, the body of Balashov. He was in hell, they said, for the mortal sin of killing Matula. His corpse would pollute them. Mutz pointed out to Skripach, their new elder, that by killing Matula Balashov had saved the town, and Skripach nodded and said that it was true.

'Do you think he really believed he was going to hell?' said Mutz.

'Yes,' said Skripach. Beside him, Drozdova had been crying.

'Then he made a sacrifice for you and for us so much greater than his life. Are you not ashamed?'

'No,' said Skripach. 'He should have remained pure, an angel, and submitted himself to the will of God.'

'But does God not love self-sacrifice?'

'He loves humility more.'

'It doesn't make any sense,' said Mutz.

'You have sense, we have faith,' said Skripach. 'There's no thinking, only belief.'

Samarin had disappeared.

Mutz went to see Anna. They kissed each other on the cheek and Anna told him that Alyosha was on the mend.

'You seem happy,' said Mutz. Her colour was high and her smile came and went.

'In spite of my husband dying, you mean?' said Anna. 'I've been in mourning for five years, remember.'

Mutz told her about the castrates and how they wouldn't take Balashov's body.

'Well then, we'll bury him ourselves, on the edge of the forest. I know a place,' said Anna. 'The wind always drives waves of leaves over it in autumn, tides of leaves. You and me and Broucek. You'll make time, won't you?'

'Of course.'

'I'll say something. What shall I say? I know that look! You think I should be more sad, more respectful of his sacrifice. I'll say: "Once I had a husband and a lover and Alyosha had a father and that man died. Gleb Balashov couldn't replace that man and he didn't try. Sometimes he reminded me of my husband, and perhaps, sometimes, I reminded him of a woman he had loved, an equal length of time ago, but we could only keep our distance, and it was killing me. I'm sorry Gleb Balashov is dead, and I'm glad that on the last day of his life he tried to change into something more like a man of mine, the one I loved in 1914. But I don't intend to mourn for another five years because a man sets aside his vicious religion for my sake in his last few hours. Gleb, you're not in hell or heaven, you're at peace now, asleep. We remember you.'

Mutz nodded, fidgeting with a telegram, rolling it and smoothing it. He looked out of the window. He didn't want to look at Anna. She wouldn't meet his eyes, now.

'Will you and Alyosha come with me to Prague?' he asked.

'I can't, Josef. I'm so sorry. I'm going to work as a photographer with the communists.' She glanced at him guiltily. Even though he'd expected it, she saw how shocked he was. She truly had been so resolved the day before to go with him. Was a mood so profound still a coat you wore for a day and changed? What was her real nature, when she could not, like Samarin, see all her selves at once and choose?

'I knew yesterday that you'd change your mind, even though you believed what you were saying yourself,' said Mutz. 'But I'm surprised how much it hurts.'

'Josef,' said Anna, able to look at him now. 'It isn't attractive to protect yourself by having doubts. Perhaps if you hadn't doubted me yesterday I wouldn't be doubting myself now.'

They sat in silence for a while. Mutz could feel what he now recognised as love shining over into friendship and wondered whether, if they lived in the same town long enough, the memories of that new tamer feeling might smother the older and it come to seem that there had never been anything else.

They talked for a while about the things they had done together, about Anna's face on Matula's money, about what a communist Russia might be like. Mutz asked if he could sleep on Anna's divan. He slept for four hours, then went to see about the digging of a grave for Balashov. In the late afternoon Mutz and Broucek carried the body of Gleb Alexeyevich in a sheet to the grave, followed by Anna, and they interred him. They placed the photograph of Anna which Samarin had stolen from him over his heart. Mutz had hoped Anna would offer it to him, but she didn't think of it, and he didn't ask. Anna made her funeral oration as she had rehearsed it, but with less anger, and, at the last moment, opened the shroud to see her husband's face before the earth covered it.

In Yazyk over the next few days Bondarenko and Gorbunin, in their different ways, tried to explain the nature of their new liberties to the castrates, and how under communism everything belonged to all people equally, while the castrates explained to them how they lived a life in common already, as demonstrated by the speed with which they combined to rebuild the houses damaged in the fighting. The villagers kept their dairy herd hidden. The Land Captain and his wife were made examples of as the only available representatives of the oppressor class. Their home was seized and they were thrown out. Their maid, Pelageya Fedotovna, was given a red armband and the task of turning the building into a House of Culture.

One day, a winter's day in earnest, when a short blizzard had lifted the temperature above minus ten, Mutz held the Czechs' last parade at the station, close to their repaired locomotive, which had built up steam and had a borrowed carriage with broken windows attached. The Land Captain and his wife, former people to the Reds, were already on board. They hoped to emigrate. Mutz read out to the survivors of Matula's company the telegram appointing him acting captain till they reached Czechoslovakia. When he said the word 'Czechoslovakia' one of the Czechs began to sob. Mutz did not read out the final sentence of the telegram, advising him that on arrival in Prague he would be returned to his proper rank of corporal and would be expected to account for the unit's actions at Staraya Krepost.

'Let's go, brothers,' he said. 'We're leaving.'

He had wondered if anyone would raise a cheer. No-one did. He stood by the steps to the carriage to count the men off as they boarded. No man could be left behind now. To his surprise and embarrassment, as the first man shuffled through the silencing powdery snow to the steps, he stopped, embraced Mutz, shook his hand, and said: 'Thanks, brother,' before embarking. So it was with each of them, a long, tight embrace, a word of gratitude, sometimes a handshake, sometimes a kiss, a salute from one or two of the old fashioned. The last to pass was Broucek.

'Did you arrange that?' said Mutz.

'They wouldn't have done it just because I asked them, brother,' said Broucek. 'They like you, and they're grateful.'

Mutz was the last to board. He looked down the station road, in case anyone should come running up it towards him, begging him to stay, or to take them with him, but he had already said goodbye to her, and she wasn't coming. He climbed up the steps and closed the carriage door. When the train began to move the Czechs did cheer, then, screaming and drumming their feet and rifle butts on the floor and beginning to laugh and tell stories as if they were already growing back into their homeland.

Mutz stood in the corridor watching Yazyk disappear. The train moved slowly, jolting and shrieking. They passed the smashed trolley. Samarin had never been found. It didn't seem likely he would return to trouble Yazyk. Why should he? His desperation to escape the town and travel west suggested that he and the likeminded had already decided to work to destroy the new Red order. Unless the same spirit of destruction had decided that it could find its best outlet within, rather than against, the communists. Why assassinate a few bureaucrats, after all, if you could terrorise and exterminate them as a class, hundreds of thousands of them? Within such horrors, there was a deeper mystery, that the subversive himself was being subverted, that the very spirit of destruction was being gnawed at from within, that the same hideous mind which could so perfectly imagine an Arctic labour camp which did not yet exist was travelling to a real White Garden with equal ruthlessness but for a quite different reason, a reason which concerned a particular woman he knew, and would do anything to reach.

'I miss Nekovar,' said Broucek, standing next to Mutz.

'It is cold,' said Mutz, without thinking.

'Not just because he'd fix the heating in here. Being with a woman will never be so satisfying, knowing he won't be there later to ask me questions all day long about how it works.' Broucek hesitated. 'Don't think about the widow, brother. I know a place in Irkutsk which'll help you forget.' Broucek began to list the bordellos and dance halls on their route, which they might visit while they were crawling their way east along the Trans-Siberian through the great White rout, through Krasnoyarsk, to Irkutsk by Lake Baikal, through the Yablonov mountains just north of Mongolia, skirting the Chinese border along the River Amur, to the Sea of Japan. It might be months before they reached Vladivostok, and their journey would still only be half done.

'I'm worried about crossing America by train,' said Broucek. 'What if we have to fight our way, like here?'

'I don't think we will.'

'Isn't it the same? I've read about it. I've seen films. Flat plains and forests, Indians instead of Tungus, snow and heat, Rockies instead of Urals, cowboys for Cossacks. Don't they have Reds in America, brother?'

'Yes. But they aren't roaming Colorado in armoured trains.'

They passed Develchen, the albino, moving north, away from the tracks, leading Omar through fetlock-deep snow. The shaman's body was lashed to the horse. Of all Mutz's persuasions, getting the Reds to part with the stallion for the albino had been the hardest. The horse wouldn't survive long. It didn't matter. Mutz was unsure exactly what the albino intended, but the shaman's burial would consist of the shaman being suspended from a tall larch in a cocoon of birch bark, and being left to swing. Was it that Omar, too, would be wrapped in bark and hung alongside the shaman? And that this would be the shaman's mount, the steed he'd craved, on which he would fly to the Upper World, outpacing reindeer and his own drunkenness? With his talismans singing in the astral wind, his three eyes aglow like forges, a drum in one hand, a bottle of moonshine in the other and the smoky froth of chewed mushroom on his gums, the spirit of Balashov's horse would carry the shaman where he wanted to go, by his will and against theirs, to the Upper World, to laugh in the face of the gods.

Acknowledgements and Notes

I am indebted to two books in particular for my knowledge of the sect of castrates, known in Russian as 'skoptsy'. They are *La Secte Russe Des Castrats,* a French translation of the 1929 work by Nikolai Volkov, with its excellent introduction by Claudio Sergio Ingerflom, *Communistes Contre Castrats;* and *Khlyst*, by Alexander Etkind. The castrate hymn towards the end of the novel is taken from the former work. Repressed as it was by the Soviet authorities, the sect appears to have survived into the mid-20th century. Ingerflom refers to a Russian book published in 1974, *Iz Mira Religioznovo Sektantsva* (*From The World Of Religious Sects*), whose author, A. I. Klebanov, met castrates in 1971 in Tambov, Crimea and the North Caucasus. A 1962 issue of the Soviet academic journal *Nauka I Religiya* (*Science And Religion*) carries an article, *Fragments Of A Wrecked Ship,* describing a number of acts of religious castration carried out since the end of the Second World War.

Judging by recent conversations with Czechs about it, the story of the Czechoslovak Legion is not widely known in the Czech Republic today outside academic circles, at least not by the younger generation. Most historians of the Russian civil war refer to it in passing but the only full account I have come across in English is a 1991 monograph by John Bradley, *The Czechoslovak Legion in Russia, 1914-1920.* He reports that a convoy of Japanese ships carrying the last of 67,739 members of the Legion left Vladivostok on 2 September, 1920, bringing their Siberian odyssey to an end. Readers familiar with Jaroslav Hasek's *The Good Soldier Svejk* may know that he (Hasek) was one of those Czechs who took part in the civil war in Russia, but on the side of the Reds, not with the Legion. His exploits in Russia form the basis of the short stories collected as *The Red Commissar* and translated by Sir Cecil Parrott.

The practice among escaping Russian and Soviet convicts of taking a naïve companion with them for food is documented. An entry in Jaques Rossi's *Gulag Handbook* under the heading *korova* (cow) begins: 'A person designated to be eaten; suspecting nothing, any novice criminal, invited by his elders to join them in an escape, is fit for this role . . . if, during their flight, the escapees' food supplies are exhausted, without prospect of renewal, the "cow" will be slaughtered . . .' Rossi notes that the practice predated the Soviet Gulag system, being recorded in a Russian medical journal as early as 1895. It was Ruben Sergeyev, in the *Guardian*'s Moscow office, who first told me about this.

I am grateful to the president of the Arun organisation in the town of Tura, in the Evenk Autonomous Region ('Evenk' is the name of the native Siberian people formerly referred to by Russians as 'Tungus') for her gift to me of *Evenk Heroic Epics*, a gift which, at the time, I ungraciously tried to refuse, thinking I would never read it. I was wrong. I am grateful to the people of Tura, Krasnoyarsk, Yeniseysk, Norilsk, Novosibirsk, the Kuzbass and Chukotka for their hospitality and patience during my visits there, and to the *Guardian* and *Observer* for making those visits possible.

Russian readers may recognise in Samarin's song my attempt at a translation of a poem by Innokenty Annensky from 1901.

I first came to know it in the much later version set to guitar by Alexander Sukhanov. I subsequently found that Sukhanov made slight changes to the original text, but it is his version I have translated. Anna's song is, of course, Bulat Okujava's *Vashe Blagorodiye,* written long after the events described in the book and, I hope, its only blatant anachronism.

My apologies to Czech- and Slovak-speaking readers for my decision not to include diacritical marks in rendering Czech and Slovakian names. I've also followed the usual English literary practice of spurning accents to show which syllable should be stressed in Russian names. 'Samarin' should be stressed on the second syllable, 'Balashov' on the last.

I would like to thank the people who gave me places to write away from big cities, namely Tanya and Slava Ilyushenko, and John Byrne and Tilda Swinton; Leslie Plommer, for a berth in Berlin; Duncan McLean, Eva Youren, Lenka Buss, Marion Sinclair, Michel Faber, Natasha Fairweather, Susan and Russell Meek, and Victoria Clark, who read the book in manuscript and gave precious support and advice; Jamie Byng and Francis Bickmore at Canongate; and my dear Yulia, for correcting my Russian, tolerating my absences and feeding me jokes.

James Meek
London 2004